JAMES VELLA-BARDON is the author of five books,
including *The Cream of Chivalry, Mad King Robin,
Hero Of Rosclogher* and *A Rebel North*.
His debut, *The Sheriff's Catch*, was the winner
in the 'best novel' and 'best historical fiction' categories
at the International Royal Dragonfly Book Awards 2019.

"The new king of historical fiction"
– *The Scotsman*

"Remember the name of rising author James Vella-Bardon"
– *Reader's Digest*

"Reminds me of works by today's masters such as
Bernard Cornwell, Conn Iggulden and Wilbur Smith"
– *Yorkshire Evening Post*

"Has what it takes to become a literary giant"
– *The Star*

"Sheer quality, historical integrity and emotional resonance"
– *The London Economic*

"A master storyteller, moving Abel through
a land of wonder and danger"
– *The US Review Of Books*

"The pacing is superb;
non-stop all the way until the end"
– *The Wishing Shelf Book Awards*

"Gripping, vivid historical fiction told
from an unfamiliar perspective, the book is packed
with characters with complicated relationships,
and filled with difficult human emotions"
– *Manchester World*

"Impressive level of historical exactitude"
– *Lancashire Post*

"Vella-Bardon's style is wonderful,
his language is era-appropriate"
– *The Pigeonhole Book Club*

"If you liked Outlander you'll love this"
– *Goodreads reviewer*

www.jamesvellabardon.com

TRIALS IN TUMULT

PART FOUR

of

THE SASSANA STONE

Pentalogy

JAMES VELLA-BARDON

TEARAWAY PRESS

Cover design and typesetting by Rafael Andres
Editing by Hatch Editorial Services

To the late Mario 'Craxi' Briffa,
"one man in his time plays many parts"

Cast of Characters

The MacGlannagh Tribe

Tadhg *Óg* MacGlannagh, Gaelic chieftain of the Mac-Glannagh tribe.

Dervila Bourke, Anglo-Norman wife of Tadhg *Óg*.

Muireann Mac an Bhaird, widow of Tadhg *Óg*'s late son, Aengus *Cliste*.

Lochlain, only son of Aengus and Muireann.

Cathal *Dubh,* Tadhg *Óg*'s marshal (cavalry commander) and nephew.

Donal *Garbh* MacCabe, Scottish constable of the tribe's gallowglass troop.

Redmond O'Ronayne, a Jesuit and a qualified physician.

Nial *dhá chlaíomh* Ne Dourough, a bondsman in the service of Tadhg *Óg*.

Spaniards

Francisco de Cuéllar, a sea captain shipwrecked in Ireland.

Abelardo de Santiago, a widowed marksman shipwrecked in Ireland.

SASSENACHS

George Bingham, English sheriff of Sligo.

John Gilson, an Irish renegade lieutenant in the service of Bingham.

Treasach Burke, an Irish renegade sergeant in the service of Bingham.

THE DEAD

Aengus *Cliste*, only son of Tadhg *Óg* and Dervila, husband of Muireann; father of Lochlain.

Cathal *Óg*, previous chieftain of the MacGlannagh tribe and called *An Faolchù* (The Wolf). Also the elder brother of Tadhg *Óg* and the father of Cathal *Dubh*.

Elsien van der Molen, late wife of Abelardo de Santiago.

Maerten van der Molen, late brother of Elsien.

Reynier van der Molen, late father of Elsien, Maerten and Pieter.

THE STORY SO FAR...

In the year 1588, Abelardo 'Santi' de Santiago, a veteran of the Spanish Army of Flanders, finds himself a reluctant member of the Spanish Armada which sets sail for England. Following the Armada's defeat by the English fleet at the famous sea battle of Gravelines, Santi's ship is wrecked on the western coast of Ireland. Santi somehow reaches the shore and journeys inland, where he quickly discovers a country that is oppressed by heartless English troopers that the natives call Sassenachs, which to Santi's Spanish ear sounds like 'Sassanas.'

Santi is himself hunted by English troopers, who have orders from their queen's viceroy in Dublin to capture and kill all Spanish Armada castaways. He is eventually captured by the brutal English sheriff of Sligo Town, who imprisons Santi and has him tortured. But thanks to an unlikely twist of fate, Santi flees Sligo with an invaluable emerald ring. As he flees his captors through the wilds, Santi also rescues a revered Irish bard named Muireann Mac an Bhaird. Muireann leads Santi to her tribe's rebel kingdom of Dartry, where Santi receives the protection of its rebel chieftain, Tadhg Óg MacGlannagh (the MacGlannagh). The MacGlannagh soon learns of Santi's exceptional sharpshooting ability, so Santi is ordered to train the chieftain and his bodyguards daily in marksmanship.

As more Spanish Armada castaways reach Rosclogher, Santi and Muireann are soon tasked with a dangerous mission: to rescue a Spanish sea captain, Francisco de Cuéllar, from captivity. Santi and Muireann succeed in rescuing Captain de Cuéllar, yet upon returning to Rosclogher they are horrified to learn that the English viceroy has left Dublin and is travelling west at the head of an army which is two thousand strong.

The MacGlannagh instantly orders his subjects to withdraw to the mountains to flee the viceroy's army. Yet Captain de Cuéllar tells the chieftain that he will remain behind in Rosclogher to defend its tower house with the other Spanish Armada castaways. Santi thereby finds himself part of the stout defence of the Rosclogher tower house, along with nine other defenders. After a relentless siege of the tower house, the viceroy's troops eventually withdraw to the west of Ireland as winter sets in, so that Santi and the other defenders are celebrated as heroes by the returning MacGlannagh tribe.

Yet all of the tribesmen's goodwill towards the Spaniards vanishes when the popular Captain de Cuéllar unexpectedly proceeds to secretly depart from Dartry to return to Spain. Santi seeks to regain the tribe's respect by joining a raiding party led by the MacGlannagh himself, which attacks the English garrison town of Boyle. During this raid, the MacGlannagh's second-in-command, Cathal, becomes detached from the main force and is almost slain by English troopers at the gates of Boyle. Yet Santi heroically intervenes to miraculously rescue Cathal, although he is himself badly injured while doing so.

After the MacGlannagh's force returns to Dartry, Santi receives treatment for his wounds in the infirmary at Rosclogher. Meanwhile the MacGlannagh is so impressed by Santi's display *of bravery at the gates of Boyle that he declares Santi a true hero of Rosclogher and proclaims that he will adopt him as his son.*

"He who shall England win, let him in Ireland begin."

– David Wolfe (1528 – c. 1578),
leader of the second Jesuit mission to Ireland

XXXVI

Rosclogher, Dartry, County Leitrim

7 – 12 March 1589

When at last I could return to my feet, I took up the Jesuit's suggestion to visit Cathal. Everyone in the town considered me to be the tanist's rescuer, and although I was relieved that he had survived the attack on Boyle, it was most important to feign public concern by visiting him at his bedside. So it was in broad daylight and towards midday that I walked over to the tanist's cabin. Many heads were turned as I passed, since my act of bravery had greatly elevated me in the esteem of the Dartrymen.

The hopeless horseboy Pirib accompanied me, and together we followed Muireann's son, Lochlain, who had been asked by O'Ronayne to escort us. The wily Jesuit had no doubt requested the prince to accompany us because of my unlikely hero status, which would encourage public support for Cathal's wooing of Muireann over that of the loathed gallowglass constable Donal MacCabe. Four swarthy blue jackets escorted us as they always did, until we reached the tanist's wood cabin along the banks of Lough Melvin. Two more kerns of a grim cast were posted outside, with their spears and daggers held at the ready.

Both of them bowed deeply at the sight of the red-headed prince and let us through the doorway after ensuring that Pirib bore no arms. Upon entering the cabin I saw the tanist wrapped in wolfskins, with one of his charred hands held in those of Muireann, who knelt beside him. The bandage around Cathal's head had pulled away the hair from his heavily scarred face, which was rendered more hideous by its colourless pallor. Having escorted me, Lochlain left our presence after saluting his mother with a kiss to her cheek and a curt bow, since he had been summoned to the keep by his grandmother, Dervila.

As his bodyguards shuffled out after him, I could tell from Muireann's red cheeks that she had been weeping, and she stared at me fearfully. I was so accustomed to her severe expression that her vulnerability left me feeling unnerved. She rose and unexpectedly flung herself at me, leaving me to hold her in an awkward embrace while she sobbed upon my shoulder.

'Forgive me,' she eventually whispered, and I realized they were the first words she had spoken to me since the feast of Brigid.

The ollave then withdrew her head, her expression at once contrite.

'You are a different quality of man from de Cuéllar,' she said. 'I misjudged you.'

The thought of the ring plagued me as her hair brushed my face when she turned away. She quietly returned to Cathal's side and reclaimed his hand. I suddenly recalled Lochlain telling me that his mother had stayed by the tanist's side ever since we had returned to Rosclogher. I could see that Muireann still fought sleep as her head slightly trembled.

'Get some rest, my lady. I can watch over him.'

'I shall not abandon him,' was her immediate reply, 'for even now do I fear for his life. There are those who would readily end it!'

'I take it you refer to your other suitor,' I replied as I dragged a stool to her side, 'but what of the guards outside?'

'Guards are all too easily bought,' she said, 'or overcome. I know Donal and his men. They would not blink at the chance to slit Cathal's throat in his sleep.'

'And you would offer a stouter defence of his person?' I asked, aimlessly seeking to keep the sarcasm out of my voice.

She met my remark with a level stare which was as severe as it was dismissive.

'They would not dare to lay a finger upon one of our queen's ladies.'

The logic of her words was immediately apparent to me then, which left me wondering why the thought had not crossed my mind earlier. Cathal's breathing was barely discernible, and as the light played on his haggard face, I enquired after his condition.

'Has he stirred from slumber?'

'But a handful of times. We have exchanged some words, but his injury has left him light-headed.'

'How long until he recovers?'

'Father O'Ronayne thinks that he should mend soon, perhaps within a week. I dread to think what might have befallen him, had you not intervened.'

'The shot was fortunate,' I said with shrug. 'It is very difficult to use a rifle on horseback.'

Silence fell between us once more, which was only interrupted by Cathal's ragged breathing and the crackle of a small peat fire in the middle of the cabin. As I observed the sparse furnishings of the tanist's quarters, I recalled my last visit to it with de Cuéllar until Muireann spoke again.

'Do you miss the army?'

I met her question with a dark chuckle, then did my best to provide a level-headed answer.

'The army taught me everything. But you only miss those things that you love.'

Muireann appeared confused by my reply.

'But surely you yearned to defend your people?'

The innocence of her question was almost galling as I recalled the years I had wasted in the Lowlands, spent fighting a war which had no bearing upon the safety of the Spanish people. It had been a fight that was neither just nor necessary, unlike the struggle of the Irish rebels.

'When I was born, three paths lay before me. Soldier, sailor or priest. It was a paltry choice I'll admit, and what boyhood I had was denied to me by fate. My voice had not yet broken when I joined the struggle against the Turk upon the bastions.'

'So you would rather not fight at all?' she asked with a suspicious squint. 'My son, Lochlain, told me that you were delighted to be reunited with your bandolier...'

The thought of the ring prodded my conscience again, as I shifted awkwardly in my seat. Then I smiled bitterly and whispered the words of a song often hummed in the Spanish army:

'...my want drives me to war; if I had money, forsooth I should not be here...'

No sooner did I sing it than I met her stare again and resumed our discussion in Gaelic.

'To achieve one's ambitions one requires the means. Sharp-shooting is my trade. It is all that I know.'

'Quite the scholar too,' she observed. Her head tilted sideways as a frown grew on her face. 'But of what ambitions do you speak?'

'A world where there are no wars,' I replied cautiously, 'where commoners may live like kings. A place where the rivers are awash with gold and the hills shine with silver.'

Muireann sighed.

'Such a place is not of this earth.'

'But it is, my lady; I know men who have seen it. They say that people live there in happiness, far from warring kings who would use them as pawns.'

'So you would leave us, like the captain?'

The viciousness of her tone caught me by surprise, and I found myself seeking to backtrack on my words.

'The captain returned to Spain, yet I only seek a new beginning. Would you begrudge me that?'

Muireann's glare slowly vanished as she composed herself.

'And what of a new beginning in Dartry?' she said at last. 'The whole of Ireland has been a new world to many. Not for nothing is the heretic trying to subdue us, for they have achieved great wealth in this land. Here you have comrades, men who have spilt blood with you, spilt blood for you…'

Her voice trailed off as her eyes fell to the ground, and she nodded once in acknowledgement when I replied, 'and what of the army of heretics who want us dead?'

'Do not abandon hope. They may yet be overcome.'

'Hope is a two-edged sword,' I said, so that she glared at me again.

'Perhaps you have abandoned hope in everything. Perhaps it is why you would cross the sea and leave all that you know behind. Perhaps you are just a coward who prefers to flee the world of men instead of making a stand.'

'Perhaps,' I replied wearily, for her words had cut deep and I could not talk for a while thereafter. Cathal had still not stirred from his bed, and we sat alongside him in silence for what must have been at least half an hour.

'That day,' she said at last, 'when we first met. I was shocked by your actions. A man had never dared to touch, let alone strike me.'

'I had no choice,' I replied gruffly, feeling irked to be at-tacked once more, 'and it saved your son from being an orphan.'

'We abandoned Aengus!' she snapped.

'We had no choice.'

'For days afterwards I was shocked by your coldness,' she replied. 'Would you also have turned and fled if I had been in his place? Left me behind to die alone?'

I sighed at her question as I sought in vain to bridle my outrage.

'Your husband was wise and special to you,' I replied, 'but he was not the first ally I was forced to abandon! Many were the fields in which we left our companions behind, amid terrible gore and extreme suffering. Left to die in killing fields where men had turned into beasts. You ask if I miss the army, yet the men who glorify the march to others are those who have themselves not walked half a mile! For years beyond count did I partake of a fight in which I wanted no part, and I am only alive because I am a marksman; a sharpshooter purposely kept away from the brunt of battle by his commanders, while being ordered to pick off cannon masters and officers. You would not survive a single day in the clash of large armies if you paused to retrieve every wounded comrade. Not while hundreds of enemies are closing in about you and you are caught deep behind their lines.'

Muireann looked away from me and sounded strangely subdued when at last she spoke again.

'I have wronged you once more with my accusations, grey wolf, for yours was a difficult choice which saved my life.'

I stared at the ground until she addressed me again.

'It was also an act that introduced me to the first alien I ever met.'

I was not sure what to say while she continued.

'I remember being a girl in MacSweeney territory when we lived by the sea. My heart still pines for the coastal breezes and the breathtaking views of the ocean. I often wondered about the lands beyond it, to which my kinsmen travelled. Many times did I travel inland in the company of my father, yet our return home found me watching out for and listening to the stories of returning fishermen and merchants. I was amazed by the lands of which they spoke, and often wondered what men they met there.'

She suddenly turned to the tanist, who had stirred slightly, and removed a frond of hair from his unsightly face. I felt a prick of envy before she addressed me once more.

'Many years have since passed, during which I was sent to Dartry. It is now my home, and that of my son, Lochlain. But never for a moment did I think I would befriend a man from those distant lands beyond the ocean...or find myself widowed and forced to choose between a disfigured lord or a ruthless soldier of fortune.'

Her voice faltered when she spoke again.

'What should I do, Spaniard? Who should I commit myself to?'

She covered her face with her hands.

'What shall I do?' she said in exasperation. 'There is no time left!'

'Do not despair, my lady,' I replied as I rested my hand gently upon her shoulder. 'Perhaps some other course may yet present itself to you.'

'What other course?' she cried, as she shook my hand off and bared her teeth at me in a fury. 'Would you have me flee across the ocean to another world?! I cannot abandon my lord and kin!'

I drew away from her in shock while her outburst continued.

'How foolish I must appear to you! I, who would not so readily abandon others to their fate!'

Upon finding himself an unwilling witness to her outburst, Pirib scurried to the door when I nodded at it. I engaged in a small bow to the ollave, then followed closely on his heels. In truth the accusations of the ollave had wearied me, as much as

I understood the difficulty of her situation. A muffled apology was heard through the door, yet it went ignored as I returned to the outhouse. My hurried step never wavered until I was halfway through the town, when a giant shadow fell across my path. The towering appearance of Donal MacCabe's son, Brogan, brought a lump to my throat, and immediately my hand fell to my sword pommel as I took a step away from him. Brogan MacCabe was a looming, silent figure covered in chain mail, his grin betraying sheer menace as it spread across his mottled, black beard like a sunlit dagger's slash.

When my composure was regained, I whispered 'Ne Dourough' to Pirib.

Yet as he made away, I seized him up by the shoulder and pulled him towards me. More Scots had stepped into the alley and encircled us. The passing tribesmen cast swift glances in our direction, then turned their head away as they sped off on their errands. Amid the distant hammering of an anvil, Donal MacCabe himself stepped towards me. His coarse face was the picture of unmasked hatred as he stopped a couple of steps before us, which was as comforting as being within striking distance of a muzzled bear.

'How fares the woman?' were his first words.

As confused as I was by his concern for Muireann, I sought to answer him directly to avoid provocation.

'She is well recovered from the raid upon Boyle, although still somewhat distressed.'

MacCabe grimaced.

'I meant the *tanaiste* and not the *ollamh*. I mean our little lord Cathal: he who led a glorious charge upon Boyle before falling from his horse like a befuddled oaf.'

His men instantly issued a vicious bark of laughter, which left my hair standing on end. Once the fear had passed through me, a sudden anger replaced it, at their open slight of my protector. Blood pounded in my temples as a swift rebuke left my lips, and beneath my palm I could feel the horseboy twitching.

'It ill becomes you to speak thus of your kinsman,' I replied.

Donal's voice strained beneath heavy sarcasm as he leered at me.

'*Our* kinsman you mean? The assembly of freemen has voted to adopt you. You now need an Irish name, friend Eoin.'

The revelation left me speechless as I fought hard to meet the stare of the unlikely bearer of the tidings. MacCabe immediately saw that I had not yet learned of the vote taken by the assembly.

'Do not look so sombre. You are now a member of the derbfine, and free to choose your own destiny. Yet if you choose to join my band you may become feared again, and not confine yourself to teaching the use of arms to men and boys. We have wenches to do that now, thanks to you.'

I bristled at his open slight as his men chuckled aloud, and my blade was already half drawn from its sheath. The blackguards eyed me hatefully while MacCabe continued as if he were completely ignorant to my obvious annoyance.

'Men of your skill do not grow on trees. With your rifle, we could rid ourselves of the O'Reilly himself.'

In that instant I recalled the orders of the O'Rourke. The overlord of Dartry had warned us that due to an impending struggle against the Sassenachs at hand, it would be in our interest not to provoke any neighbours who were allied to them. He had told us to avoid any cattle raids until the conflict with the heretics had abated.

'The O'Rourke has ordered us to let O'Reilly be.'

Donal snorted as he fixed me with a hard stare.

'The O'Rourke himself attacks traitors. With Maguire he destroyed O'Ferrall's country in Meath. And how else are my men to be properly fed? These cursed Dartrymen claim to need our protection, yet swiftly hide their food when we enter their homes. My men will do as I command, regardless of the whims of a distant overlord. And remember to keep your place, for being a Dartryman does not make you a chieftain.'

The Scot's arrogance left me feeling shocked beyond belief. The blood instantly rose to my head, as I spoke thoughts that would have been best kept to myself.

'You do not think of your men, but only of yourself. I would rather eat shamrock than bear arms with you against fellow believers.'

Donal MacCabe's pale-blue eyes smouldered in his rugged features for what felt like an eternity. I sought not to shuffle awkwardly when his low growl reached me.

'You want money Spaniard? I can give it to you. You also wish to return home?'

His words caught me unawares and I squinted at him curiously.

'What do you mean?'

'I can give you safe passage back home or wherever else you wish to go. The Indies, perhaps?'

I was overwhelmed by outrage as I took a step forward and sought to push him away, yet the gallowglass constable was built like a rock, and my shoving did not move him an inch.

'You eavesdropped!'

MacCabe's voice was raised as he pointed at me with his forefinger.

'Soft popinjay, you spurn the tradition of centuries. Raiding one's neighbours is not to be so easily slighted by someone as bad as a Sassenach coward.'

My blood boiled again while his thralls gathered about him with their axes already raised. Seeking to ignore their provocation, I turned on my heel and stalked off through the ring of gallowglasses with a contemptuous rebuff.

'You are wrong.'

MacCabe shouted at me angrily.

'You will never truly be one of us! You are false ally! You shall abandon us - vanish like the captain!'

My face must have been the picture of fury when I stopped in my tracks with balled fists, for his words cut deep like dagger thrusts.

'The O'Reillys are deep in the pocket of the enemy, fool! You make pathetic excuses so as not to fight!'

It was all I could do to shrug off his taunts as his threat rang in my ears.

'I shall teach you, Spaniard! No one spurns Donal Mac-Cabe!'

I returned to the outhouse with as brisk a pace as I could manage, which was fast enough to get me away from the Scots yet not so hasty as to indicate cowardice. Yet upon entering my quarters I fell upon my bed and hid myself underneath the blankets, since it was all I could do to stop myself from shaking. Having witnessed the brutality of the gallowglasses first hand, I tried to think of ways in which I could flee Dartry unharmed. I snatched up the bandolier and took the ring out of it, holding it close and feeling reassured by its value. I hoped that it would one day place me beyond the threat to life and limb and the petty intrigues of military men.

After it was returned to its hiding place, I fell into a deep and dreamless slumber, which was interrupted during the late afternoon when the bondsman returned to the outhouse. I hastily told him of my encounter with the gallowglasses, and a look of concern flashed across his face.

'The Scots are not lightly crossed, yet Donal is careful when choosing his victims. The constable knows that you are to be adopted by the chieftain this week and will not risk incurring the MacGlannagh's anger needlessly.'

'But what if he attempts to harm me while hiding his hand?'

Nial nodded his understanding as he picked up a candle and placed it between us. The light flickered against his face as he stared at me intently.

'I do not think you have much to fear, at least not until Muireann openly commits herself to Cathal. My guess is that Donal wanted you to join his number in the hope that it might impress the ollave. His hopes of wooing her become slimmer by the day, for although he has a mind for gaining power through force, he lacks tact or subtlety. His manners towards you may have appeared forceful, yet that is as gentle an approach as he can manage. I do not think he meant to cause you any real harm, and you did after all leave their company unscathed.'

'And what happens when Muireann commits to Cathal?' I asked nervously.

'That may change things,' he sighed. 'Although by then you will be a son of Dartry, maybe even form part of the chieftain's bodyguard, if that is also your will.'

My inclusion among the bluejackets was not something I had ever considered, although I knew the members of the exalted force well from my time spent training them in the use of the firearm. On the one hand I desired the added protection that joining them would afford me, though I dreaded the lack of private space in the ringfort.

'It is my will,' I replied after a few moments.

'Then we shall see it done upon the completion of your rite of passage,' he said, as a broad smile grew on his face.

'What rite of passage?' I asked, feeling both curious and fearful.

'Has no one mentioned it to you?' he asked in surprise. 'Ah well, then I suppose that it falls to me to tell you. Towards the end of winter, those boys among the tribe who are on the cusp of manhood are led deep into the forest, where they swear an oath of fealty to the chieftain and the tribe. They are then commanded to claim prey that they shall feast on with their fellows, after a brief ritual to mark their passage.'

So it was that the following Sunday after Mass, the boys who had come of age were gathered at the door of Saint Mel. I shuffled awkwardly among their number, which included the boy-prince Lochlain. Muireann's son and his handful of peers cast me baffled looks as I appeared with a rifle upon my shoulder. This was the only deviation from the traditional appearance of a kern which had been permitted to me. The cassock and other English clothes, which I had donned ever since the siege of Rosclogher, had long since been abandoned at the bondsman's insistence, and I had my old tunic and mantle fluttering about my shoulders instead.

The chieftain and the larger part of the assembly were gathered in front of us. I could see that Cathal *Dubh* had since returned to his feet, and stood behind Manglana like some crooked, broken shadow. Dervila and Muireann stared at Lochlain with fearful expressions as the bard Fearghal stepped forward with a fierce gaze. He delivered an ode about the boy named Sétanta, the nephew of King Conor of Ulster, who gained the revered name of Cu Chulainn when he slew the hound of Culain.

As the sunlight streamed through the fragmented clouds overhead, we were all transfixed by the bard's words until at last his account was ended. Fearghal then passed his eyes over us one by one before speaking again.

'It was the slaying of the beast which rendered Cu Chulainn a man. And it shall be the slaying of a beast today which shall pronounce you all fighting Dartrymen, ready and willing to serve your liege lord upon the battlefield and to protect the borders of our kingdom.'

Cathal the Black then stepped forward and turned towards the parents of the boys around me.

'Bid farewell to your sons, O worthy mothers and fathers, for the proverb is as old as the mountains: that a son is a son until he comes of age.'

Some wept openly as they embraced the boys for a last time, and Lochlain was caught in the embrace of his mother and grandmother. At last the chieftain raised his sword to salute us, addressing us in a voice which boomed across the town.

'Return as Dartrymen, or do not return at all!'

Nial ordered us to follow his lead, and a troop of bluejackets escorted us as we commenced our descent towards the lake. Swift ferries bore us to the woods across the water, over which there hung slight tendrils of fog. We marched through the trees in silence, and we had hardly covered a third rise full of trees when I noticed that the young prince had fallen in behind me.

'Are you scared, Spaniard?' he whispered to me beneath his breath.

'Why should I be scared, boy?' I scoffed, wondering why he had said that.

'You look upset, but in truth there is not much to fear from today's endeavour, except for the shadows of the night.'

'Ah, so you suspect that I share your fear of the dark?'

'No,' he said, taken aback that I was indifferent to his show of sympathy, 'yet I thought you may require some reassurance, since you are an alien and new to our ways.'

'My thanks, princeling,' I said, with as little contempt as I could manage. 'I am deeply grateful for your concern on my behalf.'

'Never fear, Spaniard,' he added earnestly. 'I know that by the end of the day, you shall have earned your passage into manhood.'

His words left me feeling greatly irked, since I was already deeply frustrated at having to be led along into the woods on a senseless caper with a bunch of whiskerless lads. I had also renounced my comfortable English clothes in the bargain. Lochlain was surprised when I stopped and turned towards him, my face the picture of profound annoyance.

'I was easily two years your junior when I killed my first man. I still remember him, a snarling, mustachioed infidel, hanging by one hand to a wall of Saint Elmo. Afterwards men slapped me on the back and told me that it had made me a man and a defender of the cross, but it made little difference to the weight on my soul. I can still see his face now, if I close my eyes and try hard enough. I can still see the stone with which I smashed his fingers, leaving him to fall back upon a spear raised by one of his own fellows. Impalement is never a pretty sight, no matter how it happens.'

'A-and why do you tell me this now, Spaniard?' muttered Lochlain.

'Because no amount of boars, deer, pine martens or wild rabbits will ever replace what it means to kill a man!' I growled. The boy's jaw dropped as he beheld my dark stare. 'Do not forget that, regardless of how many of them you slay tonight while you run around the woods with dreams of becoming your Cu Chulainn!'

Lochlain could not find words to reply, and his expression appeared both wounded and fearful as Nial's voice could be heard calling out to us from the hilltop behind me.

'Make haste, you two! Do not delay! We must make camp before the hunting can start!'

Our march ended upon the banks of the river Drowse, where we set about erecting tents and bivouacs. A few of the bluejackets kept watch around our encampment, while a serious air overcame the boys, who sharpened their spears and practiced drawing their arrows on newly fitted bowstrings. The scouts returned towards dusk, then held counsel with Nial, who listened to their words intently before addressing us.

'The woods are full of beasts,' he said, 'and free of enemies and dangerous wolf packs. You shall each be assigned a bugle before you depart, to use if you encounter inordinate peril. Yet do not resort to it lightly, for it will mean delaying your passage into manhood by another year.'

One by one the boys departed with sword and spear, after receiving a horn from the bondsman. I hesitated to walk up to him, so that he walked over to me himself.

'Friend Juan,' he said, as I looked back at him with a wry grin.

'The chieftain asked me to remind you,' he said, 'that if you undergo this rite, you shall henceforth be fully bound by the laws of this land.'

I did not display any acknowledgement of his words, although my mind raced as to the implications of this. Upon once more concluding that I had no choice but to accept, I nodded back at him.

'It is as I assumed.'

'And do you choose it freely?' he replied, watching me closely for any hints of doubt.

'Yes,' I said firmly.

'Then Godspeed, and may the Lord guide you towards worthy prey,' he said, passing me the last horn he held.

He turned back to his companions who were gathered about their fire. I reluctantly slung the bugle upon my shoulder, and turned towards the surrounding trees, making for the distant silhouette of Lochlain who had been the last of the Irish boys to make his way into the woods. One of the bluejackets served me with a slight smile and a nod as I walked away from the camp, yet I ignored him as I entered the forest, hoping that some large creature might swiftly present itself. I longed to be finished with the whole ridiculous business and to return to the town.

As the sun descended, I took soft steps into the thickening copse, wary of snapping twigs that might disturb any unsuspecting prey. The slightest rustle had me turning towards the sound with my rifle raised, yet it was all too often caused by the wind in the trees. At least two hours were spent this way, with the leaves overhead sometimes thinning enough to reveal tufts of grey cloud. After abandoning the fading prints of a badger, I wandered for a time in search of another trail, and my heart leapt when at last I saw the unmistakable signs of a boar, made evident by the outline of hooves in the low grass, which proceeded clearly into a great thicket up ahead.

My spirits were raised by this discovery, since the prize of the pig was considered a symbol of great bravery. Swinging the rifle off my shoulder, I held it before me as I made after the tracks, listening carefully for the sound of my quarry. My pursuit of a crooked passage through a tree-covered descent brought me deeper into a darkening wood, until the tracks were lost on a floor covered with rubble and tree bark. With a curse I kept to my awkward descent, but I had all but despaired of finding the beast when I picked up its trail once more.

I spotted one hoof print which resembled a devil's head, then held my breath when I came upon another score of them in the mud, which ran down a shallow gully. A shrill, grunting sound made me halt abruptly; I fell on my knees and crouched low among the tree roots. I crept towards the provenance of the sound and attempted to snatch a glimpse of the hog as I drew nearer to it. This task was rendered impossible by the trees, which grew beyond the ridge itself and made a clear shot impossible. Upon reaching the edge of the natural ditch there was no further course left open to me except to slide down softly into the gully itself, a trying task given the growing darkness in the dense forest.

A low snort to my left suddenly revealed a monster of a pig, which stood well within range of my gun as it tore tree roots out of the edge of the gully. Its head bobbed furiously as it gobbled its fare, the size of the beast leaving me stunned. Its unnerving presence reminded me of the immediate peril of my position, where only a clean shot through the hog's heart would allow me to emerge from the gully unscathed. My fear was instantly lessened when I thought of the praise which would greet me if I returned with the pig to camp. My arms were steadied as I leant onto one knee and slowly drew back the doghead, reciting my psalm in my heart for fear that I might alert the beast to my presence.

The constant bobbing of its shoulders delayed me training my sights upon it. I was about to pull the serpentine when a loud rustle was heard above me, and I was startled to see the figure of man standing above my right shoulder. It was one of the horseboys of Brogan, the huge son of the gallowglass constable MacCabe. A wide grin was spread across the boy's face as he raised a large branch and held it out before him, then brought it crashing down across his knee.

The sound was as loud as it was sickening, leaving me to fumble with the gun as I redirected my aim at the wicked boy. Yet no sooner was his vile errand achieved than the Scot swiftly vanished. I next noticed the onrushing boar, which had abandoned its feeding. I took aim at it, but no sooner was my desperate shot fired than I knew it was in vain, for the pig's charge never wavered as the ball bounced off its head.

My rifle was held across my knees as I returned to my feet, and the blow of its gnarled tusks flung me out of the gully like a skyward falcon, the rifle spinning out of my hands and beyond my sight. The wind left my breast as I crashed to the ground, so that it was a few moments before I could shake off the ensuing daze and rise to my feet. As I grimaced from the pain in my side, I was grateful that my insides had not been ripped open, yet these thoughts were swiftly abandoned when the pig charged out of the ditch towards me.

I caught sight of the rifle, which had fallen but a few steps away, and I was instantly on my feet and running towards it. A glimpse over my shoulder revealed that the pig had torn out of the gully and was making straight towards me. I had barely reached the rifle, when my left leg was butted out from below me. I was sent flying backwards again, and the bottom of my tunic was ripped open by the pig's sharp tusks.

I was utterly winded from my second fall, so that I at first barely noticed the growls and barking which followed. Then I saw the boar caught between two large wolfhounds, which held it by the ear and tail. I could hardly believe my luck. I drew my dagger as I hurled myself upon the bristled back of my prey, then slammed the blade upwards, behind the creature's right foreleg, as I sought to pierce its heart.

No sooner was this blow dealt, than the boar ripped its ear from the mouth of a hound, and dealt the dog a sideways stroke with its tusks that sent it rolling over the ground with an agonised yelp. As the other dog held on to its tail, the pig wriggled about with furious intent. Its sudden movements wrenched the dagger from my hand as I wrapped my other arm tightly about its haunches in a pathetic attempt to keep it from moving. For long instants the remaining hound and I thrashed about in a flurry of leaves, seeking to restrain the boar's powerful throes until we were both splattered with blood. Despite our efforts, the cursed pig somehow wrenched itself free and shot off into the brush.

'Whoreson,' I gasped.

The dog was after the boar like a shot, and I did all I could to keep up with it, despite feeling faint from the number of blows I had received. It was not long afterwards that I came upon the two creatures beneath a great oak tree, with the hound snarling at the boar which had its back to the trunk behind it. The trail of blood it had left behind it had been abundant, and the great heaving of its sides made it clear that my thrust had been mortal. When it finally collapsed I stepped over towards the hound and sought to pull it away, but the dog withdrew when it heard a single phrase hissed behind me.

'*Tit siar! Tit siar!*'

The provenance of the two wolfhounds was revealed as I turned to find Lochlain standing but a few feet away from me, a smile on his face.

'Good thrust, Spaniard. Almost clean.'

I was dismayed at having been rescued by a mere lad, but I exhaled wearily and tore my stare away from him. I stepped back towards the boar to retrieve my knife from its chest and swiftly end its suffering. As my blade severed its windpipe, warm trickles of blood ran down my forearm, so that it almost felt as if I were being filled by the blood of a new life. The pig stiffened, leaving me to return to my feet, my ears ringing from the sound of its recent screeching. I felt ablaze in a sudden rush of emotion, flushed by the realisation of what the kill had just achieved, my limbs throbbing from their cuts and bruises.

'That was a good stab to the heart,' said Lochlain. 'It was clean, I saw it.'

'Hardly,' I gasped, having still not regained my breath. 'I have stabbed pigs before, just not wild ones. It was not the heart that was pierced, but an artery.'

'A kill nonetheless!' exclaimed the princeling. 'And a valiant effort!'

'I would have killed it with a single shot,' I said, gritting my teeth at the recollection of the Scottish runt who had disturbed the pig, 'were it not for that whoreson of a gallowglass!'

'Which gallowglass?'

'Did you not see him?' I growled at the boy, who appeared genuinely surprised. 'Brogan's horseboy alerted the beast to my presence just when I was about to despatch it!'

'They dared interfere in the rite of passage?' whispered Muireann's son to nobody in particular. He appeared visibly shaken. 'But that is impossible. Surely even the gallowglass wouldn't dare...'

'I swear by the Virgin's honour that it is the truth,' I snapped, 'and as soon as I return to the village...'

'Do not act in haste Spaniard,' said the boy. 'The gallow-glass are not to be taken lightly.'

'What other course is open to me? It is clear that they want me dead.'

During our discussion more youthful faces had appeared behind the chieftain's grandson. Lochlain raised his arm, signalling to them to keep their distance so that we could resume our private discussion.

'I will speak of this treachery to my grandmother,' he said, 'for the Scots are a law unto themselves in Dartry, but she holds some sway with their leader.'

'My thanks for your generous offer, prince,' I replied, 'but why should she care about what has passed?'

'She will care,' he snapped, seizing me by my blood-soaked forearm with sudden passion in his voice. 'The gallowglasses have never gone this far. And she holds you in high esteem. But you must promise me that you shall say nothing of what happened.'

'Then how do I explain my wretched state?' I replied, leaving Lochlain to observe my tattered tunic and bloodied limbs.

'Say that you were on the trail of another pig before you were attacked by a sow. Say that you unwittingly came between her and her young.'

I stared at the dead pig, realising that I had indeed slain a sow, before grinning at the princeling's quickness of thought.

'One learns swiftly to think on his feet,' he said, 'after years spent in the retinue of my grandparents.'

Then he smiled and turned to his fellows, shouting at them to bear the sow away. We went in the direction of the gully, where Lochlain drew his dagger to end the life of his wounded hound which still whimpered in agony. I drifted away from the boys when I spotted my rifle lying across the grass. As I stooped over it my hand fell upon the last powder charge on my bandolier, and I breathed a huge sigh of relief to find the ring still inside it.

Thereafter I returned to the company of the Irish youths, who had recovered the slain sow and bound her legs to a pair of long spears borne by four of their number. With the ridge to our backs we rejoined more of their number in a small clearing but two musket shots' distance from the gully. To my astonishment I saw two more slain pigs hung from the branch of an oak tree. My sow was clearly the largest as it was slung up alongside them, where it also bled freely from its throat.

Following our travails during the hunt, I rested with the boys-turned-men who eventually cut the pigs down and bore them back to camp. We were received by loud cheers from the bluejackets in Nial's company, and the bondsman appeared overjoyed by our return, walking over to each youth and serving each of them with affectionate punches on the shoulder.

That night the forest was full of the new Dartrymen's cries as we feasted on our prizes around a huge fire and slaked the pork fat on our throats with mead. As always, I drifted away from the boisterous company as fights broke out amid peals of laughter, staring into the immense darkness that lay beyond the firelight. I shuddered to think that I would soon have to flee into the wilds again, before the Scots could claim my life.

XXXVII

Rosclogher, Dartry, County Leitrim

13 March – 8 April 1589

The following morning the new men of Dartry were kicked to their feet by the bluejackets. I found the sight of the youths' wretched awakening amusing, especially when I thought of their exuberance the previous day. This was coupled with a tinge of pity as I did my best to help the bleary-eyed youths strike their tents and bivouacs, then pack their belongings. The choice cuttings of boar were already salted and placed in a small barrel, which was entrusted to Lochlain to bear to his lord grandfather.

Our first day of manhood was bright and clear, and many of the townsfolk appeared to greet our return. After crossing the lake back into the town we made our way towards the abbey, with throngs of villagers milling about us and crying the nicknames of Lochlain and his returning band. Dal Verme and the Canarians were also present, and returned my salute with a nod as they beheld the happenings along the water.

Upon entering Saint Mel we heard Mass delivered by O'Ronayne, then knelt in line before the altar as he anointed us with an oily cross on our foreheads while leading us on in prayer. We blinked at the brightness of daylight as we gathered outside the abbey before making our way onto the green, where the chieftain waited for us on horseback in the company of his entire retinue. A varied cluster of expressions greeted us, and the pride on the faces of Lochlain's grandparents and mother contrasted with the bard's frown.

Donal MacCabe's scowl left me bristling with rage, so that only my respect for Muireann's son kept me from seizing up my rifle to serve him with a mortal shot. Upon noticing the baleful hatred in my stare, the constable served me with an odious grin. He ignored the approach of the princeling who covered the last few yards to his lord grandfather, then fell on his knees and held up the best cuttings of the three pigs we had slain in the woods. He gestured but once to the seven new Dartrymen behind him, and we also fell to our knees and recited the oath which Nial had taught us:

'Through the blood of our offerings
We have been made men,
Bound of our will
To the laws of our land.

To its protector our king
The knee shall be bent.
To our last drop of blood
Our lord shall be upheld

*Our shields shall be borders
For our kin and heads.
Our spears shall drive
The foes from our lawn'*

When this was done the chieftain nodded to his steward, Malachy, who made his way towards us. At his back were two servants, one of whom bore a load in his arms that was furled in woollen blankets. The other stepped forward to take the barrel of pig flesh, and the steward ordered us to rise to our feet. One by one he stepped before us, staring us firmly in the eye as he spoke in a loud voice.

'Our lord accepts your desire to serve.'

So saying, he reached out to the burden carried by his lackey, and drew a scabbarded sword, which he handed to Lochlain.

'Our lord bequeaths this sword unto you, on your first day of manhood. It is a mark of your oath of fealty.'

After we were each awarded a blade, the chieftain and his party withdrew to the tower house, and the newly armed youths returned to their homes and families. Nial appeared with a smile on his face as he rested his hand upon my shoulder.

'A proud day for us both, my friend.'

'Should I henceforth reside in the ringfort?' I asked. 'No!' he exclaimed, frowning as if he found the thought repugnant. 'My private quarters are still yours to share for as long as you desire them. You are still under my command to do as you please, unless otherwise decreed by our lord.' No sooner did he say this than I immediately retired to the outhouse, where I fell into the deepest and most dreamless slumber.

The days which followed were largely without incident. Nothing much seemed to have changed by my becoming a Dartryman, save that the gallowglasses suddenly seemed to avoid me as if I had the pox. I was unsure whether to be heartened by or suspicious of the Scots' change in attitude towards me, and on a couple of occasions I could have sworn that I noticed a pair of them eyeing me from far off. Yet no further bother came of this, and I was left to endure my own daily boredom unhindered.

It was not two Sundays from the day of my return from across the water that a barefoot kern appeared at the outhouse to ask me to visit his master Cathal *Dubh*. So following my daily instruction of the kerns in the ringfort, I made my way through the town towards the great wooden cabins along the lake. A tranquil air seemed to hang over Manglana's town, with the general mood among the tribesmen almost cheerful at the prospect of the approaching summer months.

The tanist seemed possessed of the same disposition as I made my way past his guards towards his bedside. I found him seated upright, with his long, dark locks flowing about most of the shrivelled flesh on his face. Once I had sunk to one knee alongside him, my arm was held in the firm grip of one of his charred hands, his voice shaking when he spoke.

'On your feet, worthy Spaniard. I owe you my life.'

'Hardly, sire,' I replied after I had hung my head in shame for a few moments, which he evidently mistook for humility. "Tis after all but repayment of my long-standing debt to you.'

My stare broke away from his unsightly, broad grin, as he fell back on his rushes and patted the back of his head with his hand.

"'Twas a heavy blow to the head that I suffered. There is nothing I recall beyond the charge on the gate of Boyle.'

'A most tragic moment, sire,' I replied, 'with not much worth recalling thereafter.'

'I disagree, Spaniard,' he replied, 'for your gallantry is not to be overlooked.'

'But alas, sire, many more gallant than I perished that day, as we fought to rescue you from the field.'

'True,' he said as he nodded his head vigorously. 'True. Five fine sons of Dartry perished that day. And I have compensated their families for their grievous loss.'

We both fell silent at the memory of the fallen until he spoke again.

'I have called thee to share my gratitude, but also my joy at your recent tidings.'

'The adoption?'

'Yes, the adoption,' he said, smiling broadly once more, 'for what greater honour is there for us than to count upon you as our kin? De Cuéllar may have flown long ago, friend Juan, yet I would rather have one of you, than a hundred of his double-dealing sort.'

'You are too generous in your praise my lord,' I replied, 'for it is I that am honoured by my adoption into so worthy a tribe.'

Further pleasantries of this sort were exchanged, which would be both laborious and wearisome to recount further. Our conversation mercifully moved on to the benefits that I presented to the tribe and how the chieftain would regard me as an important advisor in the fighting months of summer. The tanist then touched upon the challenges of the tribe and how the days which lay ahead might be the most treacherous and uncertain period that the MacGlannaghs of Dartry had yet faced.

'The Binghams will have no rest until we are subdued. Our spurning of the Composition has left them furious. They want our resistance broken, for they have enemies among their own people in London who are fast spreading the word against their brutal methods. The allies of the O'Rourke in Dublin tell us that these words have reached the ears of the English queen, whose viceroy in Dublin is no friend of theirs either.'

'Then some respite beckons, perhaps,' I said, hopeful that the threat of the Binghams might yet be dispelled, allowing me a safer escape into the Irish wilds when I finally made my way back to Spain.

'As I said,' he replied, 'nothing is certain. Other dangers lurk on our borders, for one never can tell when a neighbouring tribe might intend to strike out at us, and rustle our heads of cattle. Yet of greater concern to me is the growing threat that lurks within our number, which threatens the very person of our lord himself.'

'What threat do you speak of ?!' I exclaimed, feeling at once distressed and shaken by his revelation.

Cathal gestured for me to lean over towards him, and as my head sagged forward, he whispered in my ear.

'You know of what I speak. It is a threat that has afflicted you for the duration of your stay in the town. A threat caused by those paid to defend us but who instead distress us.'

'The gallowglasses?' I asked, raising my head and meeting his stare, and feeling at once elated and flattered that he had finally shared his concern about them directly with me.

'Yes, who else?' he snorted, then sat back again on his bed as he gestured for me to pass him the carafe on the ground. After he had slaked his thirst with mead, he waved at his page, who disappeared from the hut.

'It is hard to converse on an empty stomach, Spaniard,' he said, 'and O'Ronayne says that I must keep up my strength and not shy away from meat. You shall share it with me as we talk, for it must be hungry work listening to me for so long.'

'Why, my lord,' I protested, but he fell into disturbing chuckling and waved my objections away.

'Your manners are without flaw, friend Spaniard, but your stomach is possessed of louder protests than your tongue, much as you think that I have not heard you.'

Then the merriment in his stare suddenly vanished, to be replaced by one of cold resolve.

'Unfortunately, the threat presented by Donal MacCabe is no matter of jest, friend Juan. 'Tis no secret that he is as ruthless as he is ambitious and bloodthirsty. Yet of more concern to me is his lust for the throne of our lord.'

'He would not dare!'

'He has dared more and won,' was the tanist's instant reply, 'and he is slowly eyeing the next piece in his power game, which will strengthen his eventual claim.'

'What piece? What claim?'

The next look from the tanist betrayed both amusement and disbelief.

'Are you truly ignorant to the ambition that the constable of the gallowglass has long harboured above all else?'

Upon recalling my last conversation with the lady Dervila, my heart ached to think that Donal was closing in on Muireann's hand. This was confirmed by the tanist, who had observed the growing frown on my face with interest.

'Muireann.'

'Never!' I growled in disgust. 'She would never lower herself so!'

'Lower herself?' whispered the tanist, as he helped himself to a drink. 'The constable is a very powerful man.'

'But a low-born, mercenary cutthroat!' I spat in anger. 'There's ten a copper of his kind in every port and town!'

'Be that as it may, he is one with powerful friends. Lady Dervila is a big supporter of his. It was at her suggestion that he be admitted into the assembly.'

'Was it?' I exclaimed in disbelief. 'Yet surely Dervila would not subject her son's widow to such a monster?'

'What if Muireann's was a choice between two monsters?'

His self-effacing question left me both flushed and speechless once more, and it was a fair few moments before I recovered enough to protest his implication.

'You are not a monster!'

'Even my most loyal retainers would hesitate to agree with you.' Cathal smiled, after raising his brows at my loud protest. 'And I need little convincing that my face has long been deprived of whatever youthful fairness I may have once possessed.'

'Well your retainers are hardly loyal at all then,' I snarled, 'for you bear the scars of a terrible malady for which you had no fault! Men should praise the Lord for delivering so worthy a leader from the clutches of a deathly pox!'

The tanist's worn lips were stretched to form his unsettling smile, and he seemed overcome by embarrassment as he shifted his head sideways and kept his stare on the doorway behind me.

'You are a good man, Spaniard,' he said, 'for never before has anyone taken pity on my plight save for Aengus, who was ever a devoted and valiant ally to my cause. He and I may have been born of different mothers, yet never was a man closer to me than he, not even my own blood brothers, curse their evil souls.'

'I never knew the lord Aengus,' was my terse reply, 'although he strikes me as having been a man who knew quality when he saw it. Which is why there can be no doubt that the ollave will choose you over the Scottish cutthroat.'

'"Tis the will of her adopted father, Spaniard,' replied the tanist, 'yet will our lord MacGlannagh's preference be enough for me to secure her hand? The lady Bourke has as much sway with Muireann as the chieftain, and she bears no love for me, nor would she see my cause advanced.'

I quivered with anger at his reference to Dartry's queen, who had often mocked him before the whole assembly.

'I shall speak to the lady Bourke!' I hotly declared. 'I have her ear and can make her see reason!'

Mine was an impetuous outburst, and met with a low chuckle as the tanist rested his hand on my forearm.

'Do not commit yourself to vain endeavours on my behalf. Other tribesmen have tried to make her see reason, and to identify her deep loathing of me. It has all been for naught. Yet it is the ear of another that I would have you fill with speech in my favour.'

'But mention the name, sire, for I am in your debt many times over!'

'"Tis the prize that I seek, whose name is known to you already.'

'Muireann?' I exclaimed, instantly regretting my offer on his behalf.

'Yes, the *ollamh*. Men have told me that she holds you in high regard, and often has she been heard praising your virtues with other tribesmen.'

This was a surprising revelation, and my astonishment must have been plainly in evidence, since my deformed protector smiled once more before he spoke again.

'O worthy Spaniard, you must believe me when I tell you that her esteem of you has always been of the highest order. And the esteem in which the lady Mac an Bhaird holds you can only have risen since you elected to turn Dartryman.'

I could think of nothing other than how Muireann's son had intervened to rescue me during the rite of manhood. I could only imagine what a pathetic figure I must have seemed to young Lochlain as I tussled with the wild pig, and inwardly prayed that he had not shared the sight of my hapless struggles with his mother.

'Of a certainty my heart yearns to meet your request,' I replied with a forced smile of my own, 'yet there is a quandary which may yet prevent me from fulfilling it.'

'And what would that be?' snapped the tanist, a scowl swiftly replacing his ready grin.

'I have no means to ensure that I can be your advocate with the ollave, since I do not meet her at any regular intervals.'

'What became of your training of Lady Bourke and her ladies?' he protested.

'Alas, my lord!' I replied with as much disappointment in my voice as I could muster. 'Lady Dervila disbanded the training following the flight of Captain de Cuéllar and his band of curs. Nowadays I only see the ollave at the abbey on Sunday mass, or in passing when she teaches her charges along the lake, or returns to Rosclogher with kerns at her back after leading them through passes known only to her.'

The tanist's glare was withdrawn as he closed his eyes and frowned, mulling over my words before slowly nodding his agreement. I cautiously cleared my throat as I awaited his next words with some trepidation. The tanist had always proved a steadfast and worthy protector of the Spanish castaways in Dartry, and I dared not disappoint one of his rank among the tribe. His moments of pensiveness were interminable as we sat there for what seemed like hours. It had been a long day which had left me both weary and in need of refreshment, and I soon found my eyelids meeting as I drifted off into a slumber that was both untimely and impolite.

'I have it!' he suddenly barked, in a voice so loud that it had me sitting upright again and observing him as if I had never nodded off. 'The solution has presented itself to me as clearly as the brightest day!'

His voice and stare were possessed of a great exuberance as he explained himself further.

'You are one of us now,' he gasped, 'yet have still so much more to learn about our ways! What better gift can I bestow on the man to whom I owe my own life, than the private teaching of the *filidecht* by the *ollamh* herself?'

"'Tis a plan both subtle and perfect in its design, my lord!' I exclaimed. My heart leapt at the prospect of being in such close proximity to Muireann, though I immediately wondered whether this would really further endear Cathal to her.

Yet the tanist was as joyful as if she had already promised her hand to him. Any thoughts I had to dissuade him from his design were banished as he ordered his retainers to fetch us mead. His heart opened up to me as the honeyed brew warmed our throats, and I feigned as much interest as I could in his words, all the while thinking how to best profit from the incredible opportunity that had suddenly presented itself to me.

'Ever since the first day I saw her, Spaniard,' he said, raising his tankard as his servant rushed to serve him more ale, 'my heart has coveted her. I recall the day of her handfast to Aengus *Cliste*. Her radiant smile and the flowers in her hair. It was a happy day, one which was all too infrequent in the dark days of my true father's brief reign. I observed it all from the shadows, as glad for her as I was for her husband, certain that such a day would never be known to me.'

'And yet...' I interceded, 'and yet...here you are...'

He exhaled wearily and took a long and deep drink from his mug, as if its contents were the cure to a malady. To my dismay he proceeded to rest it on the ground and pull the hair out of his face with both hands. It was all I could do not to flinch as I stared back at him, seeing the full horror of his face revealed to me for the first time. The smallpox had scarred all of his face so that there were more marks across his cheeks than if he'd had whiskers, and his forehead resembled the hardened bark of a tree. His chin and throat were also shrivelled. Yet within the husk of his flesh there emerged features that hinted at a handsome boyishness, which was complemented at all times by the thoughtful stare of his dark eyes.

'I have always coveted the *ollamh*. Yet know Spaniard, that I would not impart the horror of my countenance upon any damsel, not unless my hand is forced by the tribe.'

So saying, he returned the long fringe from his forehead back over his face, as if he were hurling a sheet back over the decayed corpse of what had once been a man endowed with fair looks.

'Despite the mark of the pox, you are still sightlier than your rival,' I replied, feeling sorry for him. 'Besides, Muireann does not strike me as the type to be swayed by gentle looks and similar trifles. Reputation and honour will count for much with her.'

'Therein lies my hope,' he said, seizing up my wrists and looking at me closely, 'and why I will be forever in your debt if you sway her towards me. Know that I will always accord her the highest honour and protection, for once our heads of cattle are combined, I shall become the wealthiest tribesman after the chieftain.'

'And that is as it should be, my lord,' I said, rising to my feet and regarding him in awe, 'for the late Aengus needs replacing in these troubled times.'

'Ah Aengus.' He sighed, lifting his horn to his lips, and leaving me to wonder if the mention of the chieftain's late son always provoked the same reaction from the worthiest men among the tribe.

Cathal took another long swig before regaining enough composure to further address me.

'He is missed, Juan, sorely missed. A man of such valour that the hair rises on my scarred body just to think of the position which I fill, so overcome am I by my unworthiness in occupying the position of such a foremost lord. Just the memory of his knowledge and martial prowess fills me with awe.'

'Abandon it,' I said sternly, daring to seize him by the shoulder, 'for not for nowt does our lord MacGlannagh entrust you as his second-in-command. You showed scant abandon for your own life when charging the walls of Boyle, and there are few who would so selflessly confront ruin and death in the heat of battle.'

'That is praise indeed from a soldier of Spain,' he replied, 'although I fear that I made a complete fool of myself before the bridge.'

'Is not the whole of our struggle but a fool's errand?'

He turned his head towards me in confusion, before a low chuckle left his lips.

'If you lie so sweetly to the *ollamh* about me, I shall be wed to her before the booleying season is upon us.'

No sooner had I left him than he proved as good as his word. On the following day a knave appeared in my quarters, instructing me that his mistress, the lady Mac an Bhaird had agreed to teach me the *filidecht*, with the blessing and the consent of the chieftain. My first lesson took place under the old oak along Lough Melvin where I had often seen Muireann teaching Lochlain and the other young MacGlannaghs of high birth. As I sat between its roots she stared at me curiously, perhaps wondering what it would be like to teach a grown man. In the moments of silence that ensued I wondered what it might be like to be instructed by a woman in a subject other than cleaning or sewing, before returning to my feet and engaging in a curt bow.

'My thanks, ollave Mac an Bhaird, for agreeing to teach me the ways of your people.'

Her stare turned from one of passing interest to a look that verged on the contemptuous.

'These shall be our last words in Latin for the remainder of your instruction. From this moment on we shall converse in High Gaelic. There is no other tongue in which my teaching can be imparted.'

Just like the tanist, the ollave also kept her word. It was suddenly obvious why I had been kept apart from her younger charges, since it would have been useless to include me among their number if I could not understand a word they were saying. Yet although my knowledge of the tongue was not fluent, it was by that time at least rudimentary, given that I had spent almost half a year in Dartry. I had also received some instruction from Geraldine during the siege of Rosclogher. The ollave appeared greatly pleased by this and often broke into a warm smile whenever I raised my hand and closed my eyes in thought, until I had obtained the right word to describe the things she gestured at.

For just like the rainwater passes over ground until it has formed streams and valleys, so had the flow of Gaelic about me left its impression upon my mind through ears which had always been open to it. The ollave did much to increase this learning by using both carrot and stick, and I was soon attempting snatches of conversation with Nial and the other men of Rosclogher. They also grinned openly at my attempts and burst into the odd chuckle at my accent or odd choice of word. Upon overhearing my exchange of conversation with the village smith, the Milanese man-at-arms Luigi Dal Verme strode up to me with a dark look on his face.

'Dress like them if you must. Yet need you resort to such a barbarous tongue?'

'I am free to do as I choose,' I replied, 'and this tongue may yet prove to be my passport back home.'

The Milanese mercenary's lips twitched in distaste as he studied me from head to toe. I found myself discomfited by his keen observation.

'The way you're going, I doubt you'll even think of home for much longer.'

After spitting between my feet, he turned on his heel and marched off. Yet I ignored his proud words as I persisted in endearing myself further to the tribesmen and expressing interest in all their ways and customs. My grasp of their tongue proved crucial to unlocking their minds and hearts to me, so that before long the parish of Rosclogher and its environs were opening up to me in ways I had barely foreseen. My recent efforts to further ingratiate myself with the locals did not go unnoticed, and word of it soon reached the higher echelons of the tribe.

The year I had spent at the oar before my shipwreck in Ireland had left me broken in body and spirit, but my recovery in recent months had left me stronger than I had ever been before, able to avail myself of the opportunities for assimilation which began to present themselves. My invitations to Manglana's hunting expeditions became a common occurrence, and I soon found myself riding at the right shoulder of the chieftain. He often cheered aloud in delight whenever a fallow deer was felled by my shots from horseback, and these open displays of favour had the other highborn tribesmen seeking out my counsel on various matters regarding firearms and marksmanship.

They were heady days, which left me revelling in my newfound popularity. We charged through the trees, closely following the hounds on the scent. In tight throngs we closed in on quarry that skidded over the lush grass, striking it through the heart before it even had time to regain its footing. Countless beasts were slain this way after the breaking of the crisp, glorious dawns of the new spring. The freshness of the air and the sparkling dampness of the heather brought a contented warmth to the heart, amid the first hint of berries in the bushes and the loud chirping of birds in the trees.

These emerging surrounds added to my wonder at being a new Dartryman as I further appreciated the beauty of the land. The passing of the seasons was enshrined by the tribesmen's manners and customs, stirring in me an affection for the medieval society which had adopted me. The filth and despair of the trench and the city seemed but a distant memory at times, for despite the troubles and frugality brought about by the struggle against the Sassenachs, there always seemed to be enough sustenance and shelter to go round for all the inhabitants of the small kingdom.

My adoption also kindled a new interest and hunger within me for all martial matters since I was keen to guide my fellow tribesmen in their struggle. My views were also validated when the Scottish smugglers returned to our coast with the provisions that I had requested. The consignment of horns swiftly replaced the older powder flasks of wood, which in the months that followed reduced all spoilage. A dozen snaphance guns were also delivered, which were gleefully shared between the keenest marksmen among the bluejackets, who in turn gave up their lesser firearms to other bodyguards.

The guns proved very popular among Manglana's closest men, who needed no urging to train their aim for hours on end. During these sessions my presence was very much in demand, and before long the men were hitting difficult targets from respectable distances, with one even managing to split a card from forty feet. The main appeal of the new guns lay in not having to fiddle with the match cord required by a matchlock, although greater care had to be employed in order to protect the spring mechanism which operated the latest rifles.

The guns could at times be devilish devices if not looked after properly, and I often found myself summoned to examine a misfiring weapon in the ringfort. It was at times like these that the respect towards me bordered upon reverence, and men hung on my every word when I explained how the guns were to be cleaned and stored. Word of the new rifles spread quickly amongst the tribe, so that many regarded the fighting season with less fear and greater resolve. Some gifts also found their way to the outhouse, in the form of food, or even ale and clothing, and were quietly deposited by tribesmen at sundown but a few feet from our door.

They were the happiest times I had known in the kingdom of Manglana, and one evening I shared my contentment with my confidant, as I sipped the cup of brandy he had served me.

'And to think that now, despite all I have been through, there is no place in truth that I would rather be.'

'Except the Indies?' Nial asked.

My head fell back with a laugh.

'Perhaps. After all I only know what I have seen and touched myself.'

A small smile grew on the sword master's lips as he regarded me quietly from the shadows.

'We know so little about you, Spaniard. So very little about you...'

I was too drunk to reply, and in the days that followed the realisation grew upon me that I had last been so contented when stationed at Willebroek, during my first days of love with Elsien, the miller's daughter. The last glow of dusk was barely visible behind the mountains as I wandered alone alongside the lake, back towards the town. Word had reached me that the gallowglass had been stationed back at Duncarbery, which meant that I was free to wander about the town and its surrounds unmolested. In the wan torchlight of the distant sentinels, I sat cross-legged along the water, clenching the emerald ring so tightly that its edges dug into the flesh of my palm.

'To think that the New World was around me all this time, and that I failed to see it. All because I clung to a forlorn hope, that of returning to an old world of greed and inhumanity. These men share all trials and joys as one. Their ways may be antiquated, yet who is more primitive when it comes to defending one's own folk?'

My discomfort eased as I opened my hand before my face and stared at the priceless bauble.

'What would become of me,' I whispered to it, 'if any of the tribe discovered you upon my person? How much do I sacrifice for you, who come to me out of the mines across the ocean, after having passed through the hands of countless savages? What foul deeds led you into my keeping, for me to do all that is foul before you find yourself in another's possession?'

It then struck me that the silent stone in my hands was the cause of all the lies and misdeeds I had committed since my arrival in Dartry. A deep revulsion filled me at the thought of all the advantages which had befallen me ever since my stand upon the bridge of Boyle. With a hiss I sprang to my feet, my fingers enclosing themselves about the ring as I readied to hurl it into the blackness that stretched out ahead of me.

'Fly from my hand, filth!' I rasped. 'Begone from the monsters who covet you, regardless of the suffering that their desire imparts upon others! The chains of your appeal shall die with me!'

I flung the ring away with as much strength as I could muster, so that the power of the throw dropped me to my knees. Not even the slightest splash was heard ahead of me as the heaviness of my breathing slowly subsided, and to my horror I found that the stone was still held in my hand. In that moment the revulsion I felt for myself was doubled, my resolve having vanished in the moment of truth. For in spite of the great happiness which had filled me of late, a great fear still held me under its sway, which even exceeded my longing for a life of comfort and plenty in the Indies.

The memory of Willebroek or of Elsien's youngest brother Pieter could not yet be so easily banished from my memory. It was in that quiet village that I had last known love and happiness, only for war to destroy my dreams. War was also ever upon the doorstep of Connacht, and my own future in Dartry was far from secure in the fighting season which lay ahead.

Indeed, our own presence amongst the Manglanas will spell further conflict, I thought to myself, *for Burke and his Bingham masters will invent any pretext to flood these lands with more troops. And will its people be ready to meet them, I wonder?*

With a sigh I returned the ring to my bandolier and trudged back towards the town, inwardly resolved to spare no strength in preparing my fellow Dartrymen for the fight which lay ahead. Yet if the worst was to happen and our enemy prevailed in our impending struggles, then I was determined to secure a passage to the Indies, should the chance of flight present itself to me. The ring would be key to this and could not be so readily consigned to the bottom of Lough Melvin.

It was a curious eventuality that my greater learning of the Irish tongue made my tuition harder to bear. I had never been one who thrived when learning things by rote, but the sheer amount of poetry I was expected to remember was endless. After a morning spent listening to the ollave translating Irish verse back into Latin, I could bear it no longer.

'Must I learn all of this poetry to become one of the tribe?'

She started at my abrupt question.

'It will enable you to learn our ways. To my people the poem-craft is more than the utterance of sentiment. It is what binds us to our ancestors and embodies our law and history.'

'But how long will it take me to learn it all?'

She pursed her lip.

'It took me twelve years to become a professor.'

I steadied myself at her revelation while she smiled at the shock on my face.

'The *filidecht* will allow you to honour the memory of our forebears, and strengthen your resolve to protect our people. Tell me of the high kings of Tara.'

I closed my eyes in concentration as I recalled the part of a poem which I had struggled for so long to learn word for word.

'The Seat of the Kings was its name:
the kingly line of the Milesians reigned in it:
five names accordingly were given it
from the time when it was Fordruim till it was Tara.
I am Fintan the poet,
I am a salmon not of one stream;
it is there I was exalted with fame,
on the sod-built stead, over Tara.'

Muireann beamed at me after the words were recited in her lilting tongue.

'If nothing else, you have mastered our tongue. The chieftain will be pleased to hear your hard-learned rhetoric.'

I sighed, lost in the countless names of high kings, heroes and heroines.

'I hope I am not asked about it, for I have forgotten the provenance of the Milesians.'

The ollave assumed a grave expression as her lip twitched in displeasure.

'The men from Spain who conquered Ireland.'

'The Gaels from Galicia?'

She nodded.

'And Tara was their seat of power?'

'The seat of the high kings of Ireland,' she corrected me with a grave frown, 'crowned upon the stone of destiny.'

Wary of my impending recital, I asked her more questions.

'And what of Fintain?'

'He was the seer who advised the high kings of Ireland. He survived the Deluge in the form of a salmon, then turned into an eagle and hawk before returning to human form. He lived for five thousand five hundred years thereafter and left the mortal realm in the fifth century when Ireland was converted to Christianity.'

It was all I could do to appear serious when she said this, for I could see that she meant every word. I felt discomfited as I tried to make sense of the poem, recalling a name I had once heard given to her late husband.

'And the salmon means wisdom? Is that why Aengus was given that name?'

An uncomfortable silence fell between us at his mention. The ollave's face was a picture of sadness which alerted me to my mistake, and my mind raced to think of a related subject.

'And I assume that the tanist is at times called a fox because he is sly?'

'Yes,' she slowly replied, appearing even more disconsolate than before.

'A byname most apt for a man both loyal and valiant,' I declared boldly, seizing the moment to pay off some of my tuition.

The ollave's demure expression hardly brightened at these words. After snatching a quick sidewards glimpse of me she stared at the lake for a few moments of silence, broken only by the slow soughing of the wind and her own sigh. At length she rose to her feet and gestured to me to follow her.

'Perhaps we can proceed with what remains of today's lesson on horseback,' she said, then signalled to her knave, who ran off to fetch two horses.

Upon mounting our steeds, we made for the deep woods west of the lake with a troop of savage kerns close on our heels. No sooner had we wended our way about the western bank of Lough Melvin than Muireann led us on a northward track, and I soon recognised the tree-cloaked hills ahead which I had previously climbed with her, following my escape from de Cuéllar.

When we reached the summit of the hidden clearing, a handful of kerns stepped forward from the trees, one of them bearing a leather strap with which to blindfold me. The ollave waved him away as we rode past.

'But...my lady...' he said.

She frowned at him.

'Did you see my gesture?'

The aged kern kept his head bowed low as he stepped backwards towards his kind, and Muireann served him with a hard stare as she made for the thickening trees, where she dismounted. A snapping of twigs was heard below my hurrying feet when she signalled to me to follow her into the surrounding trees. When we had made our way through to the clearing, I was amazed by the loud hum of bees who buzzed about the skeps and the clusters of yellow flowers that had sprouted from the dye-plants which I had once mistaken for weeds. I regarded the glade in wonder as the ollave sat cross-legged beneath the old oak tree leftwards of the clearing. One of her kerns served us with cuttings of flesh and a flask of cider before disappearing into the trees.

'My thanks for sparing me the blindfold, my lady,' I said nervously, 'I shall not betray your trust'.

'Oft times have you shown yourself to be a man of loyalty,' she replied.

I was at first taken aback by this remark, then bowed swiftly to her in appreciation of her words.

'What poem would you have me recite?'

'None,' was her abrupt reply, 'for we both know why you are here.'

Her stare was unwavering as I fumbled for a reply.

'What say you, my lady?'

Without so much as batting an eyelid, her voice dropped to a whisper as she hissed her accusation.

'Ever since you have commenced your tuition, you have ceaselessly sung the praises of Cathal the Black!'

'But he is a worthy lord, who has only -'

'My esteem of lords is not based on petty gossip or hearsay,' she cut in sternly, 'and certainly not on the praise purchased from the mouth of an alien! One who has been with the tribe for less than a year!'

I could not reply to this, for her tirade had struck as true as one of the bolts from her bow. The rustle of a creature in the woods had me turn my head towards the trees that surround-ed us, yet when I turned back to look at her I could see that Muireann still beheld me with an unwavering, hawklike glare.

'Indeed my choice of suitor is an important one, yet I am not a trifle to be played with by men, less a pretty bird to be snared by them. Many suns have set since I was but a witless maid, easily won over by such petty means of gentle persuasion.'

Her face had by now turned a crimson hue. The sight of it left me feeling entirely unnerved as I recalled that she was no mere retiring widow, yet a powerful tribeswoman who commanded scores of kerns and cows.

'The choice of suitor is mine and mine alone,' she continued, 'to make in my best interest and that of my retainers. Whosoever enters the handfast with me will do so on my own terms, as demanded by the law of this land.'

'Indeed, indeed, my lady,' I quickly put in, 'for none would dare dream of depriving you of your will, or that of any other lawful inhabitant of Dartry, be they man or woman! My words of esteem for Cathal the Black are born of the true love that I bear for the tanist, and in no way intended to sway your own views!'

I did my utmost to maintain a pained expression, so fearful was I that the ollave might see through my ruse. Muireann did little to allay my angst; she glared at me mercilessly as if studying my face for the slightest hint of mistruth.

'May your face burst with boils if you speak not the truth,' she hissed at last, 'for I would beckon to my kerns to slit your neck if it were otherwise. You are after all an instrument of power, and one both brave and loyal, yet remember at all times that this does not render you its broker!'

With that she raised her hand towards me, leaving me to stiffen as I expected a blow. Yet instead her fingers clasped me tightly about the chin, leaving me to stare on at her in wonder as she drew my face closely towards hers.

'I would have your loyalty above all others, Juan,' she said as her stare softened. 'Promise me that I alone have your loyalty.'

In that instant I saw the glare of a hardened warrior-poet melt into the weary and fearful countenance of one who had borne too much for too long alone. The realisation of my importance to her flooded over me like an unexpected burst of seawater into the bowels of a ship.

'Of course you have my loyalty, my lady!' I replied hastily. 'With all my heart and being would I protect you from your enemies!'

The conviction in my voice surprised even me, and she took a slight breath before plunging her face into mine, once more shocking me with the intensity of the kiss that she planted upon my lips. My long-repressed desire was instantly uncorked, and my hands were all over her hair and back as we fell to the ground and rolled over the grass, still locked in an amorous meeting of the lips which had my whole body feeling weak from emotion.

'What of the men?' I gasped, as I wrenched my face away from hers, suddenly fearful that her bodyguards might relay what they saw to my protector.

'They know better than to look,' she replied.

Then our lips met once more, and we turned over to continue tearing up the blades of grass beneath us. Our hands were everywhere as we tossed and turned in an amorous fury. My lips were planted on every last freckle that spangled her face and shoulders, enthralled as I was by our exotic differences, feeling like a powder keg which was about to erupt. At the end of it our breath was heavy, and we rested back upon the grass with her head in the crook of my neck and shoulder, her thighs wrapped about my leg as the ends of her fingers stroked my chest.

Her advance had left me stunned into silence, and my heart was in turmoil from the pleasure of our union, which was coupled with a growing guilt I felt at having betrayed the tanist. As she finally withdrew from me, Muireann seemed herself to be struggling with what had just passed, and we donned our garments in silence before leaving the clearing and returning to the village.

Indeed, a passion so great had been kindled that it terrified me almost more than it pleased me. So fearful was I of our tryst being discovered, that I barely spoke a word for the rest of the day, struggling in vain to banish all memory of the impassioned moments which I had shared with the ollave. Even Nial remarked on my silence that evening. My next tuition with Muireann was but two days later, for Cathal had hired her services three times a week, in the hope that my influence on her would help him secure her hand.

Yet although I was resolved not to succumb to her advances once again, we only had to exchange glances a couple of times before we were riding towards the hills once more, the stone-faced kerns forming a secure and unseen ring about us. No mention of the blindfold was heard as we made our way towards the company of dye-plants and skeps, and once more we melted into one another's embrace, giving into our cravings and sinking to the ground in a melee of arms and legs.

Her soft hand reached beneath my waist, stirring me into a higher ecstasy as the softness between her thighs made my fingers quiver. Once more the act consumed us in a rabid desperation, then left us strewn across the grass in stunned delight. Her fingers stroked the side of my cheek as my grimy hands grabbed her waist and pulled her back alongside me. A profound sense of peace overcame me as her body rested against mine, and we kissed again and again.

'I have been alone for so long,' she said at last, in a voice filled with relief.

'As have I,' was my reply as my fingertips ran up and down her back.

The simple exchange of words seemed to curiously relieve our trepidation over the unlikely affair. Our nervousness and pursed lips gave way to constant exchanges before and after our secret unions. In this way her knowledge of the *filidecht* was still imparted to me so that at least part if not all of her tuition was received. Muireann was also keen to learn more about my largely miserable life, and she listened intently to my stories about Italy and Africa and other parts of the world where the empire had flung me, as well as other knowledge I had acquired from the books I had read.

Arguing about the ideas of writers with a woman was a practice which I found compelling, with our acts of love only serving to make our meetings all the more sublime. Where once I had trudged off to meet her with heavy feet and a lowered head, I suddenly hastened to the ollave's lessons with a keen spring in my step. Nial himself jokingly referred to my 'great love of Irish ways', and for a moment I hesitated before leaving the outhouse, wondering if he had learned of our trysts.

At first special precautions were taken. We ensured that our lovemaking was consigned to the hidden glade, during the hours assigned to my learning. Yet as spring set in we identified other parts of the wood where we would meet away from prying eyes, just a couple of hours before nightfall set in. The only men privy to our newfound relationship were Muireann's closest and most loyal retainers, who scouted the locations of our unions before and during our encounters, after which I would make my own way back towards the town in a different direction to theirs.

Our meetings became more frequent, until we met at least four times a week in the different locations which we had picked for our rendezvous. It was clear that the ollave's desire for our meetings matched her desire to count on me as her ally, and before and after our acts of love she shared many of her concerns with me, leaving me in little doubt that I was her closest confidant. On my part I was elated by the desire demonstrated by Muireann towards us, and I spent most of the daydreaming of her supple form in my hands, stirring a joy within me that made the time pass all too swiftly.

The start of April often found us curled up against one another, with my arms wrapped about her waist as her head rested against my shoulder and her soft hair brushed against my cheek. Her skin brought a warm glow to my face when I met the moistness of her lips, still craving her affection after the passionate act which rendered us a tangle of locks both brown and black, of freckled and olive skin. Her long, slender fingers often explored the jagged battlefield of my body, discovering new scars she had not noticed before.

It had been a day so warm as to allow us to tear our clothes off and hurl them to the ground, which had led Muireann to remark on the lacerations and marks across my back, which were all blamed on the brutality of Treasach Bourke in the dungeon of Sligo. Yet she gasped when she saw the mark of the spider on my left breast.

'Where did that come from?' she exclaimed suddenly.

'Sligo,' was my weary reply, as I restrained a shudder at the distant yet horrific memory.

'Another mark by which to remember Ireland?'

I nodded gently as she climbed atop me and sat on my waist, staring at me in muted astonishment. It was an effort not to gawk at her fine breasts and thighs as her forefinger stroked the irregular end of my nose, another milestone from a life lived in the storm.

'When was it broken?'

'The last time was at Lepanto. A blow from a staff that I thought had killed me.'

'And these scars?' she continued, her fingertips touching my throat.

'Got too close to a battery at Tunis.'

Her hand slowly caressed my inner thigh, leaving me to flinch in anticipation before she gently grabbed my misshapen right knee.

'Was this caused by a wound too?'

'No, by a fall. I toppled off the walls of Saint Elmo as it fell to the Turks.'

I could not tell whether or not she knew of the places I mentioned, but she bent over and served me with a long and lingering kiss.

'I have longed for you ever since we first met,' I whispered into her ear, 'when I threw you over my shoulder as you kicked me in the balls.'

'Liar,' she said as she blushed and smiled. 'You mistook me for a lad.'

We both chuckled at that, and I knew as my hand lightly stroked her hair that my words had struck home, since she was not the bashful type and had often rebuffed lewd advances by the captain without so much as blinking an eye.

'You may not wish to leave Dartry with me,' I told her as our eyes met once more, 'but for as long as I draw breath, I shall not let an enemy touch a hair on your head.'

'Liar,' she said again with a wide grin. 'You will escape back to Spain like de Cuéllar.'

'I will not! He offered me the chance to join him, which I spurned!'

She beheld me with a bemused frown before resting her head on my chest again.

'Whatever you decide to do, I shall never leave this land. I must choose a suitor as my foster father has requested. The law of couples dictates that I marry one of his status.'

I could not help feeling a twinge of jealousy at her words.

'And are you clearer in your thoughts?' I asked.

She never stirred from my chest as she pondered the question for a fair while, and I thought she had ignored it before she finally replied.

'All I know is that I could never lie with Donal MacCabe.'

'You care deeply for Cathal?' I asked.

'He is a valiant servant of the tribe,' she said evasively.

'But do you love him?'

'I knew love.'

'You do not know it now?'

Her stare was averted as she drew away from me.

'I must do my duty and obey my father.'

I grabbed her by the wrist.

'And what of us?'

Her hair fell about her shoulders as she turned to me in surprise.

'What of us? Never did I think that the loss I felt would be so swiftly appeased. Often have I agonised over it and wondered if I have betrayed him.'

'Who? Aengus?'

The ollave's words overwhelmed me as tears formed in her eyes.

'Then you are torn between love and duty,' I said at last, 'yet are afraid to choose the way of the heart.'

She sighed.

'I doubt that the assembly shall accept a landless alien.'

'But I have been adopted. Lands may yet be accorded to me, as they were to Donal.'

'Landless, nonetheless. With no heads of cows and no territories.'

'What does that matter?'

'Do you not understand? My next dowry shall secure my foster father's position.'

Her helplessness angered me, so that I abandoned all tact and subtle persuasion.

'Then leave this land and flee with me! We shall start a new life elsewhere!'

As her eyes widened in surprise I grabbed her by the arms, feeling frustrated by her resignation and wishing her to seize her destiny in her own hands.

'Often have you asked me about Africa, Italy and the world beyond Dartry. Unite with me and see it for yourself! Together we could reach Spain before the year is out, perhaps even the Indies! None could stand in my way with a woman like you behind me.'

She fixed her stare on the ground, and my heart sank upon hearing her next words.

'And what of my lord MacGlannagh?'

'What of him?'

'He must secure the loyalty of the assembly. Do you not see how Donal MacCabe counters all that he says? He knows that my foster father's position is not strong. The Scot will seize on his chance the moment it appears, to become lord of these lands himself. If I flee the tribe and spurn Cathal, then there will be no tribesman with the strength to counter the gallowglasses. Yet my union with the tanist will render my lord father's position unchallengeable.'

Her words rang true as she raised her head, and I looked away in dismay.

'You think with the heart, not your head,' she chided me before proceeding in a softer voice. 'One has a duty towards one's kin; we do not marry for love alone. I am free to leave whenever I wish, yet I cannot abandon the man who raised me. The passing of Aengus has thrust the control of his estate upon my shoulders and has made me the tiller that will direct the tribe's future.'

'Then you are slave to your own power,' I mumbled, glaring at her in bitter disappointment as Muireann's cheeks slowly reddened.

'Do not mock me, Spaniard,' she hissed, 'nor seek to confuse my mind for the sake of your own selfish desires. For the one that wields power can never be a slave to it, unlike those that do not have it. At a word from me my guards would seize you and slit your throat, flouting our laws and avoiding their sanction by secretly hurling you into a bog. Have you such control over the will of men that they would risk all to protect you?'

Words failed me as she cast me a dark stare, and a slow grin appeared on her face which left me feeling both awed and ill at ease.

'You do well to keep silent, Spaniard, for you know that what I say is true. One does not readily come by power, which is lost far more easily than it is gained. I do not meekly bend to the demands of my position. I am aware that the passing of my late beloved has made me one of the most powerful women in Connacht. I do not need you to remind me that I could easily forego the life of Dartry for one which you call civilised.'

She paused her tirade, turning her head westwards towards the distant ocean which lay beyond the trees.

'Do you recall what you said when we lay together the other day? When I asked you what your travels had taught you about the world?'

Her softer tone left me feeling somewhat more at ease, and the memory of her reference quickly sprang to mind.

'Yes, my lady. And I told you that wherever I have been, the only certainty is that all over the world, both north and south, people everywhere – be they Flemish or Moorish or whatever other nation they belong to - only crave a roof over their head and some food in their bellies, together with a safe and modest future for their children.'

'There was more to your reply.'

'Ah yes, indeed there was. There are few things that people want or ask for, yet we cannot guarantee them to most. Man has built castles, siege engines, studied the stars and written compendiums. Yet he cannot guarantee such modest essentials such as food and clothing to most of his own kin, although war and suffering seem to be in abundance.'

'Except that the Gaels could once guarantee it!' she said angrily. 'And they will again, once every last enemy is driven out of Connacht! You have seen for yourself how the tribe shares all mishaps and fortunes, and none go without as they do in the towns of other supposedly civilised nations.'

I was about to object and refer to the life of the churls, those poor wretches amongst the tribe who had no land or recognised status and who toiled from day until night for a few scraps of food and some shelter, yet I bit my tongue for fear that I had already tested the ollave's patience far enough. I was also forced to admit that even the churls did not lead a life as miserable as some unfortunates I had seen in various cities across the known world.

The ollave leant her warm body back against mine and curled her forearm across my waist. Our lips met again as she reached for my face and pulled it back towards hers.

'Yet much as I am glad for the authority that I wield, I am in truth not made for petty politics. Nor do I greatly crave more learning, although I have been taught much during my life and have a mind that easily retains it. My heart yearns for the plains and the valleys and mountains, for passage through forests during the raid or the hunt.'

'You are not a slave to power,' I said at last, 'yet you are in love with the lands of your forebears.'

'Which you can surely comprehend?' she said, staring at me keenly as if my opinion alone could justify her obvious love for land and kin.

'Yes,' I said, "tis a place as otherworldly as it is entrancing. And yet....'

'And yet?' she said, resting her head upon my shoulder and looking into my eyes.

'And yet,' I said at last, fearful of upsetting her once again, 'you are beset by an enemy both ruthless and unrelenting. I understand that the Tudors have stamped their dominion both east and south of Ireland. Why would they stop in the west?'

She did not reply to this, although she did not show any signs of anger either. After a few moments of silence, I heard a small chuckle from her, which prompted me to query its cause.

'I remembered an old tale told amongst the Irish, about Saint Gobnat during the sixth century. They say that she shook the bees out of one of her hives to ward off a gang of cattle rustlers, which were changed into soldiers by a miracle.'

'And whereabouts in this tale lies the humour my lady?'

'I was just thinking,' she said with a sigh, 'that if the old tale were true, and my lord father could turn all of the bees in his land into soldiers, that we would have little to fear from the English.'

I was not sure what to say, but just then a whistle of warning was issued by one of Muireann's guards. It was as shrill as it was short and solely intended to alert us of other men passing through the forest. Our clothes were instantly wrapped back over our bodies as we sat up and assumed a cross-legged position beneath the boughs of an oak. Muireann instantly began feigning instruction in the teaching of an age-old verse.

Heavy steps and brash laughter were heard through the brush during her recital, and I could make out a handful of gallowglass Scots crashing through the wood as they passed behind her. Among them I could see the unsettling presence of Donal MacCabe's horseboy, the rascal who had endangered my life during my trial of the pig hunt. I cast him a dark stare as he looked in our direction, pointing us out to his vile fellows and no doubt making some vulgar reference to us as his comrades burst into peals of shallow laughter. I turned my attentions back to the ollave's recital and nodded in feigned understanding, yet as the Scots wandered off, I could see the horseboy still staring menacingly in our direction.

This episode did much to unsettle the ollave. She at all times feared that our affair might be discovered, leading her to be branded a woman of loose morality, which might threaten the interest of her suitors in securing her hand. It was therefore another week before our affections were resumed, in which I found myself grumpily confined to training the chieftain's men and exchanging some debate with the bondsman at night. One particular lesson in marksmanship found me in a particularly vile mood, angry as I was at being denied the intimacy of my new beloved. The kerns were pressed hard and relentlessly, and I often yelled at them in frustration whenever their target was missed. They were therefore greatly relieved to leave the training ground, both furious and panting hard. So flustered was I at the end of my instruction that I did not realise the presence of the tanist until he was standing right behind me.

'My lord!' I blurted in fright, with a quick bow, which I hoped might mask my guilt as I felt a blush of shame spreading across my cheeks and forehead.

Cathal's black locks hid most of his face, yet from between the strands of his hair emanated his intense stare.

'It has been some time since last we spoke, friend,' he whispered. 'How does your instruction in the *filidecht* progress?'

'The ollave's teachings have further bound me to the history of our people,' I gushed, 'which is both valorous and proud. In our last lesson she taught me about the high kings of Tara, whose exploits are best portrayed in the following poem -'

The tanist regarded my awkward flow of words in curious silence but raised his hand as my lips parted to recite my verse.

'Spare me the old wives' tales and walk with me,' he whispered before stepping away from me and turning towards the lake.

As I hurried to keep in step with him, his guard of five bluejackets trailed us, which did little to quell my fears. Not a word was uttered between us until we were out of earshot of all tribesmen, walking along the bank of Lough Melvin with our backs to the town.

'So who does she prefer?' he asked at last as we bowed to avoid a low-hanging branch.

'I believe it is you, my lord.'

'Did she say as much?' he snapped, as he stopped in his tracks and whirled towards me.

'Not precisely,' I replied, fearful that I might have betrayed the ollave's trust.

'Then how can you be so sure?'

The tanist seized me by the shoulders so violently that some of his hair fell away from his face, leaving me to stare into the many blemishes on his visage. For a moment I both pitied and admired Muireann.

'Ah, you know the ways of women. They can make you understand much without a word being uttered.'

'Do not toy with me, Spaniard,' he rasped in a tone I had never heard him use before, and which left me in no doubt that he should not be crossed. 'Of what signs do you speak of?'

'Warm smiles at your mention,' I said, 'and long frowns of disgust whenever we refer to the constable.'

His lips creased into a smile both wide and grotesque, and his hold on me slackened. He suddenly seemed to recover his composure, and let his hands fall to his sides as he stepped away from me. All throughout his men had not stirred behind me, although the slight scrape of steel against leather had been unmistakable to my ear, leaving me in little doubt that daggers had been drawn at the sight of Cathal's gestures.

'Forgive me, Spaniard,' he said at last, 'I did not mean to lay hands on your person.'

He turned towards the lake, staring across the water as if at a destination he had long sought out but which still eluded him.

'Much hangs on her choice. My only concern remains the survival of the tribe. The Scots care only for land and wealth; to them we are nothing.'

'There is nothing to forgive, my lord,' I said at last, marvelling once more at his concern for his people's welfare and genuinely understanding his mistrust of the Scottish mercenaries who had been employed by the chieftain.

When he turned back towards me our discussion was resumed, during which I did all I could to relieve his fears, without actually repeating what the ollave had said to me. Despite Muireann's close relationship to Dervila, her loyalty towards the MacGlannagh was without question. She would do her duty as she always did, and promise her hand to Cathal, which would secure him both Aengus's men and cows. In this way

Donal MacCabe's wealth in Dartry would be a distant second to the tanist's, so that the position of Tadhg *Óg* MacGlannagh among his assembly would be on solid ground.

After what seemed at least an hour of this wearisome talk, Cathal was at last appeased. We walked back to the village together, where he took his leave of me with a final remark.

'I hear your lessons no longer take place along the water.'

In my surprise at these words an immediate reply eluded me, and it was a few instants of nodding at him with a smile before one finally formed in my mind.

'The ollave's love for the woods and its creatures is without compare. She has led me back and forth in these forests, often using it as a way to embellish her instruction.'

Cathal smiled knowingly.

'Until our next meeting, my friend,' he said, and after I bowed I saw that he was already a few steps away from me as he made towards his cabin.

The walk back to the outhouse seemed like the longest which I had ever undertaken, and my soul weighed heavily inside me as I pondered the consequences of my affair with Muireann being discovered. It would jeopardise my relationship with Cathal, a man who had offered me unconditional protection ever since the time his men had rescued me from the pursuit of Treasach Burke.

My unease hardly abated during the night, and I tossed and turned as I tried to forget the risks presented by my trysts with the ollave. It was all in vain, as my shame was soon replaced by an overwhelming sense of longing. In the morning I resolved that I would not lay a finger on her again and would reject all her advances, yet by the afternoon my good intentions had fluttered away with the strong wind from the ocean, which rippled away all steadfastness as it quivered through the leaves and the grass.

Once more a hidden location was identified, and once more Muireann's advances were resumed, since she had clearly missed me as much as I had craved her. The lovemaking which ensued was more passionate than it had ever been, fuelled by its absence over the past week. Yet as always it was followed by a crushing feeling of wretchedness, and hollow promises which I made to myself in order to justify my betrayal of the tanist's trust.

In time the foremost pledge was that I would flee the tribe in the summer and make my way back to Spain. This would help ensure that the affair would end, and much as it broke my heart to think about it, quiet moments spent with the ring did much to temper my distress. For it was true that the ollave had reignited the old fire which had blazed for Elsien, yet I assured myself that there would be others like her across the ocean, in a land free from the religious wars which bathed an entire continent in blood. My own assurances left me feeling somewhat uncertain, yet I had never been a cuckold, and could not see myself bedding the wife of the tanist after the handfast.

'Better to flee than share her,' I repeated to myself. 'Better to flee than to share her.'

The constant recital of these words steeled my heart against the happiness I had found in Dartry. It also made my encounters with Muireann more passionate, as if I sought to drain myself of all blazing love for her through our repeated acts of union so that my escape from Dartry might not eventually crush my soul. Meanwhile Muireann received my passion with a rekindled joy, and one afternoon had her biting her lip not to moan as she lay back on the grass and I thrust myself against her.

Our act of love had reached a height that I had never crested with any woman before, due to separations caused by travel and death. I was just marvelling at her ability to keep her silence during these meetings when a sudden scream left her lips. It was of such a distressed quality that I immediately pulled myself away and regarded her in shock. Her face was clouded with fright, and her hand shot past my shoulder as she pointed at the trees above our heads, towards something which had completely unnerved her.

A loud snapping of branches was heard overhead as her kerns rushed towards us, and my blood ran cold as I turned towards the direction indicated by her finger. The gallowglass horseboy had reached the bottom of the oak with his fellow, and together they rushed back towards Rosclogher to relay news of our affair to their master. Whether they had spied on us before I did not know, yet I seized my rifle and made after them with the ollave's guards, who had just ensured that their mistress was well and safe.

'After them, you fools!' she cried. 'Do not let them get away!'

It was a difficult pursuit through the low-hanging branches and the rugged forest floor, yet we had almost gained upon them when the horseboy's mate turned around and hurled a spear in our direction. It felled the foremost of the kerns among our number yet only served to briefly delay the chase. As we closed in on the two wretches I could see that they were already too close to the water's edge and about to make their escape on a boat. I dropped to one knee and hauled the rifle off my shoulder, catching the horseboy's shoulder in my sights. A loud gunshot resounded across the forest as my shot felled him, but when the smoke cleared I saw that his fellow had hurled himself into the water, leaving his pursuers standing along the lake bank as they stared after him in annoyance.

I swiftly reloaded the rifle once more, then caught the second Scot's head in my sights. I was about to squeeze the serpentine and rid the world of the tosspot when the gun was shoved out of my hands. The sound of a shot filled the sky, sending birds scattering from the trees. I turned around in a rage, then was taken aback to find Muireann's hands on my gun.

'What – why?' I managed, as the smell of rotten eggs engulfed us and we were blinded by smoke.

'Because you can scant afford it!' she shrieked, then pushed me away and walked back towards the woods.

'Afford what?' I asked, as I made after her in consternation.

'I do not yet know!' was her reply. She fell to her knees and held her face in her hand, while I struggled to understand what she meant.

XXXVIII

Rosclogher, Dartry, County Leitrim

8 – 9 April 1589

Cries were heard from the lake as the drowning horseboy disappeared below the brackish water. Muireann's kerns quickly clasped each other by the arms to form a human chain, with the man at the end of it wading deep into the water until he, too, was beneath it. His mates stepped back and hauled him out again, with their fellow's free hand clasping the flown Scot firmly by the hair.

'The body!' exclaimed Muireann looking about her in fear. 'We need to hide the other spy's body!'

'Why?' I replied, but it was too late for any questions as a great roar of contempt was heard from the trees to our right. Donal MacCabe and his men burst forth from the bush, brandishing their axes as they made straight for their rescued companion who lay upon his knees, coughing and spluttering at the centre of a ring of spear points.

'Withdraw your arms, you curs!' warned Donal. 'That is my man, and I'll rip out the throat of anyone who so much as scratches him!'

Muireann's kerns turned in fear at the sound of the constable's voice, as Donal fearlessly strode towards their raised weapons. He angrily shoved the kerns' spearheads away as if he were only swotting flies.

'Uallas!' he yelled with the look of one who had recovered a lost son. 'Uallas, what have these men done to you?'

The exaggerated concern which he lavished on his charge turned my stomach, and even Uallas appeared taken aback as Donal removed his cloak and swathed it around the boy's trembling shoulders. I turned to the ollave whose face had turned a pallid hue as she stared at another band of Scots who were approaching. They were led by the giant Brogan, who stopped a few feet away from the body of the dead horseboy, whose legs still quivered upon the grass. Donal's son turned to his father and scowled as he pointed a finger in my direction.

I was already priming my rifle when Donal's giant son issued a loud roar and led a dozen of his men in my direction. They were but a few feet away when the gun was finally loaded, and I issued a loud cry of warning before aiming the weapon at the hulking warrior who led their charge. Their step never slackened as their uphill run tore the leaves off bushes and ripped the grass at their feet. I clung to the forlorn hope that the fall of Brogan might dissuade his charges. My finger had tugged hard at the serpentine when once again the ollave pounced upon it, hurling the rifle skywards.

'Holy host of the Madonn-!'

My blasphemy was checked as Brogan's fist sent me flying onto the ground. It took a few moments for me to regain my senses, and I coughed up a tooth before a rain of rifle butts descended upon me, leaving me to curl into a ball and shield my face as a howl of agony left my lips. A deep fear seized me as the Scots attempted to kill me; they sidestepped my kicks at them before they delivered bone-shuddering swings of their own boots. A blow to the side of my head left my ear ringing, but still I could hear the loud protestations of the ollave, who desperately shook Brogan by the shoulder.

'Leave him be! You shall answer to the chieftain if you end his life!'

Brogan turned back towards her, shoving his face into hers with bared teeth as he shouted angrily.

'He killed one of our men! Shot him in the back like a woodland beast!'

'You are not the law in this land!' she cried. 'Leave him be or you shall answer to it too!'

The giant gallowglass found no reply to this last warning, and he sat back in silence as his master's words were heard behind him.

'Fall back! Fall back!'

My attackers checked their brutal onslaught at the command of Donal MacCabe, who advanced upon us with Uallas beneath his big, shaggy arm and another dozen Scots at his back.

'Leave him be, lads!' he growled. 'He shall meet the king's justice soon enough! He knows not what is coming to him!'

So saying he turned towards the ollave, laying one of his enormous palms upon her shoulder.

'Thank the Lord you are safe, my lady! Uallas here has recounted all that he has seen! What fortune that two of my horseboys were at hand to prevent your defiling! But fear not, for this base creature shall soon answer for his crimes!'

I turned slowly onto my back, relieved that my beating had at last subsided. One of my eyes had closed shut, yet I peered at Muireann with the remaining one. She stared at the gallowglass constable in stunned silence. His hand moved from her shoulder towards her face, and he clasped her chin between his jagged thumb and forefinger and held her face up towards him.

'What is wrong, my lady? Are you mute from fear of this vile animal's lewd advances? Be not afraid, I say again to you, for he is now my prisoner and can harm you no longer!'

A fair few moments had passed before I could talk, since my right cheek had swollen to the size of a small apple.

'What are you talking about!' I gasped in a growing fury of my own. 'We were -'

'Silence!'

The command was howled from Muireann's lips, and her apparent betrayal was a skewer which cut through my guts. She advanced upon me with a grimace, aiming a kick which barely missed me. Just then her own kerns arrived red-faced and panting to surround us, and the Scots withdrew from their spear points as Donal MacCabe summoned them away from us.

'Heed the lady's command, men! Ollave Mac an Bhaird is a woman of great strength, and has recovered enough to take the matter in hand!'

The threat of conflict was thereby snuffed out as the gallowglass gathered behind the constable with their drawn axes. A sigh of relief left me, for they were twice the number of Muireann's men, who in spite of their valour would have surely been torn apart by the Scots in a matter of minutes. Yet my own troubles had hardly subsided, for the same kerns who had once guarded my secret meetings with the ollave now hauled me to my feet by the shoulders at a nod from their mistress.

'Seeing as we have both been wronged by this man,' said the constable, 'we can march to the tower house forthwith to demand justice. We should not have long to wait, for our lord MacGlannagh is gathered in his hall with those closest to him.'

Muireann's face turned a paler hue of white as the end of her lips trembled slightly. Finally she raised her voice in reply.

'Lead the way, O worthy constable. We will shadow your steps all the way to the keep.'

Donal nodded and marched back downhill in the direction of the lake, with his men instantly falling in behind him. Muireann summoned her men to follow the Scots at a safe distance, and our return towards the town was interrupted but once, when the gallowglasses stopped to gather the body of the slain horseboy. As the dead Scot was laid across a makeshift palliasse, Muireann fell behind her men to rasp quick instructions to me.

'Whatever is said in the hall, you must keep your silence. Feign, if you must, that you were struck dumb.'

'What do you mean?' I asked, my sore head still whirling like a spinning wheel as a growing dread pierced my gut.

'Just do as I say!' she snapped. 'We have been thrust into a game that is not of our design and whose only outcome shall spell triumph for its maker!'

Thereafter she returned to the front of her party, and gave me her back all the way back to Rosclogher.

Tribesmen gathered before their huts as we finally reached the town, then made past the ringfort and cut through the westward huts towards the jetty. All went quiet at the sight of the dead horseboy borne between the redshanks before a handful dared to cheer the sight as the last Scot trudged past. A few of the gallowglasses in the rear turned their heads to snarl at the hidden offenders, yet their march never wavered as they made for the jetty.

By the time we had gathered by the water, the realisation of the ensuing humiliation had me in its grip, so that I might have fled were it not for Muireann's kerns who held me by the shoulders. My fears only worsened when the ollave retired to the Abbey of Saint Mel, only to re-emerge once the ferries had borne all of the Scots across the water. When we were finally punted across the lake we descended onto the crannog to find most of the Scots waiting outside the tower house.

We later discovered that the chieftain's guards had only permitted access to the constable and a handful of his closest retainers, observing the long-held command that only five mercenaries at a time should enter the keep. The loud protests and cries of Donal's remaining men went ignored, and only grew more outraged when all of Muireann's guards were granted access into the chieftain's hold. Her kerns formed a tight chain about me as we passed through hostile onlookers, who did not hesitate to land the odd blow to the back of my head.

They who once hailed me as a hero, I could not help thinking.

As we passed through the steel doorway into the tower, the dank air inside made it harder to breathe. We found Donal's band awaiting us atop the staircase, where the sentries blanched at the sight of the corpse that the Scots bore with them. Muireann gestured for us to stop until our presence was declared. Then the door to the hall was thrown open before us. Sweat still prickled my brow despite the warmth from the hearth, as the Scots laid their dead comrade down upon the straw.

The chieftain sat but a few paces away from the corpse, clearly confused by the Scots' appearance, while at his arm his wife also stared on in bafflement. Members of the assembly gathered about us, looking on in fear at the sight of the dead horseboy. Every last ear of influence in the tribe was strained towards us to determine whether the tidings we brought might be used for future schemes and alliances.

'Why does a dead body lie in my hall?' said the chieftain at last. 'What is the meaning of this?'

'This man found the Spaniard imputing unchastity to your daughter!'

Manglana's brows were raised at these tidings, and he slowly turned his head towards me. About him a great silence descended over the hall, so that only the crackling hearth could be heard.

'Is this true?'

My skin crawled with shame when I heard the unmistakable voice, and my stare met that of the tanist, who stood alongside the chieftain. His gaze betrayed such bewilderment that I fixed my stare upon the ground and did not look him in the face again for many a day thereafter. I kept my silence as I knelt among the hounds with my head bowed. Muireann's guards formed a half-moon of raised-spear points about me. Donal's son Brogan, roared aloud as he stepped behind me and shoved me onto my face with his foot.

'Our brother, Uallas saw him forcing himself upon Aengus's widow!' he roared. 'This lecher would have had his pleasure upon him had he not sighted our men searching for eggs in the trees! He slew poor Ronan in cold blood, and would also have shot Uallas down like a swine had we not appeared to rescue him!'

Muted mutters and low whispers spread about the hall at these tidings, and a low sob was heard behind me as O'Ronayne hurried from the lady Bourke's side towards us. He clasped the ollave in a gentle embrace as she openly wept with her face held in her hands, no doubt torn at having to abandon me to salvage the chieftain's political designs. The constable's plan was clear to me then, and I was left stunned by his ruthlessness and audacity.

'Be still, Brogan!' shrieked Dervila, as she rose from her oaken seat. 'Dare not raise another hand in this hall without my command!'

The giant Scot scowled at the chieftain's wife, but a nod from his master Donal MacCabe had him return to the company of his fellow Scots who stood gathered about the corpse. Meanwhile the chieftain's wife summoned Muireann before her, rising from her seat to hold the ollave's hands as she spoke to her in a low but audible voice.

'Tell me, my child. Was it by force?'

Muireann did not reply, but each passing moment of hesitation further indicted her as having consented to my advances. Donal smirked to himself in the shadows, and it was then evident to me that he had clearly received word from somewhere that Muireann was to choose Cathal's advances over his. By availing himself of her secret meetings with me, he had left her in a terrible position, to be publicly stained as a woman of loose morals whose hand would be rejected by all nobility. Unless she betrayed her lover to a punishment both unjust and hard.

'Yes,' I said at last, as I seethed at Donal's foul scheme, 'yes, I took her by force. She wanted none of it.'

Muireann whirled towards me with flushed cheeks, her jaw left hanging by the declaration I had uttered to safeguard her honour. With a roar the chieftain himself rose from his seat, his mantle swirling about him as he ran up to me and dealt me a kick in the stomach that hurled me onto my back. Seething intakes of breath filled the hall as his boot fell squarely upon my neck. His forehead crinkled with rage as he leaned over, his spittle striking my nose as he snarled at me.

'I shall snuff your life out like a candle, grey wolf.'

My soul was committed to the Lord as spots appeared before my eyes, and I had readied myself for a final shove of his foot on my throat when a voice was heard from among the gathering.

'You are a defender of the law, sire.'

With a loud grunt, the weight on my neck was gone as Manglana withdrew his boot and turned his head to look over his shoulder. With a cough and splutter I raised myself onto my elbows, relieved that my miserable hide had been spared by the ollave's intercession. Meanwhile Donal's voice rose from beside the corpse, crackling with malevolence.

'He freely admits the charge! He must face justice!'

The constable had failed to besmirch the ollave's honour to prevent her handfast to his rival, leaving him intent on crushing his smaller prey. Manglana's arms hung by his sides as he returned to his throne, his fingers bunched into throbbing fists. I could not but tremble when he returned to his seat, for I had never seen him raise hands on anyone. In truth the swiftness of his attack on my person had shocked me even more than his blows.

'You shall have it, as shall I. Let the Spaniard go free. This is a matter of law.'

I stared about me in surprise as Muireann's guards withdrew their spears and stood away from me. A deep exhalation was heard from the chieftain that could not have been exceeded by the largest bull in his herd. He gestured at the body of the slain Ronan.

'Get that corpse out of here and bury it forthwith.'

As the Scots set about collecting the body of their dead comrade, a hand was slipped under my armpit and I was lifted onto my feet.

'Follow me,' hissed the bondsman, and without needing further instruction I limped out of the hall after him, relieved to be finally free of the scene of my utter humiliation.

Nial's assistance could not have come at a timelier moment, since my head was light from the blows I'd received and the injustice of what had just passed. As we flew down the stairs and hurried towards a ferry, I voiced my foremost worry.

'Am I not to be imprisoned?'

'We do not jail people accused of distresses,' said the bondsman as he stepped into the skiff and reached his hand out to me.

'What will my punishment be?' I gasped, barely keeping my footing as I boarded the boat. 'Will I hang?'

'The Irish do not hang anyone,' he replied. 'It is likely to be a fine, what we call an *eineach*.'

'An *eineach*,' I said, uttering the word hesitantly, 'but I have no means. How high will it be?'

Nial sighed as he gestured to the boatman to ferry us across the lake.

'I do not know.'

'How am I to avoid trial? Can we not get anyone to put a word in for me? Perhaps bribe the judge?'

'Banish the very thought,' replied the bondsman with a look of concern, 'for it is a fact well known among us that if judges do not speak truth a blemish will appear on their face. Furthermore, all of the tribe are bound by the Brehon law, which reserves the highest punishment for those of the highest status.'

I regarded him in disbelief.

'Does that mean the chieftain would be punished more severely than his own kerns?'

'Yes. Even clerics are sentenced more harshly. Certain distresses even bar them from recovering their position.'

'Surely you are jesting.'

'I can assure you that I am not. Furthermore, offences against the property of the poor incur a higher punishment than those carried out against the wealthy.'

'What shall I do?'

Nial bit his lip in thought.

'Do not despair. Your reputation has suffered, but the Mac-Glannagh once held you in high esteem. His daughter-in-law is violated but unharmed. As father-in-law of the victim, he has full power over your fate.'

After reaching the shore we returned to the outhouse without interruption, for word had not yet reached the tribe of what had occurred in the assembly. A few of the tribesmen even saluted me as I hurried away towards the abbey with the bondsman, still struggling to believe what had just happened. When we entered the outhouse, it took three goblets of *usquebaugh* to steady my nerves, so that I could relate the events of the day to the bondsman, who sat back on his palliasse and listened intently. At the end of my account he filled my mazer once more, wearing an expression which was deadly serious.

'Your situation is desperate and far from enviable. Yet you may still emerge unscathed if you heed my advice.'

'Pray, share it,' I cried, 'for I know not what to do, and I dread the courtroom more than a troop of cavalrymen!'

Nial frowned as he produced another goblet, which he filled for himself.

'Our trials do not take place in courtrooms. Yet the Brehon judge Echna is the least of your concerns if you value your life.'

A long swig was taken from his beaker before he glared at me once more.

'Do not breathe a word of what you told me to anyone. For all we know, the chieftain might yet be your ally, but you will lose him forever if your trysts with the ollave become common knowledge. Aengus is not yet a year in the grave, and the tanist might baulk at committing himself to a woman still expected to be mourning her husband. The word will spread that she is of the promiscuous sort, for tongues are quick to spin all manner of lies when a woman's honour is openly questioned.'

He sighed aloud, then spoke again.

'Cathal the Black has previously secured a divorce on the grounds of adultery, and he would appear a hypocrite to all and sundry if he were seen to propose to a woman of loose morals. And if Cathal hesitates to propose, thereby foregoing Muireann's dowry, then the chieftain will be left in the unbearable position of having to count on Donal MacCabe as his most powerful supporter.'

Sweat prickled my forehead at this revelation, as I realised the extent to which I had compromised the chieftain's position. I slowly realised that Manglana had let me off lightly when he had all but suffocated me to death in his hall.

'Why would Cathal baulk at marrying Muireann?' I protested angrily, struggling to accept just how badly matters had gone for me. 'How does her honour affect her retainers or the number of heads in her herd?'

Nial cast me a hard stare when he spoke again.

'It is not only Spaniards who value their honour.'

I bowed my head to him, fearing that I had offended the man who suddenly seemed to be the only ally I had left.

'I pray that you accept my apology. I spoke in haste. What should I do?'

'Your trial will be held outdoors beside the cairn,' replied Nial. 'Our laws decree that you may choose your Brehon, but since Aengus's passing we have only one.'

'Echna?'

'Yes, the venerable lady Echna. She is a judge both learned and fair. You are also entitled to your own counsel.'

'Who should I choose?'

'Either of the ollave or Fearghal the bard. Your choice is evidently restricted.'

'Indeed,' I replied, upon thinking of the bard. 'It appears that my stars are no longer aligned. How much will the trial cost?'

'Nothing. Our justice is freely available to all. Now before you ask more questions, I shall summon the bard. Is there anything else I can do for you?'

In my fear and desperation it occurred to me that I should mention the secret of the ring to the bondsman. For a moment the thought of sharing its burden seemed an appealing one, and in my great distress I was about to mention it to him when at the last instant I thought better of it.

'My thanks, Nial, you have been a friend both loyal and true. Yet there is nothing more I require.'

He beheld me carefully.

'Are you certain that there is nothing more I can do?'

'Yes, I am certain.'

As Nial walked out I tiptoed towards the doorway and stuck my head through it. A dozen bluejackets had stationed themselves about the hut, and Nial later told me that they had been despatched by Manglana to avoid anyone exacting revenge on my person for the shame I had cast on the ollave or the slaying of the Scottish horseboy. The sight of them further enforced my realisation of the trouble which I had ended up in, and withdrawing into the outhouse I snatched up my bandolier and opened the lowest charger, pulling out the ring and placing it on the back of my tongue. When it was swallowed I curled into a bundle upon my bed and pulled my blanket over my head, hoping that the nightmare might somehow end.

Nial reappeared with the bard not long afterwards, grabbing me by the shoulder and shaking me hard.

'Arise, Sir Spaniard, for I have fetched your counsel.'

The bard's unruly abundance of silver hair fell over his red jacket as he regarded me like a serpent sizing up a dangerous prey. Fearghal had never welcomed my introduction into the tribe, and he wielded great respect and power amongst his kinsmen. He had always regarded every foreign influence on the assembly as a direct threat to his authority, which had made him a persistent objector to all progressive recommendations which I had made to Manglana. It made me ill to think that I was now at his mercy as I stumbled to my feet and bowed deeply before him.

'My thanks for agreeing to represent me, sire.'

'There was little choice in the matter,' replied the bard tersely, as he turned and gave me his back, 'for the law affords me no choice but to accept requests for representation, regardless how vile the misdeeds of the offender.'

My sense of foreboding only grew at his words as I wondered whether I might not be better off representing myself before the lady Echna. This was swiftly disclosed to Nial as I bent over to whisper my concerns into his ear, which he dismissed with a wave of his hand.

'No Spaniard, you must use the services offered by Fearghal. He is highly trained in the best legal verse, and to forego his services may well incur a greater fine.'

'But the man hates me!' I protested. 'What defence does he offer?'

Nial fixed me with a hard stare.

'None shall stray from the truth before a Brehon. All know that to do so will lead to blemishes upon the face, and other such misfortunes. The laws of Dartry are too complex for you to navigate alone, for even a subject such as apiaries is bound by rules beyond count!'

With a sigh I returned my attentions to the bard, who had taken to standing by the door with a wry smile on his face. His grin only broadened when he saw me turning towards him, for he had fully expected me to finally converse with him.

'Tomorrow you shall meet with justice. You know little of the Brehon law, which has guided our people since time immemorial. Be warned that you might meet with banishment, perhaps even death. Yet whatever the sentence that is declared by the Brehon, you must accept it with honour and humility.'

'What should I do?'

'You are not expected to do anything. Sit still throughout the hearing, and do not say anything but the truth.'

My heart sank at his explanation, and for a moment I thought to tell him of the ollave's consent before remembering what the bondsman had told me. Nial had appeared at the bard's shoulder, and the severe stare he cast in my direction reminded me that no reference should be made to my indiscretions with the ollave.

'So I am to be accused of rape?'

Fearghal sat on the ground and beheld me with a cocked eyebrow.

'Yes. A most vile offence, and one derived by force.'

'How can that be established?' I dared to ask, incurring a wrathful glare from Nial.

'You mean the use of force? At least one witness has said that he heard her scream when he saw you on top of her. All that is required is for another witness to confirm this, for the testimony of two witnesses cannot be overturned.'

'But she cried out when she saw the horseboys in the tree!'

O'Dalaigh sighed wearily as he lowered his head towards mine, to stare directly into my eyes.

'Answer me truthfully, Spaniard. Did she invite you to lie with her?'

Nial looked agonised upon hearing this, and his lower lip trembled as he glared at me from behind the bard.

'No,' I lied, fearing that I would further compromise Manglana's position among the tribesmen.

'Then it was forced,' he said curtly, as he sat back in his stool, 'and the fact that she screamed means that she did not want to hide the act. She was also said to be red in the face.'

My lips parted in protest, yet I uttered no words for I could tell that my protestations would all be in vain and that the gallowglass constable had long planned my undoing. I was now a mouse caught in Donal MacCabe's trap, and I could only hope to still draw breath once his design had run its course. The bard took his leave not long thereafter, since there was nothing to discuss about the charge of murder. If questioned, Muireann's kerns would all confirm that I had shot the horseboy in the back, and the ball retrieved from the dead Scot belonged to my rifle. That night there were no bad dreams as sleep was denied by my fears. My tossing and turning finally roused Nial before dawn.

'Have you not rested at all?' he muttered in annoyance.

'I must escape,' I gasped, springing off my bed and reaching for my mantle and sword, 'the Scots have sealed my doom, and I have tarried long enough!'

'You shall seal your own doom if you flee,' was the bondsman's reply, as he turned his back towards me and held his face in his hands. 'The Scots will track you down and surely kill you if the Sassanas do not find you first.'

His casual indifference to my anguish greatly distressed me.

'I shall head north,' I snapped, 'and offer my sword to another chieftain!'

'The lord north of our border is the brother of the lady Mac an Bhaird. He shall not kindly receive a man accused of raping his younger sister.'

His words stopped me in my tracks just as I was hurrying for the doorway.

'At best you can make for the northeast,' he said, 'where another chieftain may offer you protection. But you have no guarantee of this, and they shall in all likelihood return you to Dartry. Your only other hope lies in stealing aboard a ship that is bound for the Continent. Yet the sailing season has not yet begun.'

'Then my only hope lies in surrendering myself to Manglana's justice?'

Nial did not reply as he nodded off once more, and did not stir again until daybreak. In the morning his guards led us out of the outhouse on foot, as we made our way towards the trial. We walked towards the mountains in the south, then climbed towards the lofty height where Cathal the Black had been declared tanist. I had often seen men from all corners of Dartry making their way up the heights to obtain the Brehon's justice. We met some of them on our journey uphill, who shook their fists at me and called me all manner of names.

'He is still innocent until proven otherwise,' declared the bondsman as my detractors grudgingly accepted his words and made way for us to pass them by.

When we approached the cairn, a gathering of tribesmen had gathered behind us who were also making their way uphill towards the sizeable landmark. The lady judge was seen in front of Aengus's burial site, seated upon an oaken stump and holding thick vellum manuscripts which appeared to be written by different hands. I felt overcome by unease as she leafed through the folios, her fingers passing over letters of iron gall. A party of at least a hundred men silently gathered about her, staring on at the woman who would decide my fate.

The chieftain and his wife were both present, with the usual retainers clustered tightly about them. Nial positioned us at the far left of those present so that we stood in near seclusion a few feet away from the drop below us. All present quietly observed the proceedings which unfolded in front of them, so that all that could be heard was the odd sigh of the wind through the heights and the exchanges during the proceedings.

A highborn member of the assembly was fined for ill-treating a horse whilst another was punished for causing a weakened ox to break a bone by forcing it to do excessive work. The next hearing concerned a villager who was too stingy to provide his pregnant wife with sufficient food and was punished for abuse. Throughout I was impressed by the frankness and reason of the Dartrymen's arguments, and was even amazed to see women standing as witnesses and being given the same regard as the men. My interest in the trials quickly abated when I found myself the last defendant, urged to step out into the open-air court and stand before the judge, who regarded me intently.

My counsel, the bard, was next to step forward as he held a discussion with the Brehon about my rank within the tribe in order to better determine the level of punishment that I would receive. Since I was no stranger to a courtroom, I next recognised a sort of pleading which was delivered by the bard before the case was heard. To my surprise Saorla, Lady Bourke's lady-in-waiting, was the first summoned to bear witness. She instantly engaged in a furious tirade, accusing me of repeatedly trying to take advantage of the ollave.

'On the night after the siege was broken, when everyone in the castle was laid low by revelry and feasting, that was the first time I saw the Spaniard try to attack her. He was too drunk to take her by force, but we fled from him in terror, thinking that he had perhaps lost his wits.'

She turned to stare at me with a pair of blazing eyes, leaving me stunned by her dislike for me.

'He cast an enchantment upon her, of this I am certain, although I do not know how he did it. The lady Mac an Bhaird is still vulnerable after her husband's passing, yet often did she speak to me of him, expressing puzzlement at why the Spaniard entered her thoughts so often.'

This further revelation of Muireann's thoughts left me feeling both bewildered and saddened by our plight. Once more I dealt the crowd a sidelong glance, hoping to see the ollave's face. The chieftain and his wife could be seen frowning gravely, as could the Jesuit O'Ronayne, who stood at Dervila's arm. Yet Muireann and Cathal the Black were nowhere to be seen, having perhaps avoided the trial because of shame, or distress, or both.

When Saorla was finished, she stepped back towards the crowd, clearing the way for other witnesses to plunge the blade into my honour and reputation. Up stepped the horseboy Uallas, who no longer appeared the shivering, frightful rabbit from the previous day.

'I was up in the tree searching for birds' eggs,' he cried, 'when we saw the Spaniard stooped over the lady. She screamed as he pinned her to the ground with his strength, and her face was as red as dulse! His advances upon her were uninvited, and his acts made her blush! The Spaniard treated her with such abandon that he did not even apologise when we discovered him. He shot my brother Ronan, and would have killed me, too, were it not for my brothers-in-arms!'

Uallas's testimony was backed by the giant Brogan, who towered above the Brehon Judge in his glistening chainmail, a massive helm held beneath his arm.

'We were within earshot of a lady's cry,' he said, 'which was most certainly the ollave's! We raced towards the sound of the gunshot, then saw the Spaniard loading his rifle to shoot poor Uallas here. Were it not for the bravery of our worthy ollave, he would have felled another of my brethren in his cowardly way.'

So saying he raised a forefinger towards the score of armoured gallowglass warriors who stood apart from the rest of the crowd, still as statues behind their leader, the constable MacCabe. Donal could not resist a small, hateful smirk in my direction as his men buried me beneath a heap of irresistible accusations.

'Each of those men can confirm my testimony.'

Echna gently shook her head as she leafed through her pages.

'The testimony of two witnesses shall suffice to prove a matter of law. In any event, most of your men are beardless, which means that their testimony cannot bear weight.'

The yells of an onlooker were heard at the back of the throng which had gathered about us, and a few raised fists were shaken in the air.

'The arrogance of these aliens! The Spaniard should be beheaded!'

Echna raised her hand, and instantly the uproar was quelled.

'Be silent. It is the law which shall decide justice in this land. There is but one witness left whom I must question.'

Great gasps of awe were heard when Manglana himself stood forward, looking almost uneasy when he stepped before the judge.

'My lord MacGlannagh,' said the Brehon, 'I thank you for finding the courage to bear witness at a time of great trial. I understand that the lady Mac an Bhaird is unable to be here in person, yet since all are entitled to benefit of the law your rule has restored to this land, I would ask you but a single question, since the ollave is your daughter at law.'

Manglana rolled his shoulders back once while nodding at the judge who took a deep breath.

'Did your daughter invite the Spaniard to lay hands on her?'

The chieftain's face turned stonier when he replied with a voice that sounded like the scrape of gravel.

'No. She assured me that she did not.'

The Brehon bowed her head to him, which gesture was returned by the chieftain, who walked back to his place.

'It would appear that all of the witnesses have been heard,' said Echna, as she turned her attention to Fearghal, 'unless the accused's counsel has any witnesses of his own.'

The bard drew a deep breath as he stepped into the shadow of the great cairn.

'We have none, my lady.'

A great anger welled up inside me at his reply, and I was about to shout out in protest when another cry was heard from the crowd.

'Wait!'

A great tumult was heard among the gathering as the tribesmen sought to identify the source of the howl. Then a boy burst out of their number, running up to the Brehon and falling upon his knees. My mouth fell open as I made out the tear-streaked face of the princeling Lochlain, who stared at Echna in sadness as he sought to recover his voice.

'I know that I am but a beardless whelp, but the whole truth has not been heard! None know of the secret that I have kept with this worthy Spaniard, one which has yet reached no ear!'

So moved was I by the lad's intervention that my lower lip trembled. I had long rebutted the princeling's friendship, since I regarded him as a mere fop who had been born with a silver spoon thrust in his mouth. Yet his bravery left me stunned, and I could see his mother's resolve blazing beneath his late father's red locks.

'Lochlain! Come back here' roared the chieftain, gesturing at his puzzled bluejackets.

'Ronan tried to have the Spaniard killed!' shouted Lochlain, ignoring the bodyguards' approach. 'I saw it with my own eyes! We had to kill a pig at the rite of initiation, and the horseboy was secretly sent to disturb the boar just as Juan was about to shoot it! Ronan was himself dishonourable, and Juan did not kill an innocent man!'

Four of the bluejackets firmly grabbed him by the tunic as he struggled in vain to release himself.

'Wait!'

The guards' looks of bafflement only increased as they heard the Brehon's command. They turned their heads from her to the chieftain in an effort to understand what was expected of them.

'Your words are not yet admissible in this court, young prince,' said Echna, 'yet your bravery and resolve are to be commended, as is your yearning to pursue the truth. These were all traits displayed by your late father for as long as his wisdom graced this land. He was my foremost pupil, yet I fear that even he would bid you to respect our laws.'

Lochlain appeared downcast as he was led away, and a tear slipped down my nose as I stared on at him in wonder. He raised his head once more before reaching the crowd, meeting my stare for an instant before his look of defeat turned once more into one of resolve.

'Don't lad...' I whispered to myself, my eyes closed and my hands turning into tightly clenched fists.

'Do not fear, Spaniard,' he cried, 'for I know that you would never hurt my mother! I do not believe these lies, Spaniard! For they are lies, Spaniard! Only lies!'

His protests were drowned out by the great murmuring of the crowd, then lost in the howling wind as he was dragged away. An uncomfortable silence lingered over the gathering, and a quick sideways glance revealed that Donal MacCabe's spiteful mirth had been replaced by a sudden glare of outrage and frustration. At last the Brehon spoke again, inviting the bard to deliver his final words on my behalf. Fearghal strode before the throng in his screaming red coat, standing in front of me as he addressed the tribesmen. For a moment a hope stirred in me once more that Lochlain may have succeeded in planting some doubt in the minds of all present, enough to allow the bard one last proper defence of my innocence.

'This man may have erred,' he declared, 'but it is also to be recalled, O honoured Brehon, that he has selflessly defended our tribe in the past. He fought to save our keep and suffered injury when risking his life to rescue the tanist before the walls of Boyle. Indeed he is not without his virtues, and I entreat you to consider his past conduct before deciding the verdict.'

Brogan erupted at these words.

'Of what virtue do you speak, bard? Do you forget the lot of our brother Ronan! Even a lass would have killed him with more honour!'

Echna's robes fluttered in the wind as she rose to her feet in outrage, which seemed to cast a hushed blanket about her.

'Be silent! We have all heard the witnesses! This trial shall not descend into a shouting match!'

No one dared stir when she pronounced her decree.

'The lady Mac an Bhaird is a gentlewoman of marriageable age, and has never been known to be promiscuous or adulterous. She was never an unreformed prostitute, nor did she meet other men when married. The ollave screamed during acts that were uninvited. Acts which caused her to blush.'

A lump formed in my throat as the judge served me with a severe stare.

'This man has proven himself devoted to the tribe and has even been adopted as one of us. Yet I myself recall our lord MacGlannagh warning the Spanish castaways against taking advantage of our women, which means that this man acted in clear disregard of our lord protector's warning, which constitutes malice. It shall double the penalty.'

The Brehon paused to regain her breath as I braced myself for the worst.

'The lady Mac an Bhaird's father at law, our lord MacGlannagh, is owed fourteen *cumhals* in addition to the honour price of the victim. The ollave is part of the assembly of freemen, which renders her honour price an added seven *cumhals*. That is twenty-one *cumhals* in all, so the accused owes our lord seventy-three milk cows or pieces of silver.'

My shoulders slumped forward in distress before the Brehon proceeded to declare my penalty for murder.

'The horseboy was of no rank, which means that no honour price is due to his brother, Uallas. Yet the crime of murder incurs seven *cumhals*, plus an added seven *cumhals* for the malice with which it was committed. That is fourteen *cumhals* in total, amounting to fifty-two cows or pieces of silver. Once the Spaniard repays his debt to our lord MacGlannagh, Uallas may forfeit the fine he is owed and instead request that the Spaniard be put to death.'

With her judgement having been pronounced, Echna slapped shut the heavy manuscript which she held in her hands.

XXXIX

Rosclogher, Dartry, County Leitrim

9 April – 2 May 1589

My senses were beset by the smell and sounds of livestock, and sleep was only achieved through sheer exhaustion. Half of my new lodgings were crowded with pigs and fowl at night, to keep them safe from robbers and wolves. With a groan I turned over towards my left side, desperate to ignore the accompanying snores of the herdsmen and, asking myself how my stay in Dartry had so swiftly descended into so nightmarish an existence.

It had been two moons since men had jeered me before the Brehon, after she pronounced her judgement. The chieftain had immediately dismissed me from his service, and one of his bluejackets had approached me to snatch the rifle and bandolier from my shoulders.It was a painful separation, one which almost hurt as much as the wounded expressions worn by Manglana and his wife. I had endured this open humiliation without objection, as I was now marked out by the tribe as a criminal, with the law itself stripping me of any honour or its accompanying price.

The fine imposed upon me would have been hard enough to repay were I still a kern partaking of raids upon enemy tribes. My barring from the chieftain's service meant that I would miss the upcoming fighting season. In turn this spelt a lifetime working for anyone who would employ me, as I sought to repay my debt, yet my presence was shunned by all highborn tribesmen, which meant that I could only offer menial labour.

To my horror I had been reduced to a churl in all but name, one of those outlaws who toiled from day to night and who were treated worse than dogs. One employer of these unfortunates was Gorman, a brawny man with rounded shoulders whose grey hair fell over his face and chest. His first greeting to me had been a shovel which he thrust into my hands as he pointed at the piles of dung which were to be cleared from the byre.

As I set about this filthy task I was glad to have left my clothes in the care of the bondsman. Nial had warned me against keeping them, before furnishing me with a black sheepskin and cowled mantle, which were worn above a pair of torn woollen trews. It was hoped that these clothes might help me to fit in with my new employers, yet Gorman and his family were ever mindful of my identity, avoiding me at all times and ensuring that I was never left alone in the company of their women.

During my first days among them I may as well have worn the mark of Cain, and even the handful of unfree churls in their employ turned their heads away from me. In truth, my new surrounds would never have offered much in the way of lofty conversation since my employers were freeholders who ranked beneath the nobility, and who were assigned land by the assembly to mind the chieftain's cattle and fowl.

Gorman and his family toiled from dusk till dawn to ensure that Manglana's pigs, sheep and chickens were accorded the best of care. They were simple folk who had only travelled the world as far as their charges. Indeed they were as hard as the wind-battered heights around Rosclogher, yet I found them in time to possess the kindness of those who had learned to live with almost nothing and who shared every last scrap of food.

This meant that precious little envy and scheming was to be found among them, yet I soon realised that it would be near impossible to hide the ring among people of few possessions. My sentence meant that my personal privacy had vanished with my honour price, and to make matters worse, I was constantly shadowed by one of Gorman's sons. The boy was a witless oaf that the tribesmen secretly called a *druth*, who went by the name of Brian.

No sooner had I seen him than I recognised the simpleton who had approached me in the infirmary months earlier, when I had awoken to find myself in Rosclogher after the tanist had rescued me from Treasach Burke. He was always accompanied by Gorman or one of his brothers, since by Irish law it was the *druth's* family that were responsible for his actions. Brian was a large specimen with rounded shoulders who often cast a vacant stare at things while spittle dripped from the end of his lower lip. In spite of his general slowness he was capable of wreaking great damage if the fancy took him, so that his minders were relieved when I became the sole object of his attentions.

The fool was still as taken by me as when I had first reached Dartry. His eyes were fixed on me for the whole time that I lived in Gorman's hut, and he would at times burst into a fit of mindless laughter at my slightest gesture. He often poked me with a fat forefinger or pulled my nose and hair, amazed as he was by my darker southern features that contrasted so greatly with that of his fellow tribesmen.

Needless to say, these antics on his part greatly galled me, especially when they were carried out in front of the other tribesmen. His brothers would not encourage him, yet neither did they dissuade him, and it was all I could do not to strike him whenever he rushed up to me with furious giggles to tug at my beard and moustache. These antics soon became the worst torment of all, accompanied as they were by the sniggers of his kinsmen.

Hunger soon became another affliction, for the herders ate but once a day, gathered at night about their tables of fern. Their hands and mouths were wiped on grass bundles as smoke from a great candle of fat and reeds in the middle of the hut escaped through a hole in the rooftop. Our daily fare was humble and consisted of oaten bread and butter sometimes served with griddle cakes. Although my rank seemed to be just above that of the unfree, I sat with the churls during meals, and one of them snorted aloud when I asked if Gorman's family ever ate wheat.

'That is a luxury they could never afford.'

During meals the herdsmen faced the doorway at all times, with their arms close beside them. On feast days they cooked swine flesh in a hollow trunk, which was wrapped in raw cowhide and placed upon the fire. Throughout our daily chores dozens of young children swarmed about us like flies, playing with twigs and other items collected from the ground. Meanwhile the elder folk were skilled with the sling, and readily picked targets such as trees at which to fling their stones.

The end of my third week among the herdsmen found me hunched over the water of the lake, busily washing tunics. Two other churls also busied themselves with the task, and we were keenly watched by two of Gorman's sons whilst their sisters knelt a few feet away from us, cleaning their pots with straw. As I busied myself with my labour a familiar voice was heard behind me which brought a smile to my face for the first time in days.

'Your punishment has done you the world of good, friend Juan. You look the picture of rugged health already.'

Nial had spotted me from the outhouse and had approached me with a handful of bluejackets. His friendship and company had been sorely missed since I had passed into Gorman's service, and I turned to him with a laugh.

'Honest work is no punishment, friend Nial, though many would deem it such.'

A smile grew on the bondsman's face as he studied my piteous state.

'We should dress you like a seasoned laundress, with a smock drawn in at the waist.'

I laughed at his quip, then caught my reflection in the water. In that moment the sight of my bedraggled hair and filthy, torn clothes no longer felt like a laughing matter, and I frowned wearily as Nial slapped me on the back.

'Do not despair, friend Spaniard. Where life endures, so does hope. If there is ever anything I could do for you, you need only ask it.'

His words were of some relief to me, and it was with a lighter heart that I set about my duties, which also consisted of assisting Gorman's wife. One of these consisted of boiling linen in one pot while she mixed tannin and broom weed in another. When the cloth was thrown into her mix I was next ordered to stir it until it turned saffron, a colour only worn by the highborn Dartrymen.

I put my back into these hard chores, which only served to further endear me to the herdsmen. Many of them were surprised by my embrace of toil, yet a life of little privilege was nothing new to me. My resolve was also strengthened whenever I witnessed the lot of the churls in our number. They were punished criminals like me, who were worked as hard as mules and who were treated worse than the beasts in our care.

Our days of toil slowly ground along while the passing of April brought springtime warmth. Mosquitoes swarmed in the bog and tormented us, although they brought no disease. Rumour soon spread as quickly among us as the bothersome insects, telling of a rider who had appeared at dusk, seeking swift audience with Manglana. As the skiff bore him towards the keep, gossip grew as quickly as the ripples across the lake, with every last man giving his view on this visit.

Some spoke of the troubles that were spreading far west, which had been heard from the grey merchants. They told of an Irish lord, one called the Blind Abbot, who had claimed the title of MacWilliam, one which the Sassanas refused to heed. It seemed like the O'Rourke was as always lying in wait like a mountain wolf, hoping for the lands below him to clear of troopers summoned to battle so that he could swoop like a falcon and make off with as many cattle heads as his men could shepherd. Being the O'Rourke's sub-king, Manglana would be expected to commit to the conflict in whatever way he could, which some hoped would remove the gallowglasses from among our midst, since the presence of the Scots was hated more than the stink of the great middens alongside mad Orla's hovel.

'Not war again,' grunted Gorman as he helped himself to a rare slice of goat's cheese upon a hunk of bread.

'So what?' snapped his wife. 'It is all we have known, since before Brian was born.'

The burly *druth* snorted like a pig and pulled a face. His mother ignored him as she jerked her eyes in the direction of two massive gallowglasses who slept near the pig sty.

'At least we'll be rid of these hateful redshanks for a time.'

'True,' said her husband, with crumbs falling down the sides of his mouth. 'May they all be slain and their black souls committed to the hell they deserve. Yet what if the enemy turns up in force again?'

'Let them come,' snorted one of his older sons, a bullnecked specimen named Finn. 'The winter frosts have long departed, and we can spend half a year hidden in the mountains.'

Gorman shook his head slowly as he scratched at a louse in his beard.

'In truth, war cannot come too early to these lands. There are too many mercenaries heaped upon our hospitality, and the warmth is already breeding restlessness amongst them. I can already see them eyeing our daughter's ankles as they gather in bands around our cooking fires. No good can come of their loitering, so I say let them be off to earn their keep.'

'Will we also get to fight?' I asked earnestly, breaking the silence which I always kept at the end of the hut.

My blood had been stirred by talks of pretenders and fighting, since my time spent serving herdsmen had long dampened my spirits. The long days spent clearing dung and dyeing linen had led me to harbour the false hope that I may in time be allowed to contribute to the tribesmen's conversation. Yet my question was received with a blanket of silence, as if the greatest obscenity had been uttered in the hut. Finn turned towards me with a sneer on his face.

'Men without honour do not go to battle! Men without honour are barely fit to serve beasts!'

No sooner had he said this than his snarl was followed by a spade which he seized from near the doorway and flung at my head, so heartily that its end barely missed me as I threw myself upon the ground. A howl from a churl was heard behind me, who lay in a heap like a beaten dog, clutching at his freely bleeding nose. The tribesmen did not notice him as they returned to their conversation, speaking in muffled voices and swotting at the cursed insects which assaulted us in the gathering dusk.

'But will the chieftain summon all men to fight?' asked one of Gorman's daughters, who was heavy with child. 'It is not yet summer. Fair enough for the Scots to head to battle, for that is their business, but what are our men to do in the open field against Bingham's troopers?'

'That is for our lord MacGlannagh to decide!' rasped one of her younger brothers as he rose to his feet with a hand on his sword hilt.

The lad was enthused by talk of battle, having evidently seen precious little of it. He also laid particular emphasis on his reference to Manglana, which left his sister's face to slowly redden in embarrassment upon realising her casual reference to Dartry's lord. It was a custom of the Irish to always address their chieftain formally, be it to his face or behind his back, with any other reference deemed to be highly disrespectful.

'Settle down, Osgar,' growled Gorman's wife, glaring at her sprightly charge like a ruffled hound and wiping the frown right off the young pup's face. 'Would you bear arms against your own sister?'

Nervous laughter was heard about the hut as the mere stripling returned to his seat by the door. Just then, one of the neighbouring freemen popped their head through the doorway.

'Get out here, you lot,' he cried, 'for the messenger is returning across the water!'

His yell was like an invitation to a feast, for the tribesmen fell over one another in an attempt to make it out of the hut first. Gorman's loud protestations were ignored as he was buffeted about like a ship in a storm, fending his face from a fury of flailing arms and legs as his whole family vanished like a windswept fume. The churls and I were hot on their heels, joining the dozens of townsfolk who had left their huts and run down towards the banks of Lough Melvin.

Across the dark water, as oars glistened in the moonlight, the figure of the O'Rourke's messenger could be seen. He stood at the prow of the boat with his hands upon his waist and one foot raised on the boards as his dusky figure slowly grew in size. Two of the chieftain's bluejackets stood at his shoulders, raising their spears as the boat was moored to the jetty. They kept the men of Rosclogher at bay with the ends of their weapons, shouting at them to leave the envoy in peace while O'Rourke's man mounted his horse and kicked it towards the trees.

An army of children suddenly swelled about the horse's haunches, as scores of questions were howled in his direction. The rider raised his hand to the crowd behind him in a signal to leave him be, yet it was for naught as many of them had already raced to the bog to block his path through it.

'What tidings do you bear?' they howled. 'Tell us of what passes in the west!'

The rider huffed in frustration as he begged them to let him pass, yet none of the crowd would be placated as they tugged at his sleeves and the horse's mane. The moments must have seemed like hours to O'Rourke's man as he manfully fended off the assault. Finally a dozen bluejackets appeared from the ring-fort to let him through. Yet the tribesmen's attentions had not been fruitless, and a few replies were uttered by the messenger.

'Yes, the Bourkes are revolting,' acknowledged O'Rourke's man as he batted away a child's hands away from the reins, 'and the enemy has summoned many bands to its banner. Yet ask not about my master's intentions, for I would not breathe them if it meant my death!'

The man was as good as his word, and no amount of cajoling or shoving could loosen his lips, even after he had fallen off his mount. He was so flustered at this that he rose from the mud, cursing wildly, and the press of the tribesmen slowly eased as cold steel flashed from his belt. He was still cursing after Nial had appeared with other bluejackets to separate the crowd, and the air was abuzz with the rumour of impending battle as the envoy vanished into the trees alongside us.

No sooner was he gone than the gathering turned its attentions to the bondsman instead.

'Tell us, Nial, is it to be war again?'

The bondsman swiftly drew his two swords, crossing them before him like a huge pair of scissors. The gesture instantly checked the steps of those closest to him. They froze to a standstill and regarded him with open mouths. Nial's face was the picture of defiance as his blue eyes fell upon them.

'I pray you, good folk of Dartry,' he cried, 'return to your homes for the night. I would not injure the least one of you. I know not whether we shall again take up arms against the enemy, yet the decision is one that rests with our worthy protector, my lord MacGlannagh.'

Some muttering and grumbling was heard from the crowd, yet the bondsman was a respected figure among the tribe, and one who was held to be a man of his word. The tribesmen did his bidding and returned to their homes, the elderly among them hobbling shoulder to shoulder as they traded solemn nods and countless words of wisdom. All throughout this exchange I stood apart from the tribesmen with Brian gurgling and poking my back, observing the Dartrymen's belligerence and wondering how it might aid me in my escape.

For I had entertained the hope of fleeing the country in the long, hellish weeks I had endured ever since I had been committed to Gorman. I had often stared across the lake at the endless cluster of trees which skirted its opposite bank, tempted to run towards the peaks behind them, where I might make my way with the emerald ring back to Spain, and from there on to the Indies.

The following summer months of pasturing, combined with the certain prospect of war, would cause havoc, perhaps even enough for me to be able to slip away unnoticed. Brian's hefty forefinger tapped my shoulder hard, so that I was certain that a ring of black bruises was spreading across my back. It only served as a timely reminder of my lot, though a gurgle in my stomach suddenly reminded me that a more opportune moment to be alone might not sooner present itself.

A yelp was heard from the dolt at my back as I darted towards the closest ring of huts; it was followed by the inevitable heavy footsteps and anxious groans. A look over my shoulder revealed the *druth* to be a few steps away from me, close enough for him to keep up his pursuit, yet far enough for me to be able to lose him in the village.

'Be swift, Brian. Make haste,' I called out, then made towards his father's hut before taking a sudden left three huts before it and squatting between two other hovels until the fool had crashed past.

As I returned to my feet, I tore off in the direction of the middens. I ignored the loud cackle of mad Orla, as well as was the loud grunting of her latest visitor, as I scampered past the mounds of rubbish and crouched in the bushes ahead, which skirted the ring of bog. My bowels were swiftly relieved, before I engaged once more in the nasty business of finding the ring. The gem was next cleaned on the grass at my feet and held upon the palm of my hand.

'Fallen on hard times, you and I,' I whispered, prodding the trinket with my left forefinger. 'To think of all that you have put me through. But we shall soon both be free of this land, slipping through the shadows unseen until I sell you to one who is also slave to your charms.'

As soon as this was said I felt a tinge of fear and wondered whether I could ever be parted from something which had been a constant through all my misfortune in Ireland.

'Yes,' I whispered, as a tear formed in my eyes, 'all that I know and hold dear must be given up before a new start can truly be made.'

I stroked the soft and smooth gemstone in its golden casing with the knuckles of my right hand as my low voice was masked by the chirping of crickets in the thickets at dusk.

'Your place is in the old world, my friend, which is now your home. Yet my place is across the sea from whence you came, so that we can each be a guarantee of a better place in both worlds, which we can help secure for each other.'

A rustle was heard a few steps away, and I raised my head to see two bluejackets advancing in my direction with their spears raised over their heads. The soldiers had already detected my presence among the bushes, so I quickly placed the ring into my shoe. I next slowly rose to my feet, holding my hands above my head so as to show that I presented no threat. Upon recognising me, one of the kerns issued a low bark of mocking laughter, then walked up to me and shoved me away.

'Return to your hovel, you cur,' he snarled. 'What sort of mischief can you hope to achieve in the bushes at night?'

The two kerns were still insulting me as I made my way back towards Gorman's hut, where I received an instant rebuke and blows for having abandoned his dolt of a son. On his part Brian howled with delight at the sight of me, and I was almost thankful when he darted towards me and wrapped his huge arms about my body, shielding me from further indignity at the hands of his kin.

In coming weeks the number of runners and mounted messengers between Dartry and Breifne increased, until the tribesmen ignored them altogether. There was not yet any word from Nial as to whether Dartry would go to war again, but only a fool could have missed what was afoot. It was obvious to me that the rebel chieftains were watching and waiting, sitting back on their thrones and relishing the prospect of large - and soon to be scantily guarded - southern herds.

With the grazing season so close at hand, Manglana decided to commit to the raids, since his people would be safer in the mountains than they would be in their huts. Nial quickly spread these tidings among the villagers, who were glad to learn that only troops in their lord's employ would be committed to the field. Yet Gorman met these tidings with a dark scowl and shook his head.

'Our lord MacGlannagh will not use his annual right to summon all men to fight. Which means that this is only a small repast before the full banquet.'

That Sunday the Dartrymen's voices were louder than usual at Mass, as they thanked the Almighty for deliverance. Many of the highborn stood as godparents for the lower-ranked freemen, to secure the loyalty of their lowlier kinsmen. As always I cowered at the back of the abbey, stealing glimpses of the ollave Muireann who stood with her son between Manglana and Dervila.

The sting of her absence was more keenly felt whenever I saw her, for the hardest part of my punishment had been my separation from her. Often did my skin tingle at the thought of her warm touch and embrace, and the memory of the desire in her soft, brown eyes caused me to waken at night with a start. It was all I could do not to tremble at the sight of her, a sweet torture that was even denied me by the ever-watchful Saorla. The maiden was as vigilant as a hawk at Muireann's back, and stood behind her whenever she spotted me so as to shield the ollave from my line of sight.

Muireann was soon also gone from Rosclogher, and I warily stared after her as she rode out of the town alongside Manglana. I hid behind Gorman's sons when the chieftain's company rumbled past, for at their back rode Cathal the Black in helmet and chain mail as he led the highborn cavalrymen after his lord. At their backs followed the gallowglass axes, who had for so long plagued the town with their presence, and a few cheers were issued by the townsfolk as the reviled Scots made off.

'Earn your keep you whoresons!' howled Finn above a chorus of catcalls by his younger brothers. Brian whinnied in delight behind them, thinking that my hiding was a funny game. He proceeded to clap his hands and hoot like an owl, which revealed my location to the passing Scots. Their leader, Donal MacCabe had until then received all jibes with a stoic expression, yet he caused many bystanders to gasp as he reined his steed in before Gorman. The herdsmen stared up at him in fear as a great grin spread across the constable's face.

'Spaniard!' he cried, as he heftily patted the neck of his mount. 'Step forth, that I may show you my fine steed.'

With a groan I returned to my feet and tried not to tremble before Donal and his men. Brogan towered behind his father, with a broad grin also spreading across his face. The gallowglass revelled in my air of disappointment, for the constable's new mount was none other than my old black stallion, which I had stolen from the Sassenachs when Aengus was killed.

'See, Spaniard? See?' growled Donal, as he proceeded to ruffle the horse's mane. 'See what it means to spurn an invitation to join our number? I would have made a powerful warrior out of you, but clearing dung should keep you out of mischief!'

'Get you to the byre!' Brogan shouted, then laughed aloud as his father spurred his mount away and beckoned his men to follow him. Amid a loud shuffling of feet, the fearsome party of Scots trudged after their two mounted commanders, the tribesmen again hurling jeers and curses at their backs long after the gallowglasses had crossed the green and entered the trees skirting the bog. There followed great cries of joy and relief when the last axe of the Scots vanished among the trunks, for their lodging in the town had caused no end of misery and bother.

Men could now look forward to keeping their stores of food unhidden. Meanwhile the town's smith, whores and many others looked forward to the day when the debts owed to them by the mercenaries would finally be repaid, if the raids upon the enemy's herds were a success. All agreed that the fighting had not come too soon that year, for never before had the gallowglasses been harboured throughout the winter months.

Manglana's host was gone for many days, but little was heard about his movements. Rumour had it that Dartry's chieftain had joined his overlord the O'Rourke's great cattle raids in the land of Sligo. In any event, the disappearance of the gallowglass, coupled with the presence of a small force of kerns left behind, had improved tempers in the village.

Children played freely and without fear in the alleyways, and for the first time in months women were seen to walk alone from dusk until dawn. Even the churls seemed happier as they went about their endless chores. I even heard whistling whilst he worked. None of Gorman's sons silenced him, as they happily talked to one another, and ate food which had seemingly appeared from nowhere and was suddenly available in greater quantities.

As April drew to a close, the warmer weather improved the tribesmen's spirits. Despite the constant attentions of Brian, I managed to obtain greater moments of privacy, and in these moments of solitude many thoughts on how to best escape Dartry filled my mind. One such idea involved me boarding a sailing craft which would return me to Spain. Yet the design was one that was in truth impossible, for it required me to hide along the coastline until I sighted some smuggler's vessel which hailed from the Continent. A secure method of persuading outlaws to take me on board was beyond my reckoning, for it would be suicide to attempt to bribe them with an offer of the ring held in my possession.

My only other choice was to disappear into the forests north of the lake, and make my way north as quickly as my feet would carry me. A great deal of luck would be required to succeed in this endeavour since the borders of the Irish had become more heavily guarded. It was also said that the Sassanas passed freely and unhindered among the great tribes of Ulster, who had not rebelled against the English crown.

These thoughts were one day disturbed by the loud blast of a bugle, and I withdrew from my usual lakeside hideaway towards the town. The townsfolk milled upon the green, and my heart sank when I saw the chieftain's banner fluttering in the wind. I strained my ears to listen to the inevitable cheers from the tribesmen, yet they were instead filled with ear-splitting lowing and snorts, as dozens of cows were led through the trees after the chieftain's company. Men instantly set about the beasts with halters and sticks, leading off the prizes towards bawn and byre. In the corner of my eye Nial could be seen limping away from the party towards the outhouse, in the company of two knaves. I hurried after the bondsman, hoping to glean some news of Manglana's movements during the previous weeks.

'Nial! Wait!'

The bondsman's chest heaved wearily as he turned towards me. His servants bared their teeth and their daggers at my approach, though they vanished when their master bid them to go away. I could see that he had had a rough time of it of late, for his blond hair was stuck to his sweaty forehead and cheeks, and much of the mirth was gone from his dancing eyes. His mail shirt and forearms were spattered with dried blood and gore, some of which speckled his knees.

'What is it, Spaniard?' he asked with another deep sigh.

'I seek tidings of your venture,' I replied, walking up to him and resting my hands on my sides.

'There was much venture but precious little glory,' he said with a shrug, 'for the Sassanas are so absorbed by their fight in the west that they left their north and eastern flank lightly guarded. We slew many tribesmen held to be royalist. Women and children also fell beneath the blade.'

He seemed to struggle when he said this, and he stared into my face as if he were looking into a deep void.

'The chieftains secured many heads,' he continued at last, 'before Bingham marched a large army to meet us on the field. We fled before he arrived and made off with scores of heads. This is but a third of the cows we rustled, and the rest have been left behind at Duncarbery, under the watch of the tanist and the constable.'

'Were many losses suffered?' I asked, amazed by the number of cows which had been seized by the Dartrymen, which made me wish that my services had been retained by Manglana.

'But a few slight injuries inflicted by missiles, and someone lost an eye,' he replied, 'yet I pray you to save your questions until the morrow, for I am claimed by sheer exhaustion and must retire for the night.'

His scabbards bounced against his thighs as he turned back towards his lodging; the two boys behind him served me a dark stare as they made after him. The lowing behind me only grew, which tore my stare of longing away from my former lodging and returned my attentions to the green. There herdsmen could be seen leading cattle away from the soldiers amid loud cheers and laughter. The haul brought to Rosclogher numbered close to sixty strong, and I suddenly realised with a shudder that Gorman and his men would be in need of me.

His sons greeted my appearance with curses and insults as the halters of two cows were thrust into my hands. I led them back to the crowded bawn nearest the ringfort, where its bleating tenants had more than doubled within the hour. Thereafter I fetched straw and water for the cows placed in my care, grateful that I had not endured any further humiliation at the hands of my employers. The rest of the day was spent carrying out a number of other menial chores, while rumours abounded amongst the tribesmen, telling of the exploits of their chieftain.

The unexpected bounty brought to the town had heartened the tribesmen and shrouded them in great joy. Never would I see them happier. Bellies were fuller upon the appearance of so much livestock, with the chieftain and most lords having made good on a large part of their debts. Most joyously of all, the gallowglasses' debts had also been honoured, which meant that the townsfolk of Rosclogher had been freed from the burden of having to maintain them.

Manglana had ordered the Scots to set up camp outside the walls of Duncarbery, where they were to guard the coast road which passed through his land. Word had it that Bingham's advance had been checked by the O'Rourke when the overlord had passed into the Roscommon, yet Dartry remained vigilant against any future enemy incursions. Despite this threat, the absence of Donal's men was of great relief to the town. The hammer on the smith's anvil rang happily as bowyers and fletchers gathered upon the green, repairing bow strings and sharpening arrow heads.

Two days later I awoke at dawn to a stunning sight, finding most of the tribesmen gathered outside their huts and marvelling at the rising sun. Children pointed at it as if they had never seen it before, and Gorman startled me when he walked up to me with a broad smile, as I looked about me in confusion.

'Today is the feast of Beltane, Spaniard. It is a time of blossom and of fire.'

I nodded once to him and turned back to the great stirring about me. On the greensward I could see that a great maypole of birch had been erected, with many of the tribesmen dancing gaily about it. New life and fertility were being celebrated, with all celebrants engaging in scenes of great revelry. Many jumped over broomsticks of corn husks while children bedecked the doors of their families' huts with whitethorn.

Towards noon the chieftain strode before the maypole with his usual retinue and guard of bluejackets. Matters immediately assumed a more serious tone as the highborn members of the *derbfine* gathered about him. Muireann and Cathal stood among the exalted number, their eyes trained upon a kern who stepped before them with a leather bag in his hand.

'What is afoot?' I asked Gorman, whose company I had kept for most of the morning.

His sons eyed me darkly when I spoke, for none could understand why their father suddenly desired my company.

'May Day is a time when all heads of cattle are counted. Lots will now be drawn among our lords to divide the tribe's property for the coming year. The allotted portions are to be shared equally.'

I had long known that no concept of private property existed among the tribe, yet the ceremony still intrigued me. Large portions of grazing land were divided, with even the bogland being painstakingly split into identical parts. Manglana was also accorded his own lands in this way, and quietly bowed his head in acceptance when his territories were declared to him, mirroring the gesture of the other members of his *derbfine*.

When at last the ceremony was ended, the crowd proceeded towards the Abbey of Saint Mel, where the handfastings took place. It was a curious custom practised by the Irish, whereby couples pledged their intention to be wed within the year and joined hands while receiving the blessing of O'Ronayne. This ritual was observed with great solemnity by all those present, and a more sombre silence was observed when at last Cathal the Black stood forth, his black locks covering his devoured face.

Manglana observed his nephew intently, while at his right shoulder Dervila sported an open frown of disapproval. A slight movement was seen as Muireann left Lady Bourke's side and made her way towards the tanist. My heart was pierced with longing as the ollave strode towards Cathal, wearing a pale blue gown above her linen chemise. A lump formed in my throat at the sight of her high cheeks and eyes like deep pools of warm ochre. As her arms hung by her sides, her flowing sleeves fluttered in the light wind that rippled the grass about us.

Her wealth of hair was tied up in the traditional way, beneath a low-brimmed hat. So transfixed was I by her beauty, that it was a few moments before I realised a few of the glares cast in my direction. I therefore kept my eyes on the ground and listened to the proceedings from the back of the gathering as the rest of the ceremony unfolded. The exchange of consent for future marriage took place with all due solemnity and instantly brought an end to the handfasting.

'And now,' boomed the chieftain in a voice as loud as a thunderclap, 'let the preparations for the booleying time begin!'

A crackle and hiss was heard behind us, and we turned to see two bonfires bursting into flame. Two kerns scurried away from them, grinning openly, and I could tell that they had used the black powder produced in the ringfort to light the great pyres, which roared brightly as if in challenge to the afternoon sun. There followed greater revelry as the crowd dispersed. Herdsmen rushed back towards barn and byre, ushering their cattle towards the green where two great bonfires were raging.

'The twin fires of Beltane!' shouted the herdsmen again and again, then scurried towards their homes to gather the belongings they had stowed away over the previous days.

This great rustle of sacks was swiftly followed by the loud creak of fences and the bark of the hounds. All the cattle were let out of their winter shelters into the open, where the herdsmen in charge of them prodded them onwards towards the gap between the flames. The lowing quickly turned into a high-pitched screech as the cows and bulls rumbled nearer the fire, yet hearty swings of the flail and the pointy end of sticks kept the beasts to the course designed for them, with a general clamour heard among the onlooking townsfolk when the first cow hurried through the smoking pyres. Tribesmen ran among the flames, yelling about the fertility that they believed the two great bonfires would bring them. Brands were hurled into the flames or whirled over the heads of the revellers. It was a scene which left me both amused and curious, and I could not help asking my employer about it.

'Why are you doing this?'

Gorman slapped the buttock of an old ox whose deep lowing betrayed a great reluctance to approach the fire despite the many years in which it had been submitted to the ritual.

'To purify them and bring them luck,' he replied, jerking his head towards the flames, 'for those are not just any flames, Spaniard. They are the need-fires of Beltane.'

I nodded at him, then noticed Manglana's steward, Malachy, who stood at the other end of the bonfires, taking account of every single head of cattle that passed through them. When the last of the cattle had passed through the flames, I was summoned to return them to the byre. The revelry persisted for the remainder of the day, with the fires being fed until they were left to die a few hours before dusk. Great reverence was still accorded to the red cinders, with daring children running over them for luck and women stepping over them to thwart barrenness.

As the last of the daylight dwindled over the mountain peaks, I looked on as Gorman's wife and daughters gathered the cooler embers and took them back to the hut. They were closely followed by their father and brothers, whose steps were shadowed by their retainers. I stood in the doorway with the churls as I watched them feed the embers from the twin flames upon their own fire. Prayers were recited about the fire late into the night, as we nodded off one by one.

The early morning cry of a rooster had us back on our feet, hurrying to feed and water the cattle. Manglana's town was already astir as the lakeside dwellers prepared to journey to the mountains, which would be their home for the duration of the summer months. Men could be heard honing their daggers and spearheads on the whetstone while the women screamed at their children to gather their belongings.

I was swept up in the general clamour and excitement, until I saw Gorman's son Finn marching into the byre and summoning the churls to him. Those churls closest to me frowned as they cursed and muttered beneath their breath, and in vain did I try to hide, crouching behind the back of a cow.

'You too, Spaniard.'

We followed Gorman's son towards the green, where at least fifty churls could be seen gathered about the same number of large wicker baskets. The large and ragged band were closely watched by Nial and a dozen of his best bluejackets, who stood alongside a half-dozen riders led by one of Cathal's closest subalterns.

'Here are the half-dozen you were promised!' roared Finn at the bondsman, who made no sign of recognising me. 'Return them to us whole, for we've many heads that need minding.'

Nial turned his back on the herder in reply, and already the riders made towards the path through the bog.

'Where are we going?' I asked a one-eyed churl to my right.

'To pick the God-forsaken weed,' he snarled, then spat on the ground before seizing up a basket and hurrying after his wretched companions who followed the kerns and riders.

There followed a hard march through the woods and the grassland, which was only interrupted when we arrived within sight of Manglana's fort of Duncarbery. Upon arriving there, our number was bolstered by another score of churls, who were closely guarded by a dozen evil-looking gallowglasses. We proceeded along a path which at once seemed strangely familiar to me, and then I caught sight of the white billows of spray upon the ocean.

It was the same strip of coast where I had met with the Scottish smugglers, and the memory of my bartering on behalf of the tribe was still as fresh as the surf which hissed before us. It was then that I realised the purpose of our errand, as the churls wordlessly made their way towards the large and unbroken mass of black-red seaweed, which stretched as far as the eye could see along the water's edge. As the churls bent over towards the ground, their arms were plunged deep into the seaweed, picking it off the sand with their bare hands and flinging it into the baskets they had cast at their feet.

The kerns silently gathered along the grey sand while the riders dismounted and kept their own company. The gallowglasses leant upon their great axe heads and stared at the sea. My nostrils were soon full of the smell of seaweed, which was thankfully still fresh and had not yet rotted. When our baskets were full, they were slung over the backs of the freemen's horses. More baskets were then filled and slung onto our own backs.

'Make haste!' cried the bondsman as we made to leave the sea behind us. 'We shall make for Tullaghan before you return to your masters.'

The burdens on our backs were as heavy as a wounded comrade borne over one's shoulder, and I understood the dismay of the one-eyed churl on learning that we had to pick seaweed and bear it back inland. It was backbreaking work, and soon the rasp of my breath was almost louder than the sounds of my footsteps. We had covered at least half our march, with the fort already in sight, when a loud cry was heard up ahead. As I raised my head I saw seven horsemen riding hard in our direction.

A roar was heard from the gallowglasses, who snatched their axes off their backs; their horseboys joined the kerns in raising their spears above their head and readying them for a throw. As I looked from left to right I could see that many of the churls were motionless like fearful chattel. Up ahead the freemen could be seen cutting the dulse baskets off the backs of their horses as they struggled to mount them before the approaching riders reached us.

Nial's swords were already drawn as he called out to the bluejackets, who roared at the Scots and gestured at the still distant hazard. Their cries had a desperate note to them, for although the gallowglasses were able to engage with mounted men, the onrushing riders remained the worst human hazard for any foot soldier to deal with. My worries only worsened as the enemy grew ever closer. A cold fear seized me as I made out stirrup boots, lowered lances, and the red crosses splayed across white shields. The sight of the English troopers so close to the sea was too much for me to bear, with the memories of the shipwrecks not yet a year old, and the horrors of the dungeon of Sligo still plaguing my mind at night.

I unslung the basket's straps from my shoulders at once, and as my load collapsed onto the grass, I was already tearing off on a northwards run. In my panic I had chosen to flee up an incline rather than making in the direction of the water. Meanwhile the other churls cried out in fear and made off in all directions.

A look over my shoulder revealed the troopers galloping away from the gallowglasses, their shields raised to block the many spears flung in their direction. Two of the enemy swayed in their saddles as they were caught in the leg, though the foremost among them skewered a kern with his lance.

The horror of the sight left me feeling shaken, and I collapsed as the toe of my right foot got caught in a tussock, leaving one of my brogues rolling across the grass. I could not afford to recover it, and my ears were filled with the furious cries of the Irish behind me as I hauled myself back to my feet and ran off again. I inwardly cursed myself for attempting to flee horsemen in open territory. A loud crack made me peer over my shoulder once more, only to see smoking pistols brandished by the growing troopers. They had served Manglana's men with a volley while one of them gestured wildly in my direction.

My balance was nearly lost again as I noticed the beaver hat on his head.

'Holy host deliver me,' I gasped beneath my breath. 'Not that whoreson Treasach Burke . . .'

I wiped the sweat from my eyes with my forearm as I raced on, hardly believing that the renegade tracker had managed to sniff me out so deep in rebel-held territory. The prospect of fleeing him again appeared more unlikely with each desperate step that I took towards the distant trees, and the pounding hooves grew louder and louder behind me.

The ground grew rockier beneath me as I ignored the pain in my bare foot and hurried on. My heart leapt at the shrill ring of steel against stone. Pistol shots echoed as Burke roared at his men, perhaps scared that my death might spell the loss of the ring.

With my doom so close at hand, I shoved myself forwards with both hands and feet, scaling the steepest part of the incline and making for the still distant trees. A last glimpse over my shoulder made my mouth go dry as I glimpsed the whites of a rider's eyes in a scarred face contorted with rage and malice.

The Sassenach issued cries in a gruff voice, perhaps urging me to surrender. I was half tempted to end my flight, since my legs were ablaze with strain and the small copse ahead could never be reached in time. Yet the memory of my torture in Sligo Castle served as a most pointed spur, and my pace only grew as my skin prickled at the thought of the terrible death which was at hand.

I had never run faster in the whole of my life, yet the horse's breath was felt on my neck in the instant before the ground swallowed me whole. A cry left my lips as my shoulders brushed against sharp rock, for the sudden darkness was like a blanket being thrown over my head. I half twisted my ankle as I crashed onto the dank and rocky floor below, where I lay in a dazed heap for long moments. I slowly realised, to my growing dismay, that I had fallen into a deep crevasse which old wives warned of, that were said to speckle the Irish coast.

A great whinny was heard overhead as I slowly returned to my feet, feeling like a cornered rat as I looked overhead and assessed my unlikely plight. As the Sassanas spoke and laughed amid the snort of yet another horse, my hands reached out to the slimy walls of the fissure which entrapped me, which was only about wide enough for two men.

'Holy host of the Madonna,' I cursed as the unmistakable sound of a pistol being cocked reached my ears from above.

Without a second's delay I hurled myself against the bottom of the wall which sloped inwards to my left. Rainwater had eaten deep enough into the rock to afford my body some protection from any missiles which might rain down from above.

Meanwhile the talk above me grew more anxious. My enemies knew that they were not far from Manglana's keep, which the tribesmen they had left behind might have already reached. A rope was instantly thrown down, and I could not keep myself from shivering when the sound of Burke's voice followed the cord.

'Greetings, my rabbit. Crawl out of your warren immediately, if you please.'

In my helplessness I could not but dread his mockery, and it was not from cold that my hair stood on end.

'Do not make me come down there, Spaniard,' he hissed angrily, 'or I shall bear you back to the dungeon at Sligo Castle.'

At his mention of Sligo Castle I curled ever more tightly against the deep fissure's wall, cringing like a helpless dog filled with dread. At any moment I knew that the sound of boots against rock would be heard, forcing me into a terrible scrap with an armed and armoured man, with little room to manoeuvre. Not since my crawling through the waterlogged mines beneath enemy fortresses in the Low Countries had I endured such a constrained and hellish experience, and I issued prayers beneath my breath as I cowered against the rock. My skin crawled as a loud cry of rage was heard from the renegade, and pistol shots whistled against the rock but a palm's length away from my feet.

'Get out of there, you cur,' screeched Burke, 'or I will cut you to shreds and cast you into the sea!'

I barely breathed until another loud curse was heard, and my body stiffened when I heard the scrape of soles against grass overhead. I turned myself onto my back with a gasp, spotting the evil face of my tormentor as he readied to climb down towards me with a *skene* dagger clenched tightly between his teeth. Yet although Burke's eyes shone with malevolence, his head was raised at the sound of another horse's snorts; a straggler could be heard riding up to his men while shouting his head off.

'Treasach! Treasach!'

To my relief Burke vanished to answer his call, and my mind raced to guess what new devilry the heretics had hatched. There followed a loud order barked by the renegade at his charges as the newly arrived horseman muttered to him between snatches of breath. It was then that the sight of my bare foot caught my notice like a fist to the stomach, and to my great horror I realised that I had lost the very shoe in which the ring had been stowed away.

With a yelp I fell upon my knees and beat my fists upon the ground, issuing a loud howl of defeat as a cackle of laughter was heard above me. Ignorant to any danger from the heretics I beat my fists against everything until they were bloody, even striking my own face in frustration at the cruel loss I had endured after all my months of suffering in Dartry. I suddenly cared no longer for my life and safety, nor for the sound of chargers galloping away overhead.

Everything I had risked had been for nothing, and my rage soon turned to sorrow as tears welled up on my cheeks. My sobbing was rudely interrupted when something heavy crashed into my shoulders and smacked my cheek against the dirt underfoot. In the darkness I first thought that my enemies had contrived to hurl a boulder down upon me, so heavy was the weight on my back. Then Burke's evil voice was heard once more as he snarled his farewell and goaded me in his triumph.

'Do not fret, Spaniard, for you are no longer alone. The cold corpse of Bingham's cousin shall provide you with good companionship until you starve to death. No one will hear your crying out here, for I have barely heard you myself.'

My rage at the loss of the trinket had me wriggling about in anger as a last imprecation left my throat.

'Bastard!'

Another high-pitched, mocking laugh was heard, accompanied by the unmistakable cock of a pistol. I made myself as small as I could, with my arms and legs pulled tightly against my chest and stomach as more shots rang down into the hole. Once the shots were fired, a gob of spittle followed, together with the unmistakable trickle of piss.

'Ah, 'tis indeed a beauty, Spaniard,' said Burke as he relieved himself. 'One that would fetch a king's ransom. To think of the wealth it shall bring me as you rot in this pit.'

When he was finished he bent down to one knee, and his hands were cupped about his mouth as he poured the last of his scorn upon me.

'You may leave your shell again, crab, for I shall waste no more shot on you. Die with the unbearable knowledge of what you so foolishly lost.'

Then the screech of a horse announced his departure, although I dared not move long after the last dripping sound had subsided. It must have been at least an hour until I dared to stretch my limbs again, and I somehow wriggled out from beneath the corpse, which had been flung down upon me and which had reddened my tunic with the blood which had gushed out of its severed windpipe. As I shoved the stiff corpse of the dead Sassenach away from me, I could not but feel the slightest pity for another fellow unfortunate who had crossed the path of a most irresistible and deadly ring.

XL

DARTRY MOUNTAINS, DARTRY, COUNTY LEITRIM

3 May – 3 July 1589

Summer was a time beloved by the Manglanas. Herdsmen abandoned their trews for the kilt, and took breaths of fresh air heavy with pollen as they savoured the fragrance of furze. Our creaght first retired to a large cattle booley in the heights of the Dartry mountains, which consisted of a round cabin whose roof was supported by a bog pine pillar. The rest of the structure was composed of earth and thick stone walls, a rough construction where Gorman and his wives resided while his sons and churls led the chattel from pasture to pasture.

The tribesmen leapt from crag to crag like agile mountain goats during the day, building huts from sods and branches in the evenings. At times we retired to a circle beneath a starlit sky with our feet thrust towards an open fire, lying upon rushes and using logs for pillows. As they retired for the night, some of the Dartrymen engaged in the curious practice of steeping their mantles in water, then pulling them over their heads and bodies. One night a fellow churl insisted that I observe the practice, and I discovered to my surprise that when heated by the fire, our soaked coverings kept us warm long after the flames had gone out.

Our days spent watching the beasts were idyllic. We ate stirabout which was washed down with buttermilk. The air was often full of the tunes of harpists and pipers; storytellers appeared at other times to recount their tales. Pedlars with pack horses sold tools that were needed by the tribesmen, the latter of whom delighted in the fair weather so that their disposition had even softened towards the churls.

I found my own disposition towards the herders mellowing as our bond slowly grew while we cared for Manglana's cattle. It had been at least ten days since I had managed to scramble out of the deep fissure into which I had fallen. A pair of bluejackets had heard my hoarse cries a day after the corpse had been flung upon me. A length of sheep gut had been thrown down to me, which I seized like a drowning man, so desperate was I to be free of the prison in which I had spent a hellish night and morning.

Upon emerging from the hole, the cause of my bewildered cast had been mistaken for thirst and hunger. Dried blood also besmeared my hair, face and tunic, and one of the kerns was so distressed at the sight of me that he instantly shoved his water flask and a piece of bread into my hands after helping me climb out. Then my rescuers' heads were turned away in shame as I stumbled upon the shoe which I had lost and promptly burst into a flood of furious tears, so enraged was I at the renegade who had robbed me of the ring.

Thereafter I ambled aimlessly after the kerns, my thoughts a whirl of loss and desperation. Life without the prospect of wealth and freedom had entirely lost its sweetness, and upon reaching a small stream I stepped into it without calling out to the kerns, who turned to see me sloughing off the blood, saltwater and the strong odour of seaweed which lingered even after I had washed. Upon emerging from the water I kept to the heels of the bluejackets all the way to the large keep of Duncarbery, where many of the other flown churls had assembled after the attack of Burke's riders.

They were gathered in a barn choked with fowl and pigs, with two kerns standing outside the door. I threw myself upon the straw and fell into a deep yet haunted sleep, only to find myself shaken awake shortly before dawn. The gold locks of the bondsman fell on my face as he held me firmly by the shoulders, so that for a moment I mistakenly thought that I was still sharing the outhouse of *Doire Mel* with him.

'You are alive!' he exclaimed with a grin. 'I feared the worst when I saw you running up that hillock!'

I said nothing as I returned his stare, for the memory of my loss still rankled with me, and I could not share in his joy. His face was suddenly serious when he saw me looking away from him.

'What is wrong, Spaniard? Have you suffered injury?'

'Does it even matter?' I asked in a tone both sarcastic and aggressive, given the treatment I had endured since my mistrial.

He flinched at my question, then rose to his feet and stepped away.

'It is true that you have endured much,' he said, 'yet you still have friends that intervene on your behalf.'

'Do you speak of the cows and the *druth* Brian?' I asked. 'For they have intervened often in my life, but scarcely on my behalf.'

Nial sighed aloud at my insolence, though any anger he felt at my words was tempered by his understanding of my predicament. He held out his right hand to me, which held nearly a pound of ox flesh.

'Take this, for you must be still hungry.'

To his surprise, I turned my head away, for despite my fasting I had no appetite, and I was still feeling sick to my guts from the loss of the ring.

'Do you not want it?' he exclaimed. 'It is all that remains of the alms given to the vagrants by our lord MacGlannagh at Beltane!'

As my hand was raised, I heard him taking a large bite of it himself.

'Did Burke injure you?' he asked between mouthfuls. 'Did he say anything?'

'No,' I lied, 'for I was mercifully spared from his bloodlust after my fall.'

The bondsman took another bite of the meat and then wiped his mouth upon his sleeve.

'Why did he follow you?'

I shrugged. 'That I do not know. They did not tarry after I fell into the hole. Yet how did they even enter this land?'

'That is an even more puzzling question, for the chieftain has almost doubled the watch on his borders since the great cattle raid south.'

This information meant little to me, except that it further barred any escape I might have contemplated from Dartry. Nial stepped before the doorway to the barn and appeared pensive as the stream of daylight fell over his bearded features.

'Some think they were ferried to Mullaghmore by boat,' he said, 'and subsequently worked their way in secret through the great forests. Clearly they were after something, the identity of which is as yet unclear.'

'Perhaps they were but testing the guard on your borders,' I finally offered, more to end the conversation than to prolong it.

'Maybe,' said Nial, 'yet now you must rest, Spaniard, for Gorman and his sons are already in the mountains, and I have given them my word that I shall guard you until they come to escort you and their other retainers to the cattle booley.'

I felt a tinge of sadness when he left me alone, for in spite of my bitter words I had missed his companionship during the long days spent herding beasts in Gorman's employ. Like most Spaniards I had held many idyllic dreams of pastoral life, all of which had been swiftly dashed. Although there was an enviable calmness to minding cattle, it was also a most perilous occupation when performed in the open country, where dangers of all kinds lurked. Foremost of these was the terrible wolf *An Faolchù*, who was said to be the malicious spirit of the Manglanas' former bloodthirsty and deranged chieftain.

The following day I waited with the churls as our employers appeared from the mountains to collect us. There was no greeting from Finn when he appeared with three of his brothers, who were all heavily armed following the news of Treasach's appearance.

'Your holiday is over,' he grunted before gesturing for us to follow him outside our lodging.

There followed a long walk to the foot of the Dartry mountains, after which we slogged up narrow and stony passes towards the cattle booley. All throughout I kept my silence as the ring took over my thoughts, leaving me ignorant to the sight of other blackened pyres which had been need-fires lit along the mountain passes. The laughter of women and children did little to move me upon our arrival, although they moved even the hardest-hearted churl to a weary smile.

Indeed the theft of the emerald had left me entirely downcast and miserable, so that I scarcely managed to pay mind to the cows in my charge. Most of my time was spent sitting cross-legged and far away from the churls, who sat in small groups with their dogs as the cattle happily devoured the endless sea of green grass which spread all along the hillsides. When I was not mourning the loss of the ring, it was Muireann who took up my lovestruck and lonely thoughts.

On one occasion I spotted her out on the hunt with Manglana's wife, wearing a dress of dyed blue. My heart leapt at the sight of them chasing the summer herds of red deer and bighorn, before I remembered that I had come to form part of a different world belonging to a lower rung of Irishmen. A loud cry behind me drew my attention to one of the more mischievous calves which had strayed from the herd, leaving me to seize up my staff and beckon to one of the dogs as I ran off to recover it.

Most evenings we herded the beasts in small pens that were built or repaired during the day, then retired to one of the small cabins of turds and turf which dotted the grazing plains. We never tarried far from the booley, where we often returned with the cows so that they might be fully accounted for by Gorman and his family. Nightfall was generally a most droll and carefree affair, with tall tales of battle and past adventures recounted by the fire as food and drink were passed around.

Wandering gamblers called carrows sometimes made their appearance at dusk, treating the herders to games of dice and cards in exchange for some meat and drink. They were often in the company of minstrels who also travelled alone and who played songs beloved of the Dartrymen. The carrows also bore tidings from other kingdoms. The most popular of these travelling musicians was named Allán because of his striking good looks. All of Gorman's daughters vied for a place at his feet, listening to the silvery sound of his voice with wide eyes of adoration.

When his playing was over, the red-haired bard sat at Gorman's side as a beaker of buttermilk was brought to him, with a serving of oatmeal dressed with cuttings of beef. The bard bowed deeply to his hosts as he laid his harp aside and gratefully helped himself to the fare on offer. He was allowed to eat most of his dinner in silence before Gorman and his other sons asked him for tidings from afar.

'You would have heard of the rebellion by now,' said the minstrel. He gobbled his food quickly to be able to speak un-hindered.

'The rebellion is now old tidings, fair Allán,' grunted Finn with rough discourtesy, 'and over a week since it was relayed to us by a carrow.'

'That is well,' said the minstrel, as he swallowed another mouthful and cast Gorman's son a severe look, 'for there is much more which has since come to pass. Ours are tumultuous times indeed, and the portents have been held by the wise to be fair and foul in equal measure.'

'Without a doubt it shall be foul,' said Gorman with his usual note of resignation, 'if the Sassenachs are involved.'

The minstrel nodded but once and took a swig from his beaker. I found myself rising from the ground onto my elbows in anticipation, for I had overheard the exchange from the back of the hut.

'A month has passed since the great cattle raid of O'Rourke and Manglana in Sligo, with the MacDermots of the Curlews and the Bourkes in the west also revolting. The viceroy sent peace commissioners to Galway, but the leading rebels ignored their calls for peace, and the O'Rourke withdrew to the Roscommon. Bingham chased him out of there, too, then turned on the Bourkes, whose cattle were driven to the sea and isles.'

'So O'Rourke has fled the enemy unharmed, and the Bourkes have kept their cattle,' remarked Gorman as he slowly nodded. 'That is indeed good tidings, fair bard.'

'And what of the Bingham bastards?' growled Finn. 'Where are they now?'

'An apt question, Finn son of Gorman,' remarked Allán with a wry smile, 'for it is just what I was about to mention. After chasing the Bourkes into their fastnesses, Bingham returned to the plain to rest his men. Yet at Cong he received word from the viceroy in Dublin, who forbade him to further prosecute the rebels and ordered him to disband most of his troops. The commissioners were ordered to deal with the rebels until the viceroy travelled west.'

'The viceroy is to travel west?' stuttered the young Osgar, suddenly too scared to reach for his sword, as he usually did. 'When?'

'He is already here,' said the bard with a grin.

'Wh-what?' cried Gorman's stripling, whose hand had finally reached his pommel. 'Then must we hasten to retire to the mountains again?'

'We are already in the mountains, you fool,' snapped Finn, who looked as fearful as everyone else in the hut.

'Yes, that you are,' said the bard with a half chuckle, 'and the viceroy is in Galway.'

'What is he doing there?' asked Gorman, just as Finn blurted, 'Does he have an army?'

'It appears that he does,' replied the bard, 'although it is said to be smaller than the one which razed Dartry in the winter.'

A shiver ran through the herdsmen. None spoke until, after a while, Gorman shrugged.

'That is but his usual escort,' he said. 'He must have travelled there to parley.'

'Or to buy time,' remarked his wife, who, unlike her daughters, had paid more attention to the bard's words than his looks.

Her words were no surprise to any of us, for everyone but the *druth* knew that the enemy might be feigning peace to better prepare for battle. Yet the unspoken question that lingered over the hut like a bad smell concerned the terms of that peace, which at times bore consequences as bad as those of war itself.

'What has been offered?' I blurted aloud at last, entirely forgetting my place because of the cold fear that prickled my forehead with sweat, which I could no longer endure.

Over a score of men, women and children turned to look at me, then turned their heads back towards the bard. Together we stared at Allán, who shifted uncomfortably upon his backside as his head turned from left to right.

'Speak, man,' said Gorman.

'They are but rumours,' said the bard in a shaky voice, 'of which I have no proof.'

'What are these rumours?' I cried as I rose to my feet and stepped towards the centre of the hut.

I surprised myself with this act of boldness, for it suddenly seemed that the loss of the ring had returned my old brashness. Gorman's kin also appeared entirely stunned by my daring, yet none stirred or barred my path.

'Word has been uttered to me by another wanderer,' said Allán, eyeing me warily, 'that the rebels are resolved to pray for redress. They want the removal of the Bingham butchers from Connaught, and immunity from martial law. They want men of their own to collect rents and to serve as sheriff for the Sassenachs. The Blind Abbot also wants part of the profits of the MacWilliamship, which were allotted to the house of Castlebar.'

A roar of laughter was heard at these words, for the claims of the rebels in the west were as audacious as they would prove unacceptable to the enemy.

'And the O'Rourke?' asked Gorman. 'Is he also to travel to Galway?'

'The last I heard was that the O'Rourke and his army are escorting as many cows as his men can mind back to Breifne, after fleeing the Roscommon.'

Peals of laughter were heard after this revelation was made, for it was no secret that O'Rourke's raids of Sligo had provided him with as handsome a bounty of cattle as had been won by Manglana, his sub-king from Dartry.

'That wily *na Múrtha!*' laughed Finn. 'He was always as crafty as a mountain wolf!'

The merriment which followed was as welcome as it was heartwarming, since good tidings had of late been hard to come by, and the terms of the commissioners – if true and if observed by the enemy – would provide the Dartrymen with some overdue respite. Yet I sensed that a thorn was still hidden beneath the beautiful bud of good tidings that stemmed from the bard's lips, since he had refrained from mentioning the terms which had been requested by the English viceroy.

'And Viceroy FitzWilliam?' I cried above the cheery din. 'What does he want?'

A frown appeared on the bard's face, and he pretended not to hear me until I shouted the question again and again. It was soon echoed by others gathered among us, with Gorman himself piping up until Allán raised his hands for silence.

'Peace, my good Dartrymen! Peace! Again 'tis but rumour that has reached my ears. Yet they say that the rebels have written three books of outrages, two of which contain accusations against the devil Richard Bingham himself, and one against the sheriff of Sligo, his brother, George.'

The mention of George Bingham left me feeling disturbed, as I recalled both his look of hatred when he had me committed to Burke for torture and my subsequent treatment of his French whore.

'They are ready to present them to the viceroy in Galway. In return it is said that they will honour any pledges he will nominate, which shall no doubt consist of a request to make good all spoils until a certain day and to pay whatever fines he will prescribe.'

Allán paused to take a long swig from his beaker, then wiped his mouth with a forearm and looked straight at me. In my heart I feared the worst the moment he did this, for already I knew what he was about to say.

'It is also expected that the rebels will be asked to surrender all Spaniards.'

Once more the voices and whispers died about me, and a nervous chuckle was heard. The last of the viceroy's likely requests should have come as no surprise to me, yet I felt as if a spear had been thrust through my guts. It was all I could do to hide my distress, some of which must have shown in my face when the red-headed minstrel spoke again.

'And now you have the tidings which you so greatly desired, Spaniard. I am sorry to have been the one to utter them, for I did all I could to refrain from mentioning them.'

I could see how I had misjudged him for being a fawning pleaser of his hosts, when he had in fact attempted to ignore claims for further news to keep from causing me distress. For he was, after all, a man with nothing in the world but his harp, and I had to accept that I had never seen anyone in the tribe as happy as they had been ever since he had reached our cattle booley. Positions and titles were of no appeal to him at all, and I had heard that he had even spurned the advances of one of Gorman's youngest daughters out of respect for her honour.

Allán nodded after I bowed deeply to him, before hobbling to the back of the hut, fighting the great dread brought about by his tidings. The churls looked at me in awe as I crashed to the ground between them, for none of them had ever dared to speak over Gorman and his sons. Yet it mattered nothing to me, for the threat of being surrendered to the enemy weighed heavily on my mind, so that much restlessness was endured that night until I finally fell asleep.

As the summer days wore on I thrived without the burden of the ring, no longer keeping apart from the other tribesmen at every opportunity for fear that my secret might be discovered. One by one the sons of Gorman assumed a less guarded attitude towards me, with some of them even greeting me with a grin where they had once scowled at me. My wanderings with the Irishmen were happy and carefree, with the smell of pollen and fresh grass thick in the air as we led the cattle across the various grazing places. Soon the easier days of summer became so warm that the sun's appearance caused me to sweat beneath my tunic, and no longer did I pull my mantle around me as I lay on the rushes at night.

In the improved weather we strayed further from the cattle booley, wandering far and wide to ensure the nourishment of the chattel in our charge. With each passing day, my cast increasingly resembled that of a wild Irishman, with my hair hanging about my face and the soles of my feet becoming almost as hard as leather. Everything was shared among our creaght, since food and drink were often as scarce as people during our wanderings through the mountain passes.

At times our stomachs grumbled so loudly that one of the herders would open a cow's vein with the point of his *skene* dagger, filling a cup with the beast's blood and mixing it with sorrel leaves before passing it round among us. As this unholy brew slipped down my throat, I strained to overcome my revulsion at it before realising that the pain in my belly had eased. This meagre diet ensured that I was soon as lean as a mountain goat. My chest often burned with breath, and my cheeks were ruddy and my forehead glistening from the toil of the uphill run.

'You have learned how to run with us, Spaniard!' called out the one-eyed churl with an evil cackle.

I smiled back at him, for I had indeed become a fleet-footed specimen, able to endure as much exertion and toil as I had weathered during my prime in the Army of Flanders. Soon I was so healthy that it felt as if time had been reversed, and the summer heat had even returned the old olive hue to my skin, which had become as pale as that of my hosts during the winter months.

All in all it was glorious living, and no longer was the tribesmen's joy at the feast of Beltane lost on me. Summer was a season also beloved by the highborn, who also travelled to the heights. One evening we were herding a score of heads back to the byre when I noticed a group of churls and herdsmen pointing at another small gathering further uphill. When I walked up to them one of them pointed out a small trail of smoke, where two score of bluejackets could be seen, surrounding a man who lay upon his back, as devoid of cares as the simplest shepherd.

'A happy distance between him and his vixen wife,' muttered one of Gorman's nephews, which drew much chortling and sniggering from his listeners.

I suddenly recognised the man on his back as Manglana, from the horse hitched to the log beneath his feet. As we moved the cattle along the rise a few of his guards nodded towards us, and for the first time it seemed to me that a smile spread across the chieftain's face. In that moment I almost pitied him, since I suspected that he would have readily traded his position for that of a commoner, so great was the burden of leadership which had been thrust upon his shoulders.

News of the viceroy's appearance in Galway had no doubt reached his ears before ours, and the prospect of more fighting would have weighed heavily on a man who was resolved to appear a strong protector of his small kingdom. Rumour abounded that his flight to the mountains in the winter had led some of the more unruly creaghts to question his rule. The recent raids of his overlord O'Rourke in Sligo had restored some of Manglana's wealth and reputation, yet Dartry's king was forever occupied with containing those forces which sought to challenge his leadership in greatly trying times.

Despite the simplicity of pastoral life, the prospect of conflict always reigned across the land. At all times the herdsmen were armed with spear and sling, ready to repel wolves and any enemy tribesmen who might attempt a raid after slipping through Dartry's borders. The mark of the spider on my breast served as a constant reminder of the consequences that should await me if I were captured by the enemy, which had almost occurred during my last brush with Treasach Bourke.

These thoughts assailed me one afternoon as we made our way out of the cattle booley and down towards the plain. We could not have been walking for more than a half hour when the churls ahead gestured wildly behind me, and I turned to see a mischievous calf hurrying away from the rest of the herd. With a low curse I rushed after it, calling out to the creature and doing my best to gain up on it.

'Vile cur! Haste you back!'

Upon reaching the beast, I coaxed it back along the path it had abandoned, kicking it angrily in its backside. In a moment all of my romantic notions of pastoral life vanished because of my frustration. With a low rumble, the cow turned to rejoin the other heads. I had only just sighed wearily when the unmistakable jingle of reins was heard behind me. With a gasp I turned to find a rider in a green cloak riding towards me atop a hobbyhorse, observing me in confusion.

'Spaniard?' he whispered.

The hoarse voice belonged to Geraldine, whom I had not seen since before Manglana had departed on his latest raid of Sligo with the O'Rourke.

'Hail, Geraldine,' I replied, and bowed my head to him.

I winced as he flung himself off his steed and grasped me by the shoulder, his piercing gaze boring into my face.

'What is the meaning of this?' he hissed. 'What have they done to you?'

I did my best to meet his stare while whispering a reply.

'I have been punished.'

'P-punished?' he muttered, looking like someone had just buried his fist into his stomach. 'Punished for what?'

My eyes were planted upon my feet as I sighed heavily, then raised my head to meet his stare again.

'I am a rapist.'

Old Tom's look of bewilderment reminded me of the faces I had glimpsed whenever I had shot someone in a crowd from my perch atop a Flemish roof. After a few moments he collected himself, with a dangerous cast in his eyes as he blew his whiskers out in a fury.

'You are no rapist!' he roared in a voice that echoed across the plain. 'You are an honourable man!'

I winced at his compliment, for my guilt at having hidden the emerald ring for so long had not yet subsided and still cankered my soul. Yet Old Tom mistook my evident discomfort for humility.

'Do not doubt it,' he cried, as he seized my arm, 'for you spent a month trapped with me in a deadly siege, yet never once touched a hair on that mad wench Orla!'

He grabbed me by the throat and shoved his rageful face into mine.

'Tell me everything! And omit nothing! God help you if I discover that you have lied to me.'

So great was his fury that I blurted everything, starting with the attack of the boar during my initiation and proceeding to my hidden trysts with the ollave and everything that transpired thereafter. All throughout Geraldine listened to me intently, watching me more closely than a sharpshooter. When at last my account was ended he stepped aside, biting his fist with his eyes closed and his brows twitching in furious thought. His face slowly turned bright red, then resumed its normal colour.

'That vile, lowborn whoreson Donal MacCabe,' he said at last, then noticed me staring after the great herd that rumbled down the mountainside.

'Ride with me!' he bellowed, then rushed to his horse and climbed upon it before hauling me after him. It had been weeks since I had ridden a horse, and the great thrust of muscle beneath us left me half hoping that Geraldine would gallop off to Breifne with me. As the distant figures of the churls grew larger, I felt a nudge in the thigh as the Anglo-Norman offered me a *skene* dagger with a black handle of bog oak.

'I cannot take it,' I replied as I gently pushed his arm away, 'for I am a criminal and cannot bear arms.'

"Tis but a working knife!' he hissed. 'Do as I say, you stubborn, ox-headed fool! And tuck it away beneath your navel!'

So fierce was his outburst that for a moment I feared that he might stab me with the blade if I did not do as he ordered. After we had galloped through the herd, Geraldine reined in his mount before Gorman's son Finn, who led our party downhill. The burly herdsman's jaw dropped as he saw me dismounting from the Anglo-Norman's horse, and Geraldine cast him a withering look as he spoke his last words to me.

'Have heart, Spaniard, and hold on while you must. Remember that you are a worthy hero of Rosclogher and that you have friends who shall not abandon you to your current plight!'

'Will I be surrendered to the viceroy?' I asked, voicing my greatest fear as my feet met the grass below.

Old Tom's scowl was replaced by a broad grin of bewilderment, and his head was hurled back as he issued loud peals of laughter that seemed to resound across the very mountaintops.

'Ours has been the queerest meeting of all,' he giggled as he wiped the tears of mirth from his eyes, 'yet queerer still are your questions. The viceroy shall receive no Spaniards from us, friend Juan. Indeed he does not yet know what is coming to him.'

His last words were accompanied by a steely expression of outrage. Then he whirled his horse about and thundered down towards the plain.

'Until our next meeting!' he cried, and soon became a speck which vanished into the distant trees.

My encounter with Geraldine revived my spirits, so that I endured the trials of the upcoming days with relatively good cheer. This further endeared me to the churls who had often regarded me with suspicion, and word of my friendship with one of the O'Rourke's most trusted aides quickly spread amongst the herdsmen, so that their scorn was swiftly replaced by awe. All of this ensured that my stay among them became ever more bearable in the months that followed, as none looked me in the eye again and all stayed out of my path.

Gorman no longer had me watched, while also ordering that his *druth* son be kept from harassing me. This alone greatly eased my existence, which became almost pleasant. Yet as June turned to July I received a timely reminder of my concerns about lingering too long in Dartry. It was a day like any other, and we were ushering the cattle towards fresh plains along the borders of Breifne. Gorman himself had joined us, and his sons happily gathered about him as he led us towards the new pastures.

Meanwhile, our ears were full of the sounds of distant gunshot that could be heard in Breifne, which I could recognise as that of troops being trained, and which served as a reminder of the prospect of war. We had hardly sighted the temporary huts where we were to lodge for the night before we saw two riders approaching us at a canter, with a score of men marching behind them.

At first they veered away from us, seemingly disinterested in a few cattle herders and beasts, but then one of the riders gestured towards us with a muffled cry and jerked his horse's reins in our direction. As the men approached my legs turned leaden, for I recognised the approaching troop of gallowglasses. Donal and Brogan grinned with malice as they drew closer towards me, and the constable's huge subaltern openly mocked me.

'How do you fare, hero of Rosclogher?'

As a heavy hand landed on my shoulder, I turned in surprise to see Gorman himself staring into my eyes to issue a low warning.

'Ignore them.'

'To think how much he suffered during the siege,' declared Brogan in a loud voice, as Donal and the other Scots encircled us, 'with his feet by the fire while we were bitten by the mountain frost.'

Despite my best attempts to keep calm, this slight left me feeling furious. For although it was true that I had fought to save my own skin and the ring which was now lost, I had nonetheless fought bravely during the siege of the Rosclogher tower house. Furthermore, I thought it ill befitted mercenaries to make light of one who had been wrongly punished by their own evil designs.

'What do you want from me?' I shouted angrily.

The constable beheld me as if regarding a worm on the ground.

'We want nothing from you yet. For the chieftain counts his heads at Hallowtide and severely punishes those who lose his cattle without just cause.'

A groan was heard from the mischievous calf as one of the Scots walked up to it and whacked the flat of his great sword against its buttocks. The malicious act left me speechless, but the giant Brogan spoke up.

'And if you attempt escape before then, your head shall topple off your shoulders before you reach the Erne.'

I struggled to keep from replying as Uallas strode through the horses. I glared at the evil horseboy, who had disturbed the boar which had almost killed me and who had caused my fall from grace.

Gorman and I stiffened, as we rightly expected the worst. Uallas grinned as he stepped in front of me. Then his fist shot out, striking me in the belly and dropping me to my knees. The cursed horseboy's words dripped with scorn.

'On your knees before the constable, rapist.'

As I whipped Old Tom's dagger out from beneath my navel, the onlookers gasped, and the roar of the *tercios* left my lips as I returned to my feet.

'For Saint James!'

The knife's oaken handle was clenched tightly in my right fist as I punched Uallas straight in the mouth, and a spatter of blood whipped into the air as he fell back with a moan of disbelief. Gorman's hand was shrugged off my shoulder, for in that moment my rage was so great that I was ready to take on the constable and his whole troop with a knife.

Donal MacCabe was already off his horse. He did not stir as I raced towards him, intent on sinking the length of my blade through his throat, so great was my fury at my hopeless plight. The constable was a burly and rugged specimen, yet he moved with the speed of a snake as he snatched my dagger hand. His fingers felt like a steel trap as they closed about my wrist, so tightly that the dagger was released from my grip and fell to the ground.

He kneed me in my already bruised stomach, then crashed his forehead into mine, leaving me sprawled across the grass. Through my fast-swelling right eye Gorman and his sons could be seen howling abuse at the Scots, their spears held threateningly above their heads. With a snarl Donal spat on me, then aimed a kick at the middle of my back, which sent me rolling over the dew-drenched grass.

'Take back your cur,' he snarled, 'for I'll not waste my men's strength to pinch out his miserable life. Even the dead are better off than he! There remains plenty of time left to cleanse our land of this Spanish filth!'

Two horseboys dragged the groaning Uallas away as Mac-Cabe climbed back atop his mount. I scowled at the constable from the ground as Gorman and his sons encircled me with their spears still raised, yet Donal only looked at them and laughed.

'The fires of Beltane close in on you, Spaniard! You will not last long beyond our next meeting!'

I did not stir from the ground until the sound of gallow-glass hoofbeats vanished. I finally accepted the offer of Gorman's extended hand as he hoisted me back upon my feet. The herdsman sighed deeply as he kept me from falling over again.

'You have fallen afoul of the wrong people.'

'It has always been my greatest gift,' I replied.

A low guffaw was heard from my master, and my lips parted in surprise when he handed me Old Tom's dagger.

'I cannot,' I muttered, but he waved my protestation away.

'It is for the task that I shall assign to you tonight.'

He proved as good as his word. An hour later we reached a hut, and I was allowed to rest for most of the morning and afternoon. A hand tapped my shoulder as the sun started to set, and through my less swollen left eye I could make out the youthful features of Osgar.

'Mother has summoned you, grey wolf.'

I issued a sharp hiss through broken lips when I rolled onto my back, for the bruise from the constable's kick felt like a coffin nail had been driven between my shoulders.

I limped out of the cabin with my arm rested upon the boy's shoulder as the dusk furled us in its nightly blanket. I noted that we had moved to a pasture on a lowland bog, which had dried out in the summer. Gorman's wife and his daughters sat a few feet away from us, busily working the flax within sight of a small lake which was embowered by trees. Some of the women regarded my ungainly approach with a sorrowful expression while others quickly returned their attentions to their handiwork.

Gorman's wife's cheeks were ruddy with tears when I stood before her, and she gestured at the body of a dead ewe which Osgar dragged out from behind a bush. With a nod of understanding, I grabbed the carcass from its hind legs and wordlessly heaved it away from the women and towards the water. Osgar seemed excited by the task at hand, as he followed closely on my heels.

'Have a care, Spaniard,' called Gorman's wife, 'for they say that a *dhobar chu* inhabits those waters!'

'What in God's name is a *dhobar chu?*

'They say it is half wolf and half otter,' whispered Osgar, 'and they also say that kelpies have been seen in these parts.'

'Kelpies?'

'Yes, grey wolf,' he replied earnestly, sidestepping the dead sheep, which was dragged alongside him. 'They are black ponies which appear as beautiful maidens, but which feed upon the flesh of men!'

I suppressed a snigger at the old wives' tale, but Osgar seized my forearm and beheld me in all seriousness.

'Have strength, Spaniard!' he whispered warily. 'You must not be seduced by the wiles of women!'

I met his stare for a few moments, then made for the banks of the lake.

'I am afraid it is too late for that, friend.'

When the dark lake water was reached, I set about the task which had been assigned to me, mostly thinking of the greasy substance which might be collected from the animal. For in a land where people did not have two coins to rub together and all trade was based on barter, the sheep's fat could be easily exchanged with tribeswomen who moulded candles for other items. In turn these items might one day be traded for other valuables, which might eventually meet the price of my first cow and would go towards repaying my *eineach* fine.

I cut off one of the ewe's shoulders and lay it beside us. Osgar watched me with interest as the creature's neck and breast were also cut off, to be used for a broth flavoured with roots and shamrock. When most of the cutting and cleaning was done, I dug a hole in the ground in which to boil a pot which Osgar fetched for me.

As the soup boiled, its scent drew a few of the herders closer towards me, with some of them burying firkins of butter into the marshy ground to eventually form cheese. Their spears were always kept close at hand, for being on lower ground we were mindful of the greater danger that might lurk in the open. The constant howling of wolves around us served as a timely reminder.

As darkness fell, we made our way back towards the two cooking fires raging in front of the booley. Osgar bore the pot of soup while I dragged the cuttings and what remained of the sheep behind me. I had hardly set about stringing up the beast's hide over one of the flames when great cries were heard about me, and men readied their spears and slings. Ahead of us the shadows of a party of riders could be seen as the dying sun flared crimson.

After my last brush with Burke I feared the worst, and the dagger trembled in my hand as I readied to flee. Then a voice was heard that was both warm and familiar, and I instantly recognised Nial as he walked towards the flames, a grin playing on his lips.

'Can you spare us a seat by the fire, friend Juan?' he asked.

As I stood aside to make room for him, a flurry of exclamations were heard about me, and Nial's smile returned as a red-headed boy stepped out from the shadows behind him and raised his arm in salute to the gathered tribesmen. Gorman instantly fell to one knee, and all present took his lead as the princeling Lochlain strode towards me, a look of concern on his face.

'What happened? Did you come across a band of Sassenachs?'

As I raised my head and squinted at him through my left eye, I realised that he was referring to my swollen face and head. For a few moments I could not reply, for I tried to understand whether telling the truth might incur greater wrath from the gallowglasses, who seemed to be a law unto themselves in the land.

'We came across the Scots,' said Gorman, whose voice bristled with barely contained fury.

Lochlain could barely mask his outrage as he took in the tidings, yet somehow he managed to remain silent as he took a place by the fire. In the two months since my sentence had been pronounced, I saw that he had more of a man's sober cast about him. I could not help but feel a surge of pride at his growth. Our conversation soon turned to the matters which unfolded in distant Galway, where the viceroy was still said to be residing as he laboured to reach a peace agreement with the enemy's commissioners.

'FitzWilliam has gathered the books of outrages and complaints against the Binghams and has sent them to Dublin, where it is said that they will be sent back to England. Meanwhile the terms of both parties have been formally accepted, although it remains to be seen what happens in practice. The peace commissioners are to parley with O'Rourke on the borders of Breifne.'

'Have any Spaniards been surrendered to the enemy?' I asked, with the trepidation in my voice only thinly disguised.

'That is why we are here,' said Nial suddenly, leaving me to squirm in discomfort until all those present burst into loud peals of mirth.

'No, Spaniard,' said Lochlain, barely able to contain his laughter. 'None have yet been surrendered, and the O'Rourke shall never surrender his Spanish allies.'

'How can you be so sure?'

'It is a badly kept secret,' said Nial, 'that the Spanish king has long made gifts of silver to the O'Rourke to aid in his resistance against the Sassenachs. *Na Múrtha* shall not surrender a hair from a single Spanish head.'

'And what of the Binghams?' asked Gorman with a wary expression. 'Have they withdrawn yet from Connacht?'

'Not yet,' said Nial, 'although strong rumour abounds that the viceroy intends to bring them to trial. What is certain is that he is to hold sessions at Sligo and Roscommon, to examine further complaints brought against them.'

'Butchers trying their own?' exclaimed Gorman's son Finn. 'Why, that is a most welcome turn of events!'

'Yet will they find a witness I wonder?' said the bondsman. 'For this peace has been secured by the viceroy only in name, and none trust the Binghams' retainers to grant safe passage to any who would appear against them.'

"Tis but a ploy,' I snorted with a dismissive shrug. 'The viceroy and the Binghams feign to fight with one another, only to win time in which to prepare to fight us.'

'That is unlikely, Spaniard,' said Lochlain, 'for O'Rourke's spies have said that the viceroy is intent on ridding the Binghams of their tenures, and they have been seen to exchange heated words. FitzWilliam has refused to meet them since. His dealings with the natives have been thorough, with no stone left unturned to gather evidence against both Richard and George.'

'Then some petty rivalries are at play, or else the viceroy wants to free up positions for his own loyalists.'

'Rumour has also reached us that there is more to it than that,' said Nial as he fixed me with a piercing stare.

'Oh?' I asked, attempting to look as fascinated as I could, already guessing the cause of the dispute amongst our enemies.

'They say the Binghams have something that the viceroy wants,' continued Nial, never once looking away from me. 'Some valuable was washed ashore with the Spaniards, which he believes the Binghams have hidden away.'

I nodded, feigning a slow understanding of what was implied while hoping that the bondsman might look to the other herdsmen. Yet Nial was still staring at me, as was everyone else, and I quickly spoke up again in order to further reinforce my pretence of complete ignorance.

'What valuable would that be?'

'No one knows for certain,' said Nial, as he finally looked away and reached over for a cup of buttermilk, 'but whatever it is must be worth a king's ransom, if the Binghams are ready to risk so much for it.'

The subject of our conversation then turned to the fighting season, with many of the herdsmen curious to know if our visitors had heard word of a rising out. Yet I was still thinking about the viceroy's dispute with the Binghams, for it seemed to me that Burke had not yet surrendered the ring to the Binghams. The fact that the renegade had slain one of his own to keep it secret strongly implied this. I dared not think of what George Bingham would do to his sergeant if he learned of this treachery.

'As the weather warms up, so will O'Rourke's temper,' said Nial, as I abandoned my thoughts of the ring and listened to the Dartrymen's chatting. 'Already Old Tom has relayed a message to our lord MacGlannagh from *na Múrtha,* who has ordered that we gird ourselves and make ready. For this year the fighting season shall set in early, and our overlord the O'Rourke in Breifne itches to further avail himself of our enemies' troubles in the west and among themselves.'

'Yes,' said Finn with a dark grimace, 'we have ourselves heard gunshots from beyond the O'Rourke's borders.'

Lochlain nodded slowly at these tidings, then looked at me.

'His Spaniards are training a troop of musketeers. Soon every fighting man shall be needed.'

After he washed down his last morsel of meat with his last swig of buttermilk, the princeling rose to thank Gorman and made ready to return to Rosclogher. My master noticed me raising an eyebrow at him, and so he remembered to present the princeling with a skinned hare.

'This is part of the fine owed by the Spaniard,' said the herdsman as Lochlain took the carcass with a look of puzzlement, then stared back in my direction.

'May we have a word, Spaniard?' he asked.

I walked him back towards his hitched horse, with Nial and his highborn retainers walking closely about us.

'My lord grandfather misses you, friend Juan,' said the boy, 'for he has none to teach his men to load a rifle as swiftly as you. Now that my mother is betrothed to Cathal, he would have Echna waive your fine in an instant. Yet his hand is forced against you by the gallowglasses, whose help he needs in the months ahead.'

'Do you mean that he bears me no ill will?'

Lochlain sighed.

'My mother told him the truth of it, yet he cannot have her honour besmirched. My guess is that he will wait until August to free you of your debt to him, when the attentions of the Scots will be taken up by battle. Until then, you must bide your time.'

My annoyance at his words was kept in check as I reassured myself that I would long have escaped before then. I somehow managed a low bow to the princeling, who had always proved a true friend to me. After mounting his horse, he passed me a scrap of vellum.

'From a loyal admirer,' he said, then rode off into the darkness with his highborn retainers close behind him. A prick of loss was felt at the departure of the princeling and the bondsman, though it was slightly tempered by the familiar smell of roseate water upon the message I had received. I instantly recognised the handwriting upon it.

'*Despair not, beloved, for fabled fighting brews.*
Gaelic Ireland will once more come alive.
The bard's words summon it from the smoke
– and music and blood.
Rings shall sparkle about warriors' arms and necks,
With blades of their grandsires' grandsires
thrust through their belts,
Amid the strumming of harp strings and the beat
of the goatskin head of the bodhran,
All shall be summoned from our lord's hall to battle and glory.'

Muireann's words stirred me as I made back towards the flames, upon which I hurled her note to preserve her honour. Yet my hopes began to wane and were abandoned as the days became weeks. With the descent of each moon and the rising of each sun, it seemed to me that the only action I would see in coming months would be the moving of cows between hill and plain.

XLI

ROSCLOGHER, DARTRY, COUNTY LEITRIM

4 – 25 July 1589

Two weeks of toil passed without mishap, yet all was set to change on the morning that found me strewn across my pallet, enjoying some rare rest which had lasted beyond dawn. Yet I rose to my knees with a gasp when a thunder of hoofbeats was heard outside the mud huts we had reached the previous night. The stripling Osgar poked his head through the doorway, screeching like a skewered hog.

'Horsemen approach! A half-dozen at the least!'

I instinctively reached for a gun, then cursed aloud and whipped out the *skene* dagger instead. Whether due to my recent pursuit by Treasach Burke or the ridiculous weapon I carried, my skin prickled with fear as I hurled my blanket aside and emerged from the pungent smell of ashen peat onto the sunlit plain. Gorman and his sons were armed with spears and slings, yet they lowered them as the advancing riders slowed to a canter and their leader raised his hand to us.

'Peace, brothers! Do not fear! We come in peace!'

Relief washed over me like a pail of warm water, and my heart slowed and my normal breathing was regained. The party of riders was largely garbed in yellowed tunics, and I stowed the knife away beneath my garments before any of the freemen could see it.

'The bondsman visits us yet again,' whispered Gorman behind me.

Nial's usual smile was glaringly absent as he dismounted and walked towards us, making it clear that something was afoot. For a moment I feared that the Dartrymen had decided to surrender me to the enemy, as the bondsman addressed me without greeting.

'You are summoned to Rosclogher.'

'Now?'

'Yes, at the earliest. My lord MacGlannagh has ordered it.'

For a moment I feared that my suspicions were founded, and I stepped back hesitantly.

'Why?'

Nial's stare darkened as his hands fell upon his sword pommels.

'I swear that I know not. Yet join us you must, whether by your own will or by force.'

In that instant I turned to look at Gorman, who served me with a slight lifting of his brows which served to affirm that I had little choice in the matter. Herdsmen gathered about us in fear and confusion as I followed Nial back towards his exalted band of riders, one of whom had brought a hobby for me from

Manglana's town. I recognised some of the men as Cathal's retainers; they all turned their heads away from me without betraying the slightest emotion as Nial led us downhill, then steered us north.

Countless questions raced through my mind as we hastened to the chieftain's call, yet Nial rode too far ahead for me to be able to speak to him. When the higher pastures were left behind us, we dismounted and walked in a single file through the thicker forest towards the ring of bog. After we crossed the marsh, I felt somewhat moved by the sight of the greensward.

Upon the large lawn, two bands of kerns were engaged in a hotly contested game which the Irish called hurling. Big clods of mud were thrown up as their sticks struck the earth more often than the ball; the odd limb also smacked by wood, at times accompanied by a crack of bone and a piercing howl of agony. As Nial hurried us along to our mysterious errand, I could recognise many of the kerns from the town at play, yet the other half were strangers and not known to me at all.

'Where do the other lot hail from?' I asked one of the highborn, yet my question was entirely ignored.

I wrapped my mud-spattered mantle tightly about me as we made our way towards the door of the keep. It all felt surreal, as if the last three months had never taken place. I was claimed by a great sense of shame at my forlorn appearance, and held the mantle closely over my shoulders so that my face was all but concealed by it. The highborn freemen accompanying Nial formed a tight ring about me as we wandered through the gathering in Manglana's great hall.

At the centre of the hall we came to a standstill, met by the sight of two men who were possessed of a stark difference in height. Both wore tanned leather jackets and held morion helmets with tall crests. As the shorter of the two turned towards us, I felt the hands of six clasping my arms and shoulders as Curro Ramos served me with the briefest of glances. The tall man alongside him also cast a glance at me, revealing himself to be the forest Croat, Dario Ohmunevic. My blood boiled at the sight of my old sergeant, yet Ramos turned back towards Manglana, who sat alone upon his dais, furled in his crisp and newly washed *lèine*.

'Is that him?'

'Aye.'

Ramos turned again and cocked a suspicious eyebrow in my direction as I shook with rage in the hands of the freemen.

'What in the name of the Blessed Virgin happened to you?'

A gruff voice rose in reply, revealing Constable Donal MacCabe beside the hearth.

'He serves his punishment amongst the lowborn herders and churls.'

'Punishment?'

'He forced himself upon a woman. He has no right to even be in this hall.'

The cynical narrowing of Ramos' and Dario's eyes left me wondering if Geraldine had spoken to them after my meeting him in the mountains. As my anger slowly subsided I hung my head at the constable's words, wondering what devilry would befall me with both him and Ramos in the hall.

'That is ill tidings indeed, friend Scot,' replied Ramos, 'for my master the O'Rourke has requested his skills.'

My head was swiftly raised at his words, and in my disbelief my jaw fell open.

'R-requested my skills?' I muttered in disbelief.

'But he must repay his debt!' said MacCabe, a hint of outrage in his voice.

'Our enemy sends outlaws and tosspots to fight us,' replied Ramos. 'We should at least afford this man a choice as to how he intends to repay his fine, be it by minding either cows or troopers.'

'He has no choice,' snarled Donal, 'for no troop in Dartry will have him!'

My head fell forward again, yet Ramos spoke up almost instantly.

'I will have him.'

MacCabe's cheeks turned crimson, and he half grinned in disbelief as he spoke again.

'Have you no honour? Hiring a rapist? His crimes also –'

'I am not a judge but a soldier,' cut in Ramos, 'and the fighting season is upon us. We have more need of fighters than cowherds. This man shall not be relieved of those fines imposed upon him by the laws of Dartry. He shall merely pass from the byre into the O'Rourke's service.'

I had never seen Donal MacCabe's lower lip tremble, and for a few moments his grizzled expression resembled that of a child who had lost his favourite puppy. His head turned from left to right as he sought out the dissent of another freeman, then issued a low growl when he realised that none was forthcoming.

'And what of the other criminals and churls in Dartry? Are they to also abandon the herds to be pressed into battle?'

'That is for your Lord to decide,' said Ramos in a low voice, as he fixed his eyes upon the ground with a shrug, 'for I am but the bearer of my own lord's instructions.'

'And will his fine be paid if he is to serve another lord abroad?' insisted MacCabe. For a moment I feared that the Scot had finally blocked my passage into the O'Rourke's army.

Ramos slightly pursed his lips, leaving me to dread that he had no reply. Yet when he spoke again it was obvious to all present that my former sergeant had arrived in Dartry girded with a quiver of counterarguments, with which he could shoot down the inevitable objections of the gallowglass constable.

'His fines will be reduced from next year's tribute that is owed by your lord MacGlannagh to the O'Rourke. The overlord of Dartry has declared that he will gladly acquire this debt in exchange for the Spaniard's services.'

A violet flush slowly claimed Donal's face; it started at the bottoms of his cheeks and spread to the rest of his rugged face like tentacles. The slightest hint of a smile appeared at the ends of Ramos' lips as he regarded the Scot's growing fury with a calm and inquiring look. Meanwhile the knuckles in MacCabe's bunched fists whitened, and in his despair he blurted a final retort.

'But the judge said that no one else is to pay his fine for him!'

Ramos cast Donal a look which verged on the suspicious, as if to imply that the last words of the Scottish constable had been wide of the discussion at hand. He made much show of clearing his throat before replying.

'The O'Rourke is not to pay a single groat of the fines to your Lord. He is only to reduce the salary owing to the

Spaniard for martial services from the annual tribute that is owing to him from Dartry. In any event, my lord constable, I believe that the verdict passed barred anyone *in Dartry* from paying these fines. Is that not the truth, O worthy Brehon?'

Much as I loathed the man, for a moment I could not help but admire Ramos for the speed with which he had understood and worked out the ways of a society which I still grappled to understand. My admiration turned to relief as the elderly Brehon Echna rose to her feet to affirm Don Curro's words. Some of the freemen chuckled, openly admiring Ramos' appreciation of their law, while others scowled openly at the way in which I had been relieved from the lowly duties of a herdsman. All throughout the chieftain had not betrayed a whit of sentiment, but the constable roared his final words of disgust in a malicious bid to get Manglana to change his mind.

"Tis a travesty of justice! An utter disgrace! Woe that one of my daughter's rapists be ever let off so lightly! But pray tell us, Brehon, will our fine-feathered Spaniard also be relieved of a death penalty, should Uallas forego the fine owed to him once our lord's *eineach* is repaid?'

'No,' declared the Brehon, as many heads turned towards her.

'Ah.' Donal grinned to my dismay. 'Then justice may yet prevail in this land.'

Manglana cast the Scot a dark look at that, for everyone knew that the chieftain prided himself on having restored law and order to the confines of his kingdom after he had succeeded his brutish elder brother. MacCabe fell silent, leaving Ramos to pipe up again unhindered.

'Then that appears to be the end of our argument. The man Juan shall be bound to the O'Rourke until your lord's debt is paid.'

The chieftain accorded Ramos the slightest nod of acquiescence, as his retainers – which included Cathal *Dubh* and O'Ronayne – stared at me in wonderment and confusion, as if beholding a two-headed salmon. Never had events conspired so neatly to relieve a criminal of his miserable lot, and the great helping of fortune which had just been served to me could not be easily underestimated. Just when it seemed that all objection to my passing into the O'Rourke's service had ceased, another voice of dissent was heard from a most unexpected source.

'And what if the Spaniard escapes whilst in your service?'

The low whisper belonged to Cathal *Dubh*, who stood among Manglana's closest retainers, at the chieftain's left shoulder.

'Escapes?' said Ramos, uttering the word with distaste and appearing entirely taken aback by the tanist's suggestion.

'Indeed!' roared Donal with a grin of triumph. 'For you Spaniards are known to abandon their allies at the earliest opportunity! Our tanist has lost a fair few heads on wagering otherwise!'

Cathal did not rise to the taunt, and silently glared at us through the fronds of hair which fell across his face. I could not enter O'Rourke's service soon enough, for the outrage of Dartry's most powerful men had been directed against me. I had been so preoccupied with the Sassanas and the gallowglasses that never for a moment did I consider the ill will borne towards me by the tanist.

During the weeks spent serving Gorman I had only seen Cathal on three occasions, each time leading a troop of cavalry through Rosclogher. He had been too preoccupied to notice my swiftly vanishing presence, as I ducked behind a mud hut or a cow in my care to avoid his line of sight. I became flushed with embarrassment at his open disapproval, for in truth he had only suffered personal setback and disappointment ever since we Spanish castaways had first appeared in Rosclogher. De Cuéllar's disappearance from Dartry at his expense had long rankled him, only for it to be eclipsed by my raping his intended wife, also at his expense.

'My men shall watch him at all times,' declared Ramos in his haughtiest tone. 'I give thee my most solemn oath.'

He drew his sword from its sheath when he said this, then planted the lengthiest of kisses on its blade, so as to affirm the seriousness of his vow.

'May my remaining arm fall limp by my side if I fail to keep this man in my power.'

There was nothing more that could be said to this, since Ramos had once more proved the master of turning his weaknesses into advantages. Both Cathal and Donal glowered at him with an ill-suppressed malice, which greatly soured the ensuing silence until the chieftain finally spoke.

'Is that the sole purpose of your visit, Spaniard of Breifne?'

The tall Dalmatian who flanked Ramos spoke in his stead, the low timbre of his voice echoing across the hall.

'We also bear our lord's instruction to you from Ulster, where he is plotting a new attack on the colonists. He has bid me to tell you that a time of great change is at hand, in which we have no choice but to act. A chink of light has appeared in the darkness, for as I speak, it is rumoured that the Binghams will face trial in Dublin. It is said that the Blind Abbot is to achieve his MacWilliamship, without which peace cannot be secured in Connacht.'

Donal snorted aloud at these words despite the tribesmen's ears being trained towards the message from their overlord.

'What trial?' growled the Scot. "Tis but a farce for our enemy to strengthen for war.'

MacCabe was swiftly silenced by the incensed freemen gathered in the hall, all of whom were keen on listening to the rest of O'Rourke's message. After resting his fists upon his hips as a clear sign of impatience, Ramos served the constable with a look of revulsion before turning to the chieftain once more.

'What we know for certain is that the viceroy has not been satisfied with what he found in Connacht. His concern with the Binghams' methods are genuine, since their brutality is only spurring the tribes to assist Spanish castaways and Jesuits in other parts of the country who have managed to stir up the latest rebellion. The messages of these rebel tribesmen to my lord O'Rourke have been clear. We must persist once more with our raiding, since the conflict is costing our enemy much in coin but delivering precious little in tax. Bingham's purges have destroyed the country to the west, devoiding it of man and beast. Yet the English queen has spent much on their own armada, which is poised to attack the Spanish mainland, so she wants no more outlay from the Crown towards quelling further uprisings in Connacht.'

The sergeant's words struck a chord among the tribesmen, as the elders in the assembly regarded each other with severity and disbelief. Manglana himself shifted slightly in his seat as he picked at his beard and spoke the thoughts of most present.

'So we are to enter into league with the viceroy? Accept his peace while the Binghams are led to trial in Dublin?'

Ramos could not restrain a chuckle.

'Hardly so, my lord. Hardly so. Have I not said that our lord O'Rourke prepares yet another attack?'

'I have heard tell,' said the chieftain with a slight frown, 'that the viceroy's peace commissioners are preparing to ride out from Galway to meet with him.'

'Your spies have spoken the truth, lord,' replied Ramos, 'for my lord O'Rourke also prepares to meet with them upon the borders of his own land. Yet he has hundreds of men under the command of his son, who are ready to strike out yet again and hustle many heads during the parley. This should help the enemy understand that peace will not be won by words alone and thus should further compromise the Binghams' position so that they may be cast out of these lands.'

Ramos' address had swathed the hall in a hushed silence, and all that could be heard was the heavy and expectant breathing of his listeners.

'Viceroy FitzWilliam has gathered the books of outrages that were given to him by the rebels. Our rebellion has not been in vain, and we may be rid of butchers like the sheriff of Sligo and the likes of Treasach Burke and John Gilson. The O'Rourke asks that you answer his summons. We must strike again whilst the iron is still hot.'

Great cheers of approval were heard, for the passions of Dartry's highborn had been rekindled by their recent raids in Sligo, which had grown both their heads of cattle and their bellies. Upon witnessing these cries of consent, Ramos was swift to deliver the last of his master's message.

'My lord O'Rourke retains gold sent to him by our rightful King Philip of Spain. He offers blood money for your losses and shall make good on any other debts you incur. An opportunity like this shall not present itself again soon. For years the Binghams have tried to subdue you with force and lies. This time you shall be rid of them once and for all.'

Some of the elders fell over one another upon hearing this, punching the air and crying their assent. O'Ronayne's face was spotted amongst their number, and the Jesuit shouted at the top of his voice.

'Blessed be the words of this Spaniard! Let us be rid of the butchers! By the grace of God we shall drive them all back into the sea!'

Manglana observed the general tumult in his hall with his bearded chin rested upon his right fist. When the cries died down, he slowly rose to his feet, then drew his sword from its scabbard and held it out before the gathering.

'Then let us ready our hafts and sharpen our blades!' he cried, with his eyes wide and his rotten teeth bared for all to see. 'We shall unite with the host of our overlord and unleash merry hell among our foes!'

Shadows flickered across the hall as the men roared their approval. I shuddered at the natives' ferocity. Amid the passionate uproar, Ramos walked up to me and grasped my shoulder, his nose twitching as he hurled me towards Nial. I was so outraged by this treatment that my hand fell to the handle of my *skene* dagger and I whirled about in a fury, only to find Nial's gauntleted hand gripping me by the shoulder as

Ramos beckoned to O'Ronayne, who approached us with his face still flushed.

'Give this mud-sodden mongrel that bath, for the love of the Virgin.'

The Jesuit and the bondsman spirited me out of the hall, a handful of bluejackets at their heels. We silently made our way back down the steps and ladder, then boarded the ferry which bore us back across the lake. No one spoke during our trip across the water, and I kept my silence while O'Ronayne flashed me dark glares of confused outrage. Upon reaching the edge of Manglana's town, they rushed me towards O'Ronayne's quarters at *Doire Mel*, and once inside his house I started at the sight of a large, wooden tub full of steaming water, which was still being filled by two old maids.

The two servants scurried off with their pails at a gesture from O'Ronayne; then one of the bluejackets slid the length of his *skene* dagger between my back and the collar of my tunic, pulling the length of the blade towards him as he ripped the filthy tunic off my back. The servants next pulled my trews off so that I stood as naked as a babe; Old Tom's dagger fell to the ground.

'Pretty little thing,' observed Nial, scarcely paying the blade any notice.

The household kerns next slid their arms beneath mine, dragging me towards the tub and hurling me headfirst into it. As my head was raised from beneath the hot water, I gasped for breath as fits of laughter rang in my ears. Nial and his men slapped their knees in mirth as O'Ronayne beheld them disapprovingly from the doorway. After the bruising months of toil spent serving Gorman's kin, I could almost feel my bones creaking into place as the heat of the tub revived me, though its water swiftly turned the colour of pitch as several weeks' worth of mud and filth slid off my limbs. Nial and his men still laughed as they cleared out of the house, leaving O'Ronayne alone in the doorway.

'You are the first man to use my bathtub,' he snarled, furious at the treatment accorded to me, 'but do not make yourself too comfortable yet. You are a man of O'Rourke's now, and he is always in the brunt of all fights with the enemy. Should you fall into the enemy's hands, you may yet receive the punishment I would have served you on the day of your trial!'

So saying, he stepped outside and slammed the door behind him, leaving me entirely discomfited by the extent of his phlegm as I slid back into the healing water. It had been years since I had taken to a tub, so all fears and preoccupations were dispelled from my mind as I resolved to enjoy every last moment of my unexpected wash. I picked up a piece of black soap from the ground, and I almost purred with delight as I scrubbed it against my face and shoulders, my arm pulled back as far as I could to also scrape it along my back.

By the time the soap had melted away, the water became even darker, and I lay upon my back in a trance, the rafters above me becoming darker as my eyes closed and I drifted away from consciousness. The water was colder when at last my heavy eyelids were parted, and as I wiped my eyes with my forearm I made out the familiar figures of two men.

'Good day to you, my wrinkled little lovebird.' Ramos grinned. 'Went and lost your head over a native all over again?'

'It was consensual.'

'That's what they all say.' The sergeant snorted with a smirk, but the tall Croat behind him maintained a stoical expression when he spoke.

'You are not the first rogue in our charge. We have gathered many churls into our company, all men who have paid their fine, yet are still without status or honour price.'

He passed the fingers of his two hands through each other, then pushed his palms out towards me, prompting a loud crack of his knuckles which brought a lump to my throat.

'Since entering our command, all of them have learned not to put a foot wrong. And from this moment on, have a care to do the same.'

Despite my relief at having been readmitted into military service, I served them both with an indignant glare as I resisted the temptation to shower them with sharp insults.

'Where were you?' I spat, somehow refraining from swear words and curses.

'There were other matters to discuss with *MacGlannagh Abù*,' said the sergeant, as he made mocking reference to the Dartrymen's favourite war cry, 'and we can only hope that the old bullock-head understood most of it.'

'What matters?'

'That does not yet concern you, Abelito. Now get out of that tub and get dressed. You have not been enlisted to float about all day in a tub.'

'I pray that you return in an hour,' was my retort, 'for I am enjoying myself in here, and your company is unwelcome at the best of times.'

Ramos sighed at my insolence, then exchanged a glance with Dario as they stepped towards me. At the sight of their approach I sat up in fear, worried as I was that violence might be forthcoming, then yelled out in protest as together they gripped the sides of the wooden vessel and heaved it once and upwards. I bristled with rage like a soaked tomcat as I rolled across the floor of the Jesuit's abode and the bathwater ran all over the ground.

'That's a pretty thing with which to impress the lasses,' remarked the Croat as I rose back to my feet with bunched fists, glaring at the two men who had noticed the spider's mark on my breast.

'I do not recall you bearing any special affection for the spider,' said Ramos. His one eye shone mirthfully at my naked appearance.

'I was branded by the enemy in the dungeons of Sligo, you idiot!' I roared, then regretted what I had said the instant it left my mouth.

Ramos was swift to turn his head sideways as he mulled over my outburst, all the while serving me with a keen stare.

'I did not recall hearing that you were tortured in Sligo either,' he whispered.

With a grunt of annoyance I brushed past him, making my way to the other side of the lodging as I looked for clothes to wear.

'Have they left me no tunic?' I snarled. 'Or mantle?'

'What is this talk of Irish garb, Abelito?' cried Ramos. 'You are a Spaniard and not a savage, man! A soldier of the king, by God!'

'Be silent, you fat fool! I deserted the Army of Flanders over three years ago!'

Ramos appeared to heed my command, but only because he was too angry to speak. When at last he calmed down, he spoke again, so irritated was he by my searching the Jesuit's house for garments.

'Your clothes are on the bed of rushes near the door. There you will find both shirt and trews.'

I found my old English clothes where Ramos said they were, gratefully pulling them on and feeling relieved as my feet slipped into the kersey stockings once more. Upon seeing me fully dressed, Dario walked to the doorway, beckoning to one of his men, who brought him a sack and a long object wrapped in linen. My jaw dropped like that of an awed child when he handed over both items, and I instantly recognised a Marquardt rifle as my fingers wrapped themselves about the linen.

So sweet was the feeling of reunion with the firearm that for a fleeting moment I almost forgave Ramos for everything. I swiftly drew it out of its cover and held it to my shoulder again, taking aim at the Jesuit's bookcase. My attentions were next turned to the heavy sack, from which I drew a burnished cuirass which I slipped over my shirt. This was followed by my newly polished bandolier, which I instantly swung about my shoulders. A surge of pride flared through me at the sight of the trooper's boots, which reached past my knees. A Spanish helmet had also been provided.

After I donned this last piece of armour, I could see Ramos' chest swelling like that of a proud father. His face was crinkled with emotion when he stepped forward and clapped me on the back with his one hand. He ran his remaining eye over me as a broad grin grew across his face.

'By God, if we were not born to fight side by side. We are the last of our *camarada*. No longer will we flee the enemy like scurrying rabbits; it is time to show these heathens what Flanders' *tercios* are made of. And our account with the Sassenach shall be paid in full, Abelito.'

His one eyed bulged with sentiment when he said this, and his one hand rested itself once more on my shoulder. I shrugged it off with a growl and pushed Ramos away from me, so hard that he fell backwards and all but toppled over onto the ground.

'Begone from my sight, you cur! I may have to fight with you, but I shall not hear talk of *camaradas* from a double-dyed, lying whoreson! Our *camarada* died the day you and your three whoresons killed Elsien and Reynier at Willebroek. You should already be dead by my own hand, just like the other three tosspots, and I should be with Maerten and Pieter in the Indies!'

Dario stepped before the sergeant with a huge, outstretched palm.

'Peace, Spaniard. There is no need to come to blows.'

'What's this?' I fumed. 'A personal bodyguard?'

In my rage I lunged at him with a fist, which Dario gently caught before slipping his thumb onto the back of mine and pushing it downwards until my legs gave way beneath me and I cried out for him to stop. He only did this at Ramos' command, and as I recovered my hand, I glowered at the sergeant.

'Leash your dog or you will pay for this!'

Ramos wearily nodded to Dario again, who promptly kicked me in the stomach, leaving me writhing upon the ground and gasping for breath.

'We can do this all day, Abelito,' sighed the sergeant, 'yet believe me when I tell you that I would prefer that you largely be left undamaged.'

'Go fuck yourself!'

At another nod from Ramos, Dario seized my right wrist and used it to twist my arm behind my back, pulling it up and backwards whilst he slammed the sole of his boot down between the blades of my shoulders. I sought in vain to strike him with my other arm, which only made him push down even harder. Ramos crouched low as he approached me, bringing his face close to mine while waving at me.

'Truce?'

'Why do you mock me with that child's gesture?'

'Because you are behaving like one.'

Just then the length of Dario's leg was fully extended, leaving me to gnash my teeth and wriggle furiously as the ball of my shoulder was slowly and agonisingly lifted out of its socket.

'Very well then, truce! Truce!' I cried, batting his hand away. 'Whatever you want. I'll kill you later!'

'Swear it by Fra 'Cola's grave,' persisted the sergeant, despite my frenzied wriggling, craftily referring to the beloved tutor who had raised me as a child, whom I had often mentioned to him in Flanders.

'Yeeeeeeeeeeees!'

At Ramos' gesture the cruel Croat released his grip, and my face smacked the straw-strewn earth like that of a freshly caught fish. So winded was I by the Croat's attentions that it was some time before I could stir again. When at last my head was raised, I could see Ramos reaching his hand out to me. I took it, feeling battered but also quite flattered.

'Why are you helping me?' I asked in resignation.

He beheld me carefully as he replied, as if trying to understand if I was serious.

'When Alba was recalled to Spain you were but one of a few of his retainers left behind in Flanders. An abandoned whelp, entirely forgotten by your lofty betters. Many that hated the duke would have soon been rid of you, had I not taken you under my wing.'

'I was as good as dead,' I admitted with a weary sigh, though I glared at the huge, stoic-faced Croat.

'That you were, Abelito,' he said, his stare turning harder as he proceeded with his explanation. 'War hardens a man, makes him lose his mind. No number of songs or oaths about king and country can allay that sickness. For close to a decade did I see men, some of them close comrades of mine, succumbing to it, until all they had left in the shit-strewn world we were thrown into was a death wish that they held close to their breasts at night. In their slow-growing lunacy they started to believe that a choice as to how to dispose of their own lives somehow rendered them free men again. All too often did this leave men – good men beyond count – to throw themselves into desperate hand-to-hand skirmishes they knew they could never survive, often against the orders of their own officers.'

I nodded in agreement, recalling the countless grimy faces of the Spanish legions – devoid of hope and up to the hips in rainwater – weathering yet another volley of heretical fire as they readied to storm yet another God-forsaken fort in some other beleaguered territory we had turned into a living hell. Ramos' solemn cast brightened unexpectedly into a grin.

'Perhaps it's because I've got something of the Jew in my blood, or perhaps it was my own bent of growing blooms out of stony surrounds. Throughout my life I have scarcely ever been an honourable man, yet all know that I have the stomach for a fight whenever it is necessary. Often was I tempted to go down on my own terms, to storm a trench against direct orders or run into the breach alone and ahead of the rest. Yet I desisted from doing this, for it somehow became clear to me that other ways of securing freedom existed within the war itself, if only I could become more ruthless and uncaring than I had ever been before.'

My lip was bitten in anger when he said this, since it seemed to me a poor justification for the horror he had unleashed on the van der Molens and many others, who had all perished at his instructions. Memories of Reynier's charred corpse and that of his daughter, Elsien, returned to me then, as well as the sight of the *Santa Maria de Vision,* which had perished beneath the waves, dragging the poor Maerten down with it. Ramos raised his head slightly upon noticing my outrage, yet persisted undeterred.

'I was one of the first who came up with the fire tax, of claiming rents from the people whose land we occupied in return for not burning down their houses. You know of what I speak, Santi. We took their food from their children's mouths and whored their best daughters. We lied to our dying comrades before lining our pockets with the money they had saved for so long, after tearing up their last letters to their loved ones. Our own commanders could not be trusted, seeking as they did to kill a fair few of us off so that they could then pocket the dead men's salaries.'

Ramos paused to draw breath.

'Our own king's pensioners also accepted pensions from the enemy, so that they were always late to do battle. I looked at men like Duke Adolf of Holstein with envy as well as hatred, for it was clear to me then that the man that profited most from war was the mercenary. Just like that whoreson Scottish constable, Donal MacCabe, who I wager would as soon sell his axes to our enemies should he earn more out of it. It was with this mercenary spirit that I set about accumulating all that I did during my last years in Flanders, and scaled the heights that I did in Seville. It was that same spirit which led me to muster a troop to embark upon the Armada, and now here we are.'

'Indeed, here we are,' I snapped. 'And what of it?'

I glared back at him with increased loathing, yet he did not appear to notice my unmasked look of hatred.

'Those days in Flanders were a living hell. All we had to rely on were our wits first and our *camarada* second. Which was why I was afraid when we lost old Antón on the march, after he collapsed clutching his chest and stiffened like a burning twig. We needed another member to replace him and fast, if we were to retain numerical parity with the other packs of wolves in our troops. It was then that I saw you drifting about the town, alone and white as a sheet. Someone told me who you were, and I invited you to join us for the same reason I do now.'

'Which is?'

'I need a marksman. You often got us out of trouble when an enemy scout spotted us in the woods or an unseen danger lurked amongst the leaves. At all times you were our angel, and never did I make a more inspired choice than to invite you into our fold. You must have saved my own life at least a dozen times.'

Dario beheld me with newfound respect.

'You are the best sharpshooter I have ever known,' continued Ramos, 'and you must never forget who you are. Yet never mistake my desire to retain your services as some soft act of kind-heartedness or mercy, for it is nothing more than a cold and calculated decision. We are but cold tools to one another; I warn that you must never hope for more.'

Despite my anger towards him I knew that he spoke truth, and my head was lowered in acknowledgement.

'You and I make a formidable pairing, and Dario here counts for the other three, not to mention other fierce local fighters whom I have gathered to my troop. So until we triumph in our present struggle, let all disputes be put to one side, at least until we are back among our own.'

'I have not fired a weapon in weeks,' I warned him, feeling slightly daunted by his faith in my abilities.

Ramos grinned.

'You shall not wriggle your way out of this one, Abelito. Now let us return our attentions to the business at hand, which is where to reside for the night. I have spent enough time sleeping in hastily assembled bivouacs across the length and breadth of this damned country.'

As we emerged from the Jesuit's abode, the summer wind was keenly felt against my freshly washed face. The feeling revived me despite the painful swelling in my side, courtesy of Ohmunevic's kick. Ramos and the Croat led me in the direction of the town as they shielded their eyes from the midafternoon sun; two Spanish guards outside the door fell in alongside me.

'Where are we going?' I asked.

'Keep your voice down,' growled Ramos over his shoulder. 'We don't want the tribesmen to know that we have just armed a convicted rapist. And keep the rim of that helmet low over your eyes so that the Dartrymen do not recognise you!'

'But where are we going?'

'That is for you to tell us. Where is Gorman's hut?'

I guided them to the cabin near the centre of the settlement, then crouched slightly as I entered the lengthy mud-and-wattle cabin. It felt empty and bare inside, with a few belongings lying about the blackened remains of the fire. I recognised the wooden pails used to fetch water and feed the cattle, which spent many months a year sheltering under the cabin's roof. Ramos and Dario popped their heads through the doorway, and their eyes widened in shock while their nostrils twitched at the sour odour.

'What in hell is this,' croaked the sergeant, 'the manger of Bethlehem?'

'This,' I replied testily, 'is where Gorman the herdsman and his kin reside for half the year.'

Ramos withdrew his head with the swiftness of a viper, and loud coughing and spluttering could be heard outside until he beckoned to us to follow him. In my confusion I paused in the doorway of Gorman's hut and called out to him.

'Are you returning to the camp?'

The sergeant snorted aloud.

'Yes, it would be best. We might be expected to fight like animals, yet we need not sleep in their offal.'

A few of the aged inhabitants of Rosclogher cast us forlorn glances from the doorways to their own huts. They were largely all that remained of the townsfolk, being too advanced in years to be able to undertake the journey into the mountains. Two of them even saluted us, yet Ramos ignored them as he led us on towards the score of tents which were spread across the greensward.

'That is the rabble I led here from Dromahair,' he said. 'They are largely churls and the flown sons of poorer herdsmen, and we have spent the last two months training them.'

His words reminded me of the first conversation I had held with him in Ireland, after I had attacked him in Manglana's hall following the siege of Rosclogher.

'You intend to train a militia, sergeant?'

He nodded once.

'Yes, a cross-square. Defensive formation. A hundred and twenty whoresons in all.'

'How have you trained them?'

'That can wait until tomorrow,' said Ramos, waving his hand dismissively in my direction. 'Let us first retire to our quarters.'

Ramos' tent was taller than most, and positioned at the rear of the large camp. The two bluejackets left our company and returned to the town as we entered his lodging, which was guarded by a handful of the Spaniards in his force. Upon entering the cowhide shelter we lay down upon the leather mats upon the ground, the sergeant lying alongside the Croat while I sat in a corner alongside the entrance. I eyed my fellow occupants warily as Ramos took a long swig from a skin and passed it over to me and Dario. He proceeded to kick off his boots and wiggle his toes.

'What are the whores like here, Abelito?'

'Ugly would be a compliment.'

'Then doubtless in need of employment,' said Ramos cheerily, stretching his legs out before him and waving away one of the midges that plagued the town, 'yet that can wait for now.'

He cast both me and Dario a look of annoyance when we refused the skin he offered us.

'Have your minds been rendered idle by that savage drink they call the *usquebaugh*? May I remind you both, fine sirs, that today is the feast of Mother Spain's patron, Saint James. For my sake, if not yours, we had best drain more of these skins together.'

With that he beckoned to his guards to fetch us more wine, and they swiftly returned with more skins of the cheap, grainy claret that we had just swallowed.

'Wherefrom did you secure this?' I asked.

'The grey merchants from Sligo, Abelito. Theirs is still a lucrative trade with the rebel chieftains, in spite of the heretics' hold on their towns.'

'They would still trade with us? I would have thought that they would be in league with the enemy.'

'Oh, hardly, for the Sassenachs are in arrears in their debts to them. O'Rourke's spies have told him that the merchants in the towns would rather hazard their money on the sea trade than lend to the heretics anymore.'

'That is a setback.'

'Indeed!' said Ramos, with a broad grin and his one eye alight. 'Hence the opportunity for us to strike.'

'Do you seriously intend to take on the Binghams? Sooner or later you will have to face them on the open ground. The chieftains have not the infantry or the cavalry to do it.'

'I disagree, Abelito,' said Ramos, lying down on his back and removing his helmet. 'We Spaniards have often faced worse odds and prevailed. These savages are not Spaniards, I'll grant you that much, yet they eat far less without complaint, since they are very hardy. They are also fighting to defend their homes.'

'They are only good for ambushes,' I scoffed. 'I have seen it for myself. We had best flee on a boat before we are slain with them.'

Ramos sighed.

'If I were to flee on a boat, Abelito, then I would have left you with the herdsmen. O'Rourke has realised that the rebels need to adapt their fighting methods, since they cannot fly to the mountains like hawks forever. He knows that infantrymen are now key in battle. Hence why the good Dario here and I have trained our troop for months out of our lord's purse. Hence why I am not about to abandon them now. There is a core of good Spaniards running through them, and they will all soon be a formidable force to be reckoned with.'

'It is too little too late,' I insisted. 'They will perish against the enemy's seasoned troops.'

'That is not what we face, Spaniard,' said Dario from the ground, his back turned towards me. The Croat's voice startled me, since I thought that he had been slumbering but had clearly overheard all we had said.

'What do you mean?'

'The English forces in Ireland are swelling with tosspots and ruffians, and the English have emptied their prisons of gaolbirds and beggars to press them into service in Ireland. A large part of their men are also Irish turncoats who have sought to get the better of their lawful masters. Spies report that morale among the enemy is not high, and they are also short of both arms and supplies.'

'That matters little, for they still exceed us in weapons.'

'That matters not, Abelito!' shouted Ramos as he shoved himself onto his backside and glared at me. 'What matters is that we have enough weapons and skill to match them upon the field. O'Rourke has used the gold sent to him from Spain wisely and has obtained sufficient arms from Scotland with which to arm our square. We shall soon be ready to meet the enemy upon the open field, and you will help us to achieve this, just like you did in the old days. And if the chieftains see that we are able to modernise their armies, then our fortunes will be secured.'

'I suppose they will shower us with buttermilk and *usque-baugh*,' I muttered.

Ramos' face slowly turned a hue of purple, until I feared that he would unleash his Croat upon me once more. When he spoke again it was in a voice that was lowered for emphasis, and he fixed me with a malevolent stare.

'How lightly do you pass up an opportunity that stares you in the face? Do you not see why the heretics seek to take over this place? The wood from the trees goes towards building their ships, and the taxes will be an endless stream of profit in their fight against Spain. Yet if we supplant the gallowglasses with our methods, the savages will give us everything, for they still declare the king of Spain their own sovereign. Soon our troop will turn into an army, and after we are rewarded with lands by the chieftains, we can clear the bogs and take the wood for ourselves, putting all idlers to work!'

'Leaving little difference between us and the enemy,' I noted drily.

Ramos' one eye narrowed further as his lower lip trembled for a few instants.

'Except that we are of the same faith as the Irish,' he said at last, 'and would not destroy their places of worship or hang their priests. Nor deny them their tongue, dress or any other part of their existence!'

'Why, of course not,' I muttered, taking a sheer delight in upsetting him, 'for as long as they serve us and die for our king, then they can retain all of their freedoms.'

'That is what all men do for their lord!' spat Ramos angrily. 'You have read too many books, Abelito, and filled your head with all manner of humanist nonsense. I have always told you that the world is a cruel place, not disposed to keeping us fed and clothed without a fight. And I have never once returned home from a war empty-handed!'

I quickly bit my lip, refraining from telling him that this time he would instead be returning home without an arm and an eye. Yet his ire was not yet diminished as he ranted on.

'This is a huge opportunity for us, if only you would rise to it! We did not sack England, but we might yet become masters of Ireland! This is something even I could not have foreseen when we embarked on that accursed Armada! Just look at how the Irish bear the evils of those terrible Scottish rogues, who are no better than a pack of medieval swordsmen. When they see what we can do, the savages will hail us as princes, and both the Scots and the English will be driven back into the sea!'

He was seized by the moment, back up on his high horse as he had been so many times before in Flanders, urging us on towards some vile design that would help us survive another day. An elated Ramos was a sight to behold, since he had the same expression that he wore in a fight. For Ramos could fight when he had to, and had not risen up the ranks of Alba's army through his lowborn blood.

'All men must be committed to the next fighting season,' he exclaimed, 'for this is the campaign that shall decide the fate of Connacht! Trouble is already brewing in the west over the MacWilliamship, and you would not believe the number of men that can be raised. In March O'Flaherty and the Joyces joined the Mayo Burkes with over six hundred strong from Galway. Thousands of cattle were rustled! These are the prizes to be had, Abelito, and we must seize our chance while the Binghams have been recalled to Dublin by the viceroy! O'Rourke is returning from Ulster, and all of his sub-kings are readying to go forth and sow merry hell down south. There will be plunder to be had, Abelito! Great plunder!'

He ranted on and on until dusk, telling us how his Irish troops would eventually be contracted out to the king of Spain to combat the heretics in Flanders, after the heretics were vanquished in Connacht. Ramos always came back to the riches which lay in store for us if we prevailed, and so great was his avarice that I soon felt less ashamed about my concealing the emerald ring from the tribe. Dario had long dozed off by the time nightfall set in, and at last my eyes closed as Ramos' shadow flickered vividly against a tent flap, resembling that of a greedy dragon as spittle flew from his bearded mouth and his one hand waved in the air.

XLII

Rosclogher, Dartry, County Leitrim

26 – 31 July 1589

I awoke the following morning well before the crack of dawn, wiping the sleep from my eyes as I was greeted by the low snores of Ramos. Dario still slumbered like his master, for neither possessed the herdsman's habit of stirring ahead of first light. For a moment I was tempted to silently slit their throats and flee, then decided against it, caught as I was in the middle of Ramos' camp, which was in turn fenced in by lake and bog.

With a grunt I rose to my feet, seeking to ignore the pain in my side from the Croat's kick the day before. My clothes and weapons were slipped on as quietly as I could manage before I crept out of the tent and made my way to the greensward. The remains of smoking fires lingered across the grass, and a handful of the churls were passed out about them, some still clasping wineskins and wooden cups. A shudder ran through me at the thought of the suffering they would endure in the long day of training which lay ahead.

Thereafter I paced up and down the green like a solitary shadow, observing the small signs of life in Manglana's town as some of the elderly went about their morning chores to and from the lake. I was not long alone, for barely had the bell of *Doire Mel* summoned the villagers to Mass than the head of Dario appeared above the tents, his brow knitted with strain.

The Croat appeared to be relieving himself, after which exercise he also made his way towards the abbey. I was surprised by his nod of acknowledgement towards me, which was swiftly followed by a look of anger when he noticed the few churls strewn on the ground around the dying fires. Veering away from his path to the church he walked over towards each one, charitably serving them with a kick in the ribs before snarling at them to prepare for inspection.

'A pretty looking bunch,' I called out to him.

'New recruits,' he snorted, shaking his head in annoyance, 'who only joined us yesterday. If the sergeant had seen them –'

Dario broke off his speech, and his expression turned as hard as cast iron as his hands fell to his sides. I turned to see Ramos walking towards us, just as the first rings of the anvil reached us from the town. My former sergeant was girded in steel and leathers from head to foot, accompanied by an air of austerity which usually meant that battle was at hand.

In his armour he appeared the very embodiment of Imperial Spain, that warlike kingdom which had forged an empire, stomping the length of Continental Europe beneath its heel. It was a kingdom which had brought peace to the Italian peninsula and struck terror into all heretics and infidels, as well as enemies within its own faith, for both France and Venice trembled before Imperial Spain, which had defeated the pope himself before making him kneel before the Iron Duke in Rome.

At the sight of the sergeant my arms also fell to my sides, for although Ramos could be the most jovial of fools at a feast, none could tell what he might do when a dark mood was upon him.

'At the peal of the church bell,' he fumed as he fell in beside us. 'I told them to be ready at the first peal of the church bell.'

'They feasted long into the night,' I replied. 'It must have been a hard march from Breifne.'

Ramos snorted aloud.

'They'll be worked twice as hard today.'

He then fell silent, as the first members of his troop shuffled onto the green and fell into line. There were at least a dozen of the men, a curious combination of Spanish stowaways and Irish tribesmen. They were a sorry bunch at first sight, with their ragged clothing and unshaven faces adding a defiant air to their unruly presence. Alongside me Ramos shifted slightly from one leg to the other, seemingly biting his lip as he waited for the rest to appear.

I was surprised to see Dal Verme and the Canarians appear next; they quietly took up their places in the second row of veterans. To my astonishment a drummer boy and a standard-bearer soon also materialised, O'Rourke's banner fluttering in the breeze as the two red-faced boys rushed into their positions. The sight of them filled me with a slight nostalgia, for it reminded me of the excitement I once felt as a boy at my first sight of a troop. I could not help a foolish smile at the memory of such a distant time, when I had been crushed by disappointment upon being told by my guardian that I was not old enough to enlist.

Within minutes all but one of Ramos' men had arrived. The last man left us all waiting for many minutes in fearful anticipation, until he finally made his way through the tents with a cocksure swagger and a defiant grin. The man's stature suggested that he could well afford his airs, for he was taller than Dario and almost twice as broad. I later learned that he was a young herdsman renowned for his physical prowess, who had spurned an invitation by the gallowglasses only the day before in order to join Ramos' troop.

A mane of auburn hair fell about his shoulders as he took his position at the corner of the fifth row with an air of reluctance. With his troop finally gathered, Ramos addressed them in a voice which crackled with menace.

'Where are your weapons and armour?'

There followed a hesitant silence, which was only broken by the odd whisper and stifled chuckle. A slight murmur of voices could be heard before the sergeant spoke again in a tone no less kindly.

'Since our drummer boy is the only bird to have landed in its full plumage, he alone shall remain on the green whilst the rest of you fetch your missing feathers. His drum shall beat a hundredfold, in which time you must return fully girded. God help those of you that tarry when the hundredth beat is struck.'

'Make haste!' roared Dario, and the whole square quickly dissolved as men ran back to their tents to fetch those items which they had forgotten. All seemed overcome by frenzy when the drummer boy started his beat at Ramos' bidding, except for the tardy giant who never stirred from his spot, regarding us all with crossed arms and a mocking smirk of amusement. In the corner of my eye I could see Ramos shifting furiously from one leg to the other, although he somehow kept his silence at the new recruit's insolence.

Despite their initial tardiness, the men more than seized the opportunity afforded to them by the sergeant, with the last of them falling into line before the drummer boy had struck seventy. When at last they were regathered Ramos shouted a single word.

'Stand forth, Morgho Mór!'

There was a slight rustle in the ranks as the tardy giant slowly strode forth. At closer sight his byname for being big was further justified, since at least two of me could have stood shoulder to shoulder and not taken up the width of his breast. He stood before the other men with an air that was still haughty, and for a moment it seemed to me that his stature had contributed to an arrogance of youth that had pushed him into dangerous territory.

'Sire?' boomed Morgho, his hands like heavy hams wrapped over one another as he observed the sergeant. Ramos took but a couple of steps towards him, all the while eyeing him warily.

'Where are your weapons, Morgho?'

'I have no need of them, sergeant. All know that I slay enemies with my bare hands.'

'Ah,' said Ramos, as he neared the giant and proceeded to walk around him. 'And would your bare hands counter the mounted lance?'

'My bare hands would fell man or beast,' growled the tribesman, who towered over the portly sergeant.

'I do not doubt that,' remarked Ramos, still seemingly unaware of the great physical danger of the man he had singled out, 'and yet, at the gallop, a lance will rend both flesh and bone, and also steel.'

Morgho's face was flushed at his commander's words, and it was clear then that it was youthful rashness and a lack of good guidance which had led him to disregard Ramos' orders. Secretly I hoped that the lad would swallow his pride and admit his foolishness, for despite his arrogance he was still a hefty prospect that could do serious damage in a close scrap with the enemy. Yet so secure was he in his bodily strength that further insolence flowed from his lips once he had regathered himself.

'I could snap a lance like a man's back over one knee!' he growled, pointedly glaring at Ramos who stood a couple of paces before him. 'Especially a fat, one-armed fool who assigns his best soldier to the back of his square! How could a lance reach me there, O portly salmon of wisdom?'

A few chuckles could be heard about the greensward at these words. A sharp intake of breath betrayed my horror at Morgho's outburst, but Dario never once stirred at my side as he regarded the standoff which unfolded before us. Meanwhile a sly smile had spread across Ramos' face, and his voice was steady and clear when he spoke again.

'You came highly recommended to this troop, Morgho Mór. The hills resound with tales of your power in wrestling, and it is said that your spear throw can hurl a man from his feet.'

'Indeed!' The giant grinned as he flexed the fingers of his right hand. 'With this arm I have slain many a castle rustler, and my slingshots have always slain an assailant, whenever the mark was true.'

'Ah,' said Ramos with a slight nod, 'now that I did not know. Yet it is said that you turned down the invitation of the gallowglass constable, Donal MacCabe himself, in order to form part of this troop.'

'Aye, that is the truth of it,' boomed the tall herdsman, as a look of outrage returned to his face, 'although I know not why I made such a choice, to be placed at the back of this force as if I were some puny churl barely fit for battle. Perhaps I had best return to the gallowglass, rather than serve a portly oaf with one lamp who knows not the merit of true fighting men.'

The slight chuckles of the Irish were heard once more, and they turned into deep laughs when Morgho smugly turned his head to acknowledge the mirth before returning his attention to Ramos. Meanwhile the sergeant before him had not betrayed a whit of sentiment as his raised head studied the face of his imposing charge.

'Men of Spain are never barely fit for battle,' said Ramos calmly. 'Men of Spain are always better prepared, and every last member of the square is part of a deadly unit dreaded by men across the known world. Except for Dartry, it would appear.'

Morgho's eyes narrowed as he heard these words, and his hands slowly closed to form fists as Ramos continued his address without ever stirring from where he stood.

'The men at the front of the square weather the cavalry charge. They are the most experienced men, and strong too.'

'Have you heard nothing, fool?' roared Morgho as he raised his arms to strike the sergeant. 'I am strength itself!'

'It is not through strength alone that one counters the lance,' exclaimed Ramos, 'for one requires deftness too!'

With that he ducked beneath a fist thrown by the Dartryman before executing the simplest of movements, of which every street urchin in Spain was the master. In a moment a *skene* dagger had been whipped from Ramos' belt. It plunged into Morgho's belly and rended two handspans of flesh before it was withdrawn. A howl of agony was heard as the giant bent over double and collapsed onto one knee; Ramos quickly hopped away from harm's reach. Almost as an afterthought, the sergeant leapt into the air and lunged out with his right foot, bringing his huge weight to bear upon the giant's raised leg.

A sickening crack was heard as the Dartryman's knee caved inwards, and Morgho's face was the picture of disbelief as he collapsed upon his back, his hands clasping his belly and his leg. However, Ramos was not yet finished, and his face was like that of Lucifer as he next whipped his sword from its sheath and turned back towards his victim. So vicious had been the sergeant's onslaught that Morgho's death appeared but an inevitable formality. Despite his agony the giant himself was clearly aware of this, as he shifted onto his backside and held an outstretched hand towards the man he had mocked so freely.

'Mercy, I beg you!' he cried. 'Forgive my rashness!'

The sergeant's sword blade sliced the air in a cruel arc, streaking the green with claret as two of Morgho's fingers flew across the grass. With a shriek the giant rose upon his good leg and hopped away before Ramos ran up to him and planted a hefty kick in his backside, which sent the wretch falling upon his face. A gut glistened at the tribesman's side as he lifted himself again, before swiftly snatching it up with his mutilated hand.

'Get you back to the Scots if they'll have you,' spat Ramos, 'for ours is the way of science and precision, and we have no need for the fighting relics of old wives' tales – or of barbaric, goat-humping savages!'

The sergeant turned, his face aflame as he stepped towards the trembling veterans and shrieked into their faces.

'We are men of Spain! Professional soldiers! And henceforth we shall behave as such!'

His bloodied sword and dagger were sheathed as his voice dropped, and suddenly his face was filled with both outrage and wonder.

'Today is a day christened by the blood of the unruly! A sacred day! No longer are you castaways and native beggars standing shoulder to shoulder. You are all my children, and I am a father who shall brook no disobedience. To each of you I say, remember! Remember that we serve O'Rourke out of the pocket of his overlord, the king of Spain! Philip is our master and sovereign lord, and to disobey me is to turn your back on him!'

The forefinger of his one hand was held up to the men before him.

'I read you the articles of war only yesterday. There is to be no mutiny or disobedience. Whosoever breaks them again shall also be carved from their naval to their gullet before being made to face the judgement of pikes. Morgho will have gotten off lightly, compared to how your insolence will be met. Yet obey my every last command and you shall know not fear but only triumph and plunder! The Spaniards amongst you know of what I speak. As for the Irish beggars amongst us, make sure to heed my simple instruction. Do not stray an inch from my orders, not for your brothers, first cousins twice removed, or half-brother whose father regaled your mother with a dry humping! Mark that I care not for the ties that bind you pack of inbred mongrels! You may think that to do what you will is bravery, but I will teach you how to stand in the face of death like a true soldier of Spain, instead of scampering off to the hills like a gaggle of headless geese.'

With that he turned his back on the men and strode towards me and Dario. A cheerful grin spread beneath his whiskers, and it seemed that at last the black mood had left him. At his nod the Croat cleared his throat and took a step forward to address the men.

'Ready yourselves for inspection!'

A clink and clatter filled the air as the recruits quickly adjusted their gear and armour, and Ramos turned to speak to me.

'You once formed part of my *camarada*, and I doubt any Spaniard here saw as much of battle as we did. Except perhaps for Dario.'

A loud sigh left him as he observed the men fiddling with their weapons and armour.

'So, what do you think of this force?'

'They are a pretty-looking bunch. Yet apart from the dozen Spaniards, these are but churls. They are barely capable of rounding up sheep.'

In his annoyance at my words, Ramos' teeth were slightly bared.

'Then you make sure they are capable of more than that. For a troop without men is akin to an arrowless quiver. This shall become a beautiful *quadrilla*, just like the ones we served in. If still a bit slovenly, all of these men were keen to enlist.'

'Did you pay them their three *escudos*?'

The sergeant met my jest with a dark stare.

'I do not think you are taking this seriously, Santiago. Step in alongside me and keep your eyes open.'

At his request I shadowed his footsteps through the ranks, serving each of his men with an unimpressed glance as he studied them from head to foot. Sometimes he paused to inspect the contents of their knapsacks and ball bags, or of the powder flasks upon their shoulders. As we passed Dal Verme and the Canarians I dared to quickly nod to them, and as Ramos walked past them they returned the slightest nod of acknowledgement.

The Spaniards in Ramos' *quadrilla* largely occupied the first two rows of ten, with the men who had followed him from Breifne largely occupying the third and fourth. None of the armour on display was consistent, which meant that we turned a blind eye to the odd assortment of breastplates and shoulder pieces on display, which had been collected from wrecks and the corpses of enemy soldiers. Some of the more recent recruits in the last two rows had rushed to join the troop on its way to Dartry, and were mostly barefoot and wearing torn tunics. All in all it was an unruly gathering, which had been furnished with proper arms and gear but who lacked the basic items required of an elite fighting force.

'They shall need helmets.' I frowned as we made our way back towards Dario, who stood before the square. 'Their fringes of hair shall be of no use against blade and ball.'

'Their *glibb* will have to do for now. We cannot afford helmets.'

'That is a shame, for otherwise their gear is largely good.'

'What do you think of the hackbuts?' exclaimed Ramos with a grin, seemingly warmed by my more positive note. 'Are they worthy?'

He signalled to one of the men on the sleeve of the formation, who handed me his gun. I was impressed to find it fitted with sights, and I held it aloft in both hands to gauge its dimensions.

'The barrel is long enough. It can be rested against the shoulder to help the aim. Are they good marksmen?'

Ramos cleared his throat slightly. 'Perhaps lacking in a bit of marksmanship.'

He then declared my presence to the troop, pulling me before them as if I were some prancing pony.

'This is Abelardo de Santiago, and you will never meet a finer marksman than him.'

The words warmed my cheeks with embarrassment, and such was Ramos' faith in my ability with the gun that he was ready to heap further praise upon me, although he had not seen me fire a rifle in years.

'In Flanders he was the scourge of the heretics. They named him 'the angel of death', and even now do the Dutch rebels in the Lowlands tremble at the mere mention of his name. Santiago is the best rifleman that ever served Spain. In the skirmish his comrades were further emboldened with him watching their backs from the trees, and countless enemy squares and batteries lost their officers to the death he sowed whilst unseen.'

What Dal Verme and the Canarians thought I dared not think, for never once had I revealed my identity to them. Meanwhile Ramos took a step forward and clapped me upon the shoulder, issuing a final declaration before training began.

'Learn to shoot like this man, and you need not fear a single cavalryman!'

The men were divided into groups of ten, with targets set up along the side of the green that was closest to the trees skirting the bog. We versed them in the skill of firing and reloading, and at the sergeant's bidding I passed from one group to another, gently adjusting their posture and sharing my knowledge on how to gauge distances. The men were also shown how to use their powder and protect it from the damp, as well as how best to slip the charger down the musket bore.

About fourteen commands were given from priming to firing, with reserve barrels of ammunition placed to the rear of the musketeers for recharging. Overall the men had already received some good training, but the Spanish seamen and the Irish required additional supervision, for their lack of precaution with the loose powder was startling. One of the new recruits almost grabbed a handful of it with his slow match still dangling from his wrist. He fell on all fours as I struck him in the knee with my rifle stock.

'Are you mad? If you have to kill yourself, then do not so readily take us with you!'

I insisted on a particular method of carrying powder and ball to avoid any possible accidents from occurring. Instructions on the use of the slow match were provided thereafter, and I also showed the men how to hold the match cord and the gun above their heads when carrying them across the water.

'Higher! Lift them higher!' I barked.

The Irish amongst us were well used to hardship, so their resolve was formidable, making them amongst the best troops I had trained. Ramos walked through our makeshift drill ground with a swagger, patting or slapping his recruits in the back of the head as he urged them on to greater efforts. He appeared the perfect specimen of a bravo trained upon the Continent. Perhaps for effect he swore strange oaths used by both *tercios* and *landsknechts*, and his jargon was endlessly seamed with military words and phrases picked from the languages of the many peoples who had served or fought with Spain.

After a half hour of shooting, the firing of balls was called off; peacetime target practice ended early due to the dear price of gunpowder. Ramos barked at the men to reform into a square on the greensward, after which he reshuffled the rows of men so that Morgho's spot was taken up by a churl and I could assume a position in the right sleeve along the front row, two men away from the rightmost musketeer. Dal Verme and the Canarians were right behind me.

'A freshly formed troop, one graced by the presence of the heroes of the siege of Rosclogher!' He laughed before a steely glint returned to his eyes. 'Now prepare to dig in and receive a charge.'

An exercise was then pursued which was aided by the appearance of Dario on horseback at the head of a dozen riders, a young band of O'Rourkes that had journeyed with Ramos' men from Breifne. At the sergeant's order the horsemen were made to charge towards our square from the other side of the greensward, and the pikemen in our number were urged to ready their weapons to meet the charge a moment before the whites of the riders' eyes became visible.

At the last moment the Croat's horsemen veered away from us to avoid the pointed ends of the long spears, yet a cavalry charge had been well replicated, so that a proper test of our pikemen's mettle had been achieved. Overall their reactions had been on the mark, yet as the ground rumbled beneath us a couple of the long weapons had risen late, and one had slipped from the hands of a churl and struck an unsuspecting musketeer, who still rubbed his head amid countless curses.

Ramos ordered that the charge be repeated, whilst also requesting that the musketeers in our force go through the motions of loading their weapons and attempting a volley at his command. This was attempted time and again, so that the horses soon frothed at the mouth as Dario's riders galloped towards us and then loped back towards the ringfort, before charging at us again and again. After a score of these charges, the pikemen's speed and movement, which had since improved, began to deteriorate as they wearied, with many of them suffering from their late drinking the night before. The musketeers also began to show signs of strain. The heavy rasps of their breathing were almost piteous while some of them appeared white in the face. As expected, Ramos observed their efforts with a pitiless stare of revulsion, and he roared at them to maintain their initial resolve.

'Even a dying man's cock would rise faster than those spears! Lift them high and lift them fast, or the enemy shall tear into you and cause you pain! And stop fooling around with those muskets! I want them loaded before the whites can be seen! You shall train, train and train until your shoulders are purple and you cannot stand anymore! When you feel your shoulders falling apart with strain, then ready yourselves to fire another ten volleys!'

'You heard the sergeant!' I echoed. 'Get to it!'

Our words drew added steel and resolve from the men, and I yelled at the musketeers until I was hoarse. After another five charges the gallowglasses appeared, bearing huge axes. They stood at a standstill along the green and chortled and whistled at our movements. From the corner of my eye I could make out Donal MacCabe glowering in my direction as he sat atop his steed, hatefully observing our progress in silence while his men openly mocked us. Their taunts proved a distraction to some of our men, who were once again late in priming their guns and raising the pikes.

'Ignore them,' I growled, 'for on the field of battle you shall stand alone!'

Until then Ramos had been too absorbed in bellowing orders to his men to notice the presence of the Scots. Yet hardly did he notice them than he strode to the front of our square and howled his lungs out.

'Long may those Scots mock us, for we are proof that their fighting days are over! Not one of our men shall be lost should they charge at us, yet we prepare to face far worse on the field. You must learn to shoot with a charge of mounted troopers shaking about you, and with cannonballs tearing the heads off your closest comrades!'

Thereafter the strength of the square was regained in spite of the taunts that continued whilst I bellowed at the men to prime, about, draw scouring sticks and present. Ramos kept on barking the fear of God at the men until they were so tired that they flopped about with pike and scouring stick. The odd muffled curse was uttered at the relentless sergeant, and I barely stifled a chuckle upon overhearing a man in the back rows making light of Ramos' bald pate.

Our training continued for well over another hour, until even the Scots tired of our actions and returned to their own lodging amid the odd titter and obscene gesture. Ramos called off the drill not long afterwards, more out of concern for the horses than the welfare of the men. Our efforts were broken up past midmorning, with the men ordered to return to the green at the midday peals of the church bell. As the men collapsed upon the grass and hobbled off, the sergeant strode over towards me with a broad grin as his brow shimmered in the midmorning sun.

'A hardy bunch, Santiago?'

'Yes, Sergeant, among the keenest I've ever trained. Yet they lack the training which we received in the Italian and African garrisons.'

Ramos shrugged. 'I fought with many of those savage bastards in the Low Countries. Always a handful with their backs to the wall who hate the heretic almost more than we do! When the time comes they shall show the same mettle.'

'Why are they using pikes?'

The sergeant assumed a feigned look of surprise as he covered his opened mouth with his good hand.

'Why, Santiago, you astonish me. A square without pikes is like a body without arms.'

'I think I am well aware of that. But what are we training them for?'

The sergeant grinned slyly as he turned on his heel and walked away from me, his tin arm dangling unnaturally to the left with each step that he took.

'Get some rest, Abelito. In time all will be revealed.'

The fate of Morgho must have still been fresh in the minds of the men, for despite their exhaustion all of them appeared in position when the midday peals were heard from the abbey. Dario also appeared atop a fresh horse, which nickered wildly while Ramos explained the training that was to follow.

'This time we will attempt a different drill. You shall practice marching in a loose formation, almost as if we are about to fight in the savage Irish way. The pikes shall be dragged at the trail so that they are barely visible. At my command, all must gather about me in perfect formation, with muskets at the ready and spears pricking the air.'

I had never heard of such an absurd instruction during my soldiering years, yet Ramos ignored my stare of bafflement as he assumed his place between the ensign and drummer boy and served them with strict instructions.

'At my signal, you must keep your standard low,' he warned, 'and not a beat must be played until the colours go up again.'

So saying he ordered us to march, leading us halfway across the greensward before he ordered us to stop.

'Now hear me well, whoresons. When I instruct you to fall out, the men to my left will take three steps to the left whilst those on the right shall move right. Upon ordering you to fall in, you shall resume your usual posts about me and ready your weapons.'

So saying, he ordered us to march on, then barked at us to fall out just before he came to a standstill. As expected the men ended up all over the place, with pikemen bumping into musketeers amid the odd grunt and shout. This prompted Ramos to lose his temper, and he ran about the square smacking men in the head and severely berating them.

'You are an imperial square,' he cried, 'not a gathering of chickens! What is this confusion? Can you not tell your right from your left?'

When we were all regathered into position he urged us onwards once more, then ordered us to fall out just as he was about to stop marching. The second attempt at the loose formation met with greater success, with only a handful of younger natives erring once more. After receiving their expected berating from the sergeant, none stepped out of line the third time, and the fourth and fifth efforts were nearly flawless, with men rushing back into their positions when Ramos ordered them to fall back in.

'That was nicely done, whoresons.' He beamed. 'Now it is time to do all that again, but in the face of a cavalry charge.'

At his gesture Dario galloped to one side of our training ground. Ramos led us well off it until we had reached the huts of mad Orla and her sisters. Some of the whores peered through the doorway and chuckled at us, yet none dared to return their attentions as Ramos marched us on towards the distant speck of Dario.

'Fall out,' he snapped after barely five steps, and the standard was lowered and the pikes dragged upon the ground as we distanced ourselves from him as he had commanded.

All the while our eyes were trained on the growing figure of the Croat, who could not have been more than sixty feet away from us when Ramos shouted at us.

'Fall in!'

To a man we rushed back into our positions as pikes were swiftly raised towards the sky. I shrieked orders at the musketeers, who fumbled with their chargers and guns, getting them ready to fire just as Dario veered his steed away from us.

It had not been a terrible first attempt, since the musketry had only been short of three or four commands while the pikemen had also been late when moving into position. Yet Ramos predictably shouted his head off, even going as far as to floor a tardy pikeman with a fist to the chin. With practice our positioning became more effective, until we were able to step away from him within instants before reforming about him as swiftly as the curling of a hedgehog.

The manoeuvre was tried for at least two hours past noon, with Dario replaced by two more riders, until Ramos dismissed his men again, allowing them a repose of a mere half hour. Some recruits slumped to the ground with weariness and did not stir until they were kicked to their feet again. The men were next divided into smaller groups, with Ramos and Dario overseeing training in close hand-to-hand combat. Hard sparring with wasters followed, and men bruised their hands and ribs with the wooden practice swords as they were urged on to greater efforts.

Dario also trained us in bare-handed techniques, using a belt to hurl men over his shoulder and showing us how to strike parts of the body to best effect. Thereafter the pikemen were disbanded while I was ordered to train the musketeers for another hour. In the end, I staggered away from the field dazed and winded as Ramos approached me with a wineskin held in his outstretched arm. Above him the sky was full of the clouds which had gathered in the west during the previous evening.

'Soak your parched throat.'

I snatched up the skin and poured its contents down my throat while he beheld me with a contented stare.

'I know you hate me, Abelito, but I am glad that we are back together.'

He then turned and walked away as I rasped a reply at his back.

'That last manoeuvre wasted precious time. It is useless; it has never been used.'

Ramos looked over his shoulder and flashed me a sly wink.

'He that shall England win, let him in Ireland begin.'

More of the wine was forced down my throat as I turned away from him with a grunt of frustration. I suddenly noticed five riders who had appeared alongside the green. I instantly picked out the shortest among their number, recognising the features of the princeling Lochlain. Muireann's son smiled at me, since he probably felt that the fearsome Spaniards he had heard of were finally coming to his people's aid. I quickly turned my head away from him, restraining a shudder at the open esteem with which he held us. I hobbled back towards Ramos' camp without ever once turning to look back at the boy.

My head swung from left to right as I sought to identify where I would spend the remainder of the day. I spotted Dario and his riders stretched out alongside the ashes of the previous night's camp fires, and I drifted towards them, half hoping that they might accept me in their company. A nod from the Croat duly confirmed this, and I found myself glad to seat myself at his side, for my recent elevation from churl to soldier meant

that I could not afford to get too close to the men I commanded, most of whom had gathered in and around their tents.

Dario barely stirred as I slumped upon the ground to his
right, except to afford me the swiftest sidelong glance. In front
of us, two knaves busied themselves with building a cooking
fire, and the haughty O'Rourke riders from Dromahair held
their own discourse without ever acknowledging my presence.
I could see that Dario was as lonely as I was, and he set about
offering me his wineskin.

'What did you make of the pike and shot?' he asked.

'They are keen and learn quickly,' I replied between swigs
of claret, 'yet nothing can replace the experience of standing
upon the field during a real fight.'

He quietly nodded his agreement.

'We will just have to make do.'

'And what of your riders?'

Dario sighed as he stretched his long legs out before him
and shifted his weight from one elbow to the other.

'We lack stirrups, so I cannot yet teach them the use of the
lance, yet they are very able horsemen, which is most fortunate,
given that we are reduced to skirmishes. As for their steeds,
they are the best horses to be had in this country. They are
both swift and courageous creatures, and not far removed from
your Neapolitan courser, which is widely regarded as the best
mount in the world.'

'For how long have you served as a cavalryman?' I asked,
then winced in pain as I shifted my weight off the side he had
kicked the previous day.

The Croat smiled almost ruefully at the sight of my discomfort, then jerked his head at the knaves who shuffled about with sticks that they furiously rubbed together.

'Why, of course,' I gasped in sudden realisation, then hurried towards them to light a stalk from their kindling with sparks from the wheel of my rifle.

The muddied faces of the two horseboys creased with delight at the sight of the small flame which was started at their feet, and their sticks were swiftly cast aside as they fell to their knees to gently blow upon it.

'I was never a cavalryman,' remarked Dario as I returned to his side and slumped across the grass with a groan, 'for I was enlisted in a band in Italy when I was still a boy.'

'Were you in debt?'

'No,' he replied, with a fleeting look of bitter regret, 'for my father was a wealthy horse trader in Dubrovnik, and I greatly desired to inherit his business.'

'Then why join the army?'

'I got into a fight with a nobleman's only son. Like all murderers, I had to flee justice.'

'Ah,' I replied, with a nod of understanding.

'And you?' he asked, eyeing me keenly. 'Why did you enlist?'

I cleared my throat awkwardly and took a long swig from the wineskin.

'I also fled justice in my youth.'

'So Abel de Santiago is not your true name?'

'I have been called many things in my lifetime,' I said, with the hesitation of one who has hidden his identity for most of his existence. Then I awkwardly added, 'The tribesmen call me Juan.'

Dario's severe expression returned as he stared at the growing fire. The Croat could tell that I was guarded about my past and did not press me further. I slung the rifle off my shoulder and availed myself of the remaining daylight to clean my weapon. I drew a cloth from my knapsack and set about cleaning the bore of my gun.

'It appears a fine weapon,' said Dario, observing my efforts with a passing interest.

'It is. Marquardt is a gunsmith who has few peers.'

'Was it taken from the Armada wreckage?'

'Yes. This is a unique weapon which would have been commissioned. Few in this world could have easily afforded its price.'

Dario nodded.

'Not bought off the smugglers then,' he said with a grin.

'No.' I laughed before mulling over his words, which hinted at a means of escape from Ireland across the sea.

'Have you met with smugglers in these parts?'

'Oh yes,' he replied, 'for who do you think supplied your men's arms?'

At his words I recalled the horns of powder at the belts of the men in Ramos' square, purchased from Bailey's smugglers.

'How long ago were the arms purchased?'

Dario's eyebrows drew closely together as his forehead furrowed in thought.

'We first arrived here close to a week ago, and rode with Manglana down to the sea upon the second day after striking camp.'

'Oh,' I replied. 'Did Bailey bear tidings from abroad?'

'That he did. It appears that some Spaniards have made it as far as Scotland and have sent word to Parma in the hope that he might send vessels to take them back home.'

'Lucky whoresons.'

'Hardly,' scoffed the Croat, 'for Parma did not waste any lives on the whole Armada enterprise, so you can imagine his enthusiasm to rescue a few Spanish castaways. He has his hands full with subduing the rebels in the Low Countries. Many assurances will be needed for those poor bastards to return home. They will be stuck in Scotland for months if not years. Which is not to mention the grave threat of the Dutch sea beggars, if they do embark for Spain.'

My thoughts instantly shifted to de Cuéllar, and I wondered whether he and his men had made it out of Ireland or if he had been captured or killed by MacCabe or some other aggressor.

'Did Bailey share any more news?'

Dario's eyes were narrowed once more in thought as he strove to think back to the day of the encounter.

'He did not tarry long, since he claimed that he still had many consignments to deliver. It appears that our enemy has a great need for iron, steel and brass balls.'

'He deals with the enemy?' I hissed, nearly dropping my rifle in outrage. Memories came flooding back to me of the long, hard stares of the Scottish smuggler upon the beach, and of Burke's hot pursuit upon the rocks near the same location.

'Have you ever known a smuggler who was not a double dealer?' replied the Croat. 'He is after all a trader licensed by the Scottish crown, who serves us with goods from stocks meant for the enemy.'

'Then why do we trade with him?' I blurted out loud, furious that I had lost the ring because of Manglana's affairs with one who also served our enemy.

'What choice do we have?' retorted the Croat, as the O'Rourkes beside us paused from their chatter and studied our heated exchange. 'And in any event, he serves us with information too. The rules of our meetings with him are obvious; it is all for profit and nothing more.'

'Then the enemy knows of our drills?'

'No, they do not.'

'Then why their sudden desire for so many Scottish armaments?'

Dario shrugged. 'He said it is mainly to English ports that he must supply them, for the viceroy's peace proposals with the rebels have cooled their need for arms in Ireland. The English queen is said to be hatching plans to send her own armada against Spain.'

I was distracted by the smell of cooked meat as Ramos emerged from his tent. The sergeant shuffled towards us in a native's tunic, which fluttered in the gentle breeze about the heavy boots he still wore.

'Spare some for me!' he cried, then scowled at something at his feet, which he kicked away.

It was a blackened forefinger, and the sight of it rolling across the grass was as disturbing as it was pitiable.

'Damn Morgho is still hanging around us,' he muttered, then walked over and took his seat among us.

'You did not have to maim him,' I said.

Ramos snorted at my gentle rebuke as he adjusted the straps of the tin arm about his severed stump. 'Half a hand is better than none.'

'Not for a man of his bearing. His fighting ability has been severely diminished.'

The sergeant glared at me in annoyance.

'I show my face, and you start all over again. Are you a soldier or a priest?'

'Of the two, I would most certainly have rather been the latter.'

'Well, make your mind up then,' he snarled, 'for there is no place for the befrocked in the hell we are readying to enter.'

As the cooked side of mutton was cut up, Ramos did not attempt any more conversation. Perhaps he was too tired to talk, or else other matters weighed heavily upon his mind, as he ate his food and fixed his stare on the flames before him. He even ignored the O'Rourke freemen, so that I started when he suddenly addressed me.

'So, where were those whores again?'

I gestured to the shabby huts at the other end of the greensward, which were closest to the middens. A small kern could be seen stepping out of them with a jacket over his arm. He wore a wolfish grin on his face, and the giggles of one of mad Orla's daughters could be heard behind him. Upon identifying the building, Ramos issued a low grunt as he rose to his feet.

'Very well,' he said. 'Never a better time for it than after a fight. But a day's hard training comes close enough.'

'Will you not rest?' I asked in bewilderment, finding myself amazed by his vigour after the day's exertions.

The sergeant turned to face me with a frown as his fingers tapped the pommel of his dagger.

'Do either of you care to join me?'

'No,' I replied, 'for I am exhausted and must still prepare for inspection.'

Meanwhile Dario stood up and shuffled off towards Ramos, who grinned at my devotion to his cause.

'Very well then, Abelito. I bid you good night.'

The formidable pair walked off together, with one towering over the other in the growing darkness. My attentions were returned to the Marquardt, and after I had cleaned it, I stumbled back to my tent and crumpled to the ground in weariness.

As July drew to an end our training only increased in intensity, with our demanding drill sergeant adding more exercises which prolonged our daily torment. Six musketeers were ordered to seize up the shafts of an old cart as if it were some oversize wheelbarrow before racing with it in the direction of our square. The pikemen amongst us were in turn ordered to raise their pikes towards the fast-approaching tumbrel, being forced to stick it with the end of their long spears to stop its advance. In this way the thrust of a horse was not only replicated but also exceeded, and the mettle of Ramos' pikemen was harshly tested and swiftly improved.

The curious hedgehog formation he insisted on was also repeated daily for two hours in the morning and two hours past noon, until we could have completed the manoeuvre in our sleep. Eventually the Irish charges among us questioned its use, but they were met by a scowl from Ramos, who served us with a stiff rebuke.

'Discard your feeble protestations and stand by me instead. If you obey my each last command, we shall all live to win the battles which lie ahead of us.'

Upon receiving this rebuke we doubled our efforts in training. With each passing day greater confidence in Ramos' methods was secured, as he relentlessly drove us to greater efforts, only allowing us a break from training on the last day of July, when we were allowed to march to Manglana's town at Duncarbery, where the festivities of Lughnasadh were held. The following morning we travelled to the Dartrymen's chief seat of power in the company of Dervila. As always, the chieftain's wife resided in Rosclogher during her husband's absence and only rode to join him at Duncarbery because she enjoyed the feast.

I kept my head down when Lady Bourke rode past us with Muireann and her other favourites, O'Ronayne and Lochlain riding close behind them. The usual band of blue-jacketed kerns followed them, keeping a brisk pace with countless hounds at their heels. Their eyes darted everywhere for the slightest sign of danger, their spears held at the ready. A score of highborn Dartrymen also rode in the company of Dartry's queen, as did Dario's riders from Breifne.

As we progressed along our westward path, Dal Verme and the Canarians were swift to step alongside me. I acknowledged them with the slightest of nods, for although I was no longer close to them, they were still men I respected who had fought well during the siege of Rosclogher.

'All our training, what is it for?' asked Pedro.

'For a fight, I suspect,' was my vague reply.

'Can you not share any plans with us?' asked his brother, Franco, with a hint of annoyance in his voice.

'Alas, I could not, even if I knew them. And Ramos has shared nothing with me.'

'Of course we are preparing to fight,' snorted Dal Verme hotly, 'for the fighting season is close at hand, and the chieftains will want to raid the heretics while the bastards' attentions are claimed by the Bourkes' next rebellion.'

'That is also my guess,' I replied, 'although our part has not yet been revealed to me.'

My fellow Spaniards refrained from questioning me further as we kept along the familiar route. They instead cast the odd stare at the great mountains to our left, which shone green and gold in the gentle day of resplendent sunshine. The seaward road to Manglana's keep was familiar to me, and my thoughts soon drifted towards the incredible events which had swept me up since my shipwreck in Ireland. Great anger welled within me at recollections of my treatment in Sligo Castle, and Treasach Bourke's sneer was still etched in my memory.

A shudder of rage passed through me as I recalled how he had robbed me of Hurtado's ring, and I wondered what fate had befallen the trinket after it had been taken from me but a mile away from our destination. The face of Treasach's master, the lieutenant John Gilson, also returned to mind, as I remembered him drawing a pistol on Manglana's only son and mortally wounding him.

When we arrived at Duncarbery, the town was already a hive of activity. Children ran amongst us with their cheeks full of berries, and countless sheets had been strewn across the ground between the settlement and the edge of its greensward, where countless hawkers sold all manner of crafts and clothing. In the growing sun a festival of games and dances was held upon the green, and after dismissing his men, Ramos summoned Dario and me to his side, and we watched the many reels and jigs being performed to the sound of bagpipes and horns. After days of punishing training, we felt our spirits revived by the sight of such revelry, and to a man we marvelled at the sight of one of the players, who clacked bits of bone between his fingers to the furious accompaniment of a viol and a timpani.

Many of the tribesmen had descended from the mountain passes to attend the feasting, and I recognised the faces of Gorman and his son Finn among the throngs of Dartrymen. They looked at me in confusion while their womenfolk checked items on sale. Tinkers and all manner of other sellers were showing off purses and pouches of leather, as well as candleholders, nails and other essentials. The loud haggling only increased as some of the disbanded soldiers also appeared among the stalls. Meanwhile Manglana and his bluejackets kept a close eye on proceedings, circling the greensward like hawks and ensuring that no trouble broke out among the many different folk who had gathered there from all corners of the kingdom.

The day was largely without incident, and Manglana was seen deep in conversation with the tanist Cathal *Dubh*, as well as his bard. A silence fell across the crowd as a strong guard of kerns escorted the chieftain to a cowhide pavilion erected upon the right side of the green. There he was united with his wife and her party, who greeted him with deep bows while he prepared to watch the proceedings.

His appearance marked the start of the keenly awaited annual wrestling contest, with burly contestants from across the land stepping before him to pit themselves against one another. The onlookers around us fell over one another to lay wagers on the contestants, with Manglana himself ordering his steward, Malachy, to place a bet on one of his favourites. As men ran around us to place bets, Ramos cursed aloud amid the mad swirl of their bodies.

'Holy host! I cannot see a thing in all this madness! Let us find ourselves a vantage point befitting of our station.'

With that he sauntered off, shoving men and women aside until we were closer to Manglana's pavilion.

'Are you planning to ask the chieftain for his little tent?' I asked.

The sergeant ignored me, and cheers and jeers resounded around the green as the first fighters stripped down to their breeches and locked arms in a fierce hand-to-hand struggle. Amid the sharp intakes of breath from the crowd, my stare was diverted from the sprawl of writhing arms and legs before us, swapping the all too familiar sight of struggle and filth for the fair features of the ollave, who stood between Dervila and the tanist Cathal.

Her features had not changed at all since I had last seen her upon the hunt, and when her eyes picked me out in the crowd, her hard stare seemed to somewhat soften. With all eyes taken up by the spectacle on the green, we gazed at one another for long instants, as if no one else in the world existed. Then a loud cheer caused me to return my attention to the sight of a fighter climbing off his vanquished rival and raising a mud-streaked arm aloft in triumph.

'Forget her or she will lead you to hell.'

I started at the rasp in my ear, then turned to meet the severe stare of the tall Croat behind me.

'I already have.'

It was a lie and we both knew it, yet Dario's warning rang true all the same. In vain I berated myself for having so quickly let my guard down after being freed from the creaght by Ramos. My feelings for Muireann were almost impossible to ignore and would lead me to further strife for as long as I remained in Dartry. So I turned my mind instead to a stirring display of horsemanship, as Dartry's freemen galloped across the cleared greensward when the wrestling was over.

Thereafter the handfasts were pronounced, and I stared on in wonder as Muireann led out a half-dozen garlanded maidens, with her betrothed Cathal *Dubh* leading out the same number of men. The tanist's head was lowered so that his long *glibb* masked the many scars on his face, and his long-sleeved tunic covered the scars all over his arms. Muireann wore a wreath of blackberries upon her crown, and as she drew nearer the sight of her free-flowing hair and tight, yellow tunic left me yearning for the firmness of her slender body. Her handsome face left me transfixed.

The sight of her was complemented by her proud bearing, which rendered her presence all the more striking to me than the sight of the other fair maidens at her back. So radiant was her presence that Cathal could not but regard her forlornly from across the grass, a wreath of blackberries also upon his head.

'Why are they doing this?' I whispered in annoyance, for I could see that the ollave's face betrayed no joy at her union with the tanist, although she and Cathal could be heard uttering professions to one another.

'It was the chieftain's design,' replied Dario beneath his breath, 'as approved by his overlord the O'Rourke.'

'Far too much oversight for so small a tribe,' I grumbled, and my heart lurched to see Muireann promised to another.

'One cannot blame the chieftains,' replied the Dalmatian, 'for Muireann's dowry will consist of many heads and other valuables, which will protect the tribe from the Scots' excesses.'

'That much is true,' I muttered, although I found scant solace in Donal MacCabe's disappointment.

So saying, I sought his face out in the crowd and could not avoid a feeling of the utmost cheer at the scowl which marked his face out like a scar. To my misfortune, his eyes met mine just as a smirk of triumph flashed across my face. The last words of the ceremony were uttered, and the young men and women walked away from the green and back towards the dispersing crowd. My eyes were swiftly averted from the Scot as his cheeks turned scarlet, and I felt a deep sense of dread as Ramos led us towards the hawkers.

'Let us mingle for what is left of the day,' said the sergeant, 'yet we must away to Rosclogher well before dusk, for we return to our training tomorrow.'

He had barely spoken when we found our path barred by a dozen fearsome gallowglass warriors, who drew their axes as MacCabe thrust his finger at me, his face still red.

'Avert your eyes, lecher! You have not stopped looking at her!'

My breathing instantly slowed, though my scabbard still rang as I raised my sword.

'Peace!' shouted Ramos. He rested his hand on my sword arm and stepped forward, raising his tin arm before the Scots. 'This is a day of rejoicing. Will you ruin it with words of anger?'

Donal sneered at me over the sergeant's shoulder.

'That cur of yours has already deprived the whole of Dartry of their justice. He shall not dishonour the ollave again.'

MacCabe shook his axe in my direction as he strode forward, prompting Dario to draw his own sword and step in alongside Ramos.

'I need no protection!' I protested hotly, but Ramos seized me by the collar and pulled me away as the gallowglass closed in about us.

'You would not dare assault men of your overlord!' he roared at the Scots, yet MacCabe was incensed and bent on violence.

'I will do anything to protect the honour of the MacGlannaghs!'

The tribesmen about us started at his cry, and many yells were heard as MacCabe's axe was swung down towards us, only to be clumsily parried by the Croat's blade. Things might have turned uglier for us in that instant, for the dull gleam of other axe heads was raised into the air. Yet in that moment a loud cry of protest was heard, and the Scots refrained from further aggression as Nial and a score of bluejackets surrounded us, their spears raised and ready to be flung.

'Refrain from this madness!' shouted the bondsman, with both his blades already drawn. 'Our lord MacGlannagh has outlawed duelling on this day!'

MacCabe and Ramos traded looks of outrage until the constable finally slung his axe onto his back, gesturing at his men to follow his lead.

'Just you wait, Spaniard,' he growled, fixing me with a stare of unspeakable hatred. 'Before the year is out I shall skin you myself, and braise you alive in your own hide.'

He turned on his heel and made for the great feasting held in the chieftain's pavilion, with his men making after him like a pack of rabid wolves. Our blades were uneasily returned to their scabbards, and Nial sounded shaken when he addressed us.

'Perhaps you should return forthwith to Rosclogher. The Scots are to be stationed here until the chieftains partake of the fighting season.'

'Nonsense,' chuckled Ramos with a casual wave of his arm. 'Run off with our tails between our legs over that minor disagreement? Besides, bondsman, it was not we who started it.'

The sergeant's voice was plaintive, a tone he had employed for years when addressing the Spanish army's police in Flanders. Nial observed him testily for a few moments, then tramped off with his kerns. I braced myself for a scolding from the sergeant, but none was forthcoming as Ramos continued walking towards the hawkers with the casual briskness of one who has only just run into an old friend.

'What I really need,' he declared, 'is a good belt. The one I've got is old and torn and does little to impress the men. Yet every drill sergeant needs something of fine leather, with one of those bright, shiny buckles to affirm their authority.'

'And what of your invitation to the chieftain's banquet?' asked Dario in an equally steady voice.

'I doubt he wants us there,' replied Ramos, 'and who cares for the gossip of his circle? In any event, I can always complain about the manners of his gallowglass constable if asked to explain my absence.'

Dario laughed aloud as we reached the wares displayed upon the unfurled blankets along the town's huts. The gathered sellers regarded us in suspicion as we sidestepped chickens in wooden cages and skinned hares. At last Ramos found a wizened old tinker who sold a few items of clothing that included leather goods. The sergeant snatched a brown belt and held it up in triumph, then surprised onlookers by fishing some coppers out of his doublet. He handed them to the elderly vendor, who puffed his whiskers out in surprise at being paid in money.

'Just what I needed,' boomed Ramos, 'and well worth our search! Now let us find ourselves some ale and fresh whores, for it's a few more hard days' work ahead of us.'

We were soon strewn upon the grass, our faces buried in tall cups of mead. Between large gulps of the brew we rolled over and shrieked with laughter at Ramos' lewd jokes, so that any onlookers might have mistaken us for friends.

'So, what do you make of your riders, Dario?' asked the sergeant, finally turning to more serious matters.

'They are fearless' – the Croat shrugged – 'but lack any awareness of tactics. They have yet to master certain manoeuvres.'

'I have no doubt that you shall have them ready in time.'

'That I shall. But without stirrups they cannot take on the enemy with lances, and are thus reduced to skirmishing.'

Ramos was quiet for a few moments as he considered Dario's words, then startled us with a loud burp.

'You shall teach them the use of the lance regardless,' he said. 'They shall have stirrups soon enough.'

'Besides,' I blurted, feeling suddenly emboldened by a few cups of strong drink, 'light cavalry is better than none. They saved our hide on countless campaigns, and Spain has employed them to great effect for years on end. Everyone knows that Gonzalo employed them across Naples to destroy countless French detachments in the countryside.'

Ramos raised an eyebrow at my contribution.

'What's this, Abelito? Advice on matters of command? Have you suddenly been overcome by belief in our enterprise?'

'I did not refer to our enterprise, but to Gonzalo's legendary horse. I cannot judge your endeavours until I know what you are leading us into.'

'And all shall be revealed soon!' exclaimed Ramos as he struggled onto his feet with a grunt. 'But will you now join your comrades in a search for some female comforts?'

My hand was raised in polite refusal, for when it came to the subject of women I already had my fair share of worries to chew on, torn as I was by my yearning for Muireann and my dependence on the killer of my last love. Ramos sneered at my gesture as he staggered towards me, and the mead was thick on his breath as he dared to kick me in the backside.

'Come on, Abelito, I'll foot the bill! What's the matter with you? Are you too good for a whore?'

'No,' I replied angrily, 'I am a humanist, and I don't consider women to be chattel.'

His yellowed teeth were bared, and he lowered his face towards mine until our foreheads were touching.

'You and your damn books, Abelito. I would burn every cursed book in the world if I could, what with them filling your head with heaps of bloody rubbish!'

He withdrew his reddened eyes and spat at my feet.

'What beast are you, Abelito? One minute able to shoot a half troop in the head in cold blood, the next minute with your head in the clouds, lost in a heap of childish ideas.'

In that instant it was all I could do to keep myself from striking him, which made the sound of Dario's voice all the more welcome.

'Perhaps it would be for the best if a convicted rapist avoids being seen with a woman.'

Ramos took a step back when he heard this, then nodded slowly as he appeared to be overcome by something closely resembling embarrassment.

'Quite right, Ohmunevic. Quite right. Let us be off then.'

They left me to finish what was left of the mead, then returned an hour later, having discovered that even Irish whores did not work on feast days. It was therefore not long afterwards that Ramos got bored and sent me to fetch his men, long before the hawkers would disperse before dusk to avoid the pilfering of their wares. Despite their protests at the early summons, the spirit of the men appeared to have been revived, so that a quicker step was noted among them as we trudged back to the banks of Lough Melvin. We reached our camp just before dusk, and all but a few stragglers retired to their blankets before the resumption of training the following morning.

That evening I tossed and turned in my sleep, still furious at the way in which Ramos had addressed me. I was disgusted at myself for having fallen in with him again, years after having sworn to avenge the deaths of Reynier and Elsien. The memory of Maerten's drowning also drove me mad, as did Ramos having dared to raise the subject of whores with me.

The faces of the van der Molens appeared to me but dimly, and the fact that I could not fully picture them only served to stoke my rage. I finally snatched my dagger from the ground and turned on my stomach, resolved to draw the length of my blade along my sergeant's throat and flee into the night. Yet I had hardly leaned forward when a low whisper reached my ears from the side of the snoring Ramos, which left me frozen to the spot in bewilderment.

'You have not slept all night. Put that dagger away and catch a few hours of sleep. I shall wake you a half hour before inspection.'

Dario's voice left me stunned, and for a moment I wondered whether he could see at night like a cat. Yet I heeded his instruction; the calmness with which it was delivered helped to dampen my outrage. I slept for what was left of the night, so deeply that I slumbered through the rumble of Manglana and his men riding into the town during the early hours of the day. The Croat kicked me awake, and I shielded my eyes from the sun as Ramos bellowed at us to regroup and move as one. Once more the pikes were raised against the cart, and the hedgehog formation was repeated again and again. The sergeant ordered us to perform this exercise until men could barely stand, leaving him to throw punches at them in a fury which eclipsed that of my worst drill officers in the burning garrisons of Italy and North Africa.

After five days of this training, we found ourselves at the end of our strength. On the fifth day, we had barely managed to return to our tents for the night when I saw two scores of mounted freemen following the chieftain through the town. As they emerged onto the green, Manglana and Cathal called a halt, then wheeled their own mounts towards us. They wore the hard stares of men riding into battle, and my presence was ignored as they reined their steeds in alongside Ramos.

'*Na Múrtha* awaits us in the rugged mountains,' said Manglana, 'for the Bourkes have flown into rebellion, and turned the enemy's head westwards once more. We must seize this chance to strike. We shall meet again a few days hence.'

Ramos saluted the chieftain, and Cathal surprised us all by speaking in a thin voice that seemed to rise out of the black fringe across his face.

'I would speak with your marksman, Sergeant,' he said, gesturing towards me and leading his horse away at a gentle canter.

At Ramos' stern look I warily made after the tanist, for I had not spoken to him in over two months. When we were a few feet away from the others, he slid off his horse and wiped the hair from his face, his ruined features only adding to the ferocity of his stare.

'Since you fell out of favour, grey wolf, I have had to intercede on your behalf many times.'

I knelt and then bowed deeply before him, fearful of where our discussion might lead.

'My thanks, sire. I deeply regret the distress that I caused you.'

When my head was raised once more, the tanist beheld me with an expression that was at once pained and outraged. He made as if to speak, checked himself and then spoke again after a few moments.

'My betrothed has agreed to guide your militia south. You must watch your step going forward, for I can no longer protect you. I know that you were staring at her throughout the festival at Duncarbery. If you do so again, there are many who would put a handspan of steel through your heart for the dishonour you have cast upon her.'

'I promise to heed your warning, my lord.'

'You would do well to do so. For you shall receive none further.'

I breathed a long sigh of relief when he rode back to his master, and I only stirred from my knees when the chieftain's mounted force had vanished beyond the trees along the bog. Training was resumed the following day, and the recruits fired until they could barely stand. Ramos yelled at them to resist the kick of the rifle.

'Your shoulders shall turn black as night. You shall load, prime and fire again.'

His words served to secure their obedience, and he later provided the pikemen with longbows and crossbows. The next morning the men's mettle was tested when Ramos got them to load up with Dario's cavalry riding towards them once more. His cries were deafening as the freemen galloped past our militia.

'Do not fear the horsemen! They are but highborn popinjays with silver spoons up their asses! You are made of harder stuff, yet their horses succumb to shot! Strike the horse if you cannot hit the rider.'

Despite being raw recruits, the natives had started to demonstrate the steadiness of veterans. Their quick learning lent briskness to the sergeant's step, and a crooked grin was soon embossed on his face. In an alien land the sergeant and I forced our lifetimes of experience onto his fresh-faced charges.

'Roar like a lion. Do not yell like a thieving wolf!' cried Ramos. 'You shall stand and face the enemy from here on, not squeal and turn tail!'

One of our charges laughed, so Ramos seized him by the throat and shook him hard.

'You must roar like the *tercios* of holy Spain!'

The whole column took up his lead again and again, and my ears rang until the sergeant was finally appeased. Later that night, I was roused by chatter outside the tent. I stirred to see Ramos addressed by a boy, and the sergeant's brow was furrowed in concentration. From the lad's knobbly knees and red spots I recognised the horseboy I had last seen at Boyle, but whether it was Pilip or Pirib I still could not tell. The burly sergeant clapped his hands at the sight of my face peering through the tent flaps.

'Rally the men, Abelito. We march south at dusk!'

'Are we not meant to meet with the chieftain?'

Ramos tutted sharply. 'Not yet.'

XLIII

ROSCLOGHER TO DOAGH MOUNTAIN, DARTRY, COUNTY LEITRIM

31 July – 2 August 1589

It must have been almost four years since the day I had deserted the Spanish army at Willebroek. I found myself marching once more in the company of the sergeant who had caused me to flee Flanders in the first place, after I had discovered the corpse of my wife, Elsien van der Molen. Ramos was in good spirits as he led us out of Manglana's town. He could not help humming an old ditty to himself as I marched side by side with him, beating a path into the setting sun.

In the meantime our drummer boy refrained from any taps, since the sergeant had given the express order for us to travel through the night in silence. At his instruction, our weapons had been furled in wool and cloth, so as to prevent the usual clank and scrape of armoured men on the march. In this way

233

we quietly made our way through the ring of bog and beyond without either sound or incident, and as night descended all that could be heard was the odd snap of a twig and the distant howl of wolves.

Dario and his riders followed behind us, leading their mounts on foot as we made our way towards the darkening outline of the mountains which lay to the south. Our path chiefly consisted of rugged and uneven ground, so that the odd muffled curse was soon heard from the men behind us, mostly from former Spanish sailors who had no experience of the nightly sally and skirmish.

'At least we shall not face any cannon,' muttered Ramos in the darkness, as he also struggled to keep his footing, 'for it is nigh on impossible to wheel anything around here.'

My own thoughts were chiefly focused on keeping my own footing along our gloomy path, and on my last sighting of Muireann. The ollave and a score of her loyal kerns had departed from Manglana's town an hour before us, as they had been assigned scouting duties. One of her men had tarried to guide us through the hidden passes which were only known to a few shepherds, Muireann and her closest retainers.

Eventually the evenness of the path increased, so that we were able to swiftly cover the miles which lay before us. Our march took us past the village of Rossinver and its high, narrow church with ivy-covered windows. We passed through the domains of O'Hart and other chieftains, covering forty miles in less than two nights. None save a few herdsman were encountered along the way until we were reunited with the ollave who led us through the shale and sandstone above Lough Allen. In the twilight the hills soon turned into the Iron Mountains, and when the spud of Doagh Hill was traversed, we passed the peak of the spout, which was the southernmost tip of the kingdom of Dartry.

Once past this great rise we crept left along the banks of a huge lake, then scaled a rise for almost an hour, our feet slipping in the mud and our blades ever ready to be drawn at the first sound of a wolf. Just when it seemed that we would tramp through the stunted trees and bushes on its summit, Ramos called a halt.

'We shall spend the night here. It affords me a fine view of the plain.'

Our company broke up into smaller groups of men, with the sergeant beckoning a few subalterns to his side and ordering them not to let their charges stray from the summit without his permission.

'Upon pain of death,' he warned them, 'which you shall also suffer if your men do not heed my command.'

After being served with this warning, the men clung to our hideout like kittens to their mother, and we rolled the blankets out of our knapsacks and stretched across the ground to rest. After having covered forty miles across a difficult terrain, I drifted off into a dreamless sleep the moment my eyes were closed. Hours later I blinked at the light of the setting sun, then slowly rose to my feet and stepped towards the bushes to relieve myself.

I noticed the shimmering Lough Allen, with the great river Shannon running out of it and through the grassland of the plain below us, then striking towards the distant woods. As I turned back to where the men were gathered, I saw Muireann on the other side of the summit, rolling up her blankets and talking to her guard of kerns. No sooner had I spotted her than a large hand wrapped itself around my shoulder and turned me around. Dario served me with a hard stare as a vein throbbed in the middle of his temple.

'Do not even think of approaching her. She was assigned to us on the condition that you be kept well away from her.'

'But the thought had not even crossed my mind,' I lied.

'Good,' said a familiar voice, as Ramos stepped out from behind the tall Croat, 'for your attentions shall be required elsewhere.'

'Where?'

The sergeant and the Croat traded glances before Ramos jerked his head towards the edge of our camp. A low fire had been started by some of the pikemen, but they instantly drew away from it at Ramos' approach. Dario minded the flames, and the sergeant invited me to sit alongside them while he pulled out a blanket and drew it tightly about his shoulders.

We traded some idle talk for a few minutes, in which Ramos feigned interest in my well-being and sought my views over the progress of his *quadrilla*. Dario was silent throughout, until at last he stood away from the low fire and rested a foot upon a log between me and the chieftain. He laid one hand upon his raised knee and used the other to scratch a rough map in the mud with a stick as Ramos explained the crude design.

'We are expecting a supply train which bears goods from Athlone to Sligo. It shall seek to ford the great river sometime before noon tomorrow.'

I stared at him in utter disbelief.

'And it is led by John Gilson,' he added.

'You must be mad.'

A scar on Ramos' cheek widened when he grinned.

'Oh no, Abelito. I must be Spanish.'

I eyed him warily as my head spun, and I struggled to choose my words with care.

'Last I heard, Gilson led half a troop.'

'Indeed he does!' exclaimed Ramos 'Although like every double-dyed scoundrel of an officer, he pockets the earnings of a score of dead-pays.'

'He still poses a grave danger.'

'Beyond doubt, Abelito, beyond doubt. All must work to plan or else we shall be butchered. But orders are orders, and O'Rourke wants him stopped by any means possible.'

Dario tapped the ground with his stick as I considered the sergeant's words.

'Our men are less than half trained,' I said at last, 'and they form less than half a troop.'

'Who has denied that?' snapped Ramos. 'Yet it shall also make our enemy overconfident. They have not yet seen a square on an open field in Ireland.'

He sat back and tugged thoughtfully at the beard about his chin, then proceeded with his explanation.

'Your caution is warranted, Abelito. English cavalry have prevailed time and again in this land, despite being often hindered by bog and woodland. Yet I have seen it myself that when their leader falls, their resolve often crumbles.'

'You want me to kill Gilson?'

Ramos' one eye widened at my outburst, and then he fixed me with a hard stare. A grin spread across his lips as he spoke again.

'No. We must do everything to take him alive. When his mount's canter turns into a charge, you must break its knee.'

My jaw fell slightly open as I regarded him in disbelief. 'You do not know the difficulty of such a shot.'

His widening grin was more intimidating than it was cheerful.

'I know that it is worth thirty-five *cumhals*.'

The words left me speechless. Ramos winked but once, and his gaze never wavered as he spoke again, his voice possessed of a frigid seriousness.

'If you miss you shall be returned to the creaght.'

An awkward silence followed, in which I nodded. Ramos ordered Dario to summon his five subalterns to the fire, then shared with them some of the details that he had shared with me concerning the following day's operation. Two of his subordinates were Irish and listened with widened eyes and open mouths, being both fascinated and stunned by the audacity of the proposed ambush.

'"Tis a daring plan,' said a silver-haired specimen amongst them in bewilderment, 'for that train will have a strong guard of horse. The garrans and baggage animals shall bear wheat and barley from far-off Limerick and other goods from enemy-held baronies.'

'Yes, that it shall,' said Ramos as he gently drew the edge of his *skene* dagger against his whetstone, 'yet most of their men shall be gaolbirds and beggars who would have been pressed into service in Ireland.'

'That is good tidings indeed,' said the elderly subaltern as he warily watched Ramos' steel scrape against stone.

He seemed about to further question the plan, but he kept his mouth shut when he noticed the sergeant's steely stare.

'Out with it, man,' said Ramos drily as he returned his eyes to the blade. 'You can speak your mind freely, away from the men.'

'Well, Sergeant,' replied the subaltern nervously, 'I was about to say that we shall need every advantage against Gilson, for he is a ruthless man, known to stab mothers through the heart with the length of his sword, often also passing it through the babes in their arms!'

'And he killed Manglana's son, Aengus!' cried a younger Irish officer at his shoulder. His elder countryman served him with a hard elbow in the ribs, looking over his shoulder in concern.

'Keep your voice down, Hugh, you oaf!' he hissed. 'The lady Mac an Bhaird shares our camp, and the pain of Aengus's passing still rankles deep within her.'

'Every advantage shall be afforded to us tomorrow, gentlemen,' said Ramos calmly as he held his knife up before his face and turned it from side to side, inspecting its sharpness in the firelight.

'So you harbour no fears about our endeavour?' ventured the silver-haired man in a low voice.

'Only a fool does not fear battle,' replied Ramos, 'yet I feel that we are well prepared. Now order the men to sleep, for we must be fresh and alert as hawks tomorrow, and with God's help we will clap this Gilson in chains and lead him off to meet his justice before the day is out.'

The subalterns rose to their feet and bowed, then slipped off into the growing darkness. Ramos paid them no heed as he continued to sharpen his dagger.

'What sort of brute kills mothers with babes in their arms?' he asked no one in particular, then held the pommel of his blade between his knees and gently tested its edge with his thumb.

'Surely you are not surprised?' I asked, pushing my luck.

He sighed wearily, then stared across the hilltop to where his men leant their pikes against one another, creating a makeshift frame with branches and mud. Dario took his leave to confer with his horsemen and inspect the condition of his riders' mounts, given the crucial task they were to perform upon the train's appearance. I was left alone with Ramos, and as I rose to one knee to bid him good night, I found the sergeant's hand firmly placed on my shoulder.

'Why retire so early, Abelito? Will you not sup with me?'

My stomach grumbled aloud at his mention of food.

'I must be well rested if my aim is to be true,' I replied, feeling reluctant to share his company for longer than necessary.

'Your aim will be more than sharp tomorrow,' he growled, 'for you were Alba's best rifle! Eat but a morsel before you take your leave of me, for you should not take aim on an empty stomach.'

'Very well then, but I cannot tarry much longer. The target you have set me would challenge better marksmen.'

'Nonsense!' he snorted. 'I have seen you strike heretics from thrice a distance.'

I sat back beside him again with a sigh, for he was not a man to be lightly spurned. Upon reaching the grass we stared at the distant, darkened hills, the constant wolf cries a reminder of our hostile surrounds.

'Damn curs,' grumbled the sergeant as he crossed his leg over the other. 'They'll rob the horses of sleep.'

'It has not been a long march,' I replied, 'albeit a tricky one. The mounts are rested enough.'

Ramos turned towards me and nodded slightly, and in that instant I wondered whether he dreaded the mission which we were to undertake the following day. For a moment I almost pitied him, a crippled old soldier in a war-torn corner of Europe, summoning up the courage to do the unthinkable against a merciless enemy. His master the O'Rourke had not spared much expense to equip the force at my sergeant's disposal, and any failure on Ramos' part would play into the hands of those forces within the tribes which were eternally opposed to change.

'So here we are again,' he declared at last, fiddling with the elbow straps of his tin arm, 'on the brink of yet another scrap with the heretic.'

'Yes,' I replied.

'Who would have thought, Abelito?' he carried on, a slight excitement in his voice. 'That it would be so soon after Willebroek?'

'It has been over four years.'

'Four largely good years,' he mused. 'How I wish I had left Flanders sooner!'

'As do most of us who served there,' I noted drily.

'It wasn't always bad,' he grunted. 'Damn troops went to the dogs when Alba was recalled, and even Parma could not save us. They were whoremongering whoresons, both those two, not to mention Alba's cur Fadrique. Yet they were the best when it came to leading men.'

This lament had been recited to me countless times before, by men of different ranks within the army. As always I nodded in agreement, which Ramos noticed in the scant firelight afforded to us by the low flames at our feet.

'It is ability and not blood that wins wars,' I said.

'Indeed! Indeed!' he bellowed, momentarily forgetting his strict orders of silence as he seized upon my words. 'Those fools in Madrid insisted that all army posts were to go to the nobility! That's when everything fell apart.'

'One can vanquish soldiers,' I whispered, 'but never courtiers.'

'And that is the truth of it, Abelito,' he hissed in a lowered voice. 'It's the common whoresons like us that are the sinews of mother Spain! Men like Verdugo who rose out of the gutter to lead us to glory! Alba knew it, which was why I was made sergeant. But once the commissions of captain were barred to us humble folk, then I knew that I could no longer serve my king.'

'But not before you had collected your fire-tax,' I remarked in a voice terse from the rage that welled up inside me.

For a while Ramos said nothing. Yet when he spoke again, it was in a tone that was deeply regretful.

'Yes. The men wanted to be paid. It had been years since the Crown's debts to them had been honoured. Word of Antwerp's sacking made them restless, mutinous even.'

'And murderous too?'

An awkward cough was heard from the shadows as Ramos attempted to placate me once more. He should not have bothered, for in seeking to appease me he left me feeling both patronised and further resolved to take his life.

'Murdering anyone was not my intention, the Lord be my witness. I did not know that her father was still in the house, and she ran back inside before I could stop her!'

Tears of rage welled up on my eyelids as the dusk grew, and I itched to snatch up my blade and slash his gullet.

'If you had waited but one day,' I whispered to myself as I recalled Elsien's face.

It had been a face fair even in death, yet one which I had for so long taken for granted in life. What kept me from striking out at Ramos was my desperate leaning towards self-preservation, which had kept me alive in Ireland through the most arduous circumstances imaginable. I quietly stewed with rage, yet the sergeant mistook my silence for muted gratitude, and his voice became ever more cheerful as I desperately quelled the urge to strangle him.

'And tomorrow much plunder shall become yours, as we put the heretic to the sword yet again! You should revel in the joy of anticipation, Abelito! Do you not feel a stirring to rescue Spain yet again?'

In that moment there were many things that I felt, last of which was a passion to serve the empire that had spawned the self-serving monster who addressed me. Somehow I managed a low snort, which only encouraged Ramos to rant on.

'Tomorrow we will shower ourselves with glory and gifts, for we have trained hard, and our enemy is cocksure and largely ignorant to my designs. If your aim is true and Gilson is felled, they shall scatter like geese before the kitchen hands as Dario and his men slay them all. And once their goods are ours, the fortunes we shall earn in this land will be as nothing compared to what shall follow. Whoresons beyond count shall flock to our banner from all corners of this cursed land, as the chieftains forget their squabbling long enough to provide us with more horse and munitions. We shall become *condottieri* in this far-flung place, warlords who will render the kerns and gallowglasses but a distant memory as we install a new high king of Ireland at Tara: one crowned of powder and steel, who shall swear fealty to Madrid! With our puppet king installed, we shall next take the fight to England, Flanders and every other heretical princedom beyond, and the very Huguenots in France shall tremble at our advance.'

Once he had commenced in this vein I knew that Ramos would rumble on and on in his usual manner, and although I could not see him, I knew that he would be glaring at thin air and gesticulating wildly to himself. Words about the tithes and riches which would fall our way sprang from his mouth until it was hard for me to even feign any interest. My eyes began to shut, and the snoring of some of the men reached my ears. I was roused nearly an hour later with an elbow to the ribs, only to find my sergeant sitting alongside me on the grass with the flames all but extinguished.

'And you, Abelito?' he gasped excitedly. 'What shall you do with our newfound wealth? Will you still depart for the Indies? You mentioned it a few times in the Low Countries.'

'That depends,' I croaked, as I struggled to keep my eyes open.

'On what?' he asked in curious bafflement.

'On whether I kill you first.'

He let go of me as I rolled over onto my belly, and a low chuckle left his lips, for Ramos had always been one to admire audacity. Then he leant over and whispered into my ear.

'You will never get close, Abelito. We have shared too much together. Nor shall you ever leave my side again. Ireland will be your Indies, for you can scarce imagine the horrors that await you across the ocean.'

A flicker of curiosity was sparked by his words, though it was swiftly extinguished by the onrushing tide of weariness which plunged me into slumber. I was woken by the great shuffling of feet the following morning, amid snatches of fevered chatter.

'It had better not rain today, Abelito.'

Ramos was standing right behind me as he glared at the dark skies overhead. Dario could be seen running towards us, his helmet held in hand and gasping for breath.

'They are here?' I asked.

'Yes,' said Ramos, and the Croat and I stepped alongside him and looked out towards the plain below us. Dario pointed towards the edge of a large copse, where we could make out the tiny outline of a supply train which advanced slowly in our direction. More of our men gathered about us as the small shape resembling a black caterpillar grew in size; we could make out over a score of garrans laden with panniers, shouldered by twice the number of armed horse.

'A bountiful stream of pack animals,' remarked my sergeant at last, 'which would add up to fair few carts on the muster roll.'

Dario held his chin as he studied the distant sight. 'More than forty riders; it is as our spies reported. Should I draw their party towards us?'

'Take only ten riders,' replied Ramos, 'for they should not be scared off. Engage briefly, then withdraw towards the foot of the mountain. Feign fear at their first pistol shot.'

'And the rest of the Breifne horse?'

'They should wait in the copse, then join the final raid on the supply train.'

The Croat barked at his highborn charges to gather their arms while Ramos bellowed at his subalterns to gather their men. In the commotion which ensued I had already fallen onto one knee, checking the various parts of my rifle to ensure that it was still in good working order. I felt a tinge of outrage, as the lowest charge was inspected, at the memory of the ring which had been lost to the enemy. A burning desire for revenge flared up in me as I rose to my feet and fell in alongside Ramos, who glared at the subalterns who were gathered before him.

'Are all of the men accounted for?' he asked.

'Yes,' replied his officers, and I also sighed with relief when this was confirmed, since the greatest threat to an operation of subterfuge was a turncoat or a planted mole.

Our relief turned to resolve as the Breifne riders could be heard urging their mounts down the hillside.

'Fall into a single file,' said Ramos, 'and none dare breathe a word until I release you from silence.'

His order was heeded in full as we seized our weapons and made our way down the mountainside. We clung to grass and scrub to avoid falling over and bit our tongues whenever we brushed past thistles. It was close to a half hour of tricky descent in the direction of the river. The slopes to our back concealed us throughout, until we reached the uneven plain.

'Light your match,' growled the sergeant. Half of Dario's riders made off towards the trees across the plain while the ten still in Dario's company rode with the Croat at a growing gallop in the direction of the baggage train. The men quickly lit the ends of the slow matches coiled about their forearms, and Ramos whirled towards me with quick orders.

'Get yourself among those trees, Abelito,' he snapped. 'Gilson rides a bay steed. He also sports golden locks beneath a bowler hat.'

'I know,' I replied, then ran off towards the end of the slope that shielded us from the enemy's view, intent on climbing one of the shrivelled trees which grew at the foot of the mountainside.

Upon reaching the closest trunk I hauled myself into the branches overhead, clambering upon the second largest branch, which afforded me a clear view of the plain. I was well concealed within the leaves as I slung both rifle and powder flask off my shoulder, then filled the gun's bore and flash pan with powder. My attentions returned to the sea of grass ahead of me, with the supply train quickly reappearing to my left as enemy troopers drifted away from it to meet the charge of our riders.

When I looked to the right, I saw Ramos' newly formed square still concealed by the mountainside, yet I returned my attention to the baggage train at the sound of a pistol shot and a loud cry. I made out Dario and his riders wheeling their mounts around and charging back towards us. A dozen troopers followed them, their pistols and lances jabbing the air as they spurred their steeds after Dario's riders.

I swiftly pulled the Marquart's butt to my shoulder, yet Gilson was nowhere to be seen. He had remained attached to the distant caravan, whose far-off figures I was still unable to make out. As Dario's men thundered past me, both the Croat and his riders could be seen riding low in their saddles, save for one man who had been shot off his hobby.

The enemy troopers were fast closing in on them, with the odd shot still fired from their pistols, as I crouched low behind the branches which concealed me. I resisted a great urge to pick off a heretic as Dario and his nine riders tore about the mountainside, making towards the hidden square of Ramos, who raised his sword at their approach. The enemy horse could not have been forty yards behind our horsemen when my sergeant swiftly took his men through their paces.

'Prime!'

His cries were barely audible above the din of the approaching cavalry, yet the manoeuvres were still as smooth as they had been when we last took to the training field. Powder was poured into flash pans, which were next slammed shut, and muzzles pulled back before being fed powder and ball.

'Shut your pan! Cast off! Blow!'

At his command the muskets were shaken to dislodge loose powder, and men stooped forward to blow it off the bore.

'Open charge! Charge musket! Draw sticks! Shorten stick!'

Ramos' voice rose above the rumble of hooves in the plain ahead of us. A few of his men in the last ranks trembled as Dario's riders drew closer, yet my sergeant maintained a voice so composed that I almost feared that he would run out of time.

'Put in bullet! Ram home! Blow match!'

The musketeers spat their balls down the bores of their rifles, then rammed them down with their ramrods. At their sergeant's command the pikemen also raised their spears, as had been drummed into them so many times before in Dartry. Their spears rose in unison like the bristling spines of a hedgehog, just as Dario and his riders burst past me and wheeled their horses madly around the mountainside. Meanwhile the English troopers at their back gave no sign of summoning a halt, and the armoured horses thundered ever closer as their riders' lances were slowly lowered. Their sound was deafening as they galloped past my hideout, and Ramos' orders were barely heard as he readied to do the unthinkable.

'Cock your match! Try your match! Guard blow and open your pan!'

The men each puffed on the smouldering ends of their slow matches, ensuring the right length was fitted through the jaws of their serpentines. Their movements had been executed to perfection despite the growing din of hooves.

'Present!'

In that instant Dario's riders tore around the foot of the mountain, narrowly charging past the square and causing a few of the muskets at the front left sleeve to wobble upon their stands. I prayed beneath my breath that the square's resolve would hold, for from my perch I had already observed the curved breastplate of our mounted enemies, which could only be punctured from twenty feet. Wafts of smoke swirled away from the square of pikemen that stood to my right, and the troopers commenced their own charge around the foot of the mountain. The square was barely forty feet away from them, and as the first trooper appeared, I feared that my heart might knock a hole through my breast just as Ramos shrieked his final order.

'Fire!'

Riders rose in their saddles as the pikes rose to meet them, and the deafening cracks of gunshot were heard, briefly rendering Ramos' force a greyish cloud of acrid smoke. A shriek of stabbed mounts and cracking wood inevitably followed, rising above desperate cries of agony. Then the shadows of skewered steeds could be seen twisting and thrashing about in it as swords rang from our musketeer's scabbards and they set upon the wounded enemies with drawn blades. The blurry figure of a charger kicked the air upon the square's left flank, screeching as it buckled in agony and ground its rider's broken legs beneath its back.

The sound echoed in my ears for a few minutes thereafter, as Dario's riders appeared out of nowhere to finish off the handful of stragglers. My view of the square was still blinded by the billows of fog from the guns, but as it cleared the ground was seen to be littered with the corpses of horses and men. The remaining riders fought like cornered wildcats, with the last of their number about to fire a fatal pistol shot at Dario when an arrow whistled through the air, burying itself through the back of the trooper's neck.

Although I could not make out the bowman, it was obvious to me that only one person in our number would have been capable of such a shot. I felt strangely satisfied by the fact that Muireann and her bodyguards had clambered down from the heights to observe the efforts of Ramos' men. The scrap was hardly ended when the sergeant's voice could be heard again.

'Follow me.'

Each of the men instantly heeded his command, their courage bolstered by the success of the sergeant's ambush.

All knew that a last part of the plan was yet to be played out, which would mean the difference between life and death, not to mention a huge supply of plunder. Not a man had been lost in the fray, save for one of Dario's riders, with all resisting the natural impulse to loot the dead bodies of the heretics which lay at their feet.

Dario galloped off with his nine remaining riders to re-join the rest of his force, which were hidden in the trees, and the kerns and Spaniards under Ramos' command trudged on in their feigned disorderly formation. Pikes were dragged by the trail so as to avoid being noticed, and the musketeers rested their guns upon their shoulders. Ramos' hand was held to his forehead as he shielded his eyes from the blinding sunlight, all the while growling to his men beneath his breath.

'A proper troop now awaits us, men. Let us meet their charge and claim our first victory upon the open field.'

When their cover of mountain was abandoned, my sergeant's infantrymen appeared a pitiful gathering, like almost any other bedraggled band of rash wood kerns trying their luck in the open country. Nothing about their appearance hinted at a highly drilled force, so that they were easily mistaken for a pack of fortunate ambushers. At the sight of them the remaining troopers guarding the baggage train gathered before the pack animals in two orderly banks of over a dozen men each, their petronels cocked in one hand and lances raised in the other.

At the blast of a bugle they broke into a gentle canter, which grew into a swift gallop with each passing yard. The troopers abandoned their formation as they thundered towards Ramos' men, in their eagerness to crush the Irish underfoot as they had done so many times before. The palm of my hand fell against my forehead as I desperately searched for Gilson amongst the fast-advancing riders.

The sergeant's men stopped dead in the midmorning sun as the lances of the enemy fell forward and I desperately sought out the bay horse. For a moment I despaired, but at last the rider in the bowler hat could be seen loudly urging his men on towards what he perceived to be a quick slaughter. At the same time Ramos' voice could be heard, ordering his men into position and filling me with a deep dread. I fumbled desperately with the rifle, fearing that Gilson might call a retreat or a caracole before I had time to shoot.

The powder flasks on the foot soldiers' breasts swayed amid the growing thud of hoofbeats, and the whole square turned sideways to meet the enemy charge. Rifles slid from shoulders, ramrods were quickly drawn, and another dreaded bugle blast issued as Gilson's men charged at us without showing the slightest hesitation. I had already rammed ball and wadding down the Marquart's muzzle, and I gave the spanner a quick quarter turn. While my right eye was trained upon the sights, it took a great effort for me to steady my hand. My aim was fixed upon the mount of the evil lieutenant in the plumed bowler hat, who raced neck and neck in the vanguard with another of his men.

'Blow match!'

Ramos' cry startled me just as my finger fell upon the serpentine, and for a moment I forgot the ensuing kick of the rifle, which almost flung me off the tree. My fingers clutched at a branch overhead as I lost my balance, and I held on for dear life until my footing was regained. With a low curse I searched the plain ahead of me, for fear that my shot had not been true.

A flood of relief loosened my shoulders like a river breaking through an ailing dam, just as Gilson's horse crashed to the ground and Ramos roared his last order. The crackle of gunfire went off as the twelve-foot spears were raised, the doughty pikemen shoving their spear butts upon the ground and planting their feet upon them. As they held the trail of their pikes in their right hands, these spearmen also grasped a higher part of the weapon in their left in preparation for the impending clash. The breath of friend and foe was already tart with fumes as Gilson's men hauled at their reins too late, then plunged into a hedge of sharpened spear ends. A piercing shriek was heard from the mounts.

'Fire!'

Amid the ensuing fusillade, my thoughts were occupied by Gilson's horse, which could already be seen kicking the air a few feet behind the enemy mounts caught on the raised pikes. The air was again filled with grey smoke and dancing horses, with an acrid stench of rotten eggs borne by the wind. Cries resounded around the discharged guns, and bulging haunches and flanks writhed astride the square which bristled with the reddened points of spears. The din lasted long minutes and had barely subsided when the sergeant's bellow rose above the cry of the impaled horses.

'*O'Ruairc Abù!*'

His men took up his cry and drew their blades with murderous intent just as Dario and his riders broke from the cover of trees to cut off any stragglers. Ramos' musketeers instantly broke ranks, falling upon the unhorsed and sinking their blades through throats and armpits. Only three mounted horsemen remained, and each of them succumbed to the spears of the Croat's men.

The fight was already over, with my part in Ramos' scheming having been performed as ordered. So it was with a heavy sigh of relief that the rifle was slung back over my shoulder and I climbed back down the tree. No sooner had I reached the ground below me than I hauled the Marquart off my shoulder once more, for ahead of me a man with a pockmarked face held his hands out before him. His surprise swiftly turned to rage as we recognised each other.

'Lowly horse thief,' he growled.

Gilson spat in my direction as I raised the rifle to my shoulder.

'Drop to your knees, or I'll blow your head off.'

'You wouldn't dare rid yourself of a hostage like me.'

It was both amusing and ironic to hear fluent Spanish spoken so arrogantly by a foreigner, though it was swiftly drowned out by the heavy gallop of an onrushing horseman. A white, flowing beard billowed in the wind above a fleet-footed hobby, its owner raising a leg to Gilson's back and sending the haughty lieutenant sprawling across the long grass.

'Tomás!' I exclaimed as Geraldine careered to a halt a few feet away from our prisoner, then raised his hand in salute as he dismounted.

'Well met, Hospitalarios,' he said as he drew his sword and rested its point upon Gilson's back. Its master addressed the heretic. 'At last you shall meet with justice, you cur.'

The lieutenant slapped the blade away as he whirled towards his captor.

'I should have known never to trust an Anglo-Norman! Just a pack of double-dealing mongrels!'

Old Tom received the insult with a snort and a slight nod.

'You are one to speak of treachery. The blood of the Saxon never ran through your veins.'

I shielded my eyes with my hand and peered into the distance, where Dario's riders could be seen finishing off their sword work as they rode among the pack horses like a deathly gale. Footmen and drivers cowered before them as spears flew through the air and sank into their faces and throats. A whirl of blades glistened in the sunlight as heads were severed from necks, and a scatter of armoured bodies littered the ground like headless beetles.

One of the last Sassenachs could be seen cocking a pistol towards the mounted Gaels, just as Dario rose highest in his stirrups and rent the man's head halfway off his shoulders. Gilson scowled at the sight as we drew closer to the conquered train.

'When the sheriff finds out wha –'

The lieutenant's threat was cut short as Geraldine struck him across the mouth with his sword pommel, and the booty was announced to loud cries of delight. The riders from Breifne O'Rourke cut many pannier straps, and heavy chests collapsed to the ground with loud cracking sounds. Dario's men quickly dismounted to help calm the frightened pack horses, some of whom had already bolted. Ramos' men reached the garrans a few moments later, and they rummaged through the panniers and pulled out all manner of goods. Skins, cheeses and jars of honey were held aloft, as well as priceless spices which included ginger, saffron and pepper. Geraldine held out a fist of Italian gold thread in amazement.

'Its barter would secure the upkeep of an entire army,' he gasped.

Ramos was right in the thick of it all, with Gilson's bowler hat pulled tightly onto his head as he jokingly donned a pearl necklace and blew kisses to his chuckling pikemen, who whistled and catcalled at him. The sergeant mockingly fluttered his eyelids as a kern behind him held up more prizes and cried out to his fellows, 'Sweetmeats!'

The man took a great bite from the white lumps he held up in both hands, then pulled a face and spat out scum. Dario reined his steed in alongside the dunce and snatched up the costly bars of Mediterranean soap.

'That is *not* food!'

Of greater use to us were the stacks of matchlock rifles and the many sacks of powder, not to mention the fool's gold which would have stocked ten times our number. The men were begrimed with smoke and blood as they donned some of the morion helmets, which were also in great supply; others seized satin dresses and bodices, and waved skirts of the farthingale variety in the air. Ramos held one of them out to Muireann, who quietly observed us with her men.

'For your guidance in our cause, my lady.'

The ollave scoffed at him, though a red tinge appeared upon her cheeks.

'I shall not don any garb purchased for the sheriff's wenches.'

Her open refusal of plunder caused Ramos to behold her in confusion, and I laughed aloud. As he turned to face me his shoulders also throbbed with mirth and relief, and the laughter of his black-faced soldiers resounded about us.

XLIV

The Iron Mountains to Sligo Town

2 – 4 August 1589

'Over a hundred *varas* of coarse frieze, thirty *arrobas* of honey and twelve of olive oil. There is also a quintal of soap, and seven of wax …'

Ramos' hand rested upon his sword pommel as he paced about the pile of goods as Old Tom recited the inventory which he had compiled. The fray had ended but two hours earlier, yet the rustle of grass could still be heard behind us as our men dragged corpses away and busied themselves with gathering more choice cuttings of horseflesh from the bodies of dead mounts. As more dead troopers were added to the pile, the subalterns carefully rifled through the clothes of each corpse to ensure that all belongings were accounted for.

'Enough fool's gold for ten times our number,' continued Geraldine. 'Half the number of ladles for sifting lead, and as many sieves to sift powder, rollers and snips …'

A smug smile grew across the sergeant's face.

'The Madonna of Ontanar be praised! What plunder!'

'Rollers and snips?' asked Dario, serving me with a look of puzzlement.

'To make birdshot,' I explained, 'and to cut it.'

'Oh,' replied the Croat with a slight nod as he patted the muzzle of a black stallion which nickered at his left shoulder.

It was one of few enemy horses to have survived the morning.

'Beautiful boy,' whispered Dario to it in Italian just as Ramos stooped over the mound of booty and flung something at the Croat. Dario seized it with a lightning swiftness and held up a seat made of two pillow-like humps of leather, with a tightened surcingle between them.

'There are your stirrups,' said Ramos.

'Indeed,' replied Dario as he studied the dangling leather straps with steel loops at their ends. 'These shall be of great aid to our cause.'

So saying he flung the saddle upon the destrier's bared back and climbed onto it. With a kick of his heels he thundered off across the windswept plain, and Ramos paused from his pacing as we watched the Croat making off like a gull across a green ocean.

'He is not the friendliest of sorts,' remarked the sergeant at last, 'but by God does he make a fine horseman!'

'. . . in them we also found sides of salt beef,' droned on Geraldine, who had never refrained from announcing the inventory, 'as well as rings of horseshoes, nails, lamp oil, boot leather, linen –'

He stopped at the sight of Ramos' raised hand.

'That will do, Don Tomás. It appears that we have everything under the sun.'

Old Tom's face was flushed with astonishment.

'Do you not want to hear of the cloves and calicoes? There's also a quantity of silver and silks, not to mention a surprising amount of vinegar.'

For once Ramos appeared dumbstruck by this revelation, and his lips twitched slightly without producing any sound.

'How much does it amount to, our plunder?'

'At least a hundred ducats, by my reckoning. Which does not include the horses and all we have claimed from the dead, or the prisoner's ransom . . .'

The sergeant was again lost for words, yet he recovered quickly as he relayed his last order to Geraldine.

'Gather the listed goods and anything else you might need. Assume my command of the subalterns until it is done. None of the spoils are to be touched or shared by the men until our return to Dartry.'

He turned and glared at the rippling of grass around us.

'I do not trust this place,' he growled. 'We must get out of here quickly.'

So saying, he stamped away from the sizeable mound of goods which had been gathered, leaving his men to their grisly work after beckoning to me to follow him. We wandered a few paces away and were well beyond earshot when he finally turned to speak with me.

'Everything went to plan,' he growled with a twinkle in his one eye. 'Everything.'

'It did,' I conceded, 'and none of us believed in you.'

'Harrumph!' he snorted, as if batting away the usual annoying fly. 'This is but a small prelude to the glory that awaits us.'

He then surprised me by drawing a pistol from inside his cloak, which he handed to me with a quick look over his shoulder.

'What is that?' I asked, taking the gun.

'A prize for your efforts.' He grinned. 'To mark our renewed alliance forged in blood and triumph.'

'A debtor is hardly a willing ally,' I protested, handing the weapon back to him.

'Take it,' he growled, raising his hand in refusal and taking a step away from me, 'and tell me what you think of the weapon.'

'Why? Did you pilfer one for yourself too?'

His lips were pursed as he avoided my stare, leaving me to chuckle and shake my head in disbelief.

'But you disregarded your own express order!'

Any small portion of shame that he felt was swiftly abandoned as he served me with a hideous glare, rasping a low warning as he bristled with fury.

'And have a mind not to serve lessons in leadership to me! Do what you like with my gifts, but do not mock your protector!'

At the sight of such virulent rage I swiftly returned my attentions to the pistol, finding myself genuinely impressed by the sights which were fitted onto it, as well as the cannon turns which decorated its muzzle and which ran from a barrel that was finished in black. The signature on the handle was unknown to me, yet its craftsmanship was nonetheless impressive.

'Well?' asked Ramos.

'I do not recognise its maker, so it must be English or Scottish. Probably Scottish, since it is a flintlock. They are accurate weapons, whose reputation has reached the Continent.'

'I am not acquainted with flintlocks,' said the sergeant with a disappointed frown. 'Are they any good?'

'The best,' was my reply, as I twisted the weapon about admiringly in my hand, 'yet you should not hold them too close to your face, or they might blow some powder into it.'

Ramos turned suddenly gleeful at my estimation of his gift and proceeded to unsling the bag on his shoulder, which he also held out to me.

'There's also this.'

Thinking it best not to refuse him again, I took the sack with a small nod of gratitude; it issued a jingle as it was passed to me. Upon opening it I was surprised to find three barrel cleaners and wad pullers inside. Ramos noted my surprise with a devilish smile.

'There's also a few hands of the finest silk at the bottom, which I cut from a dress which was damaged in the scrap. Of the kind that you always liked, which you said improves the aim when used as wadding.'

His recollection of my habits in Flanders left me impressed, and for a moment I was taken aback by the great esteem in which he held my deathly craft. We spent at least another hour together, in which I showed him how to load and clean his own pistol; a couple of shots were fired from the newly acquired guns before we stowed them away in our vestments. As we walked back to the men, Dario could be seen charging towards us at full pelt.

'Don Tomás has had all of the spoils gathered and packed. The militia is ready to depart at your order.'

It was a largely silent force that marched back into the hills from which we had descended. The sun was brightly obscured by cloud, so that our ascent was not plagued by its heat. To a man we felt weary from battle and were still dumbfounded by what we had achieved, so that the struggle of the uphill climb was quieter than usual. Dario and his riders also marched on foot, since few of the horses could be spared for riding, with every last charger being used to bear the many spoils and trophies which we had claimed from the field.

None were spared the burden of plunder, with Ramos himself insisting that he bear a fair few of the stolen goods. I had my own pounds of horseflesh to carry upon my back, and I endured this added weight with a soldier's silent gratitude at having survived such a vicious fight with only one casualty and with so much reward. Ahead of me the sergeant was flanked by Dario and Muireann, with her guards and Geraldine following closely upon their heels.

I noticed the darkened faces of Dal Verme and the Canarians behind me; they appeared to be in good health when one considered that they had withstood two cavalry charges. A few steps behind them, with his face as red as dulse, glowered John Gilson. The lieutenant had been tightly gagged so that he could only breathe through his nose, and his bound wrists had been hitched to the saddle of a pack animal. A broad, swarthy Dartryman simply known as Duf shadowed Gilson's every step, serving our captive royalist with hefty kicks in the buttocks whenever the prisoner showed signs of faltering or of struggling against his bonds.

Despite our general silence, our ascent of the heights was full of the clank of weapons and armour which had been taken from the slain heretics. The constant scrape of a makeshift litter accompanied our movement, since it bore the corpse of the rider which we had borne from the plain. After we had crested the top of our hideout, Ramos paused long enough to despatch the ollave and her kerns ahead of us, so that they might scout the enemy-held territory which he intended to traverse. Geraldine gasped heavily for breath as he cast his eye at the men behind us.

'These days even the lowborn must wear armour,' he said.

'They earned it,' replied Dario, 'for their spirit and gallantry is unsurpassed. Even the youngest among them showed the brass of a veteran.'

Old Tom slowly nodded his agreement. 'A quality we shall all need in the months ahead.'

Ramos called a march again, which lasted through the night. We reached the Iron Mountains at dawn, and the rising sun was but a muffled glow behind the surrounding peaks as we collapsed onto the rocky ground from weariness. A half hour was afforded to us to regain our breath, after which Ramos ordered us to gather the plunder into one pile and to set up our camp around it. Meanwhile Ramos and I walked over to where Gilson was held.

'And now to inspect the greatest prize of all,' said the sergeant.

Dario and Geraldine were also in our company, but none of us laughed at Ramos' quip as the huge kern guarding the lieutenant kicked the captive to his feet.

'Arise, you filth.'

Gilson stood up slowly and defiantly as he glared at us, as low moans were issued from his throat. At the sergeant's gesture, Duf released the linen strap from Gilson's head, and he instantly issued a spate of outraged curses, most of which were directed at Geraldine.

'Bloody Anglo-Norman mongrels! Never know which side they're on!'

Old Tom snatched Gilson by the collar and flung him back upon the grass. The old man's sword rang from its scabbard, and he rested its point upon the gasping lieutenant's throat. Our captive whined in pain as the Anglo-Norman started to lean forward on his blade.

'You are more Irish than I am, Gilson,' whispered Old Tom, 'so curb your forked tongue until you are spoken to.'

Ramos noted Geraldine's words with interest.

'Tell me something, Don Tomás. Are all of the sheriff's officers Irish renegades?'

Old Tom's attentions never strayed from our captive as he replied to the sergeant beneath his breath.

'The English queen has ordered that no more than six Irish natives form part of a royal troop, but the Binghams ignore all senior orders, given that they are a law unto themselves in Connacht. Most English soldiers want to fight on the Continent, since the plunder there is more plentiful and valuable, so the Sassenachs we get here are rogues and gaolbirds. Yet the Binghams often take their arms and disband them, preferring to recruit Irish turncoats instead.'

Ramos shook his head as he took in this explanation, his sweat-streaked countenance appearing more curious.

'Does it take much to turn them?'

'Hardly. Many natives have long-held grievances against the chieftains, and the English crown affords them the best conditions and payment of two shillings a week. Yet they moan and whinge for more all the time, doing as they please and taking whores whenever they want, even though their heretic masters forbid this.'

At these words Gilson jerked his head at us.

'You are one to talk! I see that you keep whores of your own!'

We turned in surprise to find the ollave behind us, having just returned from her scouting duties with her kerns. Her face was already flushed from her exertions, yet instantly turned violet when she heard the lieutenant's slur. Dario swiftly stepped forward and snatched her wrist, since her dagger was already drawn and she was about to pounce upon our prisoner. At the sight of their mistress being manhandled by a foreigner, the ollave's bodyguards drew blades of their own, and things might have taken a bad turn for the Croat had Geraldine not thrown himself before the furious kerns with pleas for calm.

Gilson cackled aloud at the discord he had caused among his enemies. Dario winced as he held Muireann at bay, while she screamed at the grinning lieutenant.

'How dare you refer to me thus? Your gun killed my husband, a man far above outlaws such as yourself!'

'Be silent, you whore!' snarled Gilson, just as the toe of Ramos' boot crashed into his jaw and almost knocked him senseless.

When both the ollave and her guards were finally calmed, the Croat released Muireann from his grip. She was as surprised as the rest of us when Gilson dared to speak again.

'You call me an outlaw,' he rasped, blood pouring from his lip, 'but that man stole my horse!'

At his accusation, I recalled the defiant face of our captive the previous year, when I witnessed the death of Manglana's son and rescued the ollave. I also remembered our treatment at the lieutenant's hands as my fellow Spaniards and I were led to Sligo Town in halters like chattel. I smirked back at him while Ramos sighed.

'A prisoner of war cannot accuse his captors of stealing. And an ollave must be accorded far greater respect.'

'The titles of doomed tribes mean nothing to me!'

'When we lead you back to her doomed tribe, you may find that you are wrong to think that.'

Gilson struggled onto one knee and scowled at the sergeant.

'What does it matter what I think or say? I am finished.'

'That much is beyond doubt!' snapped Muireann, but Ramos whirled upon her with a forefinger held to his lips, which secured her silence as he turned back to the prisoner.

'Pain need not be prolonged if you tell us all you know of the enemy's designs. For you are a prisoner of my master, the O'Rourke. He has accorded me the right to bargain with any of my captives, regardless of any of their previous heinous crimes.'

The ollave bristled with indignation at these words, and appeared barely able to speak as Old Tom piped up on her behalf.

'And what of the lady Mac an Bhaird's justice?'

Ramos waved his words away with a quick look of irritation, then returned his attentions to Gilson, who beheld the sergeant with a glimmer of hope in his face.

'Don Tomás here has told me that you know of a special cargo. One held by George Bingham, the sheriff of Sligo.'

A crafty smile appeared on the captured lieutenant's lips at the sudden realisation of his importance to the chieftains' strategy.

'Are you the leader of this force?' he asked Ramos.

'That I am. Why do you ask?'

'Then listen to my advice and heed it well. Gather your men and turn tail for Ulster. Once you reach Derry, use me as a hostage to secure a boat to Scotland, where you can cut my bonds in return for this advice. Playing at soldiers may have worked for you once, but if you ignore me then I assure you that you shall not see out the summer.'

Ramos turned to stare at us in disbelief, then punched the kneeling Gilson in the head so that the captive fell back onto the grass once more. The sergeant proceeded to rest his foot upon Gilson's shoulder, shoving his weight upon the squirming wretch as he spoke.

'My playing at soldiers is just the beginning, Lieutenant. My master has fourteen Spaniards training his wood kern. Your side's days of dominance upon the open field are numbered.'

Gilson issued a burst of mocking laughter which chilled us to the bone.

'Fool! The Binghams know of your plans the moment you make them! You will all be put to the sword!'

Ramos appeared frustrated by his prisoner's insolence, but Gilson stared back at him with piteous scorn. Then the sergeant pounced upon the captured renegade. I feared that he might mortally injure the lieutenant, yet before we could act, Ramos returned to his feet, shoving the prisoner aside after pulling a scroll out of Gilson's jerkin. Its seal caught my eye as Ramos held it up towards us, and Old Tom was the first in our number to recognise it.

'The seal of the governor of Connacht, Richard Bingham!'

Our sergeant nodded back at him, then broke the seal and unfurled the vellum pages. He frowned at the writing on them for a few moments before tossing them at Geraldine.

'Read it, Don Tomás, for I do not know English.'

'Let us hope they are not ciphers,' said Dario with a frown.

'I doubt it,' said the Anglo-Norman as he held the vellum close to his eyes, 'for our enemy is so arrogant that he scarce bothers to code these messages unless he is plotting against his superiors.'

Ramos stroked back his moustache while he listened intently to Geraldine's translation of the message.

'The viceroy is bent on securing our disrepute and destruction, yet he is restrained in his hostility towards us by the lack of a savage witness who can openly back the claims of the rebels in the court at Dublin. This state of affairs must endure at all costs, so that our allies in London may argue in our favour, so as to bring the trial to an end before the New Year. Gilson did well to capture this kinswoman of the O'Malley. Yet you, brother, must snuff out her life at once, upon learning who set her on her foolish quest to bear witness against us. You should also reward this lieutenant Gilson for sharing his knowledge about the viceroy's intentions . . .'

A sly grin appeared on Ramos' face as he raised a hand to Geraldine, who refrained from his reading. The sergeant then addressed the renegade.

'Pitting the viceroy against the Binghams, Lieutenant? It sounds to me like you are deep into a dangerous game. What would become of you, I wonder, if we were to send you to Dublin with this letter?'

Gilson seemed lost for words as his face paled.

'You've lost some colour,' said Ramos. 'Why will you not speak?'

'I would not dare to cross the Binghams.'

'Why not?' snapped the sergeant in annoyance. 'It appears that they are finished. The viceroy wants them out of Connacht. Would you dare risk his wrath? I have heard tell that his torturers can leave you alive for weeks before they finish you off.'

Our captive shivered upon hearing this, then spoke up in a low, shaking voice.

'Do you not know who backs them in London? Francis Walsingham is among their supporters.'

'Walsingham?' Ramos frowned, for the name meant nothing to him.

'The English queen's secretary and spymaster,' I said just as Geraldine was about to speak.

Ramos' head turned towards me as his eye narrowed suspiciously.

'And how do you know this, Abelito?'

I awkwardly cleared my throat as the others also turned to face me, and I shared my recollection of the name.

'When I was in Alba's service, I befriended an English agent of the Iron Duke, a certain Doctor John Story. Doctor Story was a Catholic lawyer who fled England after speaking up against his queen. Alba had him search English ships for Protestant literature.'

A lengthy pause followed my memory of the aged, kindly man, who was another friend I had lost to the enemies of Spain.

'One day he vanished, and they said that one of Walsingham's agents had overpowered him and spirited him back to England by sea.'

'What became of him?' asked Ramos.

'Alba later learned that Walsingham had the doctor tried for high treason. He was hung, drawn and quartered . . .'

A deep sorrow choked me up as I said this, and the eyes of my listeners widened in horror as even Dario shifted awkwardly from one foot to the other.

'Walsingham's spies are everywhere,' added Gilson in a serious tone. 'Many say he knows of things before they happen. You do not know the influence he has on the English queen. He is also a great backer of the Bingham brothers, who are in league with him.'

For a while none of us spoke. Then Ramos shrugged.

'Well,' he said, 'it remains to be seen if this Walsingham remembers his Bingham friends now that they have incurred Dublin's displeasure. The viceroy has not refrained from bringing proceedings against them, and Richard Bingham sounds desperate enough to me. In any event, both Dublin and the Binghams want all Spaniards dead, and we have little choice but to stick with the chieftains and the roll of the dice. So, what will it be, Gilson? Reveal our enemies' plans to us, or incur the viceroy's displeasure? Be warned that the chieftains have many agents of their own within the Pale who would gladly surrender you to FitzWilliam on their behalf.'

Our prisoner's face was entirely drained of colour as the choice was put to him again, and he was already shaking violently as he held his face in his hands.

'Well?' asked the sergeant sharply.

'I know not who I fear more,' wailed our captive, 'the viceroy or Walsingham!'

Ramos grunted impatiently and nodded at Dario.

'I understand,' he replied with forced empathy. 'Dario here will help you to reach a decision.'

Gilson's jaw dropped as the tall Croat stepped forward and seized him by the shoulder, with Dario's step never wavering as he trudged off with our hostage dragged behind him.

'You cannot do this!' shrieked Gilson at last. 'I am an officer of the Crown!'

'And how many Spanish officers did you spare, Lieutenant?' replied Ramos.

'The prisoner had best be gagged,' observed Geraldine. 'Otherwise they'll hear his cries from the coast.'

'True,' replied Ramos, stooping over to pick up the linen gag and handing it to Duf. 'Be a good lad and give this to Dario.'

As the kern hurried after Dario and the prisoner, Ramos invited us to be seated and ordered two kerns to fetch us some breakfast. In my embarrassment at finding myself in the ollave's company, I asked to take my leave.

'Where are you going?' asked Ramos with a dark stare.

I quietly nodded in the direction of the ollave, who sat between him and the Geraldine. Her bodyguards were seated behind her, where they glared at me suspiciously.

'I thought I –'

'Be seated,' snapped Ramos, 'and don't think! I personally guarantee everyone's safety in this militia, and you'll do precisely as I command.'

Muireann shifted uncomfortably in her seat as I returned to mine and said nothing as meagre servings of horseflesh and cheese were brought to us on wooden plates. For a while thereafter we wolfed down the food in grateful silence, scarcely noticing the distant sounds of fist striking flesh. We had barely finished our meal when we saw Dario walking back towards us, dragging the battered Gilson by the collar as the lieutenant lay upon his back in a lifeless heap.

'That was swift,' remarked Ramos without ever looking up. 'Are you losing your cruel streak?'

'Hardly,' snorted Dario as he let go of Gilson and sat alongside me, eyeing the food and plates before us. 'I hope you've left some for me.'

'Why, of course, my good Croat,' exclaimed Ramos with exaggerated offence. 'What sort of barbarians do you take us for?'

Dario ignored the sergeant's mockery as he snatched the remaining platter of meat, and I looked over towards Gilson, who still lay motionless. The lieutenant's swollen eyes and cheeks were violet. His nose bent unnaturally to the left, and the linen strap in his bloodied mouth was almost twice its previous size and of a bright red hue. He appeared to be missing some clumps of hair on his head, and the holes in his torn clothes revealing a number of gashes and bruises.

'I hope he's not dumbstruck,' I said.

'I was not gentle,' said Dario between mouthfuls.

Ramos grunted as he gestured to a passing soldier to carry away our empty plates.

'It will take more than a hiding to get that insolent tosspot to shut up.'

In that instant the ollave quietly rose to her feet, and before anyone could stop her, she walked over to the captive and spat on him.

'He is stirring,' she observed.

Dario appeared alarmed and was about to return to his feet, only to be stopped by Ramos, who placed a firm hand over the Croat's shoulder.

'That should suffice for now. Perhaps he has already made up his mind.'

'But I've hardly started on him,' protested Dario feebly, only for Ramos to insist.

We left Dario to his meal and stood around the prisoner. Gilson groaned aloud when Geraldine undid the cloth about his face, and when he spoke I could see that a few of his teeth had already been swallowed. His eyes were so swollen that they were piteous to behold, and the captive squinted sideways when he addressed Ramos.

'I shall answer all that you would have me tell you,' he croaked, 'yet I pray that you ask it loudly, for my ears are still ringing.'

The sergeant feigned sympathy as he nodded once and leant towards the lieutenant. Then he cupped a hand over his mouth and screamed in the prisoner's ear so loudly that Gilson squealed in shock.

'Start with the witness!'

'Ah, the one in the letter I take it. A brave woman, yes, and a foolish one too. You know that the viceroy in Dublin has little love for his servants the Binghams. His hate for them has only grown since the Armada landings, although none are certain why. People say it is because . . . but I digress.'

'What do people say?' cut in Ramos sternly.

I could have sworn that the sergeant's eye flickered towards me as I swallowed uneasily and shifted uncomfortably from one foot to the next.

'People say the Binghams have something of great value that he believes to be his.'

'What thing?'

'Who can say for certain?' answered the lieutenant. 'Some claim that it is silver from the Indies while others say that it is a trinket they intend to ransom.'

'Go on. And pray, leave nothing out.'

'"Tis no secret that the viceroy is going to great lengths to dishonour and rid Ireland of his own queen's servants. He has received books of outrages from the rebels and has summoned a trial in Dublin. Yet there is but one thing he lacks to finally be free of them. One simple thing and yet all too elusive.'

'A witness,' said Ramos, 'but that is not news to us.'

'Yes, a witness,' said Gilson, 'for although the Binghams are under attack by their own master in Dublin, many natives still fear them.'

'Except for a certain someone?' said Ramos, with an edge in his voice that warned of his impatience.

'Yes, one,' replied Gilson swiftly, for he had also noticed the sergeant's displeasure, 'a kinswoman of the famous Irish pirate queen Grace O'Malley, who is also related to the Blind Abbot – he whose false claim is strongly backed by her kin.'

'The Blind Abbot's claim to the MacWilliamship is not false!' roared Geraldine.

Gilson lowered his head and trembled slightly.

'Very well, Geraldine,' he stuttered. 'Be that as it may, this woman . . .'

'What is her name, serpent?' snapped Muireann angrily.

'Riona O'Malley, my lady,' said Gilson, suddenly remembering his manners, 'and also a worthy pirate from what I understand. Brave enough to sail into seas unknown, just as she tried to venture into grave matters beyond her borders. The foolish girl's family had met with foul fortunes, and she is a widow herself with young mouths to feed. So she declared to her lord that she would risk the wrath of the Binghams and travel to Dublin to bear witness against them. She would support the charges brought by the viceroy so that London should recall them.'

'And what happened next?'

The lieutenant shuddered at the anger in Ramos' voice, and it was just as well that he did not notice the tall figure of Dario stepping towards us, wiping his mouth against the sleeve of his lengthy forearm.

'Her lord sent a force of horsemen and gallowglass to accompany her north to the lands of the O'Rourkes, yet her party was routed by one of our sergeants, Treasach Burke, who ambushed them at a ford and killed all but the witness and two of her cousins.'

'And where are they now?' shouted Geraldine.

'In Sligo Town, where she is held by Burke.'

'Is Sheriff George Bingham not also there?' asked Ramos.

'Not until next week, when I was told to expect him.'

'So you are saying that the sheriff is not at his main seat in Sligo? If you are lying to us, man ...'

'No, he is not; I swear it! Last I heard he was at Galway, and my orders were to await him in Sligo and deliver the scroll to him in person.'

'Effectively sealing the witness's fate.'

'Yes,' sighed Gilson, 'so it would appear.'

Ramos traded glances with Geraldine, then nudged Gilson's thigh with the point of his boot.

'What of Sheriff Bingham's brother, Richard? What are the plans of the governor of Connacht?'

The lieutenant was interrogated for over an hour, in which he told us everything he knew without omitting a single detail. At the end of it Ramos ordered that Gilson be gagged and taken back to Duf. The new information we had learned scarcely interested me, for all I could think of was Treasach Burke. My blood was boiling and my fists were clenched in rage at the thought of Hurtado's ring, which he had stolen from me.

'The Bingham brothers are abroad,' said Geraldine as Gilson was led off, 'and a small force of men guard the town. A more timely moment shall not soon befall us.'

'The Anglo-Norman speaks truth,' said Muireann, 'but if we are captured we shall be tortured and killed. All of the goods will be lost. As well as my justice.'

'Agreed,' said Ramos. 'To even discuss this is sheer folly. I'll not risk the lives of my master's men so needlessly.'

'With all due respect, Sergeant, 'tis hardly a needless cause,' growled Old Tom, 'for this witness is the key to ridding Connacht of the Binghams.'

'Is that so, Don Tomás?' snapped Ramos. 'So we just ride to Sligo Town and knock upon the door?'

Geraldine grimaced. 'There must be a way!'

His plea hung awkwardly in the air, but Ramos was quick to insist on his disapproval.

'Far too much risk, Don Tomás. If we lose more men in an attempt to enter the bawn, then our attempts to modernise the tribes' armies will be seriously hindered.'

'Your booty has more than justified the loss of your whole militia,' retorted Geraldine, 'and there is a fair chance that we will not lose any more men. What will the chieftains say to us if they learn that we had the chance to rid this land of the Binghams, only to let it slip from our grasp?'

'Then what do you propose that I do?'

'I know not, yet some attempt should at least be considered.'

As the sergeant and the Anglo-Norman argued, I strove to ignore a slight stirring within me, despite my great fear of capture. There was the remote prospect of securing my revenge on Treasach Burke, yet that would have to be achieved within the same walls in which he had tormented me and marked me with the Spanish spider. My thirst for vengeance was only exceeded by the unlikelier prospect of being reunited with the ring, as I thought of what I would have done with it were I in Treasach Burke's shoes.

The more I thought about it, the more obvious it appeared to me that if Burke had given the ring to his Bingham masters, he would never have killed his own man who had found it in my shoe. Furthermore, news of the trinket's discovery would have also reached Gilson. The more I mused over the options available to the renegade, the likelier it seemed to me that the ring was being kept on Burke's own person. All questions or doubts on the matter were dispelled from my head until at last the only question that remained was whether Hurtado's ring was worth more to me than my own life.

'The importance of the witness's life again!' yelled Ramos. 'Yet we have not the means to free her!'

'That cannot be for you alone to decide!' railed Old Tom as his cheeks turned crimson. 'You have not suffered years of persecution at the Binghams' hands!'

'Very well then!' cried the sergeant, as he turned upon the rest of our party. 'What do you think, Dario?'

'It cannot be done,' shot back the Croat.

'And you, Lady Mac an Bhaird? You who saw sense but a few instants ago, what have you to say on the matter?'

'I have already stated my views,' said the ollave solemnly, 'that we are duty bound to free the witness, yet have not the means to do it. Not without compromising our undertaking, as was ordered by the chieftains.

'There! See, Don Tomás?' said Ramos with a smirk of triumph. He waved towards the rest of us. 'You have heard it from the others! Is your conscience now somewhat relieved?'

'A plan has formed in my mind,' I said.

The others appeared taken aback as they stared at me, and a hopeful half smile flickered upon Geraldine's lips.

'What did you say?' whispered Ramos in disbelief.

'I think your plan was best.'

'My plan?' Old Tom asked.

'That we ride to Sligo Town and knock on the door.'

'Ah,' said Ramos with a low chuckle, 'you are but jesting. Have a heart, Abelito.'

'Many years ago in Flanders,' I continued, ignoring the sergeant, 'one of our supply trains was raided by the enemy. It was undertaken by a daring party far behind our own lines, and it was assumed that they would have fled back to their own territory. Yet instead of doing this they donned the garb of the Spanish soldiers they had slain and feigned to be an imperial force. Having gained the watchword from a captive they entered a nearby hamlet unhindered, then slew all the guards and pillaged it. Not one of their men was lost in the attempt.'

Ramos winced at my telling of the story.

'And pray tell us, Abelito, were you the prize fool standing watch who let an enemy militia enter the hamlet unhindered?'

'I was nowhere close, and it was but two score of horsemen who managed the feat. The town was expecting badly needed supplies, which were borne by the assaulted train. The heretics pretended to be an advance party bearing tidings of the train's approach, and in the town's desperation the gates were opened.'

'Not a bad idea,' muttered Dario. 'If we execute the plan fast enough, we may free the witness before word of Gilson's capture reaches the town.'

Geraldine nodded his agreement with the Croat's words, but Ramos served Dario with a withering glare.

'Surely you are not buying this nonsense too?'

'It would be easier than building a Trojan horse.' The lanky Dalmatian shrugged.

Old Tom laughed aloud as the sergeant rubbed his face in desperation with the palm of his hand.

'If the horsemen from Breifne will join you, then go,' Ramos said. 'Without my blessing, of course, but the choice must be theirs alone. Not a single footman of mine will partake of this madness, for I have already spent far too much time and effort with them on the training ground for me to throw their lives away so cheaply.'

He suddenly raised his forefinger in the air and pointed it at me.

'And that goes for you, too, Abelito. My master has committed far too much towards your stupid fine for me to let you run off and play the tragic hero.'

I was taken aback by his arrogance, although it allowed me to question his authority.

'That is impossible. This venture can only succeed with me.'

'And why is that?'

'Because I was imprisoned in Sligo Town. I am the only man here who has seen what lies behind its walls.'

'Indeed you were. And most fortunate to emerge alive. Would you so readily dismiss *fortuna's* gifts?'

His question was apt, and left me speechless while I pondered what to say by way of reply. Then my eyes fell upon the comely features of Muireann, who stared at me in bewilderment.

'I would risk all,' I lied, 'to help my people.'

Ramos' expression turned from one of annoyance to one of sarcasm as he looked at the ollave.

'Be that as it may,' he finally managed, 'you are not going to Sligo Town, and that is final. *Na Múrtha* will make a purse out of my nut sack if any harm befalls you.'

'I must lend my support to this man's request,' declared Geraldine, 'and personally assure you that any loss incurred by our lord O'Rourke shall be covered by my share of the booty and all other property I own, as well as the not inconsiderable payment owed to me by our lord for the countless services I have rendered him. For I remind you, Sergeant, that I am his aide and trusted advisor, and I can personally assure you that he would want this witness freed at any cost.'

Ramos beheld Old Tom in muted disbelief, then exhaled loudly in resignation.

'Very well, Don Tomás. You shall put every word of what you have just said to me in writing and recite it on oath before the ollave, who shall be my witness. After that you may ride into hell for all I care.'

After the events at daybreak we rested for what remained of the morning, and we were stirred by the guards an hour after noon. After gathering our belongings and booty we marched after the ollave once more, clambering the heather-clad heights of the Iron Mountains, which allowed us to round steep valleys. Our march took us past the deep woods of Bally O'Rourke and towards the mountain of Cill Oiridh. It was flanked by the Rise of the Two Birds, and stood along the southern bank of Lough Gill, where I had first encountered Muireann. I swiftly dispelled the sad thoughts provoked by this memory from my head as we climbed the mountain in the growing darkness. Each step was a struggle because of the heath that was both harsh and slippery. Beyond the lake below us stood the flat-topped promontory of Ben Bulben, and the sight of the distant seaward hill to its left filled me with dread. Old Tom noticed me staring at it.

'Knocknarea, the hill of stripes,' he said, 'which bears the great cairn of Queen Maeve upon its summit.'

'Let us hope it shall not shadow your last resting place,' said Ramos.

It was midafternoon when our last hideout was reached, and we lay low in the scrub and rocks about us as we awaited dinner. I was tired from our long journey on foot, so that I sought my own company alongside a gorse bush. My nostrils were full of the smell of fresh grass instead of the usual stink of sweat and burned fat that lingered about the cooking fires at dusk. I wrapped myself in my mantle as sleep overcame me, and my great fear at my impending return to Sligo Town was swiftly banished by sheer exhaustion.

'Abel.'

As my eyes briefly opened, I wondered if the soft voice had descended from the blue skies above me just as sleep started to claim me once more.

'Abel, wake up.'

The second summons was accompanied by a gentle shake of the shoulder, and I turned to find the ollave kneeling alongside me, with two of her kerns standing a few feet behind her.

'What are you doing here?' I hissed. 'Begone or you shall get me thrashed by the Croat!'

'Calm yourself; the men are asleep. I wanted to speak with you before you depart.'

I frowned as my head fell back onto the ground.

'Whatever it is, be swift,' I said, 'for I am not meant to even look at you.'

'I want you to know, if you must indeed leave for Sligo Town, that I am deeply sorry for all the suffering which befell you. You know that I am but a pawn in a greater game. I had no choice but to enter the handfast.'

I sighed deeply and resisted the temptation to howl abuse at her. In previous days I had come to accept the unjust treatment which had been meted out to me in Dartry, since the handfast between Muireann and the tanist Cathal the Black had been in the tribe's best interests.

'Do not fret, my lady. I have endured far worse.'

Muireann appeared further troubled by my coarse rebuff.

'My choice was the lesser of two evils,' she replied. 'The tribe's safety is of the highest importance.'

'Yes,' I replied, although I sounded slightly bitter, 'Donal MacCabe is a threat to the stability of Dartry, whose people mean nothing to him. I would much rather you were wedded to Cathal the Black.'

'So you bear me no resentment?'

'Does it even matter anymore?'

'It does,' she said with great effort as she wiped her eyes. 'It would be terrible to think that you despised us. You who have done so much for our cause.'

Her sympathy made me feel ill at ease as I thought of how much suffering my hidden ring had inflicted upon her tribesmen. The thought suddenly struck me that if the night's attempt to free the witness would meet with tragedy, then no one might learn of the hidden emerald ring in Burke's keep. For too long had the guilt of the hidden trinket gnawed away at my conscience, and I yearned to confess its discovery to the ollave, that my soul might finally be unburdened.

'In truth I have not furthered anyone's cause, save my own. You have nothing to reproach yourself for, since I deserved the Brehon's punishment and worse. I of all people should more than understand secret motives.'

A small smile appeared on her face at my words.

'Your motives were more than justified, Abel, for you have done all you could to survive and have nothing to berate yourself for. The punishment you endured was wholly unjust.'

'I speak not of survival.'

The piteous smile on her face vanished, and genuine confusion appeared on her handsome features as she struggled to make sense of what I had said.

'What do you mean?'

My throat was thick with shame as I sat up, and it took a few moments for me to collect myself as I readied to share my long-hidden secret.

'Tonight I may lose my life,' I began cautiously.

'Indeed you are mad to even consider riding for Sligo Town. You should stay here where it is safe. Otherwise –'

'Be that as it may,' I cut in, raising my hand for her to let me speak, 'I want you to know that if there is one person in this world that I trust, it is you.'

Her eyes widened at my revelation, and a slight sheen appeared in them again as she fought to control the feelings of relief which welled up in her. The intensity of the moment that passed between us almost made me shudder as she gently placed her hand upon my breast and slowly rested her cheek against mine.

'It lightens the load on my heart to hear that you think so. You know that you may tell me all, Abel de Santiago.'

Somehow my eyes were wrenched away from her as old fires within me were rekindled by our proximity. I felt ravaged by the need I felt for a woman of such great intellect and beauty, and torn by the desire to share the burden of my secret, one which I had guarded jealously for over a year. At length some words were whispered beneath my breath, rasped with great strain as if I were lifting a heavy rock off the ground.

'I am not without guilt. I have threatened all that you hold dear.'

She stared back at me in confusion.

'As did all Spanish castaways that we took in.'

Before I could reply to her, a cry was heard behind us.

'Spaniard! Are you there?'

A heavy crunch of grass followed the call, and the ollave and I beheld one another in fear.

'Begone,' I hissed, 'or you'll get me killed!'

'Do not enter Sligo,' she whispered.

I ignored her warning as I slowly raised my head over the gorse bush and leant forward upon my hands, just as Old Tom nodded at me and gave me a small wave. I turned back with a low groan, but Muireann and her kerns had already vanished. Geraldine chuckled as he raised his scabbard and fell upon his back alongside me, then surprised me by pulling out a wooden pipe.

'Greetings, my old comrade in arms,' he said. 'The sheriff ordered some good leaf. Would you care to share some?'

'Is everyone helping themselves to the booty?'

'No!' he protested cheerily. "Tis but a small treat for two men who have endured impossible company of late. You the cows and me the heretics!'

He giggled to himself at his joke as he struck his tinderbox until the tobacco was lit. I observed him in awe, realising that the Anglo-Norman seemed unperturbed by the dangerous night which lay ahead of us.

'You Spaniards truly are remarkable fighters and have trained our boys splendidly. Did you see how those pikemen held? All Irish natives to a man! Who said that we could not stand in file and fight as they do on the Continent?'

'I did,' I said.

'Or beat the enemy on the open ground!' he continued, ignoring my admission. ''Pon my oath, friend Juan, 'twas truly a wonder to behold! A triumph that might yet change everything!'

His enthusiasm amid puffs of smoke was effusive, and the pipe did much to help quell our fear of what we were to undertake at night. The prospect of entering the lion's den had my shoulders feeling as though they were in the tight grip of a giant, and my stomach felt like a wringed facecloth. It was the memories of my torture at the hands of Burke that still played on my mind, much as I tried to forget them. Geraldine and I went over our plan time and again, examining every possible pitfall as the night set in.

I wondered whether it would be the last time that I would see the stars in the sky, and I berated myself for seeking to seize the scant hope I had left of retrieving the ring. At last Geraldine knocked the dottle from his pipe onto the ground and crushed it with his heel.

'The hour is at hand, Hospitalarios.'

I drew a deep breath and nodded, then rose reluctantly from the grass and walked with the Anglo-Norman to the place where the horses were hitched. Dario had already prepared the mounts, and the riders from Breifne held their stamping steeds by the bridle in solemn silence as they watched our approach. They had already donned the enemy's breastplates and helmets, and in the dimness I figured that they could easily be mistaken for Gilson's advance party. After Old Tom and I donned our armour, Ramos appeared with Muireann to bid us farewell.

'Return with some plunder, if you can get your hands on any,' said the sergeant.

Geraldine lifted his visor. 'We ride to Sligo to reclaim and not to steal. Otherwise we shall destroy all that we can.'

'Yours must be a versed performance, Don Tomás.'

'It will be. March on if we have not returned by dawn.'

'Have no fear of that!'

Old Tom raised his sword and signalled to us to pursue him. As we passed the ollave I nodded at her. She mouthed her last words to me, and in the torchlights I wondered if her face was red from weeping.

'Do not go.'

As we led our horses by the reins past the footmen, I could see Gilson bound hand and foot under the watchful stare of Duf. The lieutenant appeared to be well recovered from his earlier hiding, and he sneered at us openly.

'Ride on to your death, you fools.'

His mockery had scarcely left his lips when Dario walked over and dealt the renegade a heavy cuff around the ear, which instantly felled the wretch to our low laughs and mutters of approval. The camp shrank behind us as we led the mounts downhill, pausing but once to catch our breath until the lower ground was reached. Geraldine spoke once as our horses were mounted and our lamps lit.

'Let us away to Druim-na-scolb.'

The place he mentioned had a grim sound that filled me with further unease, and I struggled to find my courage as I spurred my horse after the Anglo-Norman. Under cover of darkness we galloped across the well-wooded demesne that men called Annaghmore. It was there that Dario and five of his riders wordlessly fell back, making their way to an abandoned barn as had been planned. The remaining ten of us rode on in silence along the edge of the forest, with the light from our lamps guiding us through the night. When the woodland was finally behind us, we burst past small patches of ripened wheat, which were variously fenced with ditches and banks.

Rude stone walls and thorn hedges formed the bounds of the locals' livestock as we approached the dim outline of the stronghold ahead, which was flanked with dark spines. All along the walls there appeared stakes topped by round ends, which I knew to be the heads of slain rebels. My hands slightly trembled upon the reins as we slowed our horses to a canter, and Geraldine spurred his mount ahead of us as we approached the bawn's gatehouse. The creak of bowstrings and the loading of muskets could be heard above us, pierced by a strident voice which ripped through the muffled talk on the ramparts. A terse conversation in English followed, in which Old Tom declared his name to be Dick Whyte and also mentioned the name of John Gilson. Finally the watchword was asked, which Geraldine was swift to provide.

'Ave Gloriana.'

An uncomfortable silence endured thereafter, as to a man we prayed that Gilson had not lied to us under duress. We breathed a low sigh of relief upon hearing the loud creak of the opening gates, and as we made after Old Tom, I whispered to him beneath my breath.

'*Morituri te salutant.*'

The Anglo-Norman ignored me as we passed through at a slow canter, making out the stables and corrals within with puckered eyes. Cattle lowed at our entry while guards carrying out the night's watch huddled together closely as they ate about their fires. We proceeded to dismount from our chargers as a portly officer waddled up to us, surprising us by addressing Geraldine in the vernacular.

'I expect you are tired from your ride.'

The Anglo-Norman exhaled wearily. 'It was indeed a long one!'

'Did you have any bother from the savages?'

Geraldine shrugged. 'The odd scrape with bandits, not much to crow about.'

A laugh was heard from the corpulent soldier, which left me feeling a bit more relieved. As I peered about me, the lamps revealed a handful of men within the bawn, who mainly consisted of guards. Ahead of me two of the riders from Breifne wrinkled their noses.

'What is that smell of vinegar?'

'The sheriff's wench needs cleaned,' said the other, and they both sniggered.

I nudged them both hard in their backs with my fists to keep silent while the officer replied to Geraldine.

'That is most fortunate, for you can rest with your men in the stables and dine with me tomorrow. It is long since we had any guests from beyond the Shannon.'

A shriek from one of the buildings ahead of us had us start in fear, but Geraldine collected himself sufficiently to address the officer again.

'I must speak with the sergeant Treasach Burke.'

'Can it not wait until morning?'

'I fear not. My master insisted that it was urgent.' Old Tom leant towards the frowning officer and spoke in a low voice. 'It concerns the prisoner.'

Our greeter's back stiffened at Geraldine's words. 'Most certainly, follow me.'

Geraldine made after the man's quick steps, then raised his hand to us. At his signal our plan was set in motion as the remaining nine of us fell into three separate groups of three. One group scurried off towards the small arsenal close to the bridge, while another made their way towards the guardhouse at the gate, within which the main force of defenders slumbered.

Meanwhile, two of the highborn O'Rourkes flanked me as we quietly trailed Old Tom's footsteps, then slipped off towards a cow pen alongside the barn where I was sure the cry had come from. Together the three of us slipped under a fence and crouched past the necks and bellies of cattle, slitting the throat of a sleeping cowherd without him ever knowing who had fallen upon him. We silently clambered onto the roof of the large bawn, in whose thatch we cut small peepholes with the ends of our *skene* daggers.

As we peered inside the edifice past the high bales of straw, we could see that the ground was littered with coils of rope and wetted skins, those lengthy drapes used to counter flaming arrows. The figure of a bound woman could also be made out. She was lying across the ground, her cheeks streaked from tears of rage. The hair rose upon the back of my neck when I saw a man standing alongside her, one foot planted upon the woman's throat. Treasach Burke maintained a cocksure pose as he called out to his minions with an upward wave of his hand.

'Higher! Lift them higher!'

In front of him two Irishmen kicked the air as they were each drawn by the neck towards the rafters with their arms tied behind them. Burke returned his attentions to the woman below him.

'All traitors swing in the end, my dear Riona. You should tell me the names of those chieftains before your own soul leaves your body.'

'It is you that should confess!' she spat, even as she gasped for breath.

'Strange you should say that,' he mused. 'I have had it said to me before.'

Ahead of him the men's kicking became even more desperate as Riona recovered her breath and pleaded desperately for their lives. Her pleas for mercy went ignored by the renegade sergeant.

'Higher!'

My eyes were drawn away from the sickening death dance as one of the riders from Breifne leant towards me and hissed in my ear.

'There's only four of the bastards inside! Let's at them!'

'Do not dare; Dario has not yet appeared. Now get up there and make ready.'

The young O'Rourke glared back at me in anger before he climbed onto the roof with his fellow tribesman. Together they drew the bladders filled with pitch which they had stowed away in their tunics, emptying their contents across the thatch. Below us Riona's cry pierced the night as the legs of her kinsmen trembled to a standstill. It was then that a knock was heard on the barn door, and Burke turned towards it in annoyance and gestured to the woman at his feet.

'Cut down those curs and string her up.'

His minions rushed to his bidding as the fat officer strode in with Geraldine behind him. Burke peered curiously at the Anglo-Norman.

'Your name and purpose?'

Old Tom removed his helmet and bowed, and I silently prayed that he would not fly into a rage at the sight of the two dead rebels.

'I am Dick Whyte, and I lead an advance party under John Gilson's command. Even now he approaches with the train in his charge, and has bid me to bear you an urgent message.'

Burke turned his back on Geraldine as he returned his attentions to his captive.

'At last the lieutenant is almost here; we shall make ready for his arrival. The sheriff's wench has been whinging for new comforts since Easter. Do tarry, friend Whyte, for you have arrived in time for a rare spectacle, and we are in exalted company. Your message can wait a few minutes more, in which time I shall be done, for the height of tonight's drama features the torment of a highborn bitch from Mayo.'

Geraldine looked aghast as Burke took a pair of shears from one of his men and flung it upon a burning brazier. I was also shaken by this unexpected turn of events, since we had expected the renegade sergeant to rush to a private venue to hear Gilson's message, where Old Tom would have killed him in private. This would have initiated the second part of our plan, but Burke had shown an unexpected disregard for his superior's order. I secretly wondered if his recently acquired bauble had given him other priorities, as he planned for a life outside of the army.

Riona cursed aloud when the bodies of her dead companions were dragged to the side of the barn. Hers was a piteous state as she swung from her bound wrists, her swollen belly adding to her suffering as she was hauled off her feet towards the rafters. Burke limped up to her and placed a scarred hand upon her stomach, leaving her to flinch and swing helplessly from side to side.

'The little savage inside you dances in agitation,' he crooned. 'Why not spare it needless torment?'

'Burn in hell, cur!' was the O'Malley witness's reply.

Burke stood away with a hand over his mouth, feigning offence. The sight of his mockery was sickening to behold, and I also found my hands itching to seize up my rifle and storm the barn. How Old Tom below me had kept his calm was nothing short of a miracle, although it was probably unspeakable anger rather than patience which had as yet prevented him from blowing our cover.

'Your obstinacy is not appreciated, madam,' said Burke at last. 'Poor Harold and Charles here have barely had any rest today, what with the number of prisoners they've had to haul into the air.'

Burke's thugs sniggered, but Old Tom did not join in as his face fast reddened. I cursed below my breath as I noticed that one of the town's watchmen had walked over to the O'Rourkes, who had stationed themselves in the shadow of the gatehouse. His voice rose in annoyance at their apparent refusal to speak to him, which they only did since they did not know English.

'Holy host of the Madonna!' I swore angrily. 'Where in Christ's name is Dario?'

The tribesmen beside me had already started loading their muskets, which prompted me to load my rifle. As I did this, Burke limped forward and placed his gnarled hands on the collar of Riona's tunic. After he ripped open her garment, the sight of her pale breasts was as degrading as it was infuriating, and for a moment my eyes were averted from the sight of them. Burke unfurled a rag which he had whipped from his jacket, and picked the red-hot shears off the coals before waving them a few inches away from the prisoner's face.

'Have you heard of Saint Agatha?' he asked.

Old Tom's hand fell to his sword pommel and trembled violently, and a lump formed in my throat as the Anglo-Norman took a step towards the renegade sergeant. So taken was I by Geraldine's movements that I failed to notice the flames which had grown beyond the walls of the town, and below me the portly officer chuckled as he mistook Old Tom's step towards Burke as rage directed at Riona. Everything then happened swiftly, as cries were heard at the gate, and a sentry raced towards the barn and burst into it, howling at the top of his voice.

'Fire at Annaghmore, sire! Gilson is under attack!'

Burke almost dropped his shears as he turned towards the man. 'How do you know this?'

'He has sent riders to our gates! Savages have waylaid the train!'

The sergeant leapt towards his men with a burst of bad language, seizing them by the shoulders and hurling them towards the door. They rushed to summon relief from the guardhouse, while the renegade shrieked at a knave who already bore his cuirass and sword to him. Old Tom also made for the doorway with a drawn dagger as he feigned to observe the sergeant's orders, yet he tarried there, seizing the fat officer by the shoulders and preventing the man from racing after the sentry. I snatched the Marquardt from my shoulder, and I shoved its muzzle through the peephole just as Burke turned in disgust towards the doorway, where Geraldine could be seen bent over the fat officer whose throat he had just slit.

'What are you fools doing? I said summon the men!'

Burke's foot was clearly in my sights, and my forefinger jerked back the serpentine as I blew off his toes. Charles and Harold were next to fall as the O'Rourkes alongside me fired their muskets, then lit the pitch on the roof. As the top of the barn burst into flames, we kicked our feet through the thatch before sliding our whole bodies through the roof, swinging off the main beam and dropping ourselves a few feet from the shrieking, twisting figure of Treasach Burke. Old Tom next appeared, bloody and shaken, before running up to the sergeant and kicking him in the face.

'Finish him!' snarled Geraldine, then ran over to the witness to sever her bonds.

Burke's head slowly rose off the straw as he touched his bloodied mouth, and his jaw dropped when he recognised me.

'You!' he croaked as he rose onto an elbow.

'Yes,' I replied, and kicked him across the face once more, 'your rabbit has crawled back out of its warren.'

Riona gasped as she fell into Geraldine's arms, lifting her head but once as she stared in disbelief at the aged Anglo-Norman.

'Who are you?' she gasped.

'Friends,' he uttered, then flung her arm over his shoulders and dragged her towards the door as my two O'Rourkes rushed over to help him.

'I'll fetch the horses,' he cried as they carried her off. 'We must make haste!'

As my Irish allies ran outside, I was left alone with Burke. The sergeant slowly turned onto his stomach and lifted himself onto one knee as his voice dripped with scorn.

'I'll grant that you have had the luck of the devil, Spaniard. Yet you shall not live to see another winter.'

His hair was snatched up in my left hand just as the crackle and hiss of the blazing roof filled my ears. The dagger in my right hand was rested against his throat as I leant closely towards him.

'Give it up, or I'll tear open your gullet.'

The sergeant stiffened and his teeth were gritted in his staunch refusal to reply, but I had glimpsed the slightest movement of his hand, which twitched protectively towards the last powder charge on his bandolier. I instantly pulled the belt off his shoulders and slung it over my head. As he turned about to curse me, I slammed my rifle stock into his cheek, causing a spray of blood and glistening tooth fragments to fly from his mouth. Burke was sent rolling across the straw. A blazing length of timber crashed onto the ground behind us as I swiftly reloaded the Marquardt. It was already primed just as Burke started to stir again.

'You know not,' he said, 'what it means.'

'What?' I asked, watching him carefully.

'The ring,' he said. 'The Binghams will not stop till they take it.'

'What have I to lose?' I replied. 'They think I have it anyway.'

'True,' he exclaimed, 'yet listen to me! Take refuge in Dartry for three more months, and they'll learn you don't have it!'

'Just three months?' I asked.

'Maybe even two! I have found a broker who is buying it tomorrow; you will soon be free of its curse! I will give you half my earnings, I swear it! It has not been easy, yet you shall receive many ducats. The ring is not any emerald bauble . . .'

'Then what is it?' I asked, as the raging heat above my head grew in intensity.

'A gift, Spaniard,' he gasped from the ground, 'from the king of Spain to the prince of Ascoli's mother! She was his mistress!'

I recalled the inscription on the ring's band, but then a flaming rafter crashed into the ground behind me, flooding me with unease.

'I'll take my chances,' I said as Burke scowled.

'You'll meet my same end, Spaniard,' he croaked. 'Those that live by the sword –'

'And what of those that live by the gun?' I cut in, then stepped over towards him and rested the rifle's muzzle upon the back of his knee.

The fire roared overhead as I drew back the trigger, and Burke howled in agony as a fleck of blood landed on my cheek. The smoke of the gun gathered about us as I tore down the door, just as more of the roof collapsed and a loud eruption was heard in the direction of the gatehouse. All was chaos in the bawn outside as cattle bucked and shrieked at the growing fires that the O'Rourkes had started everywhere, rendering the very sky red with flame. I realised that I had tarried too long inside, and I raced towards the flaming gate as terrified cattle thundered through it.

Old Tom then rode up to me on his charger with the witness seated in front of him and my hobby in tow. As I gratefully climbed atop my steed, Geraldine tossed me a sack of powder filled with shrapnel and rock shards.

'To you the honour, but be swift!'

He spurred his horse through what remained of the gate as I thundered back towards the barn where I had left Burke. Upon reaching it I wheeled my mount around, and as I dashed back towards Old Tom, I hurled the bag through the black smoke that billowed out of a window in the sidewall. The resulting blast from the barn all but flung us to the ground as my steed charged through the flaming gate and out into the open country.

XLV

County Sligo to Rosclogher, Dartry, County Leitrim

4 – 5 August 1589

We charged away from the town as though Satan himself were on our tail. All we heard was the raging crackle and hiss of the burning bawn, and men with lamps were seen gathering in the doors of their huts as we thundered past. Fearful glances were thrown over our shoulders in the direction of the town, and for a time it was every man for himself. The riders from Breifne had set fire to the arsenal holding stores of gunpowder as had been planned. Flames from the explosion still lapped at the sky, rendering our surrounds almost as bright as day.

At Annaghmore we reached the blazing barn which Dario and his men had set alight. We reined in our mounts a few feet away from the blazing building as Geraldine dismounted and approached the Croat.

'What took you so long?'

'The barn was not wholly abandoned,' answered Dario, 'for a dozen bandits had set up lodgings inside.'

'And where are they now?'

The Croat gestured to the trees to our right with his bloodied mace.

'Flown to the forest after I took care of their leader. A most disagreeable sort he was too.'

Geraldine nodded and turned to the rest of us.

'Are we all accounted for?'

A distant neigh was heard in reply, and we could see two of the O'Rourkes galloping towards us.

'We are now,' replied Dario.

Old Tom remounted his horse and risked lighting a small lamp, then set off at a brisk canter. We followed the little swinging flame ahead of us as our aged leader made for the wide outline of the mountains which loomed ahead of us. We ascended a gentle incline for at least another hour until we reached a dense underwood of wind-sculpted trees.

'Look!' exclaimed one of the O'Rourkes as he gestured behind us.

In the distance Sligo Town still blazed uncontrollably as scores of torches quivered like fireflies about its dim outline. Geraldine cursed aloud and addressed the witness behind him.

'Are you well enough to ride on?'

'Yes,' whispered Riona in a hoarse voice, 'let us away before all is lost.'

'My precise sentiments,' remarked the Anglo-Norman, then kicked his horse on as we followed in close pursuit. None of our party dared to breathe a word as we kept to his back. My fears turned to relief with each furlong we covered in the night, as we rode past ash and birch until the cover of bark and leaves was abandoned for a steeper bridle path. To a man we dismounted, with the O'Malley witness clinging to Dario's shoulder for support as we quietly led the steeds up the steep rise. At times the incline became so harsh that we found ourselves on our hands and knees, and the horses also struggled to keep their footing.

It was with great relief that the summit was finally reached, and the pre-dawn light cast us all in a pale hue of blue. When my breath was at last regained my attentions returned to the distant flicker of Sligo Town, which was so far away as to render the blaze within its bawn the size of a tallow light. The great silence about us was only pierced by the odd cry of a wolf, until a whisper was finally heard from the front of our own band.

'Can the lady still walk?'

'She is passed out from fatigue,' replied Dario from the shadows. 'I carried her up the last stretch over my shoulder.'

'Poor lass,' replied Geraldine. 'Be a good man and carry her a bit further.'

There came a rustle and a clink from the shadows as Dario gathered the witness from the ground, and one of the highborn O'Rourkes took the reins of the Croat's black destrier. Then we staggered off after Geraldine again. Everyone breathed more easily along the even path until a half circle of low cooking fires could be seen in the bushes ahead; already our nostrils were filled with the smell of cooked horseflesh. The dim figure of a wolf watcher stood out from the darkness, brandishing two spears.

'Old Tom?'

The cry sounded as high-pitched as it was incredulous, and Geraldine instantly rasped at the man to keep silent. Yet it was all for nothing as more of our guards appeared, laughing aloud in disbelief and slapping us heartily upon the backs. The witness was taken from Dario as Ramos himself appeared with a burning faggot of wood held in his right hand, which further revealed the joy on the faces of those that surrounded him.

'Be silent!' he snarled at the men. 'And return to your posts!'

When at last we were left alone, the sergeant stepped up to the Anglo-Norman and shook him heartily by the shoulder.

'Well met, old goat! I feared you were gone forever. Yet I see that your numbers have not dwindled but have instead been bolstered.'

'And we stole a few quintals of powder.'

'Good! Good! More plunder never goes amiss. Now get yourself by the fire with Dario and Abelito.'

Ramos' expression visibly changed from one of elation to one of concern as he said this.

'Is something astir?' asked Geraldine.

'We have had a visitor,' replied Ramos without elaborating further.

To a man we feared the worst, yet as we neared the fires the guest rose to his feet, and I already knew by the scabbard worn at each hip that it was the bondsman, Nial Ne Dourough.

'Juan!' he cried as he grabbed my outstretched hand and seized me in a strong embrace. 'You scoundrel! I knew you'd survive!'

'The sergeant told you of our mission?'

'He only mentioned a raid and would say nothing more until you returned. So, tell me, where were you? You smell of cow dung and smoke . . . and vinegar?'

'Is that not the smell of Dartry?' I said, then turned when my name was heard once more at my back.

'Juan?'

I instantly recognised the voice as belonging to the ollave, and I turned to find Muireann approaching me slowly, until her hands were rested upon my shoulders.

'You survived,' she whispered, and in the scant light of the dying fires behind me, I could tell that she had been weeping.

'What is the matter, my lady?' I asked, daring to rest a hand upon her arm.

She stared back at me without speaking, and her reddened eyes seemed to stare right through me. An all too fleeting hope passed through them before her gaze was averted, and she turned away from me and walked back towards the shadows and the forms of soldiers asleep on the grass.

'My lady?' I called after her, only to be ignored as she vanished into the gloom, clearly resolved to keep her own company.

With a shake of the head I turned back towards the flames and found the bondsman still standing behind me. The cheer had disappeared from his face as he regarded me with a set jaw and a grim expression.

'I fear I have been the bearer of ill tidings,' he said, 'which might explain the ollave's upset.'

'What ill tidings?'

'Let us talk while you sup,' he replied with a slight nod towards the hearth.

Many thoughts passed through my head until we were seated alongside Ramos and Geraldine, who were deep in conversation by the flickering flames.

'Ah,' said Ramos when he saw us, 'it appears that the two lovebirds have been reunited.'

Nial bristled at the sergeant's mockery as Ramos slowly rose to his feet.

'And now, my friends, I bid you a good night. It is past midnight, and a hard march awaits us in the morning. Were I your good selves I would not tarry long before bed, although I know that there is much that you wish to share.'

As Ramos wandered off, we helped ourselves to the remains of some black pudding. Not a soul stirred except for the three of us, since the men were all rolled up in their blankets and the distant howl of wolves was a constant. Old Tom had already lit his pipe and was recounting what had occurred at Sligo Town between long puffs of smoke, as if referring to some event which was already long past. Nial listened to all we said with genuine interest, only speaking up when the Anglo-Norman referred to the liberation of Riona.

'And what of Treasach Burke?'

Geraldine nodded at me.

'He is dead.'

'Dead! Are you sure of it?'

The bondsman's jaw hung open as Old Tom leant forward to light a twig upon the embers at our feet, which he used as a pipe light.

'The barn in which he lay wounded erupted,' I replied, 'after I flung a sack of powder and porcelain into its flames. No one could have survived the blast.'

Nial nodded slowly in disbelief as he lay back on the log behind him.

'Tonight must be a cold day in hell indeed if that monster finally perished.'

'Well, perished he has,' said Old Tom in a gruff voice. 'Just wait till that dog Gilson hears of it.'

He offered his pipe to Nial, who leant forward gratefully and drew a long breath of the leaf himself, surprising us by blowing a small ring in our direction as he watched the small glow of Sligo Town in the distance.

'It has been a bad year for the royalists,' he mused, passing the pipe over to me.

'Yes,' said Old Tom, 'long may it endure. And what have you to recount to us, worthy sword master?'

'I hear tidings both good and ill,' – Nial sighed – 'which I shall recount in order of occurrence. Upon leaving Rosclogher, my lord MacGlannagh's men joined the great force of the O'Rourke, which had gathered south of our borders. Together we plundered Corran and Tirerill, then moved on to Tireragh, where we ravaged the land up till Easky.'

'The Binghams shall be pleased,' I said.

Nial chuckled with his usual cheer.

'Word reached us that a force of theirs was also beaten back by the Burkes of Mayo. It seems that the tribes are in open revolt from Erris to Traholly strand. Leyny, Corran and most of the Roscommon are also up in arms, while O'Conor and the O'Hart have pledged support to the rebellion.'

Old Tom received the tidings with a low whistle.

'And we have ambushed their supply train and destroyed their bawn.'

'Yes,' replied Nial, 'yet if the Binghams avoid justice in Dublin there shall be hell to pay.'

'But that has also been seen to,' exclaimed Old Tom, 'for we have a witness!'

Nial nodded his agreement with a wry grin as Geraldine cackled aloud and clapped his hands in glee.

'Countless miseries have I endured, but never was my faith repaid as it has been today! The Lord be praised! In Connacht shall the slow encroachment of the heretic scum be stemmed, and the winds now turn in our favour!'

'What of the ill tidings?' I asked, feeling somewhat unsettled by the Anglo-Norman's passionate surge of optimism. 'Is that not why you are here?'

'Ah', said Nial, with another slow nod, 'you are not easily carried away, Spaniard.'

'Out with it, man!' blurted Old Tom, suddenly afraid that he had spoken too soon. Nial cleared his throat awkwardly.

'Upon reaching Easky, word reached us of a large troop of the hated O'Reillys. It was sighted in the lands of O'Rourke.'

'Treacherous whoresons,' snarled Old Tom.

'Indeed,' said Nial, 'and always willing to do the English crown's bidding to secure more lands which rightfully belong to the kin of *na Múrtha*. Since they feared the worst, the lords O'Rourke and MacGlannagh sent a detachment of their army north to secure the passes to their strongholds. I was hardly recovered from our days of raiding when I found myself riding with Cathal the Black, who was placed in command of a force of horse and foot.' Nial scowled as he referred to the foot soldiers, and Geraldine was quick to seize on this.

'Did the tanist's force of foot also include the gallowglasses?'

Nial nodded as Old Tom issued a low growl and shook his head in frustration.

'I think I know how this story ends, but I pray you to finish it, friend Nial.'

'Upon reaching Dartry we were separated from the men sent by the O'Rourke, who galloped east to secure their own lands whilst we rushed towards Rosclogher, arriving weary and short of breath. Yet we were relieved to discover that the O'Reillys had not yet arrived. Dervila's skeleton force at the tower house had just been bolstered by a band of kerns from our party when Cathal ordered that we push on after barely a day's rest, so that we might rout the invaders and foil their foul designs.'

Neither Old Tom nor I stirred at this news, except to lean forward slowly as we hung on Nial's every last word.

'After leaving Rosclogher behind us, we travelled east, crossing the border with the O'Rourke to the north until a few of our scouts returned, telling us that they had caught sight of the scum near the heights of Dartry. Cathal and the constable quickly laid plans, with the tanist deciding to meet the larger force of enemy horsemen upon the plain and the Scots ordered to lie in wait before they also entered the fray to secure our triumph.'

Old Tom covered his face with his hands.

'So you put your lives into the hands of mercenaries?'

Nial cleared his throat uncomfortably.

'Long did I remonstrate with the tanist over his decision, yet he would hear none of it. In fairness to him, the constable's behaviour up to that point had been commendable, and all throughout the campaign it seemed that the spoils gained from our raids had quelled the avarice of Donal MacCabe and his men.'

'So you crossed swords with a larger force,' I said, 'and awaited the relief of the Scots in vain.'

The bondsman seemed suddenly shaken at the memory of what had passed, and we beheld him in silence until he managed to address us once more.

'It was a massacre, perpetrated by an enemy both savage and merciless. Donal did finally intervene, and as always his men fought hard. Yet it was too late, and well he knew it, for the scrap had long swung against us by the time he and his men appeared. It was an act of pure betrayal, for by the time the O'Reillys fled the field, barely a quarter of the tanist's men were left standing.'

'And what of Cathal?' asked Old Tom hastily.

'He was borne away by the enemy, so that none know if he is dead or alive. At the end of the fight the gallowglasses offered us neither apology nor succour, and the constable allowed his men to pilfer the corpses of both friend and foe. In a rage I approached him with both swords drawn, only to be laughed at and told to bear word to my master that he should honour the debts which were outstanding if he desired to keep a hold of his lands. MacCabe then furnished me with a horse that I half rode to death until I met the ollave's scouts on my southward journey.'

'That is most fortunate,' remarked Geraldine, 'for you would not have travelled much further alone.'

'Yes, and fortunate that they recognised me before the arrows flew from their bows or the spears left their hands. They immediately escorted me back to Lady Mac an Bhaird, who received my tidings with a heavy heart.'

'That double-dyed scoundrel MacCabe!' fumed the Anglo-Norman. 'He has played himself into a position of greater strength. He is a ruffian without honour or scruples, and our enemies might now have a valuable hostage, whom they will use to clip our lord MacGlannagh's wings.'

'Then it is just as well we spared Gilson,' I muttered darkly.

'That is true,' said Nial, surprising me with the sharpness of his hearing, 'although the enemy might not value our captive enough to exchange him for the tanist.'

'And are we even sure that the tanist lives?' asked Geraldine.

Nial fell silent at the question as he laid his hands upon his stomach and closed his eyes. His face contorted at the memories evoked by his thoughts, as he sought to remember what had occurred in the fight that he so wanted to forget.

'The last I saw of him,' he said, finally opening his eyes, 'he was screaming in the direction of the cursed Scots, who stared down at us from atop a hill. I shouted at him to retire from the fray, but he would not listen, or could not hear me because of the great clash of arms about us. Then the O'Reillys closed in tightly about us, and from then on my thoughts were wholly taken with surviving the ensuing bloodbath.'

Old Tom swiftly changed the subject due to the bondsman's distress.

'So we march to the protection of Rosclogher?'

'Yes,' replied Nial. 'Muireann shall ride west to bear my tidings to our lord MacGlannagh, and we will make for Dartry at daybreak.'

Our conversation had lasted for over an hour, after which we rose to our feet and staggered off to find our blankets. As the Anglo-Norman snored behind me, I reached for the last powder charge in Burke's bandolier, as I had yearned to do ever since we fled the hell of Sligo Town. As the contents of the ampoule slid into the palm of my hand, I could have cried aloud in triumph as a small hard object bit into the flesh of my palm.

'You are mine again,' I whispered as the ring was returned to the powder charge. My hands shook and a tear formed in my eye at my overwhelming sense of guilt. For what remained of the night I tossed and turned upon the heath, feeling tormented by a deep unease. In the morning a kick in the hip left me blinded by sunlight, and I beheld Dario's outstretched hand.

'Get up, Spaniard. This is the third time I've kicked you.'

I clasped his hand, and he hauled me onto my feet, then left me to regain my balance. About us the whole camp was already astir as men adjusted packs upon their mounts' backs and readied to descend towards the far-off cover of forest. As we commenced our descent, the northern peak of Ben Bulben could be seen ahead, covered by trees which seemingly ran all the way to the sea. The plain of Maugherow spread beyond the table-topped mountain range, bounded by lofty cliff walls which stole their beholder's breath. When the lowland was reached I climbed onto my hobby's back, only for Dario's voice to reach me as I mounted the saddle.

'Hey, Juan! Ramos says you should escort the O'Malley witness. He said to shoot anything that gets too close to her.'

'Should she not ride with Geraldine?'

'No, for he is scouting ahead.'

As Dario led Riona towards me I quickly dismounted and bowed to her, then helped her to climb upon my horse. A guard of kerns had also been assigned to her by Ramos, and they moved in a circle about us, donning some of the plate and other pieces of armour which had been taken near the Shannon. Due to the great peril faced by Dartry, Geraldine urged Ramos to undertake a morning march.

As she silently rode atop my hobby, the O'Malley witness beheld the heights about us, whose shades and colours changed in the growing light of the sun. Her raven hair fluttered about her sharp, handsome features, her cheeks rough from harsh squalls and sea spray. As she returned my stare, I saw that the witness's eyes were red from a night spent weeping.

'Are you to be my guardian angel?' she asked amid the cry of grouse and wild ducks in the distance.

Her question was wholly unexpected and left me fumbling for a reasoned reply.

'If you consider me to be such, madam. Wherefrom did you learn Spanish?'

'My people are seafarers,' she replied, 'who have had much trade with Spain. For years did we encounter your fishermen along our coasts, and I have even sailed as far as your land.'

The disbelief on my face was ill disguised as she described her travels to the Continent.

'And where did you think the chieftain's wines come from?' she asked.

Riona spoke to me at length of her adventures aboard the pirate ships of Dubhdara, who was the great lord of her tribe. His fleets travelled so far that they had also grappled with the pirates of Barbary. I listened to the adventures of these Irish pirates in wonderment, listening to how Dubhdara's famous fighting daughter Grania had once repelled an attack of the Turks on her ship shortly after giving birth. The detail with which Riona described these stories assured me that her accounts were not contrived.

'Before the troubles with the heretics we traded no end of goods with the Continent. Wool, hide, timber and tallow. Even fruit, corn and salted fish . . .'

As she proudly displayed the number of exports upon her fingers, I could see that some of her nails were split, which was common among seamen who worked with hawsers and canvas. As the kerns led us along one of the tracks scattered throughout the country, her necklace of seashells tinkled whenever my mount struggled to find its footing.

'Have you travelled far within Ireland?' I asked.

'Only by sea,' she said, 'and never this far inland. All I know is the rocky broken land around Cuan Mó, with its lakes among the windswept hillocks. Often did I wonder what lay beyond it, for many men have fled beyond the mountains of Dartry for refuge.'

'Men such as me,' I mused.

'You are one of the castaways?' she asked.

When I replied, the O'Malley witness listened intently to how the tribe had protected me, although I left out any mention of the ring or my trial at Brehon law.

'Fortune smiles upon you, Spaniard,' she said at last, 'for many of your countrymen were caught by the English bands which searched the coast. Many of my kinsmen were also taken and put to death for helping the survivors of the wrecks, and the lands of several chieftains were seized by the Binghams. It is why the Burkes of Mayo flew into rebellion.'

'Did you say Burke?' I muttered with obvious discomfort at the memory of the evil sergeant I had killed in Sligo Town.

Riona must have instantly read my thoughts, as a deep frown appeared on her own face.

'Yes, the same kin that sired that monster of Treasach, may the devil claim his soul for all eternity. Yet it is also an unfortunate truth that many noble families have been split by the invaders or seen their sons embrace the heretic yoke.'

Her revelation left me feeling ill at ease, for it seemed impossible to tell friend from foe in a land where loyalties shifted like the wind. I next recalled the number of curious episodes which had occurred during my time spent in Dartry, from the enemy obtaining knowledge held by the tribe alone or appearing in unexpected places without warning. Riona was ignorant to these recollections which plagued my mind as I sought to identify who the mole in the tribe might be, much as I was inclined to think that it was the gallowglass constable, Donal MacCabe.

Riona then told me of the horrors endured by her people at the hands of the ruthless Bingham brothers, led by Richard, the Governor of Connacht, and his younger brother, George, who was the sheriff of Sligo and my former captor.

'Any rebel who falls into their hands is dead. It seems impossible to me that I still live.'

'When you are of use to the powers that be,' I replied, 'the incredible does occur.'

She startled me with a low, hollow laugh.

'If you are saying that I am a pawn, then know that I am one out of my own free will. When my husband was killed by the Binghams my life vanished overnight. All that is left to me is the faint hope of justice that is offered by the viceroy.'

'And what of your child?' I asked, flicking my head towards her swollen belly.

She appeared confused by my question as she stroked her belly with one hand.

'I do this out of the love that I bear for my child. The young in this land deserve a better future. One akin to the life I remember from my youth.'

'What future can your child have if your own life is threatened? Should you not seize your boats and fly to France or Spain? Somewhere where you will be free from danger?'

Riona met my concerned stare for a few moments.

'And how would I raise my child so far from home,' she replied, 'knowing that its homeland and kin are being destroyed, all because I did not act when I could?'

She bent her head slightly as we passed a low-hanging branch, and I could see that her face had assumed an angry cast; she clearly felt mocked by my suggestion.

'Home is not only about safety, Spaniard. It is also about the memories and traditions, and your friends and kin. One would not abandon it so lightly, if there were any hope, no matter how faint, of saving it. Would you abandon your own home so cheaply?'

I thought of the island of Malta where I had spent my earliest years, which had been rendered rubble and mounds of carnage by Ottoman cannon. I had abandoned it at an early age to be adopted by my dead father's brother in Valencia. At the time my uncle's invitation had appeared a blessing, but it seemed inopportune to share this with the witness.

'No, Spaniard, I am left with no choice. I want the life that I once had for my child, the one that has been threatened ever since Richard Bingham appeared with his brothers from across the Shannon. His lieutenants shall not let us have peace; they shall not rest until they have left us with nothing. Until they are gone, death is almost preferable to the life we are leading, for both at home and abroad my child's future is no better than that of a beggar's.'

It was not possible to argue with her, as memories of the poor Irishmen in the dark alleys of Spain's cities returned to mind. The term 'beggar' had often been hurled at them by the arrogant Spanish locals. Her courage and resolve left me filled with awe and gave me a deep sense of shame at having hidden the ring from my protectors.

'Yours is a most worthy endeavour, my lady. I have known few people who would show your daring.'

Riona sighed as the sunlight streamed through the copse from above the great heights to our right.

'My lord advised me not to venture forth. And long did my cousin the lady Grania insist at our last meeting that I reconsider my decision. But the path was clear to me when I learned that the trial in Dublin lacked a witness, and that the Binghams' master is resolved to be rid of them.'

I was about to warn her that the viceroy's hatred of his servants did not necessarily represent a love for the Irish, against whom he had also shown great cruelty. Yet I did not want to belittle her hopes, so I returned my attention to the uneven path ahead of us. Our march lasted beyond the noontime sun and brought us into the second valley of Glenade. We rested a good distance away from the main lake, where kelpies were said to have been sighted and which provoked more fear in the natives than any mention of wolves or Sassanas.

After a brief rest we pushed on again, leaving Trosc Mór behind us as we headed for the peak of Arroo. We maintained a swift progress throughout the last stretch of our journey, and the familiar sights were welcome as we drew closer to the place where we had spent our last days of training. Our path twisted about swamp and underwood, and we were approaching the ring of bog when we were met by the fast-approaching figure of an elderly man atop a hobby.

'Don Tomás!' called Ramos ahead of us. 'What is astir?'

'The O'Reillys!' gasped the Anglo-Norman. 'They are here already!'

At my shoulder Nial's blades rang from his scabbard, and a dark grimace spread across his face.

'Then let us at them!' he growled as he ran past me.

'Wait!' cried Ramos, as he snatched the bondsman's shoulder. 'Have you counted their force?'

'Two score,' replied Old Tom. 'They are assaulting the guards in the ringfort.'

'So they keep no formation?'

'No, it is every man to himself, for they have the sheer weight of numbers.'

Ramos fell silent for a few moments, then drew his own sword to a low growl.

'Let us engage,' he said, releasing the mantle of the startled Nial before him, 'and let us be swift. The square shall withstand a charge before Dario's horse relieves us.'

As we set forth again, Ramos assigned a guard of two kerns to Riona, ordering them to hide away and to make for Breifne the following morning if they received no further word from us. No sooner had they led the O'Malley witness away than the sergeant summoned his ensign and drummer boy to his side, ordering them to hoist the O'Rourke's standard to a loud beat as we crossed the bog. We followed his lead in single file as the last mile to Rosclogher was covered.

A brief pause was called for us to light our match cords, and as the last stretch was covered we saw that the thin plumes of smoke rising in the distance had turned into streaming billows. Many of the town's huts were aflame. Upon crossing the hidden path through the bog, we emerged from the cover of trees and were met by the sight of so many flaming cabins that it seemed that the whole of Lough Melvin was ablaze. The avenues between them were full of mounted raiders of a wild cast, who had broken away from a larger force that circled the ringfort, where a handful of beleaguered bluejackets still put up a spirited defence.

'The O'Reillys,' snarled Nial at my back, but as always Ramos was the fastest to regain his wits in the midst of the conflict.

'Form square! We march by taps!'

We fell into position while Dario's riders in the rear appeared out of the trees, hurling the plunder from their horses' backs to the grass and swiftly climbing atop their mounts. Ramos led us forward a few feet until we reached the edge of the greensward, barking his orders as the first of the O'Reillys wheeled his steed away from the ringfort, having noticed the two lions on the O'Rourke standard.

'Close ranks!' roared Ramos. 'Let us give them something to remember us by!'

The O'Reilly horseman did not instantly make towards us. Instead, he waved his sword madly above his head and beckoned to his fellows who also withdrew from the stone fort. A swift glance over my shoulder revealed that Dario and his men were finally mounted, and my good ear rang from the commands that Ramos roared at us. Musketeers grappled with their arms and jerked ramrods down muzzles, spurred on by fear as at least twenty riders charged towards us, screaming their war cry as the ground quivered beneath our feet.

'*Ó Raghallaigh Abù! Ó Raghallaigh Abuuuuuù! Ó Raghallaigh Abuuuuuuuuuuuuuuuuuuuuuuuuù!*'

Pikes were raised as the whites of our enemy's eyes were seen, just as a few of the O'Reilly horsemen started to fall away from the main body of riders. Nearly all were felled as Ramos' voice rose above the din, causing a huge cloud of smoke.

'Fire!'

The usual knock of a pike haft followed, as its owner pushed hard against two, three, four and then more horse shadows. As the foul-smelling fog finally cleared, it was all we could do to gasp for breath; the clearing air around us unveiled the usual scenes of broken bodies and cries to a distant mother. The wounds inflicted by our gunfire were horrendous, so that the slaying at close quarters which ensued was nothing short of an act of mercy. Only a half-dozen raiders had been spared in the engagement, and Dario and the O'Rourkes were hot on their tails as they thundered back towards the burning hovels where the townsfolk in their path were hacked down.

'After them!' cried Ramos. 'Break ranks! Fire at will!'

The remaining bluejackets released a huge roar as our enemy fled, then streamed out of the relieved ringfort to our left, resolved to avenge their fallen comrades. Nial summoned them to his side as he raced towards the town with both blades drawn, intent on avenging the massacre in which his friend the tanist Cathal *Dubh* had been taken prisoner. As the town was reached, his kerns flung a hail of spears at the enemy, which made whorls in the smoky haze that surrounded us. We gave a hard chase to those O'Reillys we found on foot, rushing after them past flaming cabins of wattle and straw until they found themselves caught between the town and the lake water and sought to flee along the lake's banks. Dario and his riders chased a handful of them away from the doors of *Doire Mel*, and my rifle was aimed at a wayward rider.

'Juan!'

Old Tom gestured wildly towards the keep, which stood across the water. In that instant I feared the worst, and my fears only grew at the sight of two boatloads of O'Reillys, who rowed across the Melvin towards the crannog. As my fingers returned to loading the wheellock, Dario rode up and threw himself off his foaming mount.

'Can you hit them from this distance?' he gasped.

'Not all twenty!'

He grimaced as he swung his head from left to right, then raced towards the old maypole which had been abandoned along the jetty.

'Make haste, Spaniard!'

We each grabbed an end of the heavy hawthorn, then grunted with effort as we rolled it down towards the bank of the lake, sighing with relief as it splashed into the brown water.

'Sit on it,' he snapped as he waded into the water, 'and keep your powder dry.'

I seated myself at the centre of the log and curled my legs tightly about it, wobbling slightly as Dario held the end of it and kicked the water like a goaded mule. The Croat was a strong swimmer, and the growing figures of the O'Reillys were soon within my sights as I raised the Marquardt rifle to my shoulder. One of them toppled into the water after I shot him in the back of the head, and his skiff pitched violently as a number of muskets and crossbows swirled over towards us. With a curse I hurled myself back into the water, feeling shocked by the biting cold as I cowered behind the log, which was torn by shot and bolts. We shielded ourselves with the length of the maypole as we made after the skiffs at a cautious distance, cursing again when the first of them struck the island.

Raiders hopped out of it and made straight for the door of the tower house, with another boatload soon on their heels as they snatched nervous looks towards us. Loud thuds could be heard as they attempted to break the door open. We slowly made our way to the eastern side of the crannog, where we abandoned the pole and clambered atop the island.

'Where are the guards?' I gasped.

'We are the guards!' replied Dario, as he drew his mace from his belt and ran towards the score of O'Reillys.

'But it is certain death!' I called after him, unslinging my useless rifle from my shoulder as lake water leaked from its muzzle.

'*Poziv u rat!*' he roared in his tongue, and our enemies' eyes were wide with fear as they spotted him rounding the tower house, intent on beating them into a pulp.

The sight of me wielding my gun behind him scarcely helped to settle their fears, but they finally regained their wits enough to brandish their axes and swords. Dario beat the first invader to the ground as the raiders closed in about him, while two of their number hurled roped hooks over the crenellations, then clambered up the walls like a pair of nimble apes.

'Shoot them, Spaniard!' roared the Croat as he sidestepped yet another onrushing enemy and brained him with his crude weapon.

Four more of the O'Reillys were disabled in this manner until the rest withdrew before the fiendish Croat; some readied their spears for a fatal throw while others slammed ramrods down the muzzles of their muskets. My eyes returned to the two climbers who had almost made the roof, when a woman's voice was heard from atop the settlements.

'Aim!'

At the sight of Dervila I scrambled back towards the water, calling out to Dario to do the same. The O'Reillys stared overhead at the loud cry, greeted by the sight of Dartry's queen, who raised her sword to the sky upon the ramparts as a sign to her ladies-in-waiting which were gathered upon the walls with loaded muskets. Saorla could be seen frowning in concentration, and the familiar sound akin to cracking brambles was heard along the roof. Dario had just reached the water's edge as the withering fusillade pounded our ears, and two bodies fell from the walls of the tower house as cries of agony were heard from below.

Less than a dozen O'Reillys ran back towards their boats as the highborn ladies of Dartry whooped and cheered above them, and a skiff almost went over as the raiders hurled themselves into it.

I had slumped to one knee in relief when I heard Dervila cry 'Spaniard!' above me.

I ran up to the keep's sidewall, where bodies still twitched in agony, grabbing the musket that she had flung over the roof's edge.

'Finish them off!' she shouted before also throwing down a burning match cord, a bandolier and a ramrod. I gladly snatched up the implements and ran back to the water while the women screeched insults and abuse after the fleeing raiders.

'Christ wept,' muttered Dario as he climbed back out of the water and stared at the roof in wonder. 'Now that's a pack of hellfire vixens.'

Here ends
TRIALS IN TUMULT,
being the fourth part of
THE SASSANA STONE PENTALOGY.

The fifth and final part is called
RING OF RUSE,
which tells of the final confrontation between
the MacGlannaghs and their oppressors,
and of Santiago's agonising, last choice between
his life and his redemption.

Historical Note

I enjoyed writing this part of the series for many reasons. I think it best brings out the uniqueness of Gaelic life in Ireland, the last country in Europe to be affected by Roman influences. It fascinates me to think that, less than 500 years ago, there was a corner of the world where a body of laws applied that were developed in the seventh and eighth centuries and that were largely untainted by Roman law. To date the surviving manuscripts containing these laws remain difficult to translate but we do know that they were a body of incredibly complex rules which extensively governed the tribe's way of life, down to the ownership of the last ounce of honey. Not bad for a people often referred to as savages by both their English foes and their Spanish allies and who were supposedly in need of civilising.

It is also fascinating to note that women were allowed to become judges in Gaelic society. Before the slow infiltration of Roman influence via Saint Patrick's Catholic teachings and the invasion of the Normans, women could acquire any post within their tribe, including that of chieftain. Yet the spread of the Salic law from Normandy meant that, from the Middle Ages onwards, women could no longer legally achieve the post of chieftain – although in practice women were often followed by their husband's soldiers once she divorced him, if they deemed her to be a better leader.

It is probably not a widely known fact that the Brehon law also allowed for divorce between spouses, which was legally permissible for a number of reasons, which included infidelity, impotence, obesity, infanticide or attempted abortion, being indiscrete about one's love life, spreading false stories and theft. It is doubly fascinating to consider that Brehon law permitted divorce in Gaelic society when one considers that the fervent Roman Catholic tradition in Ireland saw to it that divorce was made illegal up until 1995.

A word on the great goings on in Connacht, which form the backdrop of this novel. Gaelic life in Connacht was under great threat by the ruthless Bingham family, foremost of whom were Richard Bingham, governor of Connacht (also known as 'the flail of Connacht' because of his great brutality towards the Irish natives), and his brother, George Bingham, the sheriff of Sligo (and the titular sheriff in *The Sheriff's Catch*). In turn this partly contributed to the great rebellion by the Blind Abbot, an Irish rebel who was keen on claiming the MacWilliamship, an old and revered Gaelic title in northern Connacht.

The Binghams acted as a law unto themselves when they set about suppressing Connacht and quelling rebellions like that of the Blind Abbot. Their brutality displeased the English queen's viceroy in Dublin, William FitzWilliam, who was keen on clipping their wings. It is recorded that the viceroy collected books of outrages from the lords of Connacht before initiating a trial against the Binghams in Dublin. Of course, given the brutal reputation of the Binghams, not a single Gael dared to present themselves as a witness in Dublin, which presented me with a great opportunity to have a bit of fun and work up some of my fiction.

The plot thickens when one considers that Queen Elizabeth I in London was irked by the constant upheaval in Ireland, although this may have been due to her infamous parsimoniousness, given that she was assembling a (disastrous) fleet of her own to send against Spain. This gave the viceroy wind in his sails when taking on the Binghams, except that the Binghams did indeed have a powerful ally in the English queen's court: her trusted, competent spymaster, Sir Francis Walsingham.

For whatever reason (they were probably his agents), Walsingham took the side of the Binghams and pressed the viceroy to leave them alone. Once the trial in Dublin was disbanded, the Binghams were free to return their attentions to the uprisings in Connacht. They were greatly aided in their suppression of Connacht by the largest force of English soldiers to ever be sent overseas, for the very purpose of breaking Connacht. These events will feature in the next and last instalment of this series.

About the Author

James Vella-Bardon was born and raised in Malta, an island nation influenced by thousands of years of imperial history - from the Romans to the British - where his passion for exciting and dramatic historical events was formed. After reading law and history at the Universities of both Malta and Sydney, James qualified as a lawyer and completed a doctoral thesis on the rights and freedoms of peoples at international law.

He emigrated to Sydney in 2007 and turned his hand to novel writing. His debut novel *The Sheriff's Catch* (2018), which recounts the adventures of a Spanish Armada castaway in Tudor Ireland, won the 'best novel' and 'best historical fiction' categories at the international Royal Dragonfly Book Awards and was also named an 'Outstanding Historical' by the Independent Author Network Book Awards in 2019.

James was heralded as 'the new king of historical fiction' by British newspaper *The Scotsman*, in their review of his novella *Mad King Robin*, about Robert the Bruce.

www.jamesvellabardon.com

Also by James Vella-Bardon

The Bruce Books
The Cream Of Chivalry
Mad King Robin

The Sassana Stone Pentalogy
The Sheriff's Catch
A Rebel North
Hero Of Rosclogher
Ring Of Ruse

www.ingramcontent.com/pod-product-compliance
Lightning Source LLC
Chambersburg PA
CBHW030520120726
47904CB00005B/1557